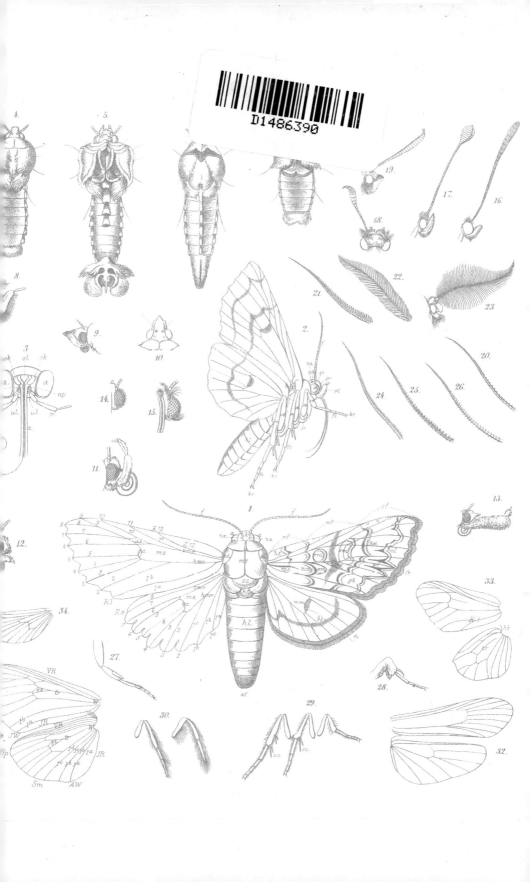

LOBSTER MOTH

by the same author

The Duchess's Dragonfly
Natterjack

LOBSTER MOTH

Niall Duthie

FOURTH ESTATE • London

First published in Great Britain in 1999 by
Fourth Estate Limited
6 Salem Road
London W2 4BU

1 3 5 7 9 10 8 6 4 2

A catalogue record for this book is
available from the British Library

ISBN 1-84115-105-X

Typeset by Rowland Phototypesetting Ltd,
Bury St Edmunds, Suffolk
Printed in Great Britain by
Clays Ltd, St Ives plc

For Doux-Doux

Almost every boy has hunted butterflies through the woods and fields, or has reared silkworms or other moths . . . And how often has the remembrance of these youthful pleasures led elderly men to return to them, and cheer the evening of their lives by a more scientific study of their early favourites! The beauty and the wonderful transformations of butterflies and moths have attracted attention and pleased the fancy from the most ancient of times. Men have even reverently traced in them the symbol of the soul, and afterwards of immortality; for there is a beautiful analogy between the graceful winged insect emerging from the dark, motionless pupa, and the spirit leaving its mortal body and winging its flight to higher regions. Psyche, the spouse of Cupid (or Eros), is usually represented with the wings of a butterfly; and her name, in Greek, denotes a butterfly, Life, and the Soul.

W. F. Kirby, *The Butterflies and Moths of Europe*, London, 1903

I

Tonight – at just after eleven p.m. on 1 June 1916 – I wish to make a proposal, and begin to provide contents, for a ten-minute pillow book.

At this stage – my recent work has been scientific rather than literary – it would be premature and possibly presumptuous to define the concept. In mind, however, I have a novel designed to be read in ten-minute spells with a soft pillow behind the head; in particular as a book for all those who find they are left with only a few minutes a day in which to read. I hope the notion is attractive.

Of course the ten is arbitrary but we can allow for variables. Among them: The fuddle of fatigue. A coming sneeze. Forgetfulness. Startling vocabulary making the reader's eyes sheer up and off the page. An intimate worry welling up through some chance word. A sudden spill. Or a suspicion that a recurrent itch by an ankle might be an insect bite. Or something wholly external, half expected but not yet formulated – the air has had a moted, clammy feel – a dazzling crack in the dark, a magnesium-bright flare of lightning across the night sky.

As blinded as by a flash bulb, I blink. The faded, damask curtains billow meekly in. A few heartbeats interrupted by a swallow and then a tremendous roll of thunder rumbles down through the chimneys of the old house to make an empty teacup dance on its saucer on the mantelpiece; about the same wild vigour in the rattle as Aubrey Gilbert uses to demonstrate how a medium worked on his very deaf grandmother. Then an erratic splatter of fat raindrops on the flag-stones outside my window, followed almost at once by the hard hiss of a downpour.

Sounds and temperature change very quickly. Those curtains are sucked a little outwards, then subside, rather lank in the hang. The rone pipes begin a mirky gurgle. The seething on the stone path softens and settles. The eaves begin to drip. Sodden, worm-drowning sounds come from the lawn. The goose-pimples on my arms sink down. Between that flare in the sky and the snaily feel of skin uncrimping on my forearms? A time of barely a minute and a half.

Back to the ten-minute novel then. Today, another convalescent here told me that modern Greeks use cigarettes as a unit to measure distance. They will say such-and-such a place is three cigarettes away, meaning about thirty minutes' walk. A pillow book, however, should not only accommodate walking or reading speeds.

For there are those who like to read from start to finish in small daily doses. Or sectionally (a stately skip along one development). Or those who like to make a private jigsaw of a book, opening first at random and then gradually filling in. Or there are even those like Lieutenant Cummins in the next room whose lights have just leant out across part of the lawn and most of the wet stone bird-bath. I saw him handle a book back to front, first riffling warily away from the conclusion, pausing four or five times as if hardly daring to read; but on reaching the frontispiece he speeded up, flicked quickly to about page 100, and began to stare, chin rising, at a half-page paragraph. Then jerking his head right back, he squeezed his eyes tight and slapped the book shut. A moment after, he glanced about him and slipped the book back on the shelf. I had no desire to pry but it did occur to me that he had moth-eaten the volume, treated a book as some moths can treat a suit, with a single hole in the fabric.

But whatever method is used this novel remains one for those who like to dip into a book ten minutes before turning off the light. Those ten minutes come at the tail end of the day. And as such they may constitute a nightcap in print. Or they may help clear the mind for sleep as certain soups help clear the palate for the next course. Or they may invoke a lost fondness for books, founts and adventures – but all are cast on undulating lidwork and mattress warmth.

Now the original or oriental pillow book includes those miscellaneous writings, lists, likes, dislikes, anecdotes and diaritic notes written by court ladies in Japan a thousand years ago when they retired to their sleeping quarters; elegant, night-time commonplace books we might say, though neither quite as elegant nor nearly as exotic as is sometimes thought – the lady adjusts her silk sleeve and in two strokes of her ink-brush has captured the essence of a firefly kind of thing. But the rain is slackening and there is a far more elementary point.

I had always understood the word 'pillow', in the original, oriental use, to be proximate to sleep and bed; in an arrangement on the floor, a Japanese cross between a headboard and a bedside table. This was because I had both seen and touched one. Made of cedar wood, it had shallow drawers (for paper, brushes, ink-stone and ribbons) and was not much different in size from a box of fifty Montecristo cigars. I was used to thinking that a necessary quality of pillows was that they were soft. But I was quite wrong. The wooden box is a night writing case *and* a pillow.

I still think the position of the head on such a stiff structure bespeaks a barely credible discipline in the art of sleeping. It resembles a meagre chopping block but for one's head the other way round, nape down, apple up. Get down and try it, however: I found my head tilted forward, chin over apple, and felt an increasingly unpleasant line of pressure across the base of my skull.

Somewhere in the next valley I understand there is an order of monks that anticipates the rest of eternity by having its members sleep in their own coffins. I find such a pose irritating. The snoring dead? I have never seen a sleeper, however exhausted, who resembles a corpse. Though I admit, I may be less concerned with the self-important elevation of the soul above worldly comforts, than with my own distaste for linking rigour and sleep. To be clear: Despite certain forms and borrowings, this will not be a traditional pillow book. And the best I can do to gloss sleep on a wooden pillow I owe to my sister. Recently, because of a distant cousin's wedding, she was obliged to sleep with her hair up and resolutely schooled herself beforehand not to move. Subsequently she was praised by the elderly for her deportment, mostly due to her neck 'feeling as though it had just come out of a month's plaster of Paris'. I would like to think that the Japanese court ladies rolled their very long hair for a black over-pillow but I doubt it.

Set sleep free. It is not a splendid slogan perhaps, but I have any number of reasons for believing in it. Let me choose one. Let us suppose, as Byron does when attacking Wordsworth in his preface to *Don Juan*, that there are some things which it is derisory to suppose. Byron thinks it weak-minded of Wordsworth to request the reader to imagine a poem narrated by 'the captain of a merchantman or small trading vessel, lately retired upon a small annuity to some inland town'. I'd be disappointed that any reader should lack the imagination to imagine a plump pillow or see her- or himself in bed when they are not. Or not accept that this book is always lit by a bedside lamp.

But enough of Japan and small annuities. Every novel requires an opening image, however tentative, however faint. The first in this pillow book would be a stone skipping across a river pool.

Now it is perfectly conceivable that the stone skips in time to the reader's pulse. It is also conceivable that the stone should blunder into a swallow dipping to drink on the wing. There is no need for the reader to feel guilty, to imagine he or she had a part in the accident by reading of it. Nor to imagine this novel is a vile dream primer.

In other words, what exercises the author, at present in the guise of a British soldier in a convalescent home called Lampenham in Dorset, is that the reader able to imagine that he or she is in bed etc. may have come with his or her own day and devices, and begun to add their own foliage to the river bank, midges to the water and have the stone, liverish and russet in colour, too big and grainy to skip well. I suppose that is any reader's right, but may I advise against it?

I would not, for example, want the reader to imagine the thrower as a boy ineptly imitating a slingshot hero while his sister agitates her parasol-free hand, not because of the stone and the swallow, but for fear of her brother disturbing their angler uncle asleep in his chair and making him dream he had caught a bird rather than a fish.

Though which would be worse, stone or hook? Is it more unpleasant to catch a swallow than a trout with a mimetic fly? The swallowed feathery bait and the metal point snagging and catching fast in the throat. The taut, transparent line linking the flustered old uncle to the frantic swallow. The beat of the struggling fish. The different pulls in air and water as registered in the sinewy tremor and tug in the nerves and muscles of the hands.

Very well. The reader should now *break that line*. Forget that boy and his plump sister clapping her hand to her mouth, and the trembling, put-upon uncle, but remember the small hook with its barb and the amazing variety of feathers from dead birds that can be tied round it to fool a fish into thinking the whole is an insect.

Let us recap – and see.

The stone skelped briskly across river water, diminishing its skip as it went until at the fourth it abruptly leapt upwards, striking first the swallow and, deflected sharply downwards, in an amazing coincidence, a rising trout. The stone splashes and as it sinks to the river bed, wavering like some enormous petrified flake of pudding-stone snow, it exerts enough pull to draw the stunned bodies of a swallow and a trout together in a slow spin, wing to fin, tail to head.

Light switch? Not yet. A few practical details first. The 'I' in this book is multiple. For instance, one 'I' agrees wholeheartedly with Byron (the library here is largish but old and stagnant) that 'no angler can be a good man'. This other 'I' would quite like to have fished himself but somehow never managed it. But both agree with Dr Henry Jekyll that man or woman is many more than 'truly two', can make up a facet of 'I's.

Now close and gently rub one eye. The rain has stopped. This is a summer night. Soothe the upper lid. Press gently on the orb.

You may obtain carbon sparks. Or a quick, miniature roundlet of aurora borealis. Or a gelatinous speckle. Or a blue so dark it resembles ink-soaked blotting paper. A few sentimental readers will, I know, have the swallow take to the air in a flurry of drops, have the trout swirl and regain the shadow of the river bank. I find that difficult to understand. But then nor do I understand the pious lie of lacking time to read when a desire not to is perfectly respectable.

The reader I love best may wish, instead of placing this small, indulgent tome by the bed, to slip it under the pillow or even into the lower side of the pillowcase. Compact book, soft pillow.

Not exactly ten minutes? And if you read aloud?

Click.

2

Imagine Narcissus from a fish's point of view. Right, let me try. I see a wide, round, convex containment of a beautiful but pained male face. It would depend on the stage of his love affair with his own reflection, but what if he is already weeping and 'tears double and redouble what is seen'?

That tear quote is from my first-ever part in a film version of a French Romantic tale in which just-dawned puberty, innocence and a copious lachrymous facility coexist in suggestions of islanded incest. Imagine Narcissus from a camera's point of view. This little Narcissus found the phrase intimidatingly difficult to pronounce. When I am nervous my mouth does not dry up, it fills with saliva and I was worried I would spray someone or, worse, make a lovely female reflection flinch. I may also have worried that it would make me look ugly; at sixteen I was fearful but stubbornly vain.

I read once in one of those flight magazines that are more gloss than content, of a notion that the stages of gestation are mirrored and extended during youth; I was jet lagged, and I think I had strayed into reading the article because our first child was about to be born, but if I remember right the article suggested that at about the age of five a child corresponds to the fish stage in the womb and in adolescence kicks. That is not exactly reincarnation. If reincarnation brings physical change to the concept of spiritual discreteness, this merely makes determinism wistful.

Flossing my teeth, I go from upper snappers to lower. Let me try to be as dry-eyed as Gilmerton. A moth that resembles a leaf twitches its wings and dislodges a drop of rainwater that falls into a pool, the consequent ripples expanding out over the reflection of a child's surprised face. The surprise widens even more as a fish rises through the reflected face to see whether the drop is an insect or motes of moth dust. Then, with a beat of its tail, the fish turns away, distorting the reflected face into elongated fragments of colour. No. I may have Gilmerton's vocabulary about right but there is something wrong with the tone. Ah, yes. 'Nature's mirror is never untrue.' Another ghastly line from that film.

The director, Dominique, treated the pair of us, girl and boy, with the briskness of an uncomfortable stepmother, until she began to suspect that I had difficulties with what she termed 'the poetic'. I tried.

'But if I am crying, what is seen is not doubled or redoubled. Wouldn't it blur?'

'My dear, it is the camera that looks, not you. Sort out your perspectives.'

'Yes.'

'But?'

'In English it sounds odd.'

'How?'

'Precious, I think.'

Dominique smiled with a charmingly controlled tremor and patted my hand.

'Whatever it sounds, David dear, it is not precious.'

Was the word I wanted 'prissy'? 'Pompous'? Dominique tapped out something morse-like on my knuckles. 'There is nothing so beautiful,' she crooned, 'except when tears double and redouble what is seen.'

Unhappily I nodded. I was filming during a summer school holiday from Edinburgh in wet season Martinique and while dreading tongue and teeth and sound I was also getting into a snorrel about the upcoming tears. Dominique took hold of my head.

'Do you have a sister, David?'

'No.'

'Then for God's sake have one! Imagine her!' And so saying, Dominique ran fluttering fingers over an outline of *my* body, as if with a tuck and a pinch and a little fleshy padding I could easily make up a sister of my own.

Dread and sulk made my eyelashes quite sticky enough for the subsequent drops (from a generous pipette). The words themselves dribbled hoarsely out of an unplosive pout and I almost swooned.

'But that's perfect!' said Dominique in that tone of hers in which her English took on traces of hankering after French. 'You see? What you have to do is make your heart [*poking me in the chest*] work through your head [*rapping my skull with her knuckles*]!'

Astringent mouthwash. Rinse, spit. Naturally the view in the film was never from underwater but a tricky mirroring of the girl's lovely face. I was a considerably shyer beauty than she. And yes, there is something about Gilmerton's injunction – Imagine Narcissus from a fish's point of view – reminiscent of exercises for budding actors. Dominique immediately gave me one. She made me stand on one leg and hold a hen's egg with the toes of my other foot.

'You have enormous feet,' she said and then, in case I missed her meaning, 'really too big to be handsome.'

While I stood on one of them she showed me the reproduction of a painting. Dominique told me that the 'manner' of the painting was German and impressionistic but that the subject belonged to Edwardian businessman's art. A basketball-tall, very slender black warrior stands on one leg but with a spear even taller than he as support, while around him lie several naked and comparatively dumpy white women in states of blowsy angst. The only standing woman is in the background, tied at the wrists and raising her eyes heavenward – or towards the rather thin top of that long spear.

'As art it is incurable,' said Dominique, 'and I want you to ignore the prurient racism.'

'He is leaning on a spear.'

'Shh. I want you to imagine what the warrior model was really doing.'

I wobbled. 'Looking after cattle?'

'Oh. That's quite good. Yes. You like women, don't you?'

'I am still standing on one leg,' I said.

Dominique looked up at me. 'My dear David, it is a question of dignity. You must be a noble savage. You are perfectly at home in nature. This is your world. You have grown up here in freedom from civilisation and consequently from any sort of humiliation.'

I cleared my throat. 'I can't put my foot down without breaking the egg.'

'Exactly! You have quite captured my thought.'

'I have?'

'Of course! Just put your foot down.'

At sixteen I was easily embarrassed but probably more easily able to consider any adult as crazy. I glanced round to see if anyone was watching us. Jerking my ankle and loosening my toes, I flicked up the egg and just managed to catch it in my hand.

'Ah,' sighed Dominique, 'you've been stringing me along. But understand my position. A director has to make everything clear. No, no, dear, from now on walk barefoot as much as you can.'

I remember being stuck with the egg but not what I finally did with it. Put it in a flowerpot? And I have now read quite a few times on flights that when a group of cranes sleeps, one of them stands on guard on one leg, gripping in the claws of the raised foot a convenient stone. Should the guard fall asleep, the stone will fall and the noise . . . ach, it is twenty years since I did that film. Reviews were dire, receipts poor everywhere except in France and Spain I think, though that had more to do with recently permitted prurient hopes than the film itself.

'You're terribly tall,' said the resolutely miserable old British actor who played our saintly uncle. All his remarks, from nature's mirror to the most trivial, were tremendously pronounced. As an actor he was also tremendously unhelpful but I learnt from him. He was the first I had encountered in the profession with a stammer and startling facial tics which only vanished when he acted. He talked insistently of approaching death but is still alive, still active, still often to be seen in the role of saintly age; perhaps I am prejudiced. His saintliness seems wilfully insincere. The lovely girl, my poor screen sister, returned to modelling clothes, made a record, I think, and committed suicide or died of an overdose four years later. She gave no sign of liking me very much. '*Mais il est écossais et tout lourd.*' Which hurt because I thought of her as amazingly self-assured and almost perfectly good-looking. A photograph I saw of her recently shows a sulky, slightly plump-faced girl with a nose not quite straight; my memory had given her a sheen, like a coloured and varnished little ghost. Francine Puy. Towards the end of shooting when I had loosened up and probably needed to be reined in, Dominique talked vaguely to me of her plan to make more Romantic films, including Benjamin Constant's *Adolphe* which she thought might suit me 'when you have more beard' but nothing came of it and the last I heard of her was when she won a prize for an advertisement in Cannes, statues delightedly depetrifying when the product passed by.

From jungle creepers and studio pools I returned to Edinburgh and was immediately asked to take part in a school production of *Hamlet*. I put my name down for the role of Horatio.

'But surely everyone identifies with Hamlet?' said the teacher in charge.

'I'd like to play Horatio, sir.'

He grunted and considered his clipboard. 'Well, we do need someone for Claudius. Now, Orr, that *is* a challenging role.'

'I'd prefer to try for Horatio, really, sir.'

The teacher took off his spectacles and gave me a ludicrously grave face as if his spectacles might hinder my impression of how serious he was. I must have been unbearable.

'I'd like, you know, to think you were pulling your weight.'

'Oh, but I love the part. I'm longing to do it.'

'Ah,' he said. He rubbed the marks on either side of his nose and replaced his glasses. 'Well. I suppose you know what you are doing.'

I have a line for that now. 'A moth it is to trouble the mind's eye.' Act One, Scene One, 'it' referring to the Ghost, often excluded but not at my school in December 1977. My tan had faded but in Edinburgh I still felt serene and cocky, something of a minstrel. And it was after that school production, when I was still in costume and with greasepaint on my face, that my father put on his pensative lawyer's face.

'I suppose you do realise that acting can lead to quite substantial remuneration. I mean, I wouldn't rule the profession out of court simply because of the risk factor.'

'The film isn't out yet. And I've an awful lot of exams this year.'

'Oh, quite. But I was thinking longer term, mm?'

I was about to hear my father crow – something I had never heard before.

'Ah, yes,' he said, whirling round for another lawyer father, grabbing and pumping his hand, 'Horatio One, Hamlet Nothing, eh?'

I went home and there in the poorly lit intimacy of conversation (silent, entirely facial) with my image in the mirror, considered not so much knowing myself as how I looked to others. It is difficult now to raise that dreamy vanity again. A large part of the thrill came from an absolute surety that I needed, both physically and mentally, scrupulous self-awareness. Surprised? I was – and practised surprise a little. I remember at that time being pleasantly frightened that I would exhaust my face, have nothing else left to see. Naturally, when I did get another part – seven months later, this time in the US – I frightened myself properly, remembering the arrogant feel of that school-hall evening almost with despair a fraction before I had to speak. My role was as an apprentice thirties gangster, shy, stammering, quite dominated by his psychotic brother. On his violent death I am the nice-looking boy with hat and long lashes who does not break down but who reaches out for a gun, lifts it, weighs it and calmly blows someone's brains over a dirty brick wall. I then test my hand – no tremble – and work my mouth – no taste – and, through my puzzlement, realise I have experimented myself into a vocation. The other gang members shuffle their feet, blink and some lips twitch. They have a new leader. My mother described my role, correctly but unhelpfully, as that of a 'violent tyke' but my father, who had felt uncomfortable with me falling in love with a sister, found it, perhaps by way of compensation, 'spot on'. The film was on television again not long ago and I thought I looked too much like a sleepwalker trying to sneer.

'Balls,' said Isabel. 'It has snap. You look tricked.'

The third entry in Gilmerton's pillow book – he had a habit of making his notes in the margins on either side of the page, an obscure sort of literary double accounting – is directly across from fish and Narcissus and is as follows: 'Less irony, *more* gall.'

3

The possibilities in a ten-minute book are as many and as invigorating as those in a summer night. Among them:

1) A childhood incident, say. The death of a ten-year-old brother in a fall from an apple tree in the walled orchard. The circumstances reviewed by a surviving sibling at different ages – twenty-four, forty-eight, sixty-six, eighty-four. The brother's emphasis on resentment, grief or responsibility shift but the incident always ends on his own desire for a juicy apple followed by a most sonorous thud on the grass, the crack of a neck.

2) Waking from a tangled dream and, while waking, watching the dream shapes calmly moving off to continue elsewhere. As a child, thrusting a stick into a fish-pond, I used to urge the refraction to detach and swim away. Recently it occurred to me – I was dull, just woken – that in memory refractions have a tendency to be recalled as coloured shadows. It is the other part, whatever casts the shadow or induces the refraction, that remains elusive. I look down. The stick becomes a swagger stick, then effortlessly forking, a rod for a water diviner.

3) The description and life history – ovum (egg), larva (caterpillar), pupa (cocoon), imago (adult) – and distribution of the (invented) Moister Moth. The Pale-shouldered Brocade, the Powered Quaker, the Heart and Dart and the Swallow Prominent all fly.

4) A literary ages of man – Dickens and candlelit grotesques till ten, Rousseau and cherries till twenty, Byron and starched turbans

till thirty, Smollett and sensitive nostrils till forty, frumpish Richardson and drooping lids till fifty, Thackeray and twitching tendons till sixty, Wordsworth and lake, pond and puddle till seventy. Styles of perception, more or less loving parodies of each author.

5) An historical venture, the shift of a word, the growth of an etymological crystal; *see also* nomenclature and clearer creatures.

Yesterday was my first walk outside for nine months. I did not go far. The drive at Lampenham forks, towards a hill on one side, towards a copse of beech trees on the other. The trees were nearer so I chose them, a distance of not more than two hundred yards. The walk was harder than I expected, accompanied after some fifty yards by a sensation as if I were leaking energy through the bones of my feet. And though the rest of my walk was at a slow, doddering stroll, interrupted by several stops to rest, I arrived at the copse in an enervated sweat, promptly flopped down with my back to a tree across the drive from a field of fat-tailed, tallow-coloured sheep. Faint, queasy, I let my lung whistle. I should have brought something to eat; my blood felt thin and skittish. I shut my eyes and breathed as deeply as I could. I groaned and nearly fainted. A prickle of panic on my skin. How could I possibly get help?

I do not know why. Perhaps my body grew bored with this little drama. Almost before I knew it, I had made do with shade, the dappling of the leaves, the smell of beech and earth and, latterly, by breaking off a small piece of moss from the tree-trunk and staining my fingers a thin, desiccated green.

And then my ears picked up the muffled sound of small, slow water. I rose like a knight in armour, slowly and with comically unoiled joints. Some fifteen yards on, behind some trees and bushes, I came across a plant-charged pool, roughly boat shaped and the size of a sunken trawler with an arrangement of stiles at the prow end, where the water dropped down a short, contrived fall. I set to looking for the entry point, moved round through the grass and wild flowers, towards the stern. A dragonfly came off its lily pad and nosed about its territory. Something aquatic plashed. A woodpigeon called from the other side of the copse. And under a thick tuft of grass and buttercups, I found a square, stone mouth from which water flowed as exiguously as treacle; any slower and the water would have been dripping. After a while I made out a variation in that flow, a slight ebb and flux as if someone nearer the source was adding small scoops of water. There was slime on the stone and, directly under the opening, in the space between flow and stone, a spider was furnishing its diving-bell with air. I stood up. The shadow of a quick cloud passed over me and then, a little ahead to my right, a beech sapling, still with its supporting stake. I saw first the eaten leaves, almost heard the stolid munching of those jaws a fraction before I saw the caterpillar itself.

Now the name Lobster Moth has the sound of old-fashioned nonsense beloved of uncles who enjoy the rhythmic squeezing of young hams.

> The Lobster Moth
> Cuts its cloth
> With pincers –
> Like this! Like this! Like this!

But the Lobster Moth is as much a moth as those that sound out of Sherlock Holmes, like the Scarce Vapourer or the Hebrew Character or the Dingy Footman; then there is that freakish Elephant Hawk-moth which can swim if it falls into water; or, with a shudder in the nursery, the Death's-head Hawkmoth whose larva can cause havoc to potatoes and which, unlike its elephant cousin, can squeak through the proboscis as decidedly as a mouse. I think it is fair to say that the death's head on the hawkmoth of that name is usually a clear representation of a skull and crossbones. Sometimes this foxes the beholder; it is one thing to make out a wooden-legged pirate with a parrot on his shoulder in a shadow on a wall, another to find that nature runs up a perfect Jolly Roger each time a certain moth issues from its cocoon. What does the coincidence mean? Nothing. It is a perfect but pointless coincidence involving camouflage in moths and a beholder who has read *Treasure Island*.

The universal name for the Lobster Moth is *Stauropus fagi*. Again, it should be borne in mind that scientific or taxonomic Latin names are still often the translation of an unscientific one – or another shorthand try at differentiation. *Arctornis l-nigrum* is the Black V Moth, *Notodonta ziczac* the Pebble Prominent. In other words moth names are always involved in similes of perception, sometimes only slightly more subtle than that of the lobster crustacean (*locusta*) which is called after an insect, the also edible locust (*locusta*).

But the intriguing thing about the Lobster Moth larva or caterpillar is that this pleasantly bizarre little creature endeavours to deceive its predators by imitating *two* others, namely a large ant and a fat grub. The ant part, intent and busily antish with its legs, rears up to get better purchase on the grub, rudimentary and recalcitrant, which writhes and drags. I had heard of this living deceit before but never seen it so I broke off the twig and took the Lobster Moth larva back with me to rear in captivity.

'That is extraordinary!' said Aubrey Gilbert as I was walking round the house. 'I did exactly the same! As soon as I could hobble out, I went and picked a flower. The smell was amazingly sweet. I felt almost drunk.'

'This isn't a flower, Aubrey.'

'What is it?'

I told him.

'My word,' he said. He skooked. 'It looks like something out of Tenniel. Isn't there something about a lobster quadrille in *Alice in Wonderland*? Though this little chap doesn't look anything like a lobster.'

'No.' I explained to him something of the caterpillar's mimetic abilities.

'I say. That's like the wrestler in music-hall who wrestles himself, as it were. The one I saw had got himself up as a Chinese and a small, straw-stuffed dragon.'

'I am thinking of something to keep it in.'

'How about a tobacco tin?'

'If it doesn't smell too much.'

'Why's that?'

'You can use tobacco oil or smoke to kill some moths.'

'Good Lord!' said Aubrey, performing a small hop on his newly tipped crutch. He asked me what I thought. 'A hop is quite expressive, but the movement tends to degenerate into a stutter.'

The Lobster Moth larva is now ensconced with its beech leaves in a scrubbed tin that once contained one hundred Craven A cigarettes. There is a thin metallic smell but no hint of tobacco. The caterpillar is now at rest, has paused in its eating, has head and tail raised, giving it that pleasantly absurd heraldic appearance, Lobster Moth rampant or whatever the term is. I have moved it away from the lamp and put it in shadow. There are still nearly thirty minutes to midnight. Lampenham is cool and quiet.

I am not sure why but I have always associated night with freedom. It is more than an association. I have, ever since I can remember, always stayed awake at night. I have a feeling of waking up at dusk, of feeling more alive then. This has nothing to do with insomnia. I sleep all right. It is simply that I find fifteen-minute naps very refreshing and two hours, preferably after a meal, preferably in the afternoon, quite enough. There is nothing grand about it. It is quite humdrum. As a child I preferred owls to eagles, moths to butterflies, slow-worms to snakes. The day I shared with others. I wished to see at night. Which is to say that I do not associate sleep with darkness and that night certainly does not come to me with grandiose or tenebrous properties. I am still asked the oddest questions. Dr Burnet here, for example, has quizzed me more than once.

'Do you have an explanation for your sleeping habits?'

'Just that. Habit. I suppose there might be a physiological element, there may be a predisposition, but my understanding is that sleep is a matter of acquired habit or routine and in that I am no different from anyone else except in the timing. What is your suspicion?'

Burnet smiled. 'No suspicions. You know, I take it, that opium eaters claim that ten or fifteen minutes under the influence is as refreshing as eight hours' sleep. It is, as it were, a particularly good quality sleep, something like a concentrate of rest.'

'Yes. But I have never taken opium and the morphine I was given made me feel awful, as if my blood had been invaded.'

'Have you wondered why? The brain certainly releases a sedative to assist sleep. They say women have similar to help them with pain.'

'I have no evidence I am particularly good with pain.'

Burnet nodded. 'Childbirth,' he mouthed. He shrugged. 'What I'd really like to know is the extent to which the dream faculty is part of the sensation of having rested. Also more on the chemical basis of some of the images we have. Do you believe in an afterlife?'

'No. You're not going to talk to me about lights and tunnels, are you?'

'No. But can I ask – did you *know* you had been wounded?'

'Ah. I remember sitting down. I am not sure I didn't go deaf. I felt someone was shrieking but that it had nothing to do with me. Then my back hurt, but no, I couldn't have said what had happened. I was told later I was knocked straight over but that is not my memory. I felt very urgently drowsy then, terribly cold. I could hear gurgling sounds, felt I was warding something off. And the rest is quick, a sort of mumble of images as I went out. I can remember two. One was of someone running away from me, over a very unbattle-like field. And just before I lost consciousness entirely I saw tiny shards of frozen water, a fountain of ice seeds and I knew they had a hole in the middle, were hollow like a crown. I don't know. The running-away part is surely belated sense. And for all I know the second image is a crude try at representing what had happened to me, the hollow being a hole in my lung and the fountain of ice alarm. I don't think being wounded leads to a particularly interesting response.'

'Damn,' groaned Burnet. 'I sometimes have an almost crystalline impression of pain, think I'll be able to capture it – but then it softens and wafts away.'

Although I have known Burnet for a very short time I am already getting quite fond of him.

4

To *try* to sleep is absurd. Sleep is not answerable to thought and decision. Sleep is the obverse of effort. And yet I have just caught myself in the bathroom mirror at a valetudinarian pottering, behaving as if I might be able to beguile sleep by bedtime routine. I once played an impotent in a farce, haughtily ignoring any localisation of blood supply but employing a desperately languid care about brushing his hair well back off his face in between keeks through the crack in the door at the girl on the bed. There are three half-foot-wide worn stone steps from our bathroom down to the creaking and uneven floor of our bedroom.

Once I am stretched out in bed, however, sleep feels attractively near by. I yawn. I have recently been looking again at Henry James's *The Ambassadors*, but not in any consecutive way. I open the book and read for a few minutes. My eyes follow the lines, my lids droop, I lose focus twice, I drift drowsily in various refracted tints. I can even, as sleep presses softly down, hear, in the way of distant cellarage, the hero's stick tapping on the stone floor of Notre Dame. Then I yawn again, but with vigour. I mean the yawn is perversely energetic, even includes the faint sound of a snarl. I wipe an eye, stifle another yawn, shut the book and put it on the bedside table by the clock and turn off the lamp. The night air is warm and still but the darkness makes it feel pleasantly cooler. Isabel wassles nearer. We kiss, amiably share lips, saliva and toothpaste. She is seven months pregnant. She rests her head on my chest and we all lie motionless. From the farm on the other side of the diminutive loch, about fifty yards away behind the trees, a sheep coughs and beats its head twice against a sheet of corrugated iron. We wait. Silence.

'Thank God for that,' sighs Isabel. I kiss her forehead and taste cold cream. 'Horses can give birth and drop dead of old age,' she says. 'You have to get up in the morning.'

She is mumbling in her near-sleep. Another kiss, this one already drier. Isabel turns on her side, I turn on my front.

Time to sleep. Slowly I slide my right hand under the pillow (I sleep on the right, window side) and push my left hand palm up along my thigh – a limp parody of a swimmer's crawl – and I begin to unache, from shoulder through to hand, from thigh down to feet, my back. Some yielding colours, left over from Mme de Vionnet probably, touches of violet and salmon pink and very white flesh, drift enticingly across my inner lids . . . and a slip-second after I find myself face down in water.

There is a slight pop of surprise but no discomfort, no sensation of holding my breath, nor for that matter any feel of wet or cold. But I can see the water, tinged as faint camomile tea, as it streams beneath me and I can separate the lovely mottling of the river bed from the shimmer and shift of surface dapple superimposed on it.

And then I pick out a fish over the river bed; it is the tail that gives it away as it beats ahead of me to the right, nearer the bank – too prosthetically beige. The rest is a pale, slimy ochre with umberish and human mole motes on its back. As I watch the fish wriggles downwards on to the river bed and stirs up small plumes of sand and grit that expand and sweep towards me. Immediately I swing leftwards, sink a little deeper, push a little further upstream, a sensation not of river current on my shoulders but of somehow heaving against cloth and flesh, as if I were in a rugby scrum. I barely have time to be puzzled. Out of the current, at first approaching quite fast, then halting to give a couple of clumsy twitches, comes a derisory hook; it is as soft and wide as a child's apprentice J, has no barb and attached to the top part are two scruffily tied pigeon feathers. I know there is danger in this absurdity. But it is no use.

Wait, wait. I am sure, at least in theory, that the dream plan is not a bad one; to sleep lulled by water, even to take advantage of that current and turn tail and sweep downstream into sleep.

No sleep. With the abruptness of released bubbles my lids spring open. My eyes, rather than my body, feel exasperatingly refreshed by the dip, are awake as if I had just slept for hours. Behind them I can feel a sluggish consciousness sliding over a few pebble-like items, leaving silverish traces on Gilmerton's fish and Narcissus and river bank, but then speeding up, dismissing images and explanations, while my body drags along and my feet and hands savour a last dunk of sleep. My eyes focus on the window, then the luminous arms of the clock. It is barely after eleven thirty. I have been asleep for two minutes. I wince but keep quite still.

We acquired this expensive, long-term bed when we married but in the six years we have had it, the thing has learnt to communicate each respective twitch or shift we make, has become an almost deliriously sensitive extension of marriage through bed-springs. Isabel normally starts three times before she is fast asleep, each start apparently descending a level of unconsciousness but with a pronounced yark. I am not sure which of the three that was but to avoid some of that twitter and twitch I turn on to my back.

I suppose my wakefulness has some novelty value. This is the first period in my life that I have ever been an insomniac. I have always been quite the reverse. When I was a child, Nanny Grizel (my name for her) or Nanny G (my parents') called me, with some pride, David Orr Sleepyhead. The lightest touch of a pillow under my cheek acted on me as Pavlov's bell on his dogs, except while they salivated for food, I dribbled on to cotton. With age, sleep's grip on me slackened, but not very much; I could easily drop off when travelling and, on long days, nap between takes. I was cheerful about admitting that this could disgust, like a glutton who stays slim, but my relations with sleep have only exercised me twice. The other occasion was on the breakup of my first marriage.

Stupid and lumpish with failure, I noted I cleared my throat a great deal, have since noted it is something other men in an emotional bind do too; it is hardly a defence mechanism but, at the price of a raw throat, it kept me at least from shuttling too close to either vomit or sobs. I swallowed, pursed my lips, nodded, went ah-hrrum again.

At great length but in the quietest of tones, almost as if musing, my first wife Kirsty refined her descriptions of my behaviour. She paused.

'Dear God,' she said, as if discovering something, 'you have been treating me as an embarrassing but *harmless* hallucination.'

I protested but she had settled on that formula and licked her lips as if licking the sticky part of an envelope. A failed marriage is an inexhaustible source of discomfort, hurt and guilt; hurt, guilty with the hurt I had caused her, guilty with relief when she left, I put my head on the kitchen table. I was, like Gilmerton, twenty-six years old but found that sealed pine surface quite as acceptable as down and linen. I slept for five hours, woke in the dark, went to bed for another eight.

Now, ten years later, I am unable to sleep. Causes? I have never before been co-producer as well as actor in a film and I suppose risk and responsibility may have joined with a characteristic of the role to keep me awake. All that is plausible enough but somehow I don't feel it is all the story. I am an actor, I am more than suggestible but I have an impression of something else. I am not, however, an anguished insomniac; in fact I quite believe insomnia can prove addictive. Nor do I feel very bad. There are times during the day when I can experience fatigue as a dispossessing weight, an experience that has made me aware of coming into possession of my mind in a way I had not known before, the weight of tiredness blotting me out for a few seconds, to be followed by a sort of reverse swoon, an upward surge into myself again. But no, I don't think this is what Gilmerton meant when he wrote to his mother at the end of May 1916, saying, 'At last I can recognise myself again when I look out.' Still, I think I might try a Gilmertonian pillow experiment, potter a little in levels of wakefulness. Lidwork and bedwarmth.

When I first met Heidi Nutall I thought at once of Gertrude Stein. This was hardly fair to either. I had only heard of Gertrude

Stein in 1981 while shooting a wet thriller in Vancouver and munching one of Alice B. Toklas's cookies and waiting for some effect (not much). Later I saw a reproduction of Picasso's 1906 portrait of Stein but it was a photograph taken in the twenties, rather Picassoish in the pose, that settled in my mind an image of her in a perpetual late middle age, squat, tilting sideways in a tweed suit, her grey hair short and Romanised, resolutely treating her knee as a bar and the camera as a barman. In other words I have only that image and pose, and a very idle impression of her as a writer interested in cubism and semantic roses, a universal but decidedly intellectual aunt.

Heidi Nutall appeared to be her clone, a resemblance so startling it made me consider – and find there was little resemblance at all. I was shaking the hand of a plump-faced, not very tall lady in late middle age who did not dye her short, brushed-back hair and who appeared shy but very determined. It is also true that she looked sensibly and dowdily dressed, was wearing stout grey-green lace-up shoes, but as she led the way to our table I appreciated that what I had taken as tweed was a much lighter material with a green and black design in the cloth so discreet as to be barely visible. And when we sat face to face I saw that her blouse, first seen as soggily cut beige was, when a fold shifted, expensively tailored, thick silk. I was reminded of a time when as a child I suddenly understood the cream in a bun was genuine and not baker's cheese. There was a pricey aplomb to the finishing on her clothes, in the buttons and angler's quality and care of the thread and sewing. The face on top, soft-water skin, no make-up, very pale blue eyes peering across the table at me. There is a reason, she said, that we eat, in an Anglo-Japanese restaurant, some thin soups and various sorts of raw and smoked fish.

'Ah.'

'I want,' she said, 'to call the film *Almost a Hero*.'

It is a good title. But she barely gave me time to consider it. Her fist clenched, her words about the project began to whizz in a hoarse, insistent whisper, the middle finger of her right hand to make small excursions from the bunch, first circling, then, like someone at ecstatic morse, pecking. She was trying hard to keep insistence away from her enthusiasm but wasn't able to manage it; she'd tut, grimace and hasten on. After some time the waiter asked us if we wanted more tea.

'Certainly not!' said Heidi Nutall. And then, 'Ah. No. No, thank you. I think . . . the bill instead?' She sat back and blinked. 'How old are you?'

'Thirty-six,' I said.

'I'm fifty-three.' She folded her napkin and put it on the table, slowly and gently, like a cloth sigh. 'I find as I get older that I need to know whether or not people have understood me.'

'In general, I think I have.'

'*Almost a Hero* is a film about what people made of and tried to make of Gilmerton. *That's the subject.* We make use of Gilmerton's own observations – he kept a laconic sort of diary – but the real matter is what other people thought or chose to remember. That's why, for example, you'll stride across the Meadows and the snow in Edinburgh in Japanese dress on your way to visit your black mistress. Not because Gilmerton did – he didn't – but because someone else liked the notion enough to write it down. Is that clearer?'

I nodded. 'You're not that someone else?'

'Good heavens, no!' she said and looked shocked.

The only benefit as an actor that I recall from my previous ability to sleep was in a humdrum TV film, as the husband and family man who has blank spells and genuinely does not know who is terrifying the neighbourhood. But that is blood on his gardening gloves, his roman-numeralled watch is haywire and his secateurs have sprung again. I spent a lot of the film as if I had just been shaken awake.

And as an insomniac? If I let my mind sink . . . yes, I see Heidi Nutall in that tatty restaurant, holding up something in her chopsticks.

'This shrimp looks ruptured,' she said and peered. 'I'm not sure it is even that. You know when a boiled egg has leaked from a crack in the shell and you get a solid white extrusion like a wee cloud? This shrimp looks to have the same consistency as egg-white. Extraordinary! It almost destroys your notion of what a shrimp might be.'

5

My dear girl, of course I have no objections. Indeed, I am grateful
you should ask. My only condition is that you allow me to remember
little by little – easier for me to tackle. Although I was not hit on
the head I sometimes have the peculiar impression that my memory
has been, as it were, winded; it has vague but resistant holes, usually
to do with a gap between belief and cause in trivial background
matters. For example, I can recall perfectly well that you were never
nurseried, that you lived in unhealthy, swagged splendour from the
earliest age – but you were eight when we left that house. Are you
saying you *never* visited the nursery? Please don't misunderstand.
This has to do with me sometimes feeling very much the simpleton
and bringing out small mental blocks of the kind – large house, few
people.

The nursery was at the top of the eastern extremity, underneath
all those turrets and ogee roofs and decorated chimney stalks, and
combined the particularities of yacht design with all the space of a
town church. The main axis was an infantile exercise area or gym-
nasium, crossed towards the far end to make two large recesses, on
one side for a schoolroom, on the other an area for eating. The
overall shape was a rectangle with bedrooms, bathrooms, cupboards
and storerooms filling out the cross.

I never really cared for the climbing ropes that hung down from
stout hooks in the cross-beams. The knots looked – and were –
false. They were additions, threaded on like beads on a string and

attached by wooden pegs, and they looked like twisted, rather sad quoits – they had something of the downcast droop you see in bread dough before it is baked. You also missed the swing and a toboggan or slide (which ended up dismantled because the width was too narrow for the height).

Some time ago I read of an aristocratic Spanish couple in the eighteenth century who made the decision to bring up their children 'on enlightened principles', a charming if vague idea. It reminded me of our father. He added another hypothetical element. As far as I know the house was finished and furnished a year *before* he met our mother. He certainly allowed for the possibilities of a very large family in his calculations. But in retrospect I am most pleased by a coincidental aspect to all the effort he expended on the design of the nursery; for five years I lived surrounded by the painstaking attentions of a father I had not met. For example, and on the same principle that those false knots on the climbing ropes could be adjusted to allow for growth, there were two doorknobs on each door, the usual thing and one placed at a height for small children. The upper was of china, the lower smooth wood.

All the woods used were Japanese and most of the furniture and toys were made in Japan though it was only later I understood it was unusual to have bricks, swing, rocking horse and so on, of one wood. Or that the letters on one set of bricks had been burnt in by a poker in the same style as the exhortative words 'Brush Hair Teeth Nails' in the four sides of the frame of my washstand mirror. I have just checked; that is still the order I follow today before shaving. Likewise all the cupboard and drawer handles were made with a poker, a moat arrangement in solid wood, leaving in the centre a smoothed round knob flush with the surface.

Our father was a devotee of Japanese hygiene but for his Scottish house wedded seemliness to cleanliness. Accordingly he designed and had made in Japan two sorts of cabinets to contain two different types of bath. They fitted together along one wall of each bathroom. On one side was a round, zinc-lined affair one could step into to soap over and be sluiced down. On the other was a round hardwood bath with an adjustable seat; one had to climb up some steps to get into it. And as an engineer, our father designed an arrangement of tanks and pipes; there was a tank to collect rainwater which connected with a boiler behind the stoves. The proposed girls' side was on the left as you entered the nursery, the boys' on the right. Yes, and there were five differently sized chamber-pots in the cupboards on both sides made of hardwood, the boys' a kind of saddle arrangement.

But I think the most striking thing in the nursery was a reversal of the normal daytime arrangement of sky and earth. In the playroom part the ceiling was reminiscent of the inside of the upturned hull of a large wooden ship. There were stout cross-beams and beyond that the ceiling was vaulted and panelled in planks of a dark, tea-red wood.

The floor, however, was a creamy tone of mushroom white, shading at scuffs into pale, moleskin grey. I could never make out the grain of the wood. Every three months or so maids would scrub it, using soft flakes of pale green soap, gleaming copper-wired brushes and always a circular motion. I do not know whether or not to trust my memory but when I crouched down after the floor had been washed, the wood appeared slightly spongiform – that is, with holes as in a network of bubbles or the cross-section of a bone – but as it dried it filled out. I had thought the wood might have been chosen because it was easy to fall on – no splinters and remark- ably yielding – but some time later our mother thought it was used 'because it soaked up sound and nails' – which will do just as well.

I certainly did not think of it then and disliked the suggestion later that there was something of Noah's Ark about the place. But it is true, though I do not know who the Charles Greene responsible for them was, that there were paintings of animals on the walls between the dado and the start of the wood ceiling. They were executed in *trompe-l'oeil* manner, but without much in the way of eye-trickery. The paints were probably oil based but the colours were by a seasick Watteau, with a bright, pallid disassociation from the subject matter. The salmon leaping out of the dado or the red deer or the half-asleep grey seal had too much light in them and a certain irritatingly, repletely coy touch about the eyes or nostrils. I remember bubbles of varnish in which a small crescent of cobalt blue cradled a smaller crescent of flake white and a point of black: nostril, pupil, the spots on the salmon's back.

There were other animals on other walls from more exotic places. All bore simple identification in clotted Gothic lettering. A wall a continent in the main, though one wall contained a duck-billed platypus and a wallaby up left while down right a kiwi peered into a corner. There was a giraffe and a gazelle. There was a capuchin monkey swinging down from the branch of a vertically halved tree with a sloth on the trunk and an armadillo by the roots. There was no Japan. And there were no moralistic nonsenses, no lions nuzzling lambs, but the overall effect was listless, a world of bone-ash walls and wrongness of tone, best seen in the flamingo which at dusk took on a green tinge like raw meat going off.

I lived there with Tsuru. I believe she was nineteen years old when I was born. By the age of five, when I left the nursery and she returned to Japan, I came up to her shoulder. I don't think *I* was aware of that intense sense of possession children can feel for their nannies until long afterwards when someone described her as 'not exactly a beauty, eh?' Of course it is true I always found particularly irritating that pleasure which a verbal vulgarian like our mother's youngest brother felt when the formula of an insult struck him as sufficiently cast with sugar – he felt a rare little crunch – but the whole thing was absurd. Not just for my being incensed enough to clench my fist. Nor for the gratuitous relish of the remark. But for the shock of an absolutely different viewpoint.

Well, I still believe Tsuru-san was pleasant to look at, in large part because she was extraordinarily and slyly self-possessed. I was going to say she was a delightful, *plump* colour but that might mislead. Her skin was a pale caramel, but that does not give the impression of smooth glaze and depth. Nor was she at all plump. She had a very firm nose of those that make me think of a clay modeller pinching his material, and eyes that struck me as admirably clearly marked at the lids when compared to the other wrinkled, deep-socketed arrangements around me. I also enjoyed her hair very much. It was very long and every morning she put it up. She began with a parting almost in the centre of her scalp which then curved, just short of a question mark, towards the crown on her left. The hair on that side was pulled back over her ear and the rest was lifted high, passed through a tortoiseshell hoop and issued as two gleaming swells. I am not an expert on long hair; when up, hers looked almost like ribbon but – I don't know if she would have been pleased – gratifyingly imperfect. She wore a succession of striped kimonos, the stripes vertical at the front, horizontal at the wide sleeves. Those stripes could look ribbed or, starting boldly, would fade towards a break I cannot now quite perceive, then resume boldly again.

How extraordinary it must have been for a girl from Kobe to land up near Brechin! Tsuru-san's English was elegantly functional rather than grammatical. She was proud of her family, as far as I know, had nothing to do with the servants. And think of the diet! By the time I was aware of it, she managed by adapting kedgeree, ate smoked fish (salmon, haddock), prepared herring, mackerel and trout herself and a variety of fish soups. I remember that I was, in winter, given cod-liver oil, followed smartly by sweet, black malt. She would join me and then suck hard at a lemon.

Tsuru means stork. She was adept at imitating insect sounds, or rather *suzu mushi*, those the Japanese call singing insects, and could make some out of paper. One called *monin* turned out to be a sword-tailed grasshopper; it had a quiet, almost mournful song and Tsuru-san would imitate it when she considered it time for me to nap.

I don't know about you but I find my memory of, say, my first four years decidedly limited, made up of a few, very possibly unreliable visual spots. Almost all of mine concern Tsuru. I know that our mother has suggested I owe my interest in biology to her tiger moth kimonos and clever imitations but I am not so sure; her imitations were of creatures unknown to me. The things I remember most sharply are exceptional views of her, not the routine. I remember her, quite silent but in tears, turning away from me, a sensation of responsibility for her catching in my own throat, but with no clue as to what might have caused her distress. I remember the shock of falling from the slide (which was then dismantled), akin to waking up but with nothing to recognise, as she ran her fingers over my limbs and head and peered into my eyes. And I remember cutting my finger with a penknife, the welling of the blood being joined by a surprising spurt of tears. She let out a hissing noise.

'Boy not cry,' she said.

'No?'

'Boy brave.'

'Ah.' I found my interest in this information overrode the shock. I stopped crying, let her tend my hand.

When I was five she returned home. When I was ten our father brought a photograph of her with her husband and two small children. He had a formal letter from her to me in Japanese and I was obliged to write back. I felt embarrassed, possibly a little ashamed at my previous affection for her. It was only later that I remembered her, if not with her due, at least better and a little more generously.

Now I wonder whether or not those insect sounds made up a limited, private language of hers to call, check or instruct me. I cannot remember. Ah. But I am not sure if the next memory is not dream. I remember Tsuru appearing one night, her hair loose, dripping water, wrapped in a linen or muslin drape, looking, rare for her, alarmed.

'I am imitating a stoat,' I said.

Tsuru shushed and sighed. 'Oh, night quiet,' she said, 'night very quiet.' I nodded and she hugged me. She smelt, despite being wet, fresh as a warm biscuit.

6

Gilmerton's pillow book is bound in a lovely, grainless, soft leather, eighty years and dyes having combined to parody the look and colour of ripe damson skin. In shadow the stuff is as dark as a blue-black bruise; take it towards the window and the bruise flushes and a ghostwork of greyish underveins appears; put it in direct sunlight and the bruise vanishes into a red-plumped purple.

A few days ago my elder daughter was thrilled to see she had left her fingerprints on the bloom of a bunch of black grapes. 'Are they mine? Really?' she asked and ate one expectantly. Here, clearly marked on the back cover of the pillow book, is a similar though printless effect, part of a left hand, the clear, pale outlines of four fingers. The spine of the book is slightly worn over the lower half and on the front cover there is an area like an elongated quarter section of a circle with pressure points on the inside of the curve. Ms Nutall considers the cause to have been a glove glued to the pillow book to help Gilmerton hold the thing.

I dare say she is right. It is a beautiful detail. But — and I am not sure why — it makes me feel squeamish. It will be in the film and I as Gilmerton have a scene in which I am, if not sticking, at least considering a black leather glove, the pillow book and a fat pot of glue. Soft hide, bound leather, gleaming black on damson. Cut. Gilmerton *putting on* a glovestuck book, *wearing* the thing, letting it hang down. The glove has two press-studs at the wrist. I loathe pressing them in amongst that junction of softish veins underneath; but I find most repulsive the sight of the book unworn, with nowhere for the thumb part to go and the buttoned wrist of the glove limply cantilevered out over the spine. Ms Nutall raised her eyebrows at me.

'We're all susceptible to something,' I said.

'Yes, yes, of course. But how extraordinary. And if I told you I had the original glove?'

Instead of using my name, Heidi Nutall often loads the word 'you'. It is an emphatically wry politeness I associate with Scots-women when they parody getting to know a man. She lifted my hand.

'It looks almost exactly the same size. Of course, the original glove is now rather thin and brittle. Resembles dried-out oil paper. Or an old snakeskin moult with a thumb stall.'

I took back my hand. 'Fine, fine. It's all right, really.'

Heidi Nutall contrived to look accommodating and doubtful at the same time.

'He must, you know, have been trying to strengthen his arm and hand as well. I think of it as being bizarre but somehow shy.'

'Shy?'

'Oh yes. Thank you. I've enjoyed your reaction very much. When I first saw the book I thought, well yes, you probably could use it as a real pillow. Or at least a firm headrest for a nap. But not much more.'

'Yes, I see, I understand, I do.'

'Don't you like props?'

'Oh yes, this will do all right. It will.'

'I had thought we could get some play out of it. Don't you think?'

'Yes, yes. If it is in the completed film.'

Ms Nutall smiled. 'You think he might be secretive about it?'

'Discreet.'

'Yes, I think that's probably better. You might say he was anxious not to take himself too seriously. The discretion would be a little humorous and self-conscious.'

On the frontispiece of the pillow book is a handwritten dedication in blue ink.

To Captain Robert Gilmerton BA, MA
Otherwise 'The Ignoramus'
And also my Darling Brother
On his Twenty-sixth Birthday
'For Thoughts, dear, for Thoughts.'
From his Adoring, Unruly and Very Much Younger Sister
Agnes May Gilmerton
Third April, 1916.

There would have been about three hundred pages of excellent quality vanilla-coloured paper but some of them have been cut out, leaving neat, even strips about a ruler wide and a fraction shorter than the very regular margins Gilmerton left when he wrote. (Heidi Nutall has her theories on this, too.) Gilmerton wrote with a fountain pen in black ink in a large, clear, unhurried-looking hand; he used a version of the 'cursive' or joined-up handwriting I recognise from my own schooldays and never skipped on loops. His s is reminiscent of an & in a mirror and his z is an n with the second leg extended downwards into the tail of a cursive y. The unhurried look, thick stroke down, light up, extends even to his field-notes.

'But you can't write up what isn't legible,' said Ms Nutall. 'And just think of how the rich of that time dressed, all those spotless, starched collars, the waistcoats, the gloves, the hats.'

Prior to Gilmerton my own world of insects was made up of the occasional miserable mosquito, the sudden appearance of a ladybird on the ironing board struggling upright, and various nondescript but otherwise occupied beetles, grubs and centipedes in the garden. I am forgetting silverfish and horniegollochs and my mother's extreme reaction to those or any other creature with more than four legs inside the house and her different horrors at bees and wasps outside. Insects, that is, were less a matter for observation than sporadically unwelcome sharing.

As for Gilmerton's mainly childhood interest in lepidoptery, I had butterflies associated with summer and as brighter and with more eye-catching flight patterns – the fluttering roller-coaster especially – than moths. What I did not know was that moth species outnumber the many butterfly species by about thirty to one. I mean that any sense of this great disproportion had disappeared into a whiff of naphthalene, the infrequent start caused by something dingy flying out when I was drawing the curtains, the smears and stray wings on the car windshield and, of course, the clank and scuff of a moth caught in a lampshade, a matter more of distraction than any desire to identify it. I am not sure I would be happier if a moth behaved like an orbiting satellite round the light bulb; I clap my hands on a mosquito, open the window for a moth, shoo it with a book. Yes, and I am forgetting the halogen snowstorm when driving over moorland on a summer night, except that the snow is live, greyish and juicy.

I start the part then from a position of ignorance – and very basic questions. Unless he could write blind, Gilmerton (or any other naturalist) must have had to take his eyes off whatever he was observing to write down what he had seen, thereby making a temporal patchwork of observation and verbal transcription; sketching does the same but is a more direct process than thinking of the precise word or colour. Do I have that right? Gilmerton does both, sketch and describe – skilful graphite creatures with arrows indicating colours in the entomologist's palette, terms like 'ferruginous' (iron-rusty) lending an initial spurious precision (at least to someone unfamiliar with the lepidopterist's colour chart) to all those ishes; brownish, greyish, blackish, purplish, whitish and so on.

What am I complaining about? Nothing. I feel more comfortable alone with a text, reading it over and over, letting it seep in, but I have had to research other roles and have done so in the same way, asking the simplest questions I can. And if the object of your study moves a lot?

Ms Nutall arranged for me to visit a lepidopterist of some fame. Such visits, even when short, are always useful. He said he could give me half an hour. When I told him Gilmerton's dates he threw up his hands and groaned.

'They were hopelessly inexact, you see. Lacked equipment. Lacked technology. Lacked science. They tried to make up for it with enthusiasm and rather wretched poetry. There were swarms of them crashing about waving nets.'

'That is, in fact, what I want to talk to you about. I have never waved a net.'

'Oh,' he said. 'Well, I can assure you, it is quite as complicated as music to represent.'

He saw me in his study, a dark, still place filled with pinned creatures and books, lit mostly by his computer screen.

'I beg your pardon.'

'Those actors who hide behind a piano.'

'Yes?'

'And roll their eyes and shake their shoulders like a woman hurrying to dry the varnish on her nails.'

I put his age at about sixty. When my eyes were accustomed to the gloom I saw he was wearing tweeds so ancient they resembled worn tapestry work.

'And it is not limited to music,' he said. 'I have often noticed that most actors are lamentably uncoordinated. The actor athlete has flat feet, the actor footballer thin legs.'

'I played squash.'

He scratched his chin. 'Any good?'

'School standard only.'

'Well, that's something, I suppose. Squash is a reaching kind of sport, wouldn't you say?'

'If you can't get your opponent to run.'

'Ah. Right. Well, that is true of collecting, too. The panters merely get hot. You *stalk* butterflies, Mr Orr, when they are at rest. It is essential to take close cognisance of your shadow. Then you use a sweeping motion and a flick of the wrist at the end of the sweep to close the net.'

It occurred to me, as he emphasised his words with a pouncing sort of mime, to ask what happens to the flower, but I did not. What's the expression? Deadheading? And if the flower is in bloom?

'And in flight?'

He raised an eyebrow at me. 'That's more tricky and depends on the flight pattern. The *Pierid* family zigzag, for example. In general, you wait and use an overtaking shot.'

37

'And the nets?'

I had had the impression he was approaching the despair of the specialist but he took this as a better question.

'Round end usually. And there's a kite end, a slightly chunky triangle. Yes, there is or *was* a thing called a scissors net, indeed like a very large wooden scissors with a net pot on one arm and a net lid on the other. I think that is probably from the time of your man.' He frowned. 'Mind you, that may be the way round your problem. Heidi said it was a comedy. Is it also a period piece?'

'Only incidentally. Have there been changes in nets in the meantime?'

'Surprisingly few. Rustproof alloys for the handles but the net is much the same. Your man used tarlatan, a muslin. Nylon tears the wings.'

'I see. One last question. I understand you use light to attract moths.'

'Not all of them, but yes, it is very common.'

'My question is: how do you see them without attracting them?'

'You use a red light.'

I don't know why but I pictured this as a pencil torch. In fact I have since seen a mothist in a miner's helmet with a blue lamp.

For Gilmerton I have been given a portly pen with a gold nib. I have found it straightforward but tedious to imitate his writing. I try to cover paper as a pond-skater covers water and it shows; following his handwriting gives me knuckle-ache. His is both larger and tighter than mine and requires a greater variety of pressure. But I can now forge it and walk (very slowly, combining a rocking movement and pensative stroll) at the same time. I have also found the glove to be more practical than I thought – no slippage and an encouraging warmth and I can imagine it allowing the thumb to tap while waiting for the right word.

7

An aunt of his christened Mildred but, he says, always known as
Tonk (from tonka bean and her addiction to snuff) has sent Sanderson a box of a dozen round tins, each one containing fifty Turkish
cigarettes. It took three British soldiers – admittedly convalescent –
and with two good pairs of hands arranged about them, some forty
minutes to make the first tin top yield. The thin, brigadier-red tab
intended to ease out the first cigarettes then parted with the startling
ease of rotten silk. Aubrey seized the tin, inverted it, secured it
firmly between Sanderson's boots and banged hard at the base with
his crutch. He left quite a dent. He had contrived to raise a solitary
cigarette a barely visible fraction above the others. For a moment
I thought he was going to hurl the tin against the floor; instead he
grimaced, asked Sanderson if his aunt had any children of her own,
blew on his fingers and with every sign of maximum effort and
strain, used the fingernails of his thumb and middle finger as pincers.
He trembled, showed us clamped teeth, started to sweat – and broke
off with a stifled roar. He nodded at us, swore as clearly and as
eloquently as an elocution teacher and waggled his fingers; but the
moment he set to again there was a slight rustle, something like a
tiny sigh, and the first cigarette slid out. He held it up, dropped it
on to my hand, then turned to the tin and shook it.

'Ah,' said Aubrey, 'but wait. Now smell that. Mm? And it looks
like a honeycomb.'

I had nowhere else to put it so slipped the cigarette into my breast pocket and leant closer. A maid was smoothing beeswax into furniture but underlying that was the scent of the tobacco, like dry heather honey mixed with ginger.

Later, by the mess, I picked up a yellowish-buff box stamped 'Psyche' in convoluted scarlet lettering and with an image of a girl in a square-necked tunic wearing dragonfly wings. The box contained waxy-looking little tubes, reminiscent of skinny, stiffened noodles, topped by small blobs of a soggy, purplish-brown colour. At the fiftieth anniversary celebration of the publication of Darwin's *On the Origin of Species* in Cambridge in July 1909, I had a conversation on Darwin's grandfather who galvanised a noodle to see if it would move – it did – and whether or not it would then be alive – it was not. We ate off Wedgwood plates. Our Edinburgh delegation was taken to see Sir Joseph Hooker; I was at the back, remember most his stupendously tangled eyebrows, the size and thickness of fetching whiskers. I was introduced to a young Huxley; self-important in a touchingly agitated way, he inhaled his laughter, a nervous reaction but a gentling 'whoa' sound, like someone slowing dray horses. A charming American from Columbia University, the noodle man and one of T. H. Morgan's team working on the genetic structure of the fruit fly *Drosophila*, described him however as 'having a terrifying faith in intelligence. He leaps from a small fly to eugenics with the promptness only self-awe can bring.' The American I joined in smoking a cigar for Darwin, lighting and relighting it with stout, whittled-looking sticks which had fat, cochineal, busby-shaped heads. The lightest scratch against the sandpaper and they crackled, a little more rasp and they hissed and flared, the flame spurting out.

In this convalescent home the side of the yellow-buff box has become dank; the first two matches I struck simply buckled and smeared on their way down. The head of the third broke off and shot across the room, trailing a little smoke as it rose, catching fire near the top of its arc before tumbling downwards and sending me after it to stamp on the Persian rug. Closer inspection of these matches under a lamp reveals that they are not wood but thin, tightly rolled strips of paper, akin to that flimsy stuff which is light enough for messenger pigeons to carry and then coated with clear wax; but the paper is still too feeble. The fourth match, however, gripped close behind the head, has struck and I have lit the cigarette at the extremity marked by Aubrey's fingernails.

At last, to the whisper of burning tobacco strands, I have sucked warm, smooth smoke into my lungs, held it there for five heartbeats and then exhaled slowly from my nose. The stuff billows around me, before settling into a slack, serpentine drift towards the window. I have also glanced down at my chest to check that smoke isn't seeping out from between my ribs.

And again. The rasp and curl of smoke in my lungs induces a light-headed version of well-being, an agreeable sensation of snagging, as if the smoke were catching on small filaments in my lungs, a feeling of tautness being lightly relaxed and controlled, the impression rising pleasantly into my brain.

I think I had better sit down, in part because my smoking and writing hand are the same. As I write the cigarette is clamped between my third and fourth knuckles and not, as with a practised smoker, between middle and index fingers; that is, when I inhale my hand has to flatten and the pen nib ends up directly in front of my left eye. And, of course, when I write, my pen, held between thumb and index finger, is more upright than usual. Let me suck in again.

If I blow out strongly, I can produce a lung-whistle like blowing through sword grass or that squeak on meat just before a bubble of fat bursts and spits. It induces a light-headedness a swim or two away from dizziness. The dryness in my throat and nose, a pasty coating on my taste buds and traces of tar in my saliva combine to give the after-taste of the tobacco undertones of clay. I sniff at my smoking hand. It is rather inkier than I expected (almost as sharp as salts), rather soapier (Pears) and the tobacco smell, though retaining something of that first honey and ginger, distinctly stale in patches.

I sit back and look around me. I had expected the smoke to be bluer, but as the stuff curls about I see the colour is more fuscous, with strands of peatish brown and small threads of white. As it shifts towards the window it takes on a uniform misty grey. A question of light. I move my hand towards the lamp. The smoke rising up from the cigarette is a silvery white, two thin currents which stream almost vertically up for about three inches before slowing into a corbel shape and twisting upwards and outwards into brisk, fantastic trees. I inhale and exhale again from the nostrils. The effect is tuskish but still silvery white on the lamp side, tarnished on the other.

I have put the cigarette down on the edge of the side table, got up and opened the curtains so that the smoke has a freer way out and the Lobster Moth larva is not troubled. This business of consuming a cigarette has reminded me, I am not sure why, of that childish pastime of placing a coin under a piece of paper and rubbing it with pencil lead until the image stamped on the coin is transferred – 'lifted' in the words of my mother – to the surface of the paper, an exercise in strokes, a clotting of light and dark grey lines, the dark, particularly when forcefully and inexpertly done, having a thick, waxy gleam and providing not a clear image of regal head and letters but what I always found to be a pleasant abstract of shadows, almost always more interesting than a numismatic profile.

Ach. By leaving the cigarette, I have made the edge of the table sweat. At least the sweat comes up; a small pale patch is left, barely noticeable on the wood. I have the cigarette back between my knuckles and have waggled it enough to even up the tip again to an approximate cone of ash and ragged flakes of burnt paper and tobacco leaf over the reddish centre, the top part of the ash whitish, the underside peppered with black specks. An uneven, charcoal-black rim creeps slowly down the cigarette paper preceded by a faint brown fore-edge, enlivened by sporadic incursions, drop-shaped surges of burn into the paper or sudden small runs of glowing red at parts of the rim.

There are some relatively attractive sidelines to convalescence; it had never occurred to me before, not quite so physically, that I could be a collection of sensations for reordering. As Aubrey says, 'One has not sprung back, has one?' It is not simply that I have not resumed where I left off. As my body heals, my mind appears to be issuing out of the past, dislodging as I go rather frail-looking memories. Why, for example, do I remember Mr Cameron setting off explosions of colour in jars of water, rattling his brushes and shaping one of them with an imperiously genteel flick, the brush held between thumb and forefinger, the others bristling out from his knuckles?

'An artist will paint you your butterfly with its soul intact. But an illustrator has no more task than to record the creature and its markings with precision.'

Both of us pause. I puff, Mr Cameron considers me, what he has just said and sighs.

'Oh, very well. The only secret is accuracy. Are you at all musical? Yes, but you know what tones are? Here it is a question of shades. Pick the darkest and the lightest. Calculate your scales, the runs of your browns, for example. Start with the darkest. Observe. And remember – there is no such thing as a straight line in nature.'

I proffered him a pinned Pebble Prominent. He grunted.

'Your world will be mottled,' he said dejectedly but immediately set his brush to twittering and clinking in jars and brown pigment.

'Never be afraid of the wet,' he said as he briskly blotched paper, 'but remember, colours can run.'

Together we watched the beginning spots of a moth dry.

Ah. One last drag. A pity. I had rather hoped my Turkish cigarette would last a full ten minutes but, having stubbed it out and picked a grain-sized bit of tobacco from my tongue, I see it has barely lasted for seven. Rather shorter than the Greek walkers. I can still get traces of smoke out of my lungs. Well.

I have risen, emitted a small belch, crossed the room and tossed the cigarette end out on to the path. The night is damp enough for dew. I have looked in on my Lobster Moth larva. It is munching tirelessly, a caterpillar's way of showing health. Evidently the tobacco has had no effect. And I have gone back to walking again.

Amongst those dislodged memories I mentioned are simplistic, panic views of myself. I woke from my nap this afternoon certain that between the ages of sixteen and twenty-one I lived in an itchy rush, an agony of possibilities, almost as if I had longed to have my lifetime done. That the impression I had sometimes had of remembering future work, future fame, was part of the same intense desire to look back on myself and recognise what shape I was and had made, what my markings were.

They say tobacco is an aid to concentration. I am at least a little sorry that my limited abilities as a painter went into moth wings; I mean I was too anxious to record what used to be called 'the perfect insect' (the imago or adult) and overlooked the caterpillar.

Ah. Though it is now after midnight someone has knocked on my door.

'Come in, Aubrey.'

'I say, has someone been smoking?'

'Yes.'

'Can't sleep?'

'I don't sleep at this time.'

'It's my stump doesn't let me sleep. So I prowl about.' He lifted his crutch; the tip was bandaged up.

'I didn't hear you.'

'Good. I'm indignant. Do you know what McKinnon said to me? He advised me to treat what had happened to me as a mere caesura in my life.'

'Is that true?'

'I couldn't invent that. How would you describe it?'

'A poetic or at least metrical lack of imagination.'

'Mm. Spondee McKinnon. I say, can I use that? The poetic part?'

8

Gilmerton's wounds, chiefly to the left arm and left side of his chest, were caused by shrapnel. 'Naturally I raised my arm and bravely ducked my helmeted head,' he says in his best older-brother style in a letter between operations. 'And of course I have been very lucky. A presumably small lump of metal was deflected by a rib the right way, as it were. Or so the hospital people say. I am not sure they are not besotted with narrow escapes.'

By the time he arrived at Lampenham he had survived pneumonia and three operations and was 'very comfortable. I imagine you have quite outgrown your liking for boiled milk and honey and cinnamon. Part of my chest looks rather like that when the milk has cooled and acquired a skin. Not unattractive, I am sure you will agree.'

At about the same time, however, he admitted, with those hypocoristic touches that make Ms Nutall narrow her eyes, that he had, in addition to the lung-whistle what he described as skin-stick. In other words, some of his skin was stuck to his ribs. His description to his mother is more lurid. 'In some spots the skin feels absurdly thin, particularly in the livid patches. Others are more like smoked beef with stretches of madder and tallow, sometimes twisted together.'

At Lampenham, Gilmerton was under the care of the person who had performed his last operation in the spring. Dr McKinnon's point was that there had been 'wastage' on the left arm, a loss of tissue and muscle, in his opinion 'exacerbated' by disuse while the bones and flesh were healing and that exercise might reduce 'the disability to its merest extent'. McKinnon also believed that exercise would 'increase circulation on the left side' and possibly help lift the skin stuck to the ribs, something Heidi Nutall describes as 'perhaps a solution in some cases of prepucial fimosis' but unlikely to have answered Gilmerton's.

Gilmerton himself called his arm 'an eighth or a seventh less in quantity' and 'a little slow'; he found some actions, like turning a doorknob with that hand, 'bizarrely complicated'. To eat he laid his left forearm on the table and used a fork as a press. It was the right hand that worked, first cutting, then taking over the fork to pierce. So McKinnon instructed him to 'become left-handed for a spell', gave him two wooden balls about the size of those for tennis 'freshly turned and with a wide grain like smoked salmon' to roll, one over the other, in his left hand, provided him with a small dumb-bell and encouraged him to find a partner for games of badminton on the lawn.

We are not quite sure of the next part. McKinnon may well have been something of a prude and Gilmerton amiably but inexpertly loud in his handling of the wooden balls. And though there is no evidence that Gilmerton found barracks humour any more congenial than the doctor, in the film McKinnon will hold Gilmerton responsible for causing jokes about lost property, worry beads and clicking false parts. It was also the case that the only willing badminton partner Gilmerton could find was Aubrey Gilbert whose lack of a leg limited his abilities as much as Gilmerton's left arm did his.

Moderate exercise in the shape of walks was also prescribed at the patient's discretion. The problem here was that Gilmerton serenely took McKinnon at his word, discretion, and since he tended to nap in the afternoon, on fine days outside with a hat over his face, he preferred to take his walks at dusk, on summer evenings very late. On the evening of 5 June 1916, Gilmerton went off for his first proper walk.

Now the imago or adult version of the Lobster Moth is dimorphic which means there are two forms in the same species. I knew of sexual dimorphism (peacock, peahen). And have heard of seasonal dimorphism (a stoat and an ermine?) But apparently neither of those is the case here and for a lepidopteral ignorant it was novel that two moths with different markings should turn out to be the same creature; that, however, is the case. At Lampenham, on the Hampshire side of Dorset, Gilmerton found both forms amongst the same group of beech trees on the same night. This is not a miracle but it is far from commonplace and the proximity ('not more than fifty feet and tantalisingly few minutes apart') pleased Gilmerton; it was the first time for many months that he had been out at night and 'years since I went mothing'.

'When I got back I found McKinnon up for poor Earnshaw. He used an uncertain joshing tone, complained about my unmilitary hours and activities. Blushing slightly, he asked me if I thought it was 'contributing to morale', since Lampenham was just as much part of the war effort as − he thought for an example and saw my torch − the Signals' Corps. I got out my Lobster Moths and explained to him what they were.

'The thing to bear in mind,' I said, 'is that British lepidoptery and German lepidoptery are radically different. In part due to the extraordinary influence of a Dr Staudinger, German lepidopterists treat butterflies and moths as natural stamps and their study as an inordinately tricky sort of philately. They ignore the law of priority, deprecate the role of the microscope and dissection in taxonomy as inimical to the sensibilities of correctly brought-up young ladies. The British approach tends more to that of biology, a more fluid perception, with the evolutionary aspects of lepidoptera seen as a process.'

Mr McKinnon squinted hard at me, then nodded.

'Ah, I see. Captain Gilmerton?'

'Yes?'

'Are you a believer?'

A charming thing about McKinnon is that he rarely listens and as Aubrey Gilbert says 'saves on replies'.

'You are an insomniac, I think.'

'Oh no, I sleep.'

He grunted. 'Of course sleep is often associated with death. Every

47

time we sleep we die a little more. Isn't that what they say?'

'Yes, I've heard that.'

'Mm,' said McKinnon. 'Of course, it is nothing at all to be ashamed of. After all, our foreknowledge that we will die is one of the hallmarks of humanity. The trick, though, is to be humble.'

This last echo of Uriah Heep (the library has every Dickens from Boz to Drood) surprised and delighted me, but somehow made him nervous.

'Oh, I wonder if I am making myself clear,' he said and I understood he was in the process of steeling himself, that the tones I had picked up were by way of preparation.

'Have you read *Alice in Wonderland*?'

'What? Ah yes, in fact it was the first book I ever read.'

'Really? Would there be a reason for that?' There was something roguishly unctuous in his voice.

'How do you mean?'

'Your full name is . . . ?'

'Robert Liddell Gilmerton.'

'And you know that Lewis Carroll was also an Archdeacon and mathematician at Christ Church, Oxford, called Charles Dodgson who told the story to a small girl, the daughter of the Dean, called Alice . . . Liddell?'

'Ah. Dr McKinnon, no one has ever claimed any relationship at all. Liddell is my mother's maiden name. Her father had a bleach factory in Perth.'

McKinnon blinked at me. 'Oh,' he said, 'oh.' I wondered who had been pulling his leg. Aubrey Gilbert probably.

'Oh, I see,' said McKinnon glumly. 'Well, well. To my point though, your insomnia. Carroll devised something he called pillow problems.' McKinnon leant forward. 'To keep away unholy thoughts, captain.'

'Are those his exact words?'

'Oh yes, dear me, yes indeed. One of the puzzles he devised he called doublets.'

'A doublet is a pillow problem? What is it?'

A doublet turned out to be simply what I already knew as word-golf, a coy happenstance in the way of shifting letters one by one to reverse one word into another, as in moth, mote, mate, late, lame, lamp. But I understood McKinnon's point. Nothing to do with my projected pillow book. His was that a distinguished bachelor academic at my old university, naturally more popular for his stories for children than for his mathematical work, helped himself ward off unspecified temptation by the mental equivalent of twiddling his thumbs. The puzzle as somnific. Sleep as hidden by a combination lock with four letters. A twitter and tumbling of letters gentling the unholy into unconsciousness.

'I offer the pillow puzzle,' said McKinnon, 'as a humble but practical aid to sleep. I certainly find it works, captain, especially when I am overtired and prone to . . . the kind of despair we all feel sometimes.' I nodded, recalled that our brief chat had included despair, temptation, a hovering impurity, word-golf, possible genetic and literary links, *Alice in Wonderland*, practical humility, death, sleep and insomnia again. I find it absurdly hard to persuade anyone outside my family of two things. I have never been to Japan. I am *not* an insomniac.

'Well, thank you,' I said.

McKinnon smiled, as if I had just taken an unpleasant medicine without fuss.

'What will you do with your moths?'

'I'll have them framed. Perhaps leave them here.'

McKinnon smiled. 'At Lampenham,' he said, 'yes. Good night, captain.'

'Good night, doctor.'

I watched him roll off down the corridor and for some reason remembered that my sister, when younger than Alice, was devoted to caterpillars, apparently considered them as live sweetmeats.

'There,' said Heidi Nutall with satisfaction, '*that's* Gilmerton! I love that "But I understood McKinnon's point"! I suppose there may be an element there of a young soldier's contempt for a plump doctor but he is mostly amiable, shy, a little haughty – and quite unable to consider McKinnon as other than more or less amusingly confused and verbose. Of course he is writing an entertaining letter but, even so, his *lack* of understanding is extraordinary.'

I looked at the letter again, addressed to a George MacFee.

'But that business about his sister's taste for caterpillars?'

'It's a confession of good-natured hopelessness. He can't make head or tail of McKinnon and shrugs. Tail, tall, tell, teal, heal, head. Unwise, though.'

I have never before been involved in the development of a script from the beginning, been used as an uneasy sounding board from the first drafts.

'You don't think he might have been offended by McKinnon suggesting he was frightened of sleep? Or by that humble business?'

'No, no. He thought McKinnon clumsy, is all.'

'Did he really find him amusing?'

'That's a good question. I think he is a little amused, but that soon shades into boredom or at least a polite insistence on separate identities. And of course he is trying to divert his friend MacFee, a vet — also wounded, by the way. He had been kicked by a military horse.'

I smiled. 'Yes. It would be quite easy to make him seem stiff and arrogant.'

'No, no, no,' said Heidi Nutall, 'not in the eyes, David.'

9

Intransitive old men have the most violent of imaginations. They combine it with a stickle-backed meanness which – and I am an old man now – quite catches at my breath. Transitive old men I take to be those bores who see in their own chochers and trembles and flatulence the death rattle of whole civilisations. I, on the other hand, resent. It is a general condition of being able to do little more than observe the decline of my faculties. With some frequency (four or five times a day) I should like to expend myself. I should like, that is, to die with the door closed and, if not painlessly, at least alone. I am eighty-three years old, an increasingly stiff and cramped fitment of shrunken flesh and brittle bones with perfectly commonplace fears to do with, in no particular order, incontinence, pain and madness.

My brain, chief organ of sense and sentences, trundles out short thoughts, drops off, starts, loses contact with the tongue; struck by the quantity of worm-casts and droppings on a lawn this morning, I said 'Damn brides', heard it, made to correct myself and merely repeated the original as a cracked echo. Then there is touch, also reduced; my fingers are dull registers. Sight is variable; without the aid of my spectacles, granulated scenes can sometimes sharpen into an acidic squint. I feel like one of the creatures I was after this morning, with hollow bones, spindly legs, ovoid belly and a nose that encroaches on my vision like some rudimentary directional aid.

Hearing is a matter of obscure, deep-dug tunnels though I am as sensitive to some sounds as a rotten tooth to golden syrup. I loathe dry, trickling sounds (a fire settling, say). And there are times the mere tone of someone's voice penetrates to the inner sides of my skeleton and flutes about my marrow and the inside of my joints. When I do not respond sharply, I often see brightly coloured scenes of carnage amongst my family, a proof against second childhoods – or perhaps not. An amiable anarchist tosses a bomb in amongst them – while I sit, safely and invisibly, watching my children's heads roll stickily on the Persian rugs or observing that a grandchild's severed hand nestles in a chandelier. No, hearing is not one of my pleasures, in part because I am obliged to compensate for my deafness. I remember a speaker tapping a silver knife on a crystal wineglass. At first I could hear nothing. Then I heard a noise as if someone timid were knocking on a door, but what I think I was doing was translating the man's expression, a plaintive rictus, into *some* sound, a rather dull, easily mistaken, makeshift arrangement.

But then there is smell! The most intense of my senses. For there are times I exist as a large, trembling olfactory organ. It is one of the reasons why, however close their relationship to me, the young lack any familiar identity. Their movements are too energetic, even if constrained by my presence, their smells too juicy and sharp. The very young smell of porridge and compotes, the old like neutered cats, all fusty lavender with an undertone of faded but persistent urine, as if they had been sleeping by a chamber-pot under a dusty bed.

For some reason, taste has not kept up with smell. I prefer game, pheasant and guinea-fowl in particular, though I will make do with grouse and quail. I like my red wines with as much vanilla as possible. I am also partial to hard little tablets of butterscotch. That is, my pleasures are few, infrequent and vague.

While I was accompanying an equally elderly lady to church the other day, she, for reasons of giddiness or frailty, leant into me, so that her breast pressed against my arm. We smiled together a while in pleasant, if resigned, complicity. The breast melted very slowly, as if it had left a damp patch on my arm to dry. My wife, walking behind with the lady's son, has become extraordinarily vain; she prefers flattering, youthful reflections on her looks to any other response. She lingers over the convex side of silver spoons, likes consommé and syllabubs. Perhaps her memories course differently. Or she does not find herself at all ridiculous.

Very well. A few months ago I became conscious that I was sometimes moved by a young woman – though the word 'moved' requires immediate qualification. Tears well in my eyes, my heart gives an atrocious wrench – but there is no emotion to accompany these appurtenances of emotion. The mechanism appears to operate simply because it is there.

Nor is the young woman one or whole. The only interest I have been able to observe is the physical peculiarity of the trigger. We have the face of Flora, Terpsichore's foot, Diana's breast – but whose arm? I am made fond by the upper arms of some young women, by that hand's breadth just before the arm turns up and round for the shoulder and just above the gloved elbow.

I suppose it is true that upper arms vary a great deal, as much, on examination, as a nose or lips; even so. I have heard men talk admiringly of a well-turned ankle or leg – French-polishers' terms – and, in theory, can appreciate their concern. But an upper arm? I even find I am becoming choosy, pernickety. Brisk and critical, I scan the ballroom. Too sallow, too fat, too dry, too scrawny . . . but there, if I am fortunate, will be that combination of pertness, slightly plumped slenderness and that beautiful, light flush of blood that sets off the second peculiarity.

It is as if I could smell what I was seeing, as if sight worked like a perfume. My nose fills with agitated molecules. A fine example of an upper arm provokes something akin to an allergy, a minging grimace, leaking eyes and a most unpleasant puff-ball sensation in my skin. It does not last long.

'Has something gone down the wrong way?' I shake my head. I wipe my eyes. I look out, full of obliging digestive gurgles while slight airs depart my lungs and I wait for my heart to wrench and for that subsequent lurch, as if my internal organs were slipping and slithering inexorably downwards into a new arrangement, possibly definitive.

*

Really? Well, my dear boy, I am of course glad that you do not take your own futured figment, me, too seriously and am nearly flattered that you give me a neuronal urgency and frequency in thinking of death. But there are different kinds of seriousness, some of them amiable and not at all dull or pompous. You call me intransitive (which may or may not be witty but which I am not sure is possible) and make me cantankerous and mean rather than, say, affable and mellow. That is your right, I suppose, though you cannot, not without a certain violent contrivance in your ironies, be ashamed of yourself half a century in advance. I did not know you had been so frightened of age as a depressed and reduced condition. It seems a little hasty and ignoble. And you miss quite important things. You do not say if I have much hair on my head. Nor do you give my watery wife a name or much presence. And then – arms?

On reflection, I take it that you are intrigued by a memory of the contrast between the flesh and those soft, very long white kid gloves women wore before the war. Women themselves have assured me that the sensual pleasure of the gloves, that sensation of snug, soft containment was short-lived; the gloves were horribly expensive and at their best only when new. Once they had been cleaned they never recovered that original, supple feel. I am not ashamed of you but I make certain allowances. I also wonder if *you* remember. Age misses but youth twists? Perhaps. But I can certainly remember your cousin Deirdre, for example, your paternal Uncle Andrew's daughter, when she was thirteen and you ten, casting shadow creatures on a wall, a giraffe, a swan, a rabbit, not inside the house, but using her long, gloved arms, summer sun and the shadow-free gaps on the orchard wall; she made that rabbit issue out of the shadow of fruit-tree foliage, said it was hot work, asked you to wipe a drop of sweat from her nose and save her gloves. Suggestive? I suppose it might have been. Though I should have thought stirring for the future might be more apt. And if you remember, it was *she* who was excited and who treated those sheathed arms of hers as if they did not quite belong to her, as if they were too splendid to be hers.

The real problem, however, is that I have no memory of finding upper arms particularly moving. You might as well have said feet. At least you knew Terpsichore. Arms are Aurora. And you suggest I have forgotten as old men will? It is possible. More likely, I have subsumed the past. I certainly remember a more direct interest in women's bodies than yours. Perhaps what I have forgotten is your poltroonishness and fear. If curiosity is a large part of desire then I suppose youthful timidity would be a large qualifier. Isn't there a phrase – to handle with kid gloves? The point being not so much gently as to avoid getting them dirty? At my age, however, I find I tend to a forthright and visionary shorthand.

I see a ballroom, not large, French panelled, containing some fifty people. The girl I see is not someone I know. She is rather flushed, has two pink patches on her very white cheeks. Her gown is electric blue, like that butterfly from Dunk's Island, off Australia, though I have never quite seen why it is called electric – it looks to me more royal-ink blue; imagine dipping a full fountain pen into an eggcup of water and squeezing the bulb. The thick surge and curl of the blue will give a better impression of the colour. You bow. You are over-impressed by the smallness of her hand in its glove, startled by her nerves – she takes a tight grip on your left thumb and does not let go. As you whirl her about, an impression rather than a fact made up from the smooth soles of your shoes, her looks and her (to you intimidating) lightness, you grow conscious of her smell. It strikes you, at the beginning, as sharp and bitter but as you turn around the floor, you find you become avid for it, an odour like sexual smelling salts, that makes you turn and turn for it again. There is a trace of lavender there but you ignore that. The material of her dress swishes and rustles, the pedestrian little orchestra saws away and your eyes begin to feel hot, your muscles tremble, you swallow when you can. The music stops. You breathe in and endeavour to smile at the same time. It occurs to you that you may have sweat on your upper lip but it is then you see a bruise on her upper right arm.

'Good God. Have I done that?'

'What's that? Oh no! I bruise terribly easily. Would you like to try?'

You ignore that last part. Instead you look at the skin of her other arm. Here the bruise is older, a faint brown.

'Is that . . . ?'

'Where? Oh no, that's just a little birthmark.'

'Ah.'

She smiles. To you she proffers both her gloved arms.

'A touch does. You'll see. Simply press. As you would to find out whether a peach is ripe or not.'

Dumb, with an ache in your throat, your eyes bright with gonadal tears, you shake your head and swallow again.

'I couldn't.'

But she has not finished. Smiling chummily, she brings her hands together, raises her right elbow a little and leans closer to you. Her smell has you open your nostrils.

'If you promise not to tell . . .'

'Yes?'

'. . . I tried to *disguise* the bruise with a little white powder.'

Your head inclines towards the bruise on the arm. Your eyes can make out no powder but you see small pale hairs in her skin. Your lips do not pout, they contract and tremble. You can feel the heat from her arm.

Smiling, the girl pulls her bruise away.

'Silly,' she says comfortably. 'I'm not as delicate as all that.'

Unfair? On the whole I think not. If you are agreeable, later on we could try other parts of female anatomy.

IO

Film is a spin, says Ms Nutall, whizz and flywheel, coeval with the
motor car. She refers, of course, to the finished article, not the
making. I read someone else (Orson Welles?) had called it a fly
cemetery that sometimes flies. I am not sure why but it is the
description I like best.

So let's see. Gilmerton's ten minutes come in usually a little short
of two hundred lines. Heidi Nutall wishes to begin at night with
mothing.

EXT. COUNTRY — NIGHT

*A summer moon. Below it a copse. Two small red lights appear four
yards apart. Actors as shadows moving carefully. One light stops.*

PROFESSOR'S WIFE

Robert.

GILMERTON

Yes?

PROFESSOR'S WIFE

Shhh. Damn! It's flown. Your way!

The other light goes off.

GILMERTON

Shhh. I have it!

PROFESSOR'S WIFE
Robert? . . . Where are you?

GILMERTON
How odd. This looks like a Mouse Moth.

EXT. LAMPENHAM — DAY

A First World War ambulance goes up the drive towards the house.

INT. MCKINNON'S OFFICE — DAY

Gilmerton, stripped to the waist, is being examined by McKinnon.

MCKINNON
Captain, would you like to breathe in. Oh, a little more, please.

GILMERTON
If I do the lung whistles.

MCKINNON
I beg your pardon?

GILMERTON
The left lung whistles. And the skin is stuck to two ribs here.

MCKINNON
Ah yes, I see. Are you in pain?

GILMERTON
No.

MCKINNON
Good. That's the spirit. And we need to build up that left arm, don't we? Well, captain, from now on good food and exercise will do us best. I'll give you some things, shall I?

INT. GILMERTON'S LAMPENHAM ROOM — DAY

This was the library. Gilmerton sits in an armchair reading. Aubrey Gilbert, missing a leg, and Sanderson, missing his right arm, come in.

AUBREY

Welcome to Lampenham. I'm Aubrey Gilbert.

GILMERTON
(*rising and shaking hands*)

Robert Gilmerton.

AUBREY

And the other member of the welcoming committee is Jeremy Sanderson.

They shake hands as they can while Aubrey considers Gilmerton.

What have you got?

GILMERTON

Shrapnel. Here.

AUBREY

You've seen McKinnon?

GILMERTON

This morning.

AUBREY

Right as rain?

GILMERTON

That's about it.

AUBREY

Are you?

GILMERTON

It's a possibility.

SANDERSON

What are these?

GILMERTON

Those are my . . . 'exercise spheres' I think the doctor called them.

AUBREY

Yes. What do you . . . do with them?

GILMERTON

I understand I am to roll one over the other in my left hand.

SANDERSON

Like very large worry beads.

AUBREY

McKinnon is a great believer in the regenerative powers of exercise.

GILMERTON

He has also given me a little dumb-bell and instructed me to play badminton with this hand.

AUBREY

Oh good. I'll give you a game some time. We thought we would show you around. Mm? It is quite a nice old place, really, especially on balmy days.

EXT. HOUSE NEAR BRECHIN — DAY

Still photograph.

GILMERTON
(*voice-over*)

My dear girl, you are absurd. Of course, I don't mind. You were either not born or too young to know. I lived in a nursery that combined the space of a town church with the particularities of yacht design.

INT. NURSERY — DAY

GILMERTON
(*voice-over*)

All thought out by our father before he had even met our mother, let alone married her. Enlightened principles. Two doorknobs to every door. One for the child, another for the adult.
   Exercise ropes. A book-lined schoolroom.

Japanese hygiene. Victorian seemliness.

And my nanny was Tsuru.

INT. GILMERTON'S LAMPENHAM ROOM — NIGHT

Gilmerton sits at his desk considering the closed pillow book and a pot of glue and a glove.

GILMERTON
(*voice-over*)

Thank you for the book. I shall try to fill it, as you say, with thoughts.

Gilmerton is seen putting on the gloved book and pressing in the studs. He tests the arrangement first, then flips the book open. He picks up a pen, tests the pen, finds it satisfactory, begins writing.

INT. NURSERY — NIGHT

Tsuru enters wet and alarmed. She speaks directly at the camera as she moves towards it.

TSURU

You were imitating a what? A weasel? Oh no, darling. Night quiet. No weasel. No bat. Shhh.

The above presents a few frames less than two minutes acted out (the camera is to move slowly down the main axis of the nursery and settle for four seconds on Tsuru in her striped kimono, before moving closer to her comb-stuck hair). But shhh. Ms Nutall is worrying at each line of the script 'as if writing my mother's epitaph'. I never know for sure if a script will work well, have done more than one which spoke splendidly on set but mumbled in the projector. And while Ms Nutall sometimes finds it convenient to have me sitting on the other side of the table — 'Just say that' — she has at other times shown some nerves. She usually made what I first thought of as general statements for my benefit but which now strike me as rather basic memos to herself.

'What we're doing is comedy, David. Any drama we carry in the comedy. The rest is an inordinate fiddle so that the spectators don't laugh in the wrong places.'

And then she'd try to get my attention away from her.

'Have you had any thoughts as to your make-up?'

It is not subtle but I do not think she is having a dig at my relations with make-up; she appears too distracted. I used to loathe the stuff. I do not mean what amounts to a garment of scar tissue in the third scene in McKinnon's office. That has merely been, like my losing enough weight to mark out my ribs very clearly, a routine of waiting and exercise, waiting for some talented and bizarre people to finish studying their forensic photographs and colour-test their plasticated version of flesh, and then submitting to the attentions of what feels like part of a very light but clammy bandage. No, what I dislike is the stifling stuff used to tan pale skin and have it blend with the wounded chest and falsely diminished arm. It is made a little more stifling by Heidi Nutall's determination that Gilmerton was not at all hairy. Boyish? Vulnerable? Perhaps even something to do with Japanese skin. At any rate, an ex-nurse called Anna has worked me over from shoulder to navel, using a bright, toy-sized cutthroat razor and slot-in blades mass-produced for countries where barbers still shave chins. 'Oh, and in National Health labour wards, before the enema.' We have had two sessions. She stretches about two inches of skin between her index finger and thumb and scrapes with very small strokes. It is like being minutely measured in strips. I end up with a tessellated look of cleaned skin and foam lines. I am then washed down with diluted antiseptic. Anna also works on body-builders and her husband has what she calls a 'corporal enhancement clinic', a tattoo shop. I mean that I try to find some interest in what is being done to me in this life for the sake of a few seconds' whizz on film. She told me waxing causes pimples but that there was always 'the risk of a pustule'. That was six weeks ago. No infections. I was scraped again yesterday, including my arms, which will save on hair-tugging when I put on the wounds. I wonder if my insomnia has anything to do with my partial hairlessness?

When I was younger I wanted to be a pure, naked actor and detested make-up. In theory I could appreciate the help with character, but appreciated rather more uncomfortably that almost all film make-up is to cover blemishes and stop the face shining, all with the aim of making the face suitable for the lighting and camera people. What I began to resent was the feel of being smothered pore by pore, of having my face marked out over and above the rest of my body, so that no matter how intent I was, an untoward lick of the lips or an itch it was inadvisable to scratch would remind me that my face was smeared and encrusted. Fear, that is, persuaded me that make-up, bib and flesh colour, was preventing me from acting as I could.

I was cured by Kirsty. She told me at once that I was suffering from 'chicken in a brick' syndrome, a strikingly apt description I thought of panic and heat. Gently, so as not to disturb Isabel, I shift limbs and bum but am still a heavy-jointed skeleton on a web of springs. Isabel stirs, in her sleep lets out an exasperated-sounding sigh. Let us just stay still for a moment or two, until her breathing settles.

There. Every actor and actress has, amongst the films that were hard or miserable to make, a favourite horror. Mine is an extension to Byron's unfinished *Don Juan* called *Juan Unbound* in which Juan (played by me) flees north from London and divorce suits to bump into Frankenstein's creation on his rampage through Scotland near Inverness, two different types of monster finding if not solace at least companionship and conversation in monstrosity. There were some good scenes: the clap and leeches, mercury and a course of horse-drawn bathing at Wallsend; consulting a witch on his resulting impotence in a castellated ruin near Jericho (a real place, not far from Gilmerton's Brechin) but deciding that magic and erections did not mix; losing his horse while crossing the White Mounth; being bound and robbed by a woman forder (who carried travellers across a fast river for a fee); his rescue by a prurient minister with a fat wife; and at least the initial conversation on irresponsible makers with a monster surprised by Juan's indifference to his large, ill-fitting appearance and intrigued by the aplomb of his quizzing. Yes, and there was a prettily meant scene on a West Highland beach when they considered the life and destiny of clams and mussels.

I was twenty-one years old, chosen I think because I was the correct age. Given the famous monster's fee and schedules, we shot the last parts first. I can still summon up a thick, pasty taste on the bud part of my tongue. There are films that turn instantly sour, become stomach-churning grinds of vulnerability. The weather was rotten, the mechanics failed, the monster wanted more extravagant make-up and kept trying to change his lines. Nothing worked. I began to feel horribly like the butt of some appallingly obscure joke, then found myself on that pretty beach, the lights finally set up, the wind dropped, suffering some new sort of subcutaneous agitation, breathing through my nose, my throat constricted, apple large and dry, brain as stolid as a dumpling, attempting to plead with my eyes. My line had to do with the quivering contents of shelly structures. I could not say it. My reaction was abysmal. I raised my hands, stared at them, covered my face and clawed my fingers through my make-up. Someone guffawed. The highly paid monster raised a mittened hand, let it drop, plodded off to his trailer asking when his press interview was. The director made a girning face and wiped an eye.

'Half an hour,' he said and then, just for me, 'That's your quota of difficulties. Right?'

I nodded. In a stubborn, if relieved funk, hanging on to myself rather than any opinion at all of shellfish, I retreated to the make-up cabin and chair.

'You have wonderful planes,' said Kirsty.

'What?'

'It's in the bones.' She laid her hand on the crown of my head. 'And your skull is beautifully put together.'

She smeared cold cream on my face. Kirsty was tall, almost anorexic slim, had soft, dark hair, green eyes and a dreamy, amiable smile.

'Look,' she said, 'I've done a de Kooning.'

She had produced a swirl of cream, jam and flesh with snub and smeared human features and half a black eyebrow. And then, exactly

64

as if the mirror were a camera, she ducked down and put her face beside what she had made of mine — I could feel the warmth of her cheek through the cleansing cream — opened her eyes wide as if surprised by a flash, and disappeared from view.

Did I drop off to sleep for a moment then? Possible. I sat and watched my face under her fingers come clear and take on Juan. I misheard entirely what was said, misread what I saw. 'Mm. A *little* depth now,' was one of her favourite expressions. But her knowledge of the constituents of make-up, historical as well as actual, was immense. She would pore over paintings and record the colours of faces with pencilled numbers, a reversal of a process that may still exist, when would-be artists miss the point but yearn for the feel of brush and paint and blotch together a landscape, a bridge or a face like a numbered jigsaw, a colourful extension of those arrangements of numbered dots which, when joined in order, reveal the outline of a swan or a giraffe to young children. Her memory for colour was unconscionable, a fantastically fine chopping of tiny differences instantly available without reference to colour cards. I once enjoyed hearing her exchange with her assistant lists of numbers in a quiet, stocktaker's murmur broken occasionally by a luscious sales name.

After the last filmed scene, of Juan finding he has the clap in an abbey in Yorkshire just at the moment Aurora Raby's guardians arrive to rescue her, Kirsty opened the door of her car and said, 'Are you getting in?' We married a couple of months later and bought a renovated, loftish place. Kirsty was five years older and we lasted five years or until my next Byronic role, this time a mix of the club-footed poet and the Minotaur on stage, when I wore a turban for him and a beautiful soft bull's head made in Paris for the Minotaur's scenes with Theseus and Ariadne. Both of us limped. Kirsty slept as little as or less than Gilmerton, usually choosing to rest in what I think is called the lotus position in yoga, sometimes in front of a black-and-white tape with the sound off. She used the word 'copulate' and pronounced it slowly, 'cop-you-late'. She ate, when she ate, mostly out of a liquidiser. We were often apart for professional reasons and our last interview took place on her return from the Far East where she had been involved in an expensive extravaganza and for which she had spent weeks examining colour contrasts in silks and baskets of exotic blooms, which she called Buddhism for Westerners. There was no irony in this.

'I dislike irony, David,' she said. 'It's rude.'

'Ah. I'm . . . fond of it.'

She looked at me in the same way she stared at smokers, a mix of disbelief (that anyone could harm themselves in such a way) and disgust (at the ash and addiction).

Oh, a failed marriage is somehow indelibly marked on one's innards. I have made a caricature of her. Was I that stupid? Or there was my snobbish mother. 'You can't marry a manicurist and expect it to last.' 'Winceful' was a ghastly word Kirsty once used, combining I suppose 'wistful' and 'wince', to describe someone's newly decorated house. When I got back to that beach, spruce and made up again, I found the real monster had had enough for that day. The line had gone and the director had decided to have me sitting on the sand looking morosely west while the monster's double leapt about rocks and rock pools in the background.

'Windsweep his hair,' said the director.

II

By far the most delightful of the medical staff is a Dr Burnet, who does what he describes as 'a round' of several convalescent homes. He is a neurologist and is compiling, here and at places in Romsey and Poole, information on violent injury. Having examined his spines and heads, he likes nothing better than to have tea on the lawn and chat about gruesome things. He wears a red-blond beard a great deal thicker than the hair on his head which he usually keeps covered by a tweed hat, has small gold spectacles that, from the skooks and squints and a gesture as if he were trying to look round them, appear to hinder as much as help his sight. He is tallish and slim, and has a languorous way of arranging himself in a chair. His hands, however, very large, very pale, move a great deal but always in strict confines about his face. He smoothes his beard, scratches by an ear, parts the centre of his moustache, keeps pushing up his spectacles, all within a few seconds. He will then place his hands together and intertwine his fingers, possibly to stop them from moving. This afternoon, while I dozed, Aubrey and Sanderson talked to him of their difficulties in finding accurate terminology to describe their respective cases, a leg gone, an arm gone.

'Neither "disarmed" nor "unarmed" are available without confusion,' complained Sanderson.

'I have a similar problem with "legless",' said Aubrey.

Burnet smiled. 'Have you considered "impaired"?'

'No,' said Aubrey. 'That's general as well. Your eyesight can be impaired but it does not mean you have only one eye.'

'Then tell me why "one-legged" or "one-armed" is not attractive.'

'They lack action and degree. How much of a limb? If someone has the leg removed at the knee, are they footless, shinless – or what? I'd also like to think that the action part was important. I was not born with one leg, the leg did not grow sick, I had it taken off, most of it rather abruptly.'

'You want a degree of violence in the description.'

'Is that unreasonable, do you think? Robert.'

'Mm.'

'How would you describe your case?'

'Shrapnelled.'

'No, I meant the part that was wounded.'

'I usually think of myself as lung-punctured.'

'That's awful. That sounds like a pneumatic tyre.'

'A tyre needs air to function.'

'Oh, I see. Try his arm and my leg then.'

'I am not sure I can. You are both amputees.'

'Oh God, that's horrible. I hate that word.'

'But why?' said Burnet.

'I don't know *why*,' said Aubrey, 'but it makes me shudder. I think of twitches . . . oh God, and gangrene.'

'All it means is leg-lopped or arm-lopped.'

'Not lopped. Not as in "pruned".'

'No,' said Sanderson, 'surely "pruned" has the idea of regeneration.'

'Doesn't "lop"?' said Aubrey. 'You lop branches off trees, don't you?'

'Yes, but I am not sure it has the same idea of cutting for the future. People lop branches to get more light now. They want an immediate effect.'

'Yes. But "leg-lopped"? I'm sorry. It doesn't sound right. Doctor?'

'Let me see if I have this right. You are looking for a brief description of your state that is expressive of . . . what would you say to "stumped"?'

'Oh, I say,' said Aubrey, 'that's quite good.'

'But isn't that a cricketing term?' said Sanderson.

'Yes, it is. I have been stumped. I was stumped at Loos. Yes, I think that might be it. Though perhaps rather better for a leg than an arm.'

'I'm not having "winged".'

'No. Robert?'

'Yes?'

'What do you think of "stumped"?'

'It all depends on your audience.'

'What do you mean?'

'Would you say "stumped" to your grandmother? Or an attractive girl?'

'Ah. I think Grandmama would get "taken off". And surely a charming sort of girl would have made discreet enquiries beforehand. Actually, I was thinking of the how-did-you-lose-yours type of conversation.' Aubrey screwed up his eyes and raised his hands. 'The problem is this, doctor: We don't want to be pitied but we don't want to sound too blasé. "How did it happen?" "I stood on a mine." It sounds somehow careless.'

'How did you lose your arm?'

'Shell,' said Sanderson.

'Now somebody,' said Aubrey, 'in a bed next to me, had his head split by a sword.'

'What are you suggesting?'

'That it sounds better. Rather more heroic than stepping on a mine.'

'But who to?' said Burnet.

'The public.'

'You mean the civilian population.'

'But there is an element of theatre in it, doctor. It is as if we were drawing lots to see who gets the best parts and lines. Losing a leg or losing an arm combines bad luck with meagre luck. An eye patch with a nice scar and a limp, even a couple of fingers missing – that is good or attractive bad luck, dashing bad luck. I heave myself along causing a kerfuffle and getting in people's way.'

69

'I feel amiss swinging one arm and I dread the prospect of revolving doors in restaurants.'

'Were you right-handed?'

'Yes.'

'Do you write well with your left hand?'

'No.'

'You see,' said Aubrey, 'we find this lack of a limb dispiriting but also embarrassing.'

'But why?'

'Well, we've sacrificed part of ourselves for our country.'

'Good God,' said Burnet, 'that is not embarrassing.'

'But in practical terms, it is. With the best will in the world, we are lopsided buffoons. Ah, there's your "lop". I knew there was something wrong with it.'

'Captain Sanderson, do you share his opinion?'

'I am engaged to be married.'

'To Gwen,' said Aubrey.

'What do you mean?' said Burnet.

'You asked me before if I could write with my left hand.'

'Yes.'

'Imagine receiving the equivalent of a five-year-old's scrawl telling you the man you will marry has lost his writing hand.'

This time Burnet did clap his hands together. 'Of course!' he said. 'What a fine example!'

I sat up and pushed back my hat.

'At night,' said Sanderson, 'I am plagued by thoughts of that nature, incompetent and beastly twists.'

'I don't understand.'

'They are absurd preoccupations rather than nightmares, as if I had got to squeeze all the juice out of my predicament, make it a dry husk. They are like loathsome long spasms but with no tears. Does that make sense?'

'Yes,' said Aubrey.

'My thoughts are shamefully ridiculous. The ridiculousness is the worst thing. I think, for example, that one side of her will always be cold. No, no, doctor, let me finish. I have made her lopsided too. It feels unforgivably as if I had let her down, misled her or not done something I said I would.'

'Ah,' said Burnet and nodded. 'I wonder if there is a link. Captain Gilmerton, have I ever talked to you of "ghost pain"?'

'No.'

'What? You don't like the expression?'

'I don't know what it means. But yes, it sounds fanciful. How do they go together? There can't be much less ghost-like than pain. Or are you referring to our inability to re-experience pain as we can a taste or smell? I don't remember ever having met or read of someone who can recall pain with the appalling accuracy necessary. We want to forget and we are probably made to forget. Is this what you mean by "ghost pain" – vague recall?'

'No. And I agree with what you say.'

'Then what do you mean by "pain"?'

'Good. I understand "pain" to be any of the degrees of physical and mental discomfort available to us – a very wide range from little more than unease to agony – as the sensation registered by the nervous system and perceived as such by the brain. To some extent we can talk of the brain translating the pain or perhaps apprehending the pain would be better. In any case, a degree of consciousness is necessary – as the use of anaesthetics demonstrates. Now as you know the anaesthetist has to work like a hangman, a rather rough-and-ready weighing up of the patient. Our problem is that we don't even have a rough way of measuring pain as we measure weight, say. And there is another difficulty in that people appear to experience similar pains differently. I had a navvy who lost his feet and who behaved with perfect aplomb. Yet the same man wept with toothache. In other words, we appear to be made up of a patchwork of sensibilities but each person may have a different arrangement and within that patchwork register pain to different degrees.'

'I think you are falling into something I did, which is a passivity in considering pain when not actually in pain. A certain amount of descriptive imagination is needed – by doctors in particular. In pain, the mind goes out to meet it or shrinks. I found that a very unscientific classification of the pains available to me helped me tackle the pains themselves.'

'How do you mean?'

'Nothing grand. There was one I called "dirty pain", akin to iron filings stirring in the flesh. "Blood pain" was wearisome and throbbing. "Pure pain" was transparent, contained, acid.'

Burnet smiled. 'And you shuffled them?'

'There was an element of that. When I could, of course.'

'As someone juggles something very hot?'

'I thought more of a railway junction and changing the points.'

'I'll remember that. Now, are you aware that in cases like Captain Gilbert's the leg that is gone is sometimes felt to be there? I had a case in which a man who had lost both legs to the thigh found his ankles hurt very badly.'

'This is your ghost pain.'

'Yes. Can you think of why the ankle and not, say, the knee?'

'What are you suggesting?'

'That the brain still thinks it has a leg and contrives to be extraordinarily precise about which part hurts.'

'Brain habit? A leg would take a deal of unlearning.'

'Yes. But why is someone seized by a pain in a part of the body they no longer have? Imagine I whacked a swagger stick down where an ankle once was. The patient would stare at me. And yet the same patient may wake screaming with pain in the same non-existent ankle.'

'So what do you do? Is the pain answerable to mime, an injection into the air where the ankle might be?'

'Good heavens, I hadn't thought of that. Are you teasing me?'

'It was simply a query.'

'We give analgesics. Do you think "ghost pain" a good term for the case?'

'The pain is real, the leg not. I don't know. "The feeling ghost" might be better. Aubrey?'

'Don't. I am terribly susceptible to suggestion. Pain in the air? It doesn't bear thinking about.'

'Sanderson?'

'What? Ah, here's McKinnon coming. Not his kind of concept, I think.'

Aubrey enjoys seeing Burnet and McKinnon together. Burnet stoops 'like a stork'; McKinnon 'resembles a dung-beetle with an invisible ball of dung, his patients'.

12

Did I drop off there? The yowl of a neighbour's piebald Great Dane sounds so close it is as if those slopping chops were by the bed-head. Startled, invaded by the smell of dog and drooling saliva, I open my eyes. Nothing. Whiff and whine fade. But I can see a small section of summer moon through the window. Piebald disc. In *Almost a Hero* I have no choice but to wear coloured lenses since the colour of Gilmerton's eyes is important. 'Quite the most heroic thing about him,' says Heidi Nutall.

Those who met Gilmerton for the first time frequently remarked on the striking and rare colour of his irises but, unfortunately, almost as often plumped on different descriptions. But I suppose we are lucky to have a list of them on one side of paper under the stark heading EYES. There are three 'butterscotch' – four, if 'buttercup' is taken as a slip – two rather fruity 'fulvous', a solitary but surely unlikely 'ochre', a 'tawny', a 'tawny buff', several 'eyes like a cat'. A couple of unhelpful 'dark yellows', a 'resinous yellow', an 'amber and yellow' and several varieties of soft, old and even tarnished 'gold'. Ms Nutall believes that women notice eyes more than men and claims to find most convincing the description given by a Miss Ravelston (Gilmerton's housekeeper in Edinburgh), namely 'saffron with tiny flecks of chopped mint'. The flecks I understood but the rest I could not imagine. So I went to our kitchen cupboards and found, in a small, clear plastic box, some wispy threads; their colour reminded me of a dry seaweed, a thick, dull, charged red. I picked out a trio of stamens, wet them a little and smeared them on a sheet of white paper. They produced an abundant red-edged yellow like clear honey laid over a base of turmeric powder. Gilmerton had eyes like that? I borrowed a coloured pencil from my daughters' box and stroked in an inner sun of dark green pips.

'Oh, that's not bad,' said my elder daughter, 'that's quite pretty.'

'The flecks are too big,' said Ms Nutall, 'and you've used white paper. But well done.'

For her contribution she took a worm of make-up foundation from a tube and rubbed it carefully alongside a red edge. She cocked her head.

'I wonder if we will have to dye your eyelashes along with your hair,' she said. 'His hair is *black*, isn't it?'

Of the five photographs Heidi Nutall has collected of Gilmerton only two show his eyes clearly and one of those is sepia coloured. The other is a black-and-white photograph taken the day Gilmerton left Lampenham. I like it very much. Partly for the incidentals; his hat on a stone urn, possibly dropped over flowers a few moments before, a crutch and its shadow leaning against the worn old brick walls of the house and a small dumb-bell that someone has placed at the base of a rone pipe. Gilmerton himself is extraordinarily slender.

'Just look at those legs!' said Heidi Nutall admiringly. 'The length of them!' They have the girth of the two eight-year-old lime saplings we planted last November. He looks to have been caught a fraction before the pose so that his surprise is amused and on the point of turning ironic. His hair is certainly dark and the cut would almost be fashionable now, very short at the sides but with two bangs that flop down to the level of his famous eyes on either side of his forehead. His cheekbones are high and very clearly marked, the nose would be snub if much shorter and he has a neat, chisel end to his chin. His slenderness and the length of his fingers remind Isabel of El Greco figures 'but without the knobbly bits'.

Now it did occur to me that it might be possible to translate shades from an old photograph into colour, even that a computer might assist, but Ms Nutall considers computer colours crude and better used elsewhere and has worried most about the lenses themselves that I have to wear. In horror and science-fiction films they are often used precisely to catch inhuman light and in their sulphur-yellow versions to show that the wearer has devilish powers and no reassuring pupils. In other colours it is also difficult to avoid what Ms Nutall calls 'that baked fish look'; in some lights the actor appears to have cataracts or an untoward glazed spot or, to give an example, a blue lens will flush deep violet. Whatever the colour, eye acting, showing the measure of intelligence and irony Gilmerton displays in a black-and-white photograph taken in 1916, becomes more than hard. When we went along to lens people, I tried, one after the other, thirty-four different shades of yellow to gold; 'Beer,' said Ms Nutall, 'piss, panther,' and put her hands over her face.

'We want the eye colour striking but credible; if not immediately attractive, at least intriguing. And *not* threatening.'

I said nothing. My eyeballs felt swollen, grazed. But I thought – stick to honey. It made little sense but provided some relief.

And what did Gilmerton himself think? In a letter to his sister he said: 'I used to consider my eyes like your hair. I remember, circa 1898, a very old lady looking agee at us. "Why Mavis, the boy has yellow eyes, the girl unruly hair." So we were yellow eyes and unruly hair. I was quite wrong to equate our particularities. I did not have to bear all those tedious and anxious jokes. I remember you, smiling with uncertain stoicism, when old Uncle Walter asked you, "When is hair musical? When it is unruly and has to have a band!" He would intersperse such stuff with hackneyed and sanctimonious lines about "a woman's crowning glory" and become maudlin and settle into a huddle all by himself – exuding a thick-throated sentiment that made us, instinctively, step back – and then recount one of the tritest and stupidest stories ever written, the one about the poor young couple, he with a watch but no chain, she with a lovely head of hair but only a comb, who go out, because of love for each other, he to sell the watch for a hairbrush, she to sell her hair for a chain. Uncle Walter never tired of telling this wretched story and always sniffled and ended as if he was giving you the most precious knowledge in the world. Naturally he was married to someone like Lydia. In that miserably gloomy time in 1904, in the weeks after our father's death, before we moved to Midlothian, Lydia decided to contribute by bringing an assortment of combs and brushes for your curls, at least one of the brushes having metal spikes for bristles. She applied this instrument with such vigour that she opened your scalp. The first anyone knew of it (I said you were stoical) was the sight of trickles of dried blood on your forehead, nape and ear. Lydia had the gall to wonder aloud as to what on earth you might have been doing. Ah, she was also, of course, the person who behaved as if our father had been unacceptably eccentric to die on the twenty-*ninth* of February. I suppose the background to this was fear – who would now look after the family's business interests? – but since I had never understood what was wrong with curls in the first place, I should have been blissfully happy to treat Lydia's face as wet blotting paper and rip it off, particularly after you had iodine applied to your scalp. It left your hair spotted and sunk with a hideous yellow for some time but I remember most your mouth opening and your inability – for about a minute – to emit a single sound. Just before I came of age Mother told me that she considered Lydia to have been "a most ferocious coward" on our father's death, but that she felt remiss; "I said nothing but I may have shown something, enough for Walter and Lydia to take offence." She was talking of money, of course, but I nodded and belatedly savoured those few weeks we were spared watch-chains and hairbrushes.'

Ah, our second, soon-to-be-middle daughter, aged two and a half, has recently taken up the habit of waking at night and asking loudly for water. She works, successively rather than rhythmically, like one of those alarm clocks that penetrates sleep by increasing in volume and shrillness.

'Daaaaa-dy. Drinkawaaaa-ta. Puh-lease, Daddy.'

We both groan. 'It's all right. I'll get it.'

'DaaaAA-dy. DrinkawAAAA-ta. Puh-LEASE. Daddy? Dad!'

I roll out of bed, walk, lifting my feet, to the far end of the bedroom where there is a door to a narrow turnpike stair to the floor above. As soon as she hears the door creak, my daughter stops and 'I listens to your feets' as they tackle the stone steps.

The floor above once held three bedrooms divided by wicker-and-clay walls but is now one large room with three dormer windows. She sleeps at one end, her sister at the other.

'Hi, Dad.' She appreciates the power in parody. There is a certain sleepy glee in her. And she enjoys mangling her English to see if we will worry. I give her the mug of water and she drinks two-handed, with noisy verve, breaking off for air.

'Have you finished?'

'No. I haven't.'

She drains the lot, smacks her lips and while wiping them with one hand, uses the other to hold out the mug, insecurely, in my direction. I take it and put it down on her table.

'All right now?'

The ritual is lengthening. She looks exaggeratedly doubtful by pushing out her wet lower lip. I sigh and comply. I lift her out of bed and sit her on my right hand. She clasps the smallest finger of my left and snuggles about my chest until she has an ear over my heart. She no longer sucks her thumb but, using a similar gesture, catches hold of her free cheek. She is, despite the sweet smell of baby shampoo, getting heavy to hold. I told her this a few days ago and she retreated outside and squatted for a few anxious minutes by the drainpipe next to the kitchen. When she returned she marched up and lifted my right hand.

'Dad, this is not a hand. It's a tractor seat.'

'Fine. Then we could get you a little tractor with pedals and then—'

'Shh.'

From the other end of the room her sister sits up and peers at us.

'Not again!'

'Shhhh!' dampens my chest. My daughter, the shusher.

I wait a little and then put her down and tuck her in. I blow a kiss to the other daughter.

'Daddy, do you think she is really asleep? Already? Or is she pretending?'

'She's not pretending. Sweet dreams.'

That daughter lies down and I go back to bed.

'All right?' asks Isabel.

'Yes.'

'This one is striking poses.'

I feel round and find a foot sticking hard up against Isabel's belly, gently rub it with the ball of my thumb. Still rigid, it stops moving, then softens quite abruptly and disappears below the drum skin.

'Ah,' says Isabel. 'Well done.'

In a few moments she is back to sleep. I have been in bed for nearly two hours. There is a clear moon tonight, though rather waxier than usual. I lie back and close my eyes. Where was I? Yes, Gilmerton's jaundiced eyes. At one of our script sessions Heidi Nutall arrived with some hyper-close photographs of famous irises. A normal hazel-brown had been transformed.

'What does it remind you of?'

'A kind of dahlia.'

'I had thought more of russet coral.'

She showed me some of the effects of age: tiny, still explosions and snags and in one very old eye, a bleached look and a mild wrinkling like that on the segments of a drying lemon half.

Ms Nutall sighed. But in fact Gilmerton's eyes were easily and successfully ordered from the US, alarmingly sized soft lenses made by the people who do eyes for ape imitators. When out they look smoked and have something of ginger in them rather than saffron, but in they work with my blue underneath, 'To intrigue the spectator but not distract her,' says Ms Nutall.

'Rather disgusting. But attractive at the same time,' said Isabel.

They feel no thicker than the thinnest onion skin but they cling to the eyeball, give a slight sensation of tugging outwards.

13

My dear girl, you reply by return! That is not a complaint, quite the contrary. I think, however, some of my replies will do better as parts of a pillow book than as mere pieces of correspondence.

Yes, I think I do know what you mean by children 'waking up'; it happened to me in the six weeks between my fifth birthday and our father's arrival on 15 May 1895, during which I was set to acquiring what Tsuru called 'creditable skills'. One of these was to eat fruit with a knife and fork. I can still remember my dismay at my first grape; it ended as two ragged blobs of luminous greenish flesh, the whole not unlike what is left of some caterpillars when wasp grubs have finished using them as a living larder.

Another task was to write my full name on three sizeable sheets of thick white paper. It was a question of scales. For my hand it was like naming a ship. Tsuru complacently showed me the instruments of Japanese writing, brush and ink-stone, and between us we painted out a wobbly run of capital letters – and then began again. I was at Liddell one evening – Tsuru had gone to fetch the apple purée you also had to eat and I had asked for lots of cinnamon – when I grew aware of a slow-fluted, quick-clanking noise somewhere above me. I was just in time to see a moth reel wonderfully fast from one of the overhead oil-lamps on a declining leftward slope towards a wall. There was no flutter. It careened along a line like a taut tent rope. Most thrilling of all, at least one hind wing appeared to be burning.

It flew so fast I flinched a fraction before it struck the wall. And when I opened my eyes again I looked down at the floor. It was not there. I looked at the wall. The creature had gone. But then I picked it out, a dark mark, like the missing piece of a jigsaw, on the painted salmon.

I got up and tiptoed over. I remember saying 'Hello' to it but quashing a movement to stroke it as being too young for me now. I put my cheek to the top of the dado and looked up.

Of course I could not have told you what I was seeing beyond the imprecise but impressive mothishness of the creature, the furry body, the ferny antennae, the large, glowing eyes and, of course, the wings. I became a mothist in the most casual and mistaken way. It was the texture of the wings that so intrigued me; the texture was rich, juicy, looked almost pleated and yet at the tips the wings had been charred and looked as fragile as burnt paper. Let me be tedious. I *think* it may have been *Lacanobia oleracea*, the Bright-line Brown-eye.

Obviously, I carried stories of fairies in my head. More recently, I had been shown 'invisible writing', lemon juice as ink. When the paper was heated by a candle flame the writing became visible, at least in blotches. But it was then – definitely too many fairies – that I had the absurd occurrence that butterflies and moths corresponded to this process, that moths might be the invisible writing and butter-flies the visible. I think that what I was really getting at was the (also mistaken) notion that butterflies had brighter wings but as thin and fragile as dried flower petals – or burnt paper. The moth wings were plumper and more satisfying. What sealed it was the following. I squinted, my eyelashes came together. Now one of the games I played at night was just that; I'd rub my eyes and squint through wet lashes to find herls and grousish peacock eyes. Here I had the same vision a little further away and gratifyingly independent of me. I haven't quite finished. Tsuru disliked moths and brushed this one off the wall and stood on it. There was a slight crunch. I saw that the moth had left a powdery silverish streak on the painted salmon. I asked Tsuru why she had killed the moth. 'Dusty,' she replied and offered me a spoonful of apple purée.

I had two framed photographs of my father in my bedroom, a formal head-and-shoulders portrait and a smaller, far more relaxed full-length shot taken on a ship in which he appears by a handrail, cheerfully acknowledging the cameraman. It was the second I preferred, the first I was instructed to kiss on completion of my prayers. I recall no particular surprise, no unfamiliarity when I first met him and saw him move, only a desire to know in what way he was different.

'My dear boy,' he said, 'how *are* you?' and hoisted me into his arms to kiss me. I found what I was looking for in his thick moustache and his smell. He smelt dry for Scotland, a mix of sandalwood and, particularly at the moustache, Japanese tobacco. Later I did kiss the glass on his formal portrait again but I also kissed my reflection in a steamed mirror. There was no discernible difference. I was delighted with his moustache and warm smell. He was also so tanned from the voyage that the wrinkles at his eyes radiated out considerably paler than the rest of his face.

I found him to be inexhaustibly patient; though nominally on leave, it was almost court he held there, and the house soon filled with family and business clients and petitioners. He did not treat me as a child. I soon learnt that if I asked him a question, he took it seriously and replied accordingly. More important, if he did not know the answer, he said so and we went to look it up. If he was dissatisfied with the answer he also said so and would, one-sidedly, talk over 'possible avenues of enquiry'.

I do not think I have to go into his public side or kenspeckle reputation. On his second visit (when you were four) he gave me the only direct advice he ever gave me. 'Don't be impressed. Don't be arrogant.' There was a pause. 'Ach,' he said, 'just make sure you decide for yourself.' This was on our way to Perth to see the bleach factory. He napped and I tried to follow suit. He spoke with many Scots expressions in a pronounced Scots accent, the accent at its most striking when he spoke to Tsuru in Japanese; same Scots tones making different words. His 'dam'd' sounded like 'dumped'. It was at Perth – I may have been an unwitting witness – that he became involved in a face-off with the Marquis of Something who accused him of not knowing the state of the country. He is supposed to have replied, 'Well, Jems, I at least have the excuse of working abroad.' I have no memory of any such incident and have heard the story attributed to many others.

What I do remember, on that first visit, is him creeping into my bedroom very early one June morning.

'Ah, you're awake, are you?' He sounded a little disappointed.

'Yes.'

'Well, I thought we might go and fish together. Are you agreeable?'

'Yes.'

He was fifty-five and did not, I suppose, have much experience of seeing children get dressed.

'Good. Now tell me something. Do you dress on your own? Or are you helped?'

'On my own, please.'

After I had struggled into my shirt he sat back and while feigning none, watched with considerable attention, particularly when I was brushing my hair. I could see him in my mirror. When I had finished he laid a hand on my head.

'Have I missed a bit?'

'No, no. But let's make very little noise. We wouldn't want to wake Tsuru-san, would we?'

This was one of the traits I liked him for. Tsuru was awake of course, but his attention was always singly given. He held out his hand and I put mine on it rather than in it because he kept his flat. And then he led me downstairs. To the early servants he whispered, 'Shh – and a very good morning to you.'

Neither of us had dressed for fishing and his only tackle was a rod and some bread he got from the cook. Leading me by the hand he took me down the yew walk, out of the garden by the far door in the wall, across the drive to the stables, through a field, along a wood-edged track, then down a slope to the millpond.

'Shh,' he said again. A few yards short of the bank he broke up the bread, gave a piece to me – 'Eat it, eat it' – and scattered the rest into the water. There was an immediate seething of fish, a gurgling of white bellies and bubbles and mottled backs. He had a very soft, slightly hoarse laugh.

'You could use a net here. We'll have to tell Baxter it is time to thin these.'

I am not aware that I had ever seen anyone fish before but even so, there was something out of place; he cast with a brisk flick, using quite a lot of the action Simpson tried to teach you with the whip and the dogcart. You would much have preferred the dog just to move. I cannot remember if he was using bait or fly.

'We are fishing for breakfast,' he said. 'If you want, of course.'

I had no time to nod. As soon as the hook touched the water a fish struck and the line took on a sudden taut slope. Our father looked around him, then yarked hard.

'I am not sure,' he said, as the fish went flapping over our heads, 'if one is quite supposed to do that. There's a question of poundage and the line breaking of course, but . . . I don't think it is considered . . . sporting enough.'

He shrugged, dropped the rod, took up the line and began pulling the writhing fish across the grass towards us. As soon as the trout was near enough, he seized it and it slid out of his hand like thick, greasy soap. He smiled and showed me the palm of his hand, smeared with slime and bright scales. Then, grasping the trout again, closing one eye as if threading a needle, he removed the hook. Shortly after, he had a second trout heaving beside the first.

'These look big enough, don't they?' he said.

I nodded.

'I should have brought a knife to gut them and give those cannibals a meal.'

I had no idea what he was talking about but felt happy to be with him. It was then I saw that a small moth, one we had possibly disturbed, was investigating the deader of the fish. It was a furry pale grey with iridescent whitish wings, for what it matters, perhaps the Muslin Footman. I do not know why but this embarrassed me acutely, a double but contradictory sensation: that the moth was an intruder, that my father was oblivious to it. He lit a cheroot, blew smoke upwards and sighed.

'They say Scotland is like Hokkaido,' he said. 'Perhaps in the Highlands.'

The moth had a swinging flight as it approached the fish and what agitated me was that it appeared interested in the rings of the mouth, still just moving. The movement stopped. The moth hovered closer.

'Ah,' said our father, 'do you know how to carry trout home when you have no basket?'

He was already bending; he took the fish by the tail and banged its head against the grass. The moth took off in a dizzying small whirl.

'No.'

'Well, hold up your left hand. Left hand? Yes. Now tuck in your thumb and keep the other four wide apart.'

By pressing he made each gill stand out like a stiff ruff, exposing the deep red branchia. I had just time to see the small moth disappear into a tuft of grass before he draped the gills over my fingers. I shut my eyes, but there was still a stinging red under my lids, a mild electric shock on the whorls of my fingers. The second trout was hooked on and then he took my other hand in his and together we strolled back to the house, the fish tails trailing in the grass.

14

My mother had the habit, always, no matter what, of crossing Princes Street. One Saturday morning in May when I was eleven we trudged off; Howe Street turned into Frederick Street and then, instead of simply turning left, into a wait at a zebra crossing. Edinburgh's main shopping street has only one built-up side. On the other, dominated by the Castle on its high ridge of rock, is what was once a loch but is now a wide green dotted with commemorative items. Invariably we would cross towards the Royal Scots Greys' memorial, then turn left and go plodding past the floral clock, the Royal Scottish Academy and go all the way to the end before crossing back again at Waverley railway station steps and shopping our way home.

Scots boys at that time (1972) and background were still schooled like timid collie dogs, to treat their mothers in public as if they were large, valuable sheep who might sometimes know better. One always walked on the outside. And while my own mother tended to traipse and had the disconcerting habit of stopping for no apparent reason, I dutifully shuffled my step to keep time. I usually understood that she was wondering whether or not she had left anything off the shopping list in her head; for some reason my mother regarded shopping lists on paper as vulgar. Sometimes, however, she would squint around her and sigh, 'But isn't this beautiful?'

On this occasion, though it was not warm and the morning sun to the right of the Castle was perfectly viewable to the naked eye, shrouded in mist as thick as muslin round a pallid dumpling, she was wearing a summer outfit of pastel blue, consisting of a buttonless coat, fairly tight under the arms but then taking on the cut of a knee-length cloak. Underneath was a matching short-sleeved dress with a round neck. There was something wrong with the hem of that dress. My mother disliked her legs, may have let the material down herself.

By East Princes Street Gardens, a little before the Scott monument, she stopped again. I had no premonition at all of what was going to happen and suspect that my memory of the unfamiliar gleam of her pale pink lipstick and an eyeshadow that looked to have flecks of turquoise in it, are observations made later when I stared back. My mother pushed the shopping bag at me.

'Open it up,' she said.

'What?'

'The bag, man, the bag.'

I opened it up. The shopping bag was made of canvas with rods, ideally like a deep letter-box. My mother dropped her dark blue handbag into it. The weight snatched a handle out of my hand. Embarrassed, I retrieved it, and looked around. The only sign of my mother was her new shoes on the pavement.

A few heartbeats later, her summer coat flew upwards on the other side of the balustrade, like a sleeved slice of impossible sky, and dropped out of sight. My coatless, barefooted mother was skipping down the path towards the Scott monument. I say skipping but it was more a juddering galumph. I don't believe I thought anything very much, except to wonder why she should be imitating a small girl and to think that her feet must hurt.

Still skipping, her elbows working from side to side, my mother disappeared behind the sixty-five-foot Gothic spire erected over the statue of Sir Walter Scott and his small dog. Further along Princes Street a man in full Highland fig started in on the bagpipes. I found something instantly dispiriting about him, in his swollen, red-faced dignity that sat sadly with the upturned bonnet on the pavement, the constant groan of the drones and the wailing fragility of the chanter. He was competing with diesel engines.

When my mother appeared on the other side of Walter Scott she was no longer wearing her pastel-blue dress but something cream and satinish with thin shoulder straps. She was still skipping but had slowed down, was flushed, looked breathless. She was moving one arm now, as if airily conducting a band, her mouth was working but if she was singing the sound was drowned out by traffic and 'Scotland the Brave'. I found I could not move my feet. In a panic I uprooted them and got away from my mother's shoes.

My mother was about to appear naked in East Princes Street Gardens. The shock of her nakedness was compounded by the speed of it, that she had not been wearing all those undergarments that normally constrained large parts of her. Mature female underthings had for me the same discretion as the contents of orthopaedic shops. I had long been aware that my mother had a peculiar pelvis; she looked to be carrying an overpacked, soft suitcase between her hip-bones. Unloosed, her thighs shuddered and her navel danced like an elastic bull's eye; her breasts she dealt with by crossing her arms in a poor imitation of those Russian dancers who squat and run at the same time. I was at an age when I thought premeditation was more shocking than a betrayal itself. The betrayal was not in her skipping naked in a public garden but in the fact that she had come prepared. She had certainly left off her underwear. Of course I was stunned by her nakedness! But somehow I kept looking or hoping for something worse. I squeezed my eyes tight and gritted my teeth.

There was movement around me, running feet and voices, a guffaw. I opened my eyes. Quite a little crowd was gathering to watch. A young red-haired woman leant on the balustrade and rocked slightly, almost as if hugging herself. On the other side of me one of a pair of striding men raised his rolled umbrella to point.

'Look, Angus, an escaped Rubens.'

A flustered policeman approaching along the gardens from the Academy received cheerful encouragement and advice.

'No, no, man! Meet her in the middle!'

But his first interest was my mother's coat which he picked up before advancing with it held up as a kind of screen, peeping round it to see where my mother was.

'Here, wife,' he pleaded, 'this'll no do. Cover yourself.'

My mother, her flesh now decidedly goose-pimpled, paused, giggled and switched direction; now she started off round Sir Walter widdershins.

'But that's a monument, hen, nae a maypole!'

Somebody pushed me. 'Here, you're too young for such an eyeful.'

That was the nearest I came to tears. I was saved by the arrival of two noisy police cars. The first disgorged two policemen and a policewoman carrying a grey blanket. As she strode down the slope, she got a small cheer. The two policemen started in on the spectators.

'Move along now. Not a public entertainment. Move on there. Move along, please. Now. Move.'

One of them bent and picked up my mother's new shoes. And shortly afterwards my mother herself sat on a step to the monument, allowed the blanket to be laid over her shoulders and let tears run down her cheeks. She turned her face up and though I could not hear what she said I am sure her lips formed 'I am *so* happy!'

I took refuge, even then shamefacedly, in my age. What possible response could an eleven-year-old have to a mother removing her clothes in an incomparably dramatic setting that also happened to be hometown Edinburgh on a Saturday morning? Then, even worse, it occurred to me that my mother might suddenly remember me and start calling out my name.

'What's going on here?'

'Ach. Just a wifie gan gyte in her birthday suit.'

Gyte? Daft. Crazy. The word operated on me like a released clutch. I started down Princes Street, shot past the busker, slipping in and out of gaps in strolling pedestrians. But it was at Waverley steps where my mother and I usually turned back across Princes Street that my reaction took its first deliberate form. Instead of left, I turned right down the long flights of steps towards the railway station, feet working like pistons, my mother's fat handbag rattling in the canvas shopping bag.

At the foot of the steps there is an elderly wood-and-iron bridge over some tracks and then a turn down more steps into the station itself. It took me a little time to get my bearings under all that iron and glass but I found the confused hush attractive. And then I fixed on a young black woman. Of considerable height and slenderness, she was wearing a tight lilac trouser suit and tremendous gold-strapped high heels. Her hair, pulled tight round her skull, burst out behind her head. She was asking a small porter for the Aberdeen platform. He pointed. She leant over and followed the line of his finger. I saw that her lipstick was purple. Instinctively it was she I followed.

I am not sure why but I had always considered Waverley station as a terminus; it was not until I saw the curving platform and the track disappearing round a high retaining wall that I really appreciated the railway went on. I don't think I had anything like a plan; it was more a rudimentary and unspecific sense of adventure taken up about ten feet away from my new black woman friend. I looked at the stone of the wall, slight traces of mist over the rails, realised I was looking north and felt almost happy.

The platform began to fill up. I had at least a substitute for a suitcase and I had a swollen handbag inside (though I don't believe I remembered it contained money). No, it just lent me a certain confidence as I waited. And I was thrilled when the black girl began to smoke a brightly coloured cigarette. The filter paper was gold and the cigarette itself was wrapped in a deep marine green. In fact, she barely puffed, soon dropped it on the platform, squashed it and put on some sunglasses.

The train from London came in after about ten minutes. I stepped backwards and when the rush had thinned and my new friend had boarded (I was tempted but did not pick up her cocktail cigarette), I tagged along with the slower passengers and started back the way I had come.

Waverley steps are steep. A year ago a charming Russian director told me that when he had first seen them he took them to be the original servants' steps and that somewhere else there would be 'an elevator, one of your Victorian marvels for high-born ladies and me'. I slowed, however, at the final flight, not because I was out of breath but because I was newly frightened of being seen.

So – about the most of my adventure – I hid at the top through two traffic-light changes and at the third sped across Princes Street and then zigzagged my way home through the New Town. I did not dawdle but I did not hurry.

Most of Edinburgh's New Town is on a north-facing slope with the result that it has long shadows in a long-shadowed place (and in winter neo-classically lined patches of frost that never clear). We lived on the south-facing side of Royal Circus. By the time I arrived the mist had thinned and the sun shone directly if not too strongly on the top half of our house. My father was standing by the open door. He waited for me without expression, put his hand very gently on the back of my neck and brought me in.

'She's with Nanny G,' he said. 'Where have you been?'

'Waverley Street station.'

His eyes opened. He nodded. 'Well, that's a sort of gumption, I suppose. The doctor's been.' He frowned. 'What have you got there?'

'It's a shopping bag.' I opened it and showed him what was inside.

He bent forward and lifted out his wife's handbag. He raised an eyebrow.

'Well,' he sighed. He leant even closer. 'Do you know,' he whispered, 'had she been drinking?'

The question struck me as shockingly unfair. He was trying to peel childhood off my back like an eggshell. I could remember an Easter egg I had rolled down Calton Hill and which I had painted green, red and blue. I mean those primary colours appeared, rolling, in front of my eyes to a sensation like the feel of cold egg-white on my skin.

'Ah,' said my father, 'it's all right. It is. Now run upstairs and clean yourself up. Good boy.'

15

My dear girl, life here is resoundingly placid. After the dawn chorus of birds a very thick quiet settles on Lampenham and its small valley ('vale' say the maids), like the aftermath of a thunderous gun. A sheep they are carting away bleats. A woodpigeon sounds surprisingly like a coy owl. The only human noise is low voices. Things liven up at mealtimes. They are announced by someone striking a large brass gong softly and repeatedly. There is something of a rush and clatter then.

The rest of the time we get better. This is perhaps more complicated than it sounds. We are put to it. The doctor in charge here likes to talk of 'positivism' – Aubrey Gilbert says it is a 'bovine posit' – and even of 'mind leading matter to health'. It depends on one's injuries and imagination, of course. I breathe deeply. I lift my little dumb-bell (my target is five hundred times a day in ten sessions of fifty). I work my fingers. I stretch. I walk (I can do about a mile and a half in one go).

There is also an unofficial roster; when the morning mist has risen we take turns to sit by those wheeled outside for fresh air. Today I sat with Earnshaw who took a fine degree in Greats about a year ago. He is twenty-two and was, like me, at Brasenose, though I have no memory at all of him. We sit like old men, though rather more puzzled and confounded than wiseacres, and we mull and we murmur. Earnshaw has enormous difficulty breathing *and* speaking so that his murmur is more mutter and only comes when he exhales;

he then breathes in two or three times before the next part. His breath usually gives out before the end of a sentence; having breathed a while, he completes it. We all pay attention; it would be churlish to ask him to repeat himself, but he can be a little obscure.

Today he talked of Daedalus and 'circuitous twists' (a whole breath for those two words). As a child he was struck that 'Ariadne was an ant' (another breath). So let me breathe for him. Daedalus is obliged by King Minos to construct a maze in Crete in which to hide the Minotaur. The secret of the maze is that it is not on a horizontal plane but is three-dimensional. To safeguard the secret, Minos refuses to let Daedalus go but the inventor devises wings for himself and his son and, though he loses Icarus on the way, escapes to Sicily. Minos discovers him by offering a reward to anyone who can thread a string all the way through a conical triton-shell; Daedalus attaches spider's silk to an ant, smears honey at the other end of the shell and the ant wends its way through all the twists and turns to get at it. That night Daedalus makes use of secret plumbing to scald Minos to death by pouring boiling water on him in his bath. Later, Minos's daughter Ariadne helps Theseus kill the Minotaur and escape; by letting a spindle of thread roll its way down the labyrinth Daedalus had built, they find both the beast and the way back.

'And who tricked who? Mm?' said Earnshaw. 'Daedalus had his pipes before he went for the honey. All nonsense, of course. But I loved the twists. To the extent that Daedalus's obsession felt familiar; I recognised it, as if it were mine.'

'You've been talking to Burnet?'

'Who hasn't? I wonder though if we *do* pursue basic shapes which we make out very early in our lives or if we are always in some way chasing our own brain chemistry, like a spider trying to learn a domed web?'

I am, like Earnshaw, eager, even grateful to remember. If Earnshaw was struck by Daedalus as a child, I had Perseus with his helmet, winged sandals and shield-mirror. I also enjoyed the Gorgons' guardians sharing a single eye and tooth among them. Childhood is a time of sticky meanings. I used to show myself my eye-teeth in the mirror of my washstand, was at first alarmed that they were not quite as white as the others, then rather proud of them, as if they were little ivory tusks. I enjoyed Medusa's viperous hair (though I had the vipers short and wormish) and the mirror movements Perseus had to make in order to sever her neck but for some reason I was not impressed by the cause of them, her ability to turn humans into stone with a direct look. No, what thrilled me was Medusa's blood. The stuff produced a warrior (whose name I am sorry to say I have forgotten) but also Pegasus, the winged horse. Pegasus caught my imagination, rising up, white wings out of dark gouts. Ah, and I soon made changes; I had his helmet not only protect him but enable him to see, allow him to pick up any light without being seen himself. Far more interested in possessing the story than having it exist in some general limbo, I changed his sickle, for reasons of heroism and cohesion, to the slimmest of gleaming steel scimitars. About the age of seven I as Perseus sliced through Medusa's neck nightly. The blood would spurt and splatter on the pale wood floor, sometimes I would even step back to save my shoes. The blood was hot, red-black and as thick as new road tar. But my point was that the blood crept and joined and slowly began to form the outline of a winged horse which then rose, the head stretching up out of the floor, the wings breaking free. I would shut my eyes and feel the buffets of air on my face and by squeezing my lids I could contrive a burst of light under them to accompany a mental image of the winged horse crashing upwards through the roof and soaring into the sky.

In my fantasies I was – I certainly considered myself as such – a determinedly realistic child; I had a similar sensation the first time I saw a butterfly issue from its cocoon, a kind of child-scale heroism in the expanding, quivering wings; or when I read 'a butterfly's blood is generally white'. I repeat, it was of course moths that intrigued me. I think it took about two years for my excitement to join with a degree of knowledge, some equipment and the realisation that other people knew little about or even saw these creatures. I remember catching myself briskly indicating to cousin Deirdre a few features of a moth found dead on a sundial.

94

The result was that when I was ten and you four, when our father returned from Japan again in 1900, I was taken aback when he asked me for my favourite myth. I had picked up the notion that the Greeks had been the privileged children of civilisation and that I had outgrown myth as striking images in narrative tosh. Nonetheless I thought back and surrendered up Perseus and Pegasus. His delight was unexpected and he made – I was not at all keen – to pull me on to his knees.

'Now Pegasus,' he said, with every sign of sharing a pleasure, 'was a ship. Imagine yourself long ago on a coast looking out to sea. You see the billowing white sails of a ship. But you do not know what it is, you have never seen a ship before. The ship rides the waves. What is it like? Instead of sails you think of great white wings. And then the prow rises, very like a horse's head – on which the Greeks sometimes painted an eye.'

He was delighted, I rather appalled. I wanted living organisms, not artefacts, Pegasus as a butterfly, not Pegasus as a ship. He eased me off his knees.

'You're getting a big lad,' he said, and then turning me round and taking both my hands in his, 'My dear boy, later on, you might care to read the Romantics.' He smiled. 'Shelley, for example. A charming, innocent, hopelessly irresponsible man, but very astute in the ways of imagination. You may have heard the expression – science is satisfying but the imagination is marvellous? You should be interested in those ways. Ah. I am forgetting. Shelley drowned, you know. I think his boat turned over in a storm. Still.'

Have I remembered that right? Or have I remembered his teasing rather better than the matter?

'I say,' said Aubrey, 'why don't I give you a game of badminton?'

'All right.'

'I don't much care for speculation.'

'What do you mean?'

'All that stuff about shells and honey and Minotaurs.'

'Earnshaw? He was remembering. And so was I. He can't play badminton.'

'Exactly. It's this place.'

'Lampenham?'

'Any military convalescent home, I suppose. You don't find it tedious? There is an absurd air of waiting to be bellicose again. But waiting is not a bellicose activity. Poor Earnshaw can't even sit up, let alone straighten up. And why do they give him a *pale* blue blanket? It hardly sets him off.'

'That's why he passes the time as he can. Serve.'

'What is it you find you miss here?'

'Is this gamesmanship?'

'Oh, sorry. No. Here.' He served.

The shuttlecock looped over the net, wavered and dropped plumb. I scooped it up. 'Sorry.'

'I meant what you miss about our life here.'

I flicked the shuttlecock back. 'A microscope, work, variety, a decent library. And you?'

'Town, I think. Bustle.'

Our badminton games are of the most listless. Given Aubrey's 'vehicular limitations' and my incompetent left arm, we try ineffectually to act counter to the idea of the game; instead of trying to place the shuttlecock out of our opponent's reach, we endeavour to make the wretched thing go directly back to the other's racquet. Rallies are infrequent and I can only remember one which lasted longer than four strokes, Aubrey spinning round on his crutch like a scarecrow in a gust of wind to deliver a fortuitous backhand winner.

'Sorry. I think perhaps we should stop. I don't want to force my luck.'

'Well, that's two nothing to you. Do you want to keep it in mind for the next game?'

'No. What was that "Ariadne is an ant" business?'

'Extrapolation. On the same lines Icarus would be a moth burnt by a candle.'

'Mm. I never much cared for myths. Well, that's not quite true. I liked the nymphs in illustrations. For the little bumps in their tunics. Oh, and I was rather wistfully religious when I was about thirteen and rather liked your butterfly idea of the soul fluttering off from the carcass. I was squeamish too, I suppose.'

'It's not my idea, Aubrey. And the analogy is horrible. The butterfly is the sexually mature version of the creature. You've never seen caterpillars mate. That's what the butterfly flutters off to do.'

'Oh,' said Aubrey, 'but there's communion, isn't there? Like nuns. And Psyche is Greek for butterfly and soul, isn't she?'

'She married Eros and they had a child called Pleasure. The only interest I've ever seen butterflies show in carcasses is as food.'

'Good God. But they don't eat human beings, do they?'

'Some like rotting meat. Last summer in France I saw a flock of Purple Emperors over a detachment of dead nuns.'

'But I thought they liked nectar and things like that.'

'The gods liked nectar.'

'Nuns!' said Aubrey, shaking his head at me. 'But you've been talking about tastes and desires, haven't you?'

'Have I?'

'Yes. Which god ate his children?'

'Saturn. Kronos the crow.'

'Does Kronos give us the word chronological?'

'The clock caws? Why don't you ask Earnshaw? He's the expert.'

A little after I heard Earnshaw laugh for the first time, a delightful staccato noise a shade away from a dry cough. As you can see, at Lampenham time hangs. Or as Sanderson said as he flopped down, 'Do you ever feel you could stir the air here, like gruel?'

16

When I was young my father's brother's wife Susan was a practising aunt, behaved as if doling out enthusiasm with a sticky ice-cream scoop. I think she saw herself as a contagiously didactic guide, loved imposing bright-coloured treasure hunts on her daughter's birthday parties. Now, despite myself, I sometimes find a trace of her in Heidi Nutall. As at that unJapanese Japanese restaurant which illustrated, by default, through the insipid food and dreary decor, that it was Gilmerton's father who was Japan or Japanese Bob. Of course Ms Nutall is much more robust than Susan, is rarely unenthusiastic for long and does not sulk if you skip a clue. For our second meeting she invited me to her house on the south Fife coast for lunch and 'to get to know Gilmerton's sister Agnes'.

The house was stone, with a pantiled roof, narrow windows with lots of astragals and surrounded by great clumps of rhododendrons; inside, an impression of flagstones, polished Edwardian panelling and not much upholstered furniture. Heidi Nutall introduced me to her housekeeper, Mrs Sempill, a pleasant, stout lady wearing a blue floral apron on top of a pink floral frock and, over champagne, to photographs of her three children, Briony, James and Rowena, the first two surnamed Muir, the third Nutall, a gynaecologist, an accountant and a silversmith respectively.

'Somehow I never took to my third husband's surname,' she said. 'That was Cunningham.'

'Ah. What was the name you started off with?'

'Adelaide Reid,' she said and both ladies laughed.

Heidi Nutall works from the entire top or fourth floor, 'somebody's idea of a Breton artist's studio'. She has a central script table and a number of other, smaller ones, 'one a character'. She topped up my glass and tilted the bottle to indicate Agnes's table.

'Gilmerton's mother died in early 1921. It took over a year to settle the estate but in May 1922 Agnes left the house in Midlothian that had been her home since 1904 and moved back to the enormous pile near Brechin where she and her brother had been born.'

Ms Nutall had photographs. The house in Midlothian was a dark stone, late Georgian affair, top-heavy with Corinthian details, the red sandstone house near Brechin 'a bizarre example of Scotch Baronial at its most ocean-going. By the way, it's rather bigger than Lampenham.'

Japan Bob had built his house on an east-west axis, the east in ship terms the towered and turreted stern, the west the lower-towered prow with a long double-storey stretch between them broken vertically only by a couple of cupolas on stalks, rather like straight, capped funnels.

'You get a better idea of the scale of the place from photographs of the servants taken when Agnes moved back.'

There were two. Dwarfed by the portico a team of maids in very white, starched aprons stare impassively or shyly back at the camera. All have their hair up and topped by a sort of doily but there are differences in the apron straps, some rising from the waist in a thick V, others plain pinafores. In the margin someone has written in very blunt pencil, 'Margaret Logan, extreme right, lived to 100 years'. The other photograph is a pose of gardeners; there are the tools of their profession – a roller, two heavy lawnmowers, a barrow – and the five gardeners shown all have caps, rolled shirtsleeves, light waistcoats, dark trousers and gleaming boots. They are scattered among pieces of clipped yew in extraordinary pastoral positions and attitudes, like clothed statues.

She handed me another photograph. It showed a tall, slim young woman perkily posed by a Rolls – 'That's a white American Brewster,' said Ms Nutall – wearing a chic black outfit and a close-fitting hat. The surprise for me was twofold. Ms Nutall did not tell me who I was going to see and it was her decided resemblance to her brother that told me this was Agnes. And then she is relaxed and exceptionally good-looking. I mean that with the photographs of servants and the talk of heroes I had expected someone stiffer, perhaps with some unfair flaw, a never-mentioned lameness or a misshapen nose. Instead I think most people would consider Agnes better looking than her brother and certainly less self-conscious when being photographed.

The only other photograph of her when relatively young, taken about 1927, is a snapshot (Agnes on a rug by rock), with far too much light. Here she shows her thick 'unruly' hair, but again she looks pretty and confident. Ms Nutall favours an ex-model for the part of Agnes; she is equally good-looking but also 'helpfully sinewy' and has to stifle her trembles when she acts. Heidi Nutall wants to take advantage of her nerves to get over Agnes's desultory but stubborn efforts to make Gilmerton a hero.

These began with her move. In a letter of explanation to her lawyers, Agnes said that, apart from her mother's death, she had also suffered, in her frostily Cervantine phrase, 'disappointment in a person I do not wish to name. In any case,' she adds, 'I made the decision some years ago.'

'Rather headstrong,' said Heidi Nutall cheerfully. 'I'm taking it that the decision to return to the house her father built was made on her brother's death. She was also her brother's age in 1922. But I suspect that what really animated her was a dinner party near Montrose. Let's say she was very surprised to learn that Lawrence of Arabia's reputation had been worked up for propaganda purposes during the war and that Lawrence himself was then encouraging the legend and had even collaborated in a touring show of his exploits, had had himself photographed in Arab dress.'

Ms Nutall loves telling stories or at least being in charge of and dealing out information. She handed me a battered, pale grey book, Agnes's copy of *The Seven Pillars of Wisdom*, Lawrence's autobiographical account of his Arabian adventures in the Great War.

'Open it at the frontispiece,' she said.

The subtitle to the book, chosen 'doubtless after thought', is *A Triumph*. Under this Agnes had added her own list of descriptive words in pencil, later and very lightly crossing out three of them. These three are 'unmanly', 'irresponsible' and 'lies', which leaves untouched 'strenuous', 'fantastic', 'dangerous', 'egotistical' and, underlined twice, 'small'. She also added, first in pencil, then over-written in ink, 'This is a disgusting confidence trick. Under the vocabulary of great endeavour lies a mystical farrago of incompetence and misogyny almost derisory were it not for the cruelty of ignoble dreams acted out.'

I think you have to have read Lawrence's book (I have not) to share Heidi Nutall's amusement. 'I can think of some people who would consider that a very respectable opinion.' But she considers it principally as Agnes's way of saying she considered her brother a better, braver, but above all, more gentlemanly man than Lawrence of Arabia.

'He had more humour too, of course.' Mrs Sempill appeared to announce lunch and as we went down the two ladies had a chat about Agnes's concept of a gentleman, agreeing on honest, restrained, affable and never, however ambitious, stooping to self-advertisement.

'But the bedrock of Agnes's gentleman,' said Mrs Sempill, 'is that he never, no matter how desperate, deceives himself – or others.'

We began the meal with toast and a leek paté that had the consistency of mousse.

'It can't have been easy for her,' said Heidi Nutall. 'Goaded by Lawrence, in a sense weighed down by her brother and his generation, all those privately printed memorial volumes of very short lives. And of course the Lawrence of Arabia stuff did not affect others in the same way. They liked it and I suspect it had something to do with that compensatory exoticism we find in anecdotes about her brother, the Japanese silks and swords standing in for Arabian clothes and dagger. Mm? There are British men who *love* dressing up, especially vicariously.'

I raised my eyebrows. We were now on a white wine with a floral after-taste made unpleasant by its persistence. I put my hand over the glass and Mrs Sempill went for the second course. A gull pewled outside the window. At the Montrose dinner party Agnes also heard that John Buchan, writer, tax lawyer, future MP and Governor-General of Canada, had been instrumental in pushing Lawrence as a hero in his wartime propaganda job.

'It was new to Agnes that heroes could be encouraged after the event.'

But then, rather oddly thinks Ms Nutall, given Buchan's role in Lawrence's fame and his production of exotic thrillers whose heroes often pass as natives and dress up in disguise, Agnes sat down and wrote him a letter, simply offering him her brother.

Buchan replied 'promptly, briefly, kindly', mentioned his own connection with Brasenose, but pointed out that the war was over, that Lawrence was still alive and 'possessed of a genius for self-promotion' and pointed Agnes in the direction of founding a Chair in Biology in her brother's name, 'whether at Oxford or Edinburgh, a memorial far more solid than the history of reputed actions'.

'Why didn't she?'

'Because she wanted a hero. She also disliked the proposal of a war memorial or memorial hall. They weren't special enough. They weren't *written* enough. Agnes paused after Buchan. And when Agnes paused she did so for a year or two. She then contacted, through her lawyers, "as reputable a literary agency as possible" and a person called Mackie spent what he called "many arduous hours" examining the possibilities of producing a biography of her brother but finally replied, enclosing his bill, as follows: "Really, Madam, it is most difficult in this day and age to make an entomologist, however bravely he died, attractive to the public eye. No one, least of all myself, could possibly doubt that your late brother was a most remarkable man by virtue of his upbringing and character. Alas, your average man sees entomologists as a cross between someone who likes creepy-crawlies and a stamp-collector with – a detail fatal to our enterprise – the killing bottle in between. It is not, unless placed in the context of a grand exploration, seen as a noble, let alone an heroic activity."

'Isn't that lovely?' said Ms Nutall. Mackie suggested a lavish memorial book, something he was experienced at and happy to arrange.

Agnes, 'puzzled and stubborn rather than grippy', paid the bill, rejected his suggestion and replied, 'It had never occurred to me that the average man was involved.' Ms Nutall wonders quite who Agnes did think was involved — heroes need a public — but also thinks Agnes 'quite right to insist her brother had been a biologist and to suspect that Mackie's arduous hours had neither lasted long nor been very penetrating'.

The second course was sweetbreads — something I had not eaten for many years — accompanied by mangetouts, broccoli, small potatoes if desired and a Mcdoc wine.

'The Mackie business, though, gives Agnes's character note. At no time did *she* investigate anything.'

'I don't know if I am following this. What was her aim exactly?'

'I don't think she knew, David. Think of her as someone in a slow swim, feeling for a solution or a way out. Oh, she pottered about a bit in heroism. For example, she was impressed, though not very usefully, by a biography of Champollion, the Frenchman who deciphered the Rosetta Stone, and in particular by the fact that the future great man, despite his normal-enough French parentage, had been so dark skinned that he was nicknamed "the Egyptian" long before his interest in hieroglyphs. The predestined child. Precocious indications of heroicity. Yellow eyes. Agnes also found out that heroes are sometimes not so in practice, are so in desire and legend. Sir Francis Drake, for example. Or the reverse could happen. In *Macbeth* Shakespeare turned an apparently competent-enough king into a monster. Agnes read some of Lord Acton's work and was taken by his remarks on sophists with sponges who follow in the wake of tyrannies. In other words, Agnes slowly began to appreciate that reputations are not only manipulable, they are *always* manipulated.'

Dessert was a lemon sorbet.

'Then in the spring of 1930 Agnes woke up one morning and found the left side of her face paralysed. All of the doctors consulted agreed that the paralysis was of nervous origin. It lasted close to eighteen months, left her always a little slow on that side of her face. She also complained of a shock of white hair on her head that grew while she was ill. During that time she wore a thin scarf wrapped round her neck and pulled over her head and left half of her face.'

Evidently Agnes felt most vulnerable. Ms Nutall considers she was ripe. Still hankering after doing something by her brother she had also been advised 'absolute repose'. Without having formulated it, she had before been looking for a biographer of genius; now she had some hasty belief in happenstance.

'Coffee?' said Mrs Sempill. 'I do hope you smoke. We have some cigars.'

Ms Nutall had prepared for her presentation. She opened her handbag and gave me another photograph. It shows a flabby, middle-aged man in pale tweeds and monocle, with a centre parting to what is left of his hair, a fleshy rectangular face, small eyes in pudgy lids and an expression both pining and pompous. He is leaning on a walking-stick.

'That's H. Gardner Price. He'd just taken a lease on a ramshackle little fortified house nearby. Can you see he has a gammy leg?'

17

This morning Aubrey decided to claim that, 'with a thick woollen sock muffling the top of my stick', he had made a night-time raid on McKinnon's office to discover our character reports. He had prepared carefully and came with a scrap of paper on which he had written his notes. He considered three characteristics to be of importance. First, that what McKinnon had written was in faint 'easily erasable' pencil. Second, that McKinnon had limited his character descriptions to one word or, at most, two. Third, that McKinnon had felt it necessary to go outside English and make the evaluation in French. I was prepared to wait but Sanderson fairly snapped at him.

'French?' he said. 'Are you quite sure?'

'Quite sure,' insisted Aubrey. 'He has described me as *farouche*. I have made enquiries. It means sullen and unsociable. But surely I am rather sociable?' He dropped his voice. 'He calls Cummins *louche* and that means shifty.'

'It also,' said Sanderson, 'means squinting – or squint-eyed.'

'Good Lord!' said Aubrey. 'Are you suggesting something physical in his descriptions? Our character *vis-à-vis* our wounds? Are you saying that McKinnon is referring specifically to my way with a crutch? I am *farouche* when I hobble?'

'Only in the most idiosyncratic French,' replied Sanderson. 'What do I get?'

Aubrey consulted. 'You're *fainéant*,' he said. 'For a horrible moment I thought it might mean fawning but it really means—'

'A do-nothing.' said Sanderson. 'Splendid.'

'And you're *distrait*,' Aubrey told me. 'It means distracted, I think.'

'Absent-minded,' said Sanderson. 'Aubrey, I can't offhand remember McKinnon ever saying anything at all in French. I am not aware he even speaks the language, likes the country or trusts the people.'

'Exactly!' said Aubrey. 'He doesn't trust us either. Don't you see? He has made us French too. Convalescents are foreigners. We're difficult and unreliable.'

For a moment I thought Sanderson was about to lose his temper but his face went red and he closed his eyes.

'What I wanted,' said Aubrey, 'was a French word to describe him.'

'*Bête*,' said Sanderson.

'Or *gauche*,' I suggested.

'That's clumsy?'

'And tactless,' said Sanderson.

But Aubrey beamed and spent his day 'spreading the word'. *Gauche* McKinnon, the medical ghost. Later he told me he was 'mightily bucked' by the general acceptance of his suggestion to include a *soupçon* more French in conversation.

'I say,' he said, 'you don't mind, do you?'

'Mind what?'

'It's just that I rather needed this.'

The result has been a twitter of lamentably pronounced French words in unlikely English sentences. *Gauche* has generated into gosh and joined *blasé*, *malaise*, *outré*, and *canard*; I even heard someone maintain that the colour *cerise* was the same as burgundy.

In the afternoon I did my best to nap.

'Worse than a plague of moths,' said Aubrey.

I opened my eyes. He grinned.

'I know French words don't behave like moths,' he said, 'though perhaps *cliché* is a bad example.'

Despite myself, I laughed.

'As a matter of interest, what *is* the French for moth?' asked Aubrey.

'*Phalène.*'

'Sounds more exotic than "moth", doesn't it?'

'Yes,' said Sanderson, 'but do you think McKinnon has ever noticed? And if he has, do you think he has associated this sudden fashion for French vocabulary with himself?'

'Oh, I do hope so,' said Aubrey. 'I want to get that thick, indignant blink of his and that slow flush of pink spreading on his face.'

Sanderson made a glum effort at a smile, tried to increase its effect by nodding, turned his head away. I had had enough and went off to get some fresh beech leaves for the Lobster Moth larva. But on my return I found Sanderson waiting for me.

'I say, do you think Aubrey's all right?'

'No,' I said, 'he's morose and agitated and has taken a possibly new development for himself as a raconteur rather too literally.'

'Ah,' said Sanderson. 'You see, I had wondered if his story of the midnight raid were quite true.'

'Well, if it is true, we should be worrying more about McKinnon, don't you think?'

Sanderson sighed. 'It's a footling business. But if his story is not true, what is he calling us?'

'I don't think we are much involved.'

Sanderson blinked. 'What?' he said. 'You're playing the understanding friend, are you? Well, damn you.'

After supper, with the curtains drawn against the evening sun, we were given a film show, three short films of one reel (of about two minutes each) and then a longer affair lasting close to forty but with intervals for reel changes. The small films were the usual capering stuff but the longer one was a little more interesting; it was German and something of a horror story. It involved a poor young woman who spent most of her part making a variety of cringing movements while widening her already wide eyes; when she rolled them they looked like hard-boiled egg-white. She was cringing from a villainous pawnbroker and his energetic shadow. Indeed the film was a shadow play with some amusing touches as when the shadow played out the villain's foul desires (shadow with knife, man smiling overfondly) or showed impatience (shadow fingers like parsnip roots tapping while the man brought the hand of flesh to his mouth in a spasm of poltroonish rage and indecision). I enjoyed a number of images and scenes: the girl's bedridden mother in her alcove; the receipt of a letter saying that a young man had been lost at sea; the pawnbroker fondling the ornately decorated bodice of an evening gown, example of the girl's art as a seamstress, or those same hands playing with blood that had dripped on to a table from a recently killed rabbit; and last, as the girl made her way ever higher in the ever more ruined house pursued by the hunched pawnbroker and his leaping shadow, the sudden appearance on a gangplank of a young sailor – 'Not "lost". Shipwrecked!' said the caption – just in time for the rescue. The pawnbroker plunged from a suspended stair to his death and, a pause later, to allow the dust to settle, his shadow abandoned the corpse on tiptoe.

When the lights came on I saw Burnet was sitting close by. He groaned. 'What dreadful tosh!'

'I rather liked it.'

'But why?'

'The actors behaved as if they were seeing themselves in a mirror for the first time. And there were some nice details, like the pawnbroker playing with mercury as blood.'

'Quicksilver? Are you serious? That blood was quicksilver?'

'Or something very like it. How else would it roll or gleam like that?'

'Ah,' said Burnet. 'I had thought film was neither art nor dream. Are you suggesting there was an attempt to leaven a creaking sort of horror with humour?'

'Surely there was a degree of parody there.'

'Mm. Can I ask you something? Are you able to tell the colours of things when presented in black and white?'

'Prime sort of colours. Nothing subtly shaded. When the girl's fat tear fell and blotted the writing, the ink was green.'

'Good God. And the gown she worked on?'

'Theatre-curtain red with gold thread.'

'Colour-blind people do not know they are colour-blind. How much of this is an imposition?'

'I imagine some. And some experience, too.'

'Quite what experience are you talking about?'

'He sees at night,' said Aubrey from behind me. I turned. Sanderson was with him.

'Is that true?' said Burnet.

'I was going to say an experience of melodrama. It wasn't difficult to work out, for example, that the pawnbroker would offer the dead rabbit to the heroine's invalid mother as a bribe, was it? The night thing is entirely relative.'

'Explain.'

'I practised a lot, particularly when I was younger. Do you know the tints in daylight shadows?'

'A coloured shadow?' said Aubrey.

'If you take a plum, put it on a table, its shadow on the wood will be plum tinted.'

'Are you saying,' said Burnet, 'that night is like some sort of stained glass for you?'

'Oh, much softer.'

Burnet laughed.

'Does this extraordinary faculty work in winter?' said Aubrey.

'Aubrey, mothing is a summer activity. In summer, particularly where I am from, it is never even properly dark and it is quite possible to identify trees and shrubs from the shade of green in their night foliage as well as by shape and leaf form.'

'Are you suggesting,' said Aubrey, 'that this ability is due to your eye colour?'

'What? No. I'm not an albino, Aubrey.'

'Do you know the first time I saw you I was appalled and thought your eyes were caused by mustard gas?'

'No, I didn't.'

'You don't think you are being excessively special?'

'I was born with them, Aubrey.'

'Yes, but then you sleep as little as a horse.'

'Or my father.'

'And then you can see at night.'

'Not as well as a horse, I assure you. And Aubrey. In Brazil, in a tropical forest at night, I couldn't see at all.'

'Ah, it is a temperate ability.'

'Because I was brought up in a temperate zone.'

Burnet smiled. 'How much are you remembering what you see, superimposing experience and knowledge on outlines and shapes?'

'To a large degree but very much on the lines of how we see in daylight, part focus and levels of light, part taking for granted, part references and cross-references. Before I mentioned a plum and its shadow. Imagine that shadow on oak. Now take a less common wood, sycamore say. It is the wood that makes the cross-reference. A plum called red might look garish, take on yellow and orange on sycamore, take on blues and blacks on oak. Now the sun goes behind a cloud. It is much the same with moon and moths. My interest made me pay attention. A moth in trees has no choice but to fly in a patchwork of shadows and night light; the rest is just some knowledge of moths, their flight patterns, favoured plants and so on.'

Burnet reclasped his hands. 'Good. So you really are saying it is the quality of attention that matters.'

'And the particular interest. If I saw a deer, for example, it would be more a disturbance with antlers than a deer. If you wanted to know about age and weight and condition, you'd do much better to ask a poacher.'

'But of course!' said Burnet. 'A poacher! The poacher's vision is made up of the habits of the animal, the ways of the moon and the lie of the land.'

'And the gamekeeper,' said Sanderson.

Aubrey frowned. 'What is the link between a poacher and a poached egg?'

'"Poacher" comes from the verb "to poke",' said Burnet.

'And the egg comes from the French for "pocket", *pocher*,' said Sanderson.

Aubrey smiled. 'Good,' he said. 'Yolk in a pocket.'

And then to me, 'I don't think I've heard you speak at such length and so vigorously before.'

We all nodded.

It is a lovely night. A ground mist has risen to form a pale scarf at foliage level on the trees. It is not quite still; the mist undulates and wisps of the stuff filter up through the leaves making the stars beyond the canopies small gobules. When the water vapour thins a little a star glimmers. A fox, with a caution as near indifference as I have seen, trots along the base of the almost black hedge and turns the corner for the path up the hill. There is a quarter moon a little to my left. And then the beat and creak of a small wing. Above the lawn bats begin to chase moths, all ragged snaps of appetite. When I was a child I first thought the squeaks of bats in the air were cries of despair when they missed their meal.

18

There used to be an exclamation, though I don't think I have ever heard it used in Scotland, of 'Great Scott!' to denote surprise. But whether spelt with one t or two, it always referred to Sir Walter at a time when his reputation bobbled close to Shakespeare's. A declining reputation and the lack of bite inherent in double euphemism have wafted the expression off. My mother's dance about the Great Scott's monument was never mentioned again and I had the perverse if leaden sensation that as an eyewitness I was expected to be man enough to be *more* silent than anyone else.

At eleven, apart from wondering that secrets could be as embarrassing as dreams or even, I think, suspecting that certain conjunctions of shame and gentility might constitute a large part of people's lives and enjoyment, I was far more concerned for myself than upset for my mother. I took parents to be as fair or as unfair as a raffle. 'There he goes,' said a friend of a big-headed sports hero, 'the Big Bang.' The notion that my parents' private parts might have anything to do with my existence I would have found absurd and unpleasant.

Five years ago I went to see Nanny Grizel in hospital. She was dying of lung cancer, had a noisy plastic tube in her neck, but otherwise was in a small row of white-haired ladies, wearing a pink-and-lace bedjacket with a crimson ribbon. She apologised cheerfully for being overdressed.

'Of course I never smoked,' she said, 'not even in secret.'

'I know, I know.'

My father had, occasionally but ineffectually, puffed at and kept having to relight a pipe, especially when handling a divorce case, and my mother had at least a posed, framed photograph of herself at about the age of twenty with a cigarette in a holder.

'My mother smoked,' said Grizel.

'Mm.'

'But it was her liver out of kilter in the end.' She smiled. 'Now *she* was frightened people'd think she had cirrhosis.' Still smiling, the tube still gurgling, Grizel looked slyly about her. 'At the beginning they treat you as if you're to blame. But then they don't like it, not when you say you never smoked.' I smiled and she winked and patted my hand. 'Now just you give me my bag,' she said. Grizel was born in the north-east of Scotland and says 'bag' as 'bug'. Grizel undid the clasp and brought out a small stack of photographs. She flipped one up.

'I'll always remember you on your first day at school. With your new cap and satchel.'

I looked at the photograph of Nanny Grizel, a quarter of a century younger, bright with pride at the diminutive manliness beside her; I seem to be looking up at the peak of my school cap. I remembered my photographer father urging 'humour' on me. Grizel flipped up another photograph. We looked at about twenty, I think, from a bucket-and-spade snap to one of me swinging a mashie. All were taken on holidays or days out and most had Grizel in them, looking more or less flustered or pleased. I leant over and kissed her.

Nanny G smiled. 'Say something,' she said.

'Thank you.'

'Ach, you know I didn't mean that.'

'I know.'

Grizel blushed and collected up the photographs on the bedspread. As she was putting them back in her bag, she said, 'We were never in competition, you know. I did the chores, your Mummy did the decoration.'

This brought me up, but she appeared to be serious.

'Has she been to see you at all?'

'Now you know she doesn't like hospitals.'

Can't abide is what my mother says. 'Are you in pain?'

Grizel considered. 'Maybe,' she said, 'just a bittie,' and winked again.

My mother, on the other hand, always affected to find me startling. I once asked her why I had no brothers and sisters.

'Good God, man, I was not prepared to go through *that* again!'

And when I was fifteen she took to calling me Jack and I understood Beanstalk. A while after, however, when a relative visited, my mother spluttered, 'Here he is! Jack-in-the-box! Dear God, Jean, he looks like a long thermometer in a woolly sock!'

I was not offended so much as bemused by my mother's blushes. She has a moonish face and capillary-shot cheeks that can deepen to a dusty beetroot. But I did not know what she had expected my height to be. She, after all, was five foot ten. And my father, even with a lawyer's stoop, was comfortably over six foot. He had a bony face and the kind of plastered-back straw-coloured hair that gave the impression of never having been thick. One lunchtime shortly before his retirement he told his secretary he felt 'rather rough', left the office, hailed a taxi and had himself driven to a private clinic. Unfortunately he omitted to tell anyone what he had done. On location in Suffolk, dressed in Vanderbank's clothes for a lush version of Henry James's *The Awkward Age* I received a telegram: FATHER MISSING STOP COME HOME AT ONCE REPEAT AT ONCE MOTHER. I called in. By that time my father had also done so and my mother airily described him as being 'in hospital for some sort of tests he wants done'. In fact my father was inoperable and had less than a fortnight to live. Those last days, however, he lived as if enchanted. He described the hospital and its routine as 'quite, quite fantastic. My dear boy, the sensation of irresponsibility is absolutely disarming. Though, for some reason, they are decidedly mean with liquids.' He had been reading the book I was filming and found 'all that corruption rather comforting'.

I did not expect my mother to visit him in hospital but nor did I expect her to go from group to group at the funeral saying, 'I told him Rileys were dangerous.' My Aunt Susan said my mother really meant, 'He had the life of Reilly.' Meaning? 'Well, dear, she feels upset and upstaged. She means he had a better time of it. I am not sure her own father didn't have a Riley. She was always very snobbish about cars.'

When my father died I asked my mother if she wanted to live with or near us. 'Oh, for heaven's sake,' she said, 'you can't be serious.'

'At least she is prompt and clear,' said Isabel. 'My mother dithers.'

So now she lives in an over-furnished flat in a converted baronial mansion where meals and cleaning are provided, the garden is walled, there is always a nurse on call, a chauffeur for shopping and where she prefers to spend Christmas and most other days with 'my friends here'. She behaves as if any conversation not started by her were a troublesome small dog at her feet and she were frightened of tripping and falling. She always calls my second wife by my first wife's name. She has no interest in her grandchildren. Did she want to hold the first child?

'Mercy on us! I can't hold a child, not in my condition.'

We told her we had given the child, as a middle name, hers.

'Marjorie? It's a horrible name. I've always hated it.'

There was a time when we considered her condition, thought of Alzheimer's or anything else to explain her behaviour, but my mother can count backwards spryly enough and a drastically selective memory and exclusive self-concern do not count as an illness. Since my father died she watches television. When I was a child she despised 'the box' and had hobbies, usually of an artistic nature. For her painting, she acquired an impressive collection of brushes and kept them bristles up in terracotta pots. I once saw her run her hand over them as if they were the arched back of a cat. But the most she ever produced were soggy little watercolours of low hills and although ready to talk of her work in technical and even exalted terms – 'I'm particularly pleased with this passage, the slightly stubbed effect I've achieved' – she became glummer, her face more moonish, her shoulders rounder on her way to that stance I associate with mother unwell – head hanging, shoulders hunched, feet splayed, hands retired.

I remember once coming home to find my father in the hall taking three books out of a paper bag. He blushed. I saw that the top book was an optimistic tome on clay modelling, the title done in strip lighting. I looked at his face, saw we were about to embark on a sheepish complicity and fled. More than once I have heard him described as 'a bit of a stick'. When I was about eight we were set to clearing out his mother's conservatory and came across a contraption that looked like a wooden tray in the shape of a round-headed tombstone. Cupped in variously sized convex fences made of small nails were some faded numbers. To one side there was a narrow channel like a thin pencil-case without a lid. My father mimed amusement.

'I think this could be described as an early version of a pinball machine.'

He dug about in some flowerpots and came up with something between thumb and index finger; it was a powdery, opaque green, like a clay pea.

'A bool,' he pronounced with that simpering relish he brought to Scots words he used.

I was accustomed to clear marbles or bools, of a sinewy twist and unlikely petals (brown, white, red) trapped in the middle of transparent glass. My father put his marble in the wooden channel and flicked with his finger; the marble rose on a rattling but leisurely curve and descended fitfully down the board, the nails giving out dull pings. He scored nothing.

'I always loved that rise,' he said. 'Reminded me of slow rockets. At your age I should have loved to have been able to fly. But the nearest I have come to that sensation is the wax in my ears. Ah. Haven't you done Icarus yet?'

'No.'

'In Greek mythology Icarus is the son of the great Daedalus. I suppose you could call Daedalus an engineer of genius. He devised some feathered wings held together by wax to enable them to fly. Icarus rose too near the sun and his wax melted.'

'Did he crash?'

'Oh yes, fatally. But it was Pegasus I liked, the flying horse.'

I was awfully literal minded and took these snuffling paternal memories in a winter conservatory most seriously. My dreams, however, linked Pegasus and the kelpie. It was Nanny Grizel who told me about the kelpie, and while I am not sure that this malignant water sprite that haunts rivers – making forders lose their footing in the current and dragging them down – is supposed to have the shape of a horse, that is how I saw it. My Pegasus rose from a river, wings folded and wet, stretching and shaking them out. I simply imagined rising up into the air on the flying horse's back, looking down on Edinburgh, the racket of the wind in my ears. Our house was slightly tricky to recognise from above, but I found it by working my bearings along Randolph Crescent, the oval Ainslie Place and the full green circle of Moray Place. I looked about me, then up towards the Firth of Forth in the distance, suddenly realised I was looking down on my own roof, felt something like alarm that I was there under it and ran off to my father's study.

'Hello,' he said. 'This is an interesting case I have. A scoundrel of a son is attempting to dislodge his widowed mother from the family home.'

I pulled up. I think I was still swimming in perspectives. As my feet petered out in the gloom of my father's study, I was suddenly aware of folds of discretion and privacy in me which felt as loose as dog's skin. But I could not stop myself speaking.

'I've been flying,' I said.

'Oh good,' he said. 'This is extraordinary. This reprobate has somehow persuaded himself that, simply as a man, he has more right to his late father's property than his father's wife and his own mother. Both deranged and ignoble, wouldn't you say?'

'Yes,' I said. I felt relieved, then comfortably anxious about keeping my various skins of privacy to myself. I think I thought that was the point of growing up.

19

Lampenham
11 June 1916

My dear girl,

For some reason – certainly not a good one nor a clear one – I recalled recently a time at the beginning of the century, after our father had gone back to Japan and you were between the ages of four and five, when you had a consuming passion for caterpillars.

I hope you have no objections to my bringing the matter up again; it occurred to me, however, to ask if *you* remembered going through the leaves of fruit bushes as intently as a monkey examines another's fur, twisting a gooseberry leaf or a blackcurrant leaf till its underside was uppermost, to see if there was a caterpillar there. You would crouch and start from the base of the bush up. I remember watching you turning leaves with your right hand while your left picked a caterpillar higher up the bush. There was almost no break in the rhythm; the caterpillar went straight into your mouth and your left hand went back to turning leaves.

I was ten and your behaviour struck me as bizarre without being particularly interesting so that I cannot now say what varieties of caterpillar you were hunting for. You must have learnt them by taste. When you began you would bite but even if the caterpillar was unlikeable you always started looking for another before you spat out. And when you had learnt you were so fast that all I can recall is that the caterpillars I saw you eat were pale shades of green; I once saw you hold one up to the sun, apparently to check whether or not it was quite luminous enough.

I was not sure whether to be indignant or aghast when our mother called me in and invited me to consider the following: might some hobby of mine have had a pernicious influence on you? I study lepidoptera, I replied, it has never crossed my mind to eat one. She raised her eyebrows and enquired if I planned to proceed through life as irresponsibly as I was living it then. I begged her pardon; she insisted: did I wish to be a gentleman or a scientist? Taken aback, I asked if the two were irreconcilable. No, she replied, but a scientist *who is a gentleman* possesses a sufficiency of imagination to accept responsibility even when he is not the whole cause of an unfortunate effect. The truly valuable imagination is a considerate imagination, a wideness of view and an unselfishness that allows someone to see, for example, that a four-year-old sister, intrigued by her elder brother's interests, as yet lacks the means, knowledge and skills to share those interests but that share them she will — in some form or another.

I felt affronted, intrigued, a touch flattered, but mostly puzzled. If humans are omnivorous, why should they not eat caterpillars? I had read that the Australian Aborigines were considered insect gourmets and there was a tribe somewhere in Peru that harvested enormously fat grubs for oil and food. But mother's talk to me had merely been one very small part in a campaign to get you to stop eating the things. You were surrounded and told that you would hatch butterflies in your stomach. You asked, with every sign of enthusiasm, 'And would they fly out of my mouth? Would they?' — and happily opened and shut your hands in front of your face and round your head.

I regret to say you did not hold out very long. They switched tack and had immediate and complete success by telling you that 'the habit' would undoubtedly give you a moustache. This may have worked because there was a maid (Margaret Logan?) who had a fascinating pale brush on her upper lip, like glued-on dandelion seeds.

As an elder brother, probably more loyal to my contempt of hypocoristic horrors than to you, I took you along the yew walk and explained that you might swallow parasites or suffer quite severe allergies but that eating caterpillars would not give you a moustache. You feared hair. You stuck out your tongue and let it feel about your upper lip. 'But the ones I've eaten,' you said, 'never had bristles, did they now?'

It may be, deep down, that this is why, even now when I am surrounded by all sorts of hirsute and not so hirsute bits and smudges, lines and snipped brushes, I remain clean-shaven. You yourself were enticed on to hairless jelly babies, green at first but then, briskly combined to your learning the names of colours, a whole bright gamut of pot-bellied creatures were distributed about the house for you to search out. Later you would round them up, invite them to tea – and bite off their heads.

You also took to calling me brother, though when you wanted something you called me Robert dear. 'Robert dear, will you help here? This dawl [doll] has lost its head.' In fact you were as fond of detaching dawls from their heads as you were of decapitating jelly babies. On principle – 'We *all* have a duty to be imaginative' – our mother insisted that you invite me to one of your teas; you sent me a piece of paper with a scribble on it by way of formal invitation. I should have preferred not to attend nor to eat a jelly baby – I was fond of striped, pillow-shaped mints that I could clonk about my teeth – but I was obliged to sit and wait for a jelly baby with a head. You offered me several incomplete babies, even claimed to be trying the sweet to see if it was all right for me but it took the time of a longish sermon to inveigle you into relinquishing an entire jelly baby with its head and bloom intact. I remember wondering what it could be about the heads as opposed, say, to the feet that might matter to you – but that was lack of imagination again. I never did let you near my collection of insects, though to be fair that was because I had also been told never, ever to let you near glass, chemicals and sharp blades.

I wonder if I can make amends now. This afternoon, while walking in the orchard with Aubrey Gilbert, I spied a caterpillar of

Smerinthus ocellata, the Eyed Hawkmoth, sunbathing on an apple tree. With the help of Aubrey's crutch we brought it down – I caught it – to find a plump, little larva, with an attractive blue-tinged green body, almost violet lateral stripes and a grey-blue horn. I ignored Aubrey's suggestion of 'introducing' it to the Lobster Moth larva I have in captivity but did take it back to my room and acquire another tobacco tin for it.

Now, as it happens, I am particularly fond of the imago of the Eyed Hawkmoth; it has, for a moth, gorgeous colours, restrained waves of pinkish brown, pale brown and bitter chocolate on the forewing and on the hindwing a strong touch of rosy pink and the eye of its English name, a large black-edged circle round a bluish-grey spot with a blackish pupil. But having remembered your appetite as a child I felt somehow stupid and cowardly. I have just written this paragraph with the *Smerinthus ocellata* worn as a moustache. I have had to raise the writing paper and pout my lips. The larva has hardly writhed at all and only briefly investigated the opening to one of my nostrils.

There. It is more comfortable for both of us if the caterpillar sits on the knuckle of the index finger of my writing hand; I got it off my lip with a small snort.

My reasons for feeling stupid and cowardly are as follows: I spent years examining insects, counted and recounted the hairs on certain legs as if counting the syllables in heroic Greek and Latin poetry, spent days finely slicing pupae of the Ingrailed Clay, *Diarsia mendica*, peered for hours down microscopes at eversible structures (scent organs) on the abdomens of certain male moths, went cross-eyed over minute regional differences in wing colours of the same creature – but at no time did it occur to me to put my own mouth to use except to talk of what my eyes saw. It never occurred to me, even with you as an example, to *taste* what I was studying. The question, 'But why should you?' is beside the point. I had never come up with a reason for *not* tasting them. Apart, that is, from the Tabby Moth larva, *Aglossa pinguinalis*, and other occasional parasites. For all these years I have followed a squeamish national tradition and combined it with the po-face of finical and apologetic science.

That is now over. I have had some difficulties. The only live food I have ever eaten would, I think, be oysters. Should I follow you and eat the larva live? And then again, dead or alive, the caterpillar would be raw. Without condiment or sauce. I believe our father developed a taste for raw squid at breakfast – but with Tabasco sauce. Should I toss the caterpillar in butter to crisp it up? But I considered cooking finally as unfair (and here at Lampenham probably impossible). Then, if I was going to kill the creature beforehand, there was the question of method. Obviously I could not use the same material and methods as when death is a preliminary to preservation. A pin or needle seemed ineffective and grotesquely like a miniature version of St George and the Dragon. No, it gradually came clear that the quickest death was to adopt your method – bite off the head and mash the creature between my molars. Oh, I admit, having shifted the caterpillar back on to my index knuckle after its progress along my finger towards the pen, that I remembered I prefer oysters with a little lemon juice but I quashed that weakness.

It also occurred to me that I had a choice of larvae. Might the namer of the Lobster Moth have been referring to taste rather than to appearance? As you know, I am fond of lobster, though I have never much enjoyed the sight of them being lulled into death by slowly heated water. Of course, there was also the possibility that I eat both larvae and compare tastes. A wine taster, a caterpillar taster? No, one was enough and besides, the Lobster Moth larva is at rest and has taken up that attractively absurd position, caterpillar rampant. So I have looked again at the Eyed Hawkmoth larva on my hand. Why wait?

Accordingly, I have broken off the horn, used my eye-teeth on the Eyed Hawkmoth's head and, with a slightly lower snuff-taker's action, have snaffled the rest in and worked my teeth once. Twice. I shut my eyes there, to concentrate on taste and texture. To be honest, not a great deal; an insipid mucal-cum-gelatinous feel with touches of fibre. My jaws have ground twice more, to more of the same – and yet, that might have been the merest hint of grass sap and, though this is to strain my taste buds, a trace of something like egg-white. And now the caterpillar is down leaving a dry after-taste, a touch of vermouth and a faint smell of lupins. Either you were a sophisticated child or you knew which caterpillars were sweet.

With much love, R.

PS. A little while ago Aubrey came to ask after *Smerinthus ocellata*.

'One caterpillar is enough,' I said and Aubrey nodded and peered at me.

'I say, I hope you don't mind my mentioning it,' he said, 'but you have a little piece of apple skin or something caught between your teeth.'

'What a marvellous letter for a sister to get!' says Ms Nutall.

I was less sure. 'Doesn't it seem fey and infantile and rather silly?'

'But of course! David, just imagine getting a letter like that! It may be one of the reasons she fell in love with some notion of him. Mm? And how much attention had big brother paid to her before? Surely it is part of what made him a hero for her!'

'He doesn't seem to have understood she was twenty years old.'

'Oh, but he does!' Ms Nutall threw up her hands. 'God, I wish *I* had had an elder brother like that!'

'Ah.'

'David, some things go *straight* in.'

EXT. LAMPENHAM ORCHARD — DAY

Aubrey uses crutch, Gilmerton catches caterpillar.

> AUBREY

What is that?

> GILMERTON

The caterpillar of the Eyed Hawkmoth. It likes sunbathing in apple trees.

> AUBREY

Are you going to keep it? Make a collection?

> GILMERTON

I'm not sure. I'll think about it.

INT. MIDLOTHIAN — DAY

Agnes opens and unfolds letter.

> GILMERTON
> (*voice-over*)
> I wonder if you remember a passion you had about the age of five for eating caterpillars?

Agnes smiles.

> It has made me think of my own cowardly behaviour. All those years and I have never tasted my hobby . . . So I have decided to eat an Eyed Hawkmoth larva.

Agnes reacts.

INT. GILMERTON'S LAMPENHAM ROOM — NIGHT

Gilmerton chews, considers, writes.

> GILMERTON
> (*voice-over*)
> Grass sap. Egg-white? Perhaps a trace of . . . vermouth.

Aubrey enters.

> AUBREY
> What have you done about the orchard caterpillar?

> GILMERTON
> I thought one was enough.

> AUBREY
> Yes. I say, I hope you don't mind my mentioning it but you have a little piece of apple skin stuck between your teeth.

> GILMERTON
> Really?

He rubs, looks at his finger.

> Ah yes. Thank you.

He sucks finger.

INT. MIDLOTHIAN — DAY

Agnes is delighted.

20

Along the length of a noble gallery which contained exquisite bowls & lacquered screens, the walls cedar panelled, the pillars clad in gold leaf & a green marble like malachite, the dim light necessary for precious artefacts given a cavernous, almost marine stillness from the green alabaster censers, past, at the far end, the life-scale model of a horse & sixteenth-century Samurai dressed for battle, then vertically on a wide stone spiral staircase, oil-lamp flickering on ashlar walls, my guide led me towards the turrets & towers of the great house, to the locked & studded door.

I had been aware of her restraint & dignity but not of her anguish until – no, no. Better would be, yes – As Thomas de Quincey says of the early scenes of the *Orestes*, with *particular* reference to Electra 'covering her face with her robe', so my guide did likewise &, in bowing her head, unlocked that studded door & stood to one side.

Problem: although Miss G wishes to be 'resolutely excluded' from the biography, it is my impression she might accept a something. If the compliment were not over-crude, naturally.

Now, how to describe briefly what the open door revealed? Museum is not applicable since the word implies a marked notion of display & order. A tomb requires a body. A mausoleum can, as well as a tomb, also be a monument, but one specifically designed for that purpose. Here was a modern warrior's burial chamber. There was no coffin but there was still something pharaonic about it. I held up the lamp & proceeded like an archaeologist in the chambers of a pyramid, revealing as I went glimpses & outlines of a treasure trove of objects.

I lit more lamps. With the help of rods I pushed back shutters. The next difference with the above was that the objects had been placed, as it were, retreating out of those rooms, without regard to function or separation. I remembered Tennyson's great poem *In Memoriam* & his notion of the body as a house from which life has gone.

But was that the effect? As light revealed the contents of those rooms, the impression was rather the reverse, of possessions dispossessed of their owner, the life brief, the possessions extraordinarily crowded, despite the largeness of the space. There is also the matter that the rooms had been built as a nursery, the first stage in life. Who was it said 'childhood peeping out from behind the man'? At twenty-six years of age half a life is as a child. Or again, that nursery had been built for several children, now reoccupied & supplemented with the objects of the rest of one life. But here there was no sense of legacy, no sense that others might ever use those objects.

My eye fell on a peculiarly stout rocking horse. On a table beside it stood a row of his own nine microscopes. In one bathroom I counted thirteen trunks. Clothes at all his ages leaked, bulged from wardrobes – though for some reason his army captain's dress uniform had been draped over a full-length mirror on a stand. & everywhere, on tables & shelves & packing cases were small bowls of mothballs. A breakfast table was entirely covered by his adult shoes & boots (twenty-nine pairs) in their trees & bags. On a tray table were scattered a safety razor, a cutthroat razor, a silver shaving bowl (the soap, barely begun, looked to have shrunk & the bubbles to have petrified), a shaving brush, two ivory-backed hairbrushes, stuck together at the bristles & bearing the initials RLG, three combs, tooth- & nailbrushes, a tin of tooth powder, a pair of small scissors & a dull grey spatula eaten by acid at one end. All his own books were there, over five thousand of them, his boyhood collection of butterflies in their glass-topped boxes (some cracked, some specimens made dowdy with age), notebooks from his time at Edinburgh & Oxford Universities so numerous they had been tied together with green gardening string in batches of ten & twenty & stacked in tilting piles, the furniture from his set of rooms in Edinburgh, a whole domestic ménage, including a dinner service for twelve on a dining table for twelve placed under a wall with a salmon painted on it, a child's bed with a stuffed animal (some sort of raccoon?) attached to the bed-head – in short, *everything* that could have been called his was confined there. & is it not curious that the dining table was carefully set? Or was it simply a way of discovering whether or not there had been any breakages during shipping? & yet on several of the dining chairs were small columns of hatboxes & on a chair at the top of the table, thick clutches of shirt collars. Here was a drawer full of gloves; two others could barely open over the handkerchiefs packed in them; the next contained many small boxes of cuff-links & collar studs. The effect was – there were, bathrooms included, nine rooms in all, the central one very large – overwhelming, partly due to the sheer quantity of possessions, partly due to their having been gathered in one place, partly due to their disorder.

Accordingly, there were some incidentals that stood out like gestures. A silk shirt for a very small child lay over the top of a wing chair. Or there was a five-pound note beneath a book on which in 1913, on 5 September at 3.20 p.m. when the London-to-Oxford train stopped 'a little before Didcot', Robert Gilmerton had sketched a butterfly that had wandered into his compartment, part of the train window & a suggestion of the view beyond, with the information *Colias hyale* – Pale Clouded Yellow, Male. I glanced at some photograph albums – the young man in a planter's hat during his visit to Brazil in 1907 – looked around at a *sheaf* of Persian rugs with another bowl of mothballs balanced precariously on top, the very precariousness revealing to me only then that all the bowls were finger-bowls, filled not with water but with naphthalene. I began to experience a pervasive feeling that I was an intruder; the movement of my shadow on polished wood, my distorted reflection in the top of a tarnished silver serving dish, catching a view of myself in the corner of a tilting mirror, led me to be increasingly puzzled & dispirited by my surroundings, at that air of desuetude & inclusivity, that odour of countless mothballs & dust, so that my glance back at the door had something of appeal in it.

My guide was still there, her head still bowed, her face still draped, standing patiently, waiting, *meo periculo*, for me to understand her relation to that nursery turned life-warehouse & also, I fancy, for me to understand what she expected of me. & as I looked I saw, just by the entrance on a narrow table or console, a pale, almost grave-shaped mound. I took up my lamp again & moved down the central aisle towards it & my guide; I made out first that the table was heaped with letters; a few more steps & I saw that the top-most envelopes & some, as it were, on the side slopes, were not even opened, that others had fallen to the floor. I stooped & picked one up & saw that it bore the imprint of my own shoe. & it was *then* I understood that such was my guide's reluctance to enter that suite of rooms that she could only open the door to them, lean a little forward & drop any mail concerning her dead brother on to that table. That was the inclusivity; my guide had confined all matters relating to Robert Gilmerton to this space because she could not bear to see them dispersed.

I believe that my reaction, something akin to envy, was only natural & manly. It is something we poor survivors have had to become accustomed to: that we can make no sacrifice to match that made by better men, but must bear our lot with humility & resignation & with a keen sense of justice towards those who died so that we should live. I have witnessed few more affecting scenes; the young lady, her face partially veiled at a door she could not bear to enter, while I stood in the vast crowd of inanimate possessions of the young life she mourned. I knew then what my task was to be; to provide a measure of order, elegance & discretion to indicate, beyond the overwhelming mass of personal objects, the principal features & characteristics, the spirit, of a brave, talented & noble young man.

'I took up my lamp again,' sighed Ms Nutall. 'I had been thinking I was becoming sentimental about stupidity, but Gardner Price has proved a rest cure. Did you like the epistolary Man Friday part?

And the fairy-tale beginning? And Electra? And all that queasy syntax? Quite unable to state anything correctly but always at a turgid quiver. And look, mauve ink for his fat hand. And surely there is something of the comfortably incompetent cuckoo in his using the dead man's spare notebooks?'

I smiled. 'What does *meo periculo* mean?'

'At my risk, on my authority. His use is off-key. Dear God, he even lacked the stamina to provide ten minutes' reading.'

I laughed; I am not sure I have ever met a scriptwriter who has enjoyed so much complaining about a character.

'Where did he come from?'

'Wales. He was born, in his own revealing but inane phrase, "on the very cusp of wealth".'

'Meaning?'

'Something fatuous. Oh, "if only I had had real money", I think. All whingingly relative, of course. His family were able enough to send him to Oxford in 1903. But there he spent his allowance on having a volume of his own poems privately printed. His reaction to his father's anger was tremendous. He abandoned poetry and country in a craven huff, went to Russia, did some tutoring and returned to Britain in 1915 with little or no money and a gammy leg.'

'Do you know how he got it?'

'It was something he refused to talk about.'

'You suspect something ridiculous?'

'No, no, and we won't worry about that for the film. With a limp and a monocle he is fine.'

'But presumably he had written something before Agnes took him on?'

'Oh yes. He came back because his father had died and he had been left a small private income. For the next fifteen years he dribbled north, East Anglia, Yorkshire, Scotland. In 1921 he published a travelogue on Chechnya and in 1927 a squeamish account of Pushkin's and Lermontov's fatal duels. Neither book was well or even widely reviewed. He was forty-five when he rented a little tower house near Brechin, largely because he got some work from a

Dundee magazine publisher on Scots in Russia. He also had the intention of writing a biography of Dostoyevsky, but with a salary from Agnes nothing came of it.'

Heidi Nutall turned to the next page of the notebook. All it contained was 'Dear Miss Gilmerton'.

We agree. Gardner Price is a gift of a part for an actor to play. He himself went on using up pages with little method and sometimes with very little on them. Having written 'Exceptional men often have exceptional parents' he turned the page and made a list of published references to Gilmerton Senior, including one article called *The Shipyard Samurai*. I also like 'Fourth son of a Presbyterian minister, born Perth, 22 April 1839, died as a result of a fall during ship trials on 29 February 1904. Apparently there exists a most scurrilous article suggesting he was helping the Japanese in their war against Russia on no more evidence than a coincidence of dates.'

And then again: 'Miss Gilmerton'. Further along what would be the same line is a tiny doodle. At first sight it looks like a simple flower but if you look closer — 'Squint, squint,' said Ms Nutall — you see the doodle started out as a diminutive moth.

21

Somehow our entertainment for this month has been crowded up and arranged a day apart. This afternoon in the great hall at Lampenham we were treated to *Hamlet* performed by a Mr George Marshall and his makeshift company who had previously acted for other soldiers in Alton, Portsmouth and Poole. We were told that Mr Marshall himself (in the title role) had enjoyed a national reputation as a stage villain in the 1880s and '90s and had now, with most of his company, come out of retirement for our benefit. We were assured, as if we might think the cast were skulkers, that the remaining actors were well below military age.

'But isn't this delightful?' said Aubrey Gilbert. 'The aged leavening of a school play. It could be marvellously eldritch. Do you suppose that the Player Queen will be a boy? However the poor child does I shall praise him and the historical accuracy of the casting just to fluster McKinnon. Brav-O!'

A full complement of nurses had placed us either in the recess under the great hall window, beneath the mullions and leaded lights and coloured heraldic glass high up, or along the walls on either side of it. Apart from the difficulties of performing the play itself in an unfamiliar place without a backstage (the hall has a screen stage right, a sombre sort of elongated banister, here in part draped with cloth for an arras; stage right was our usual entrance, here curtained), the actors also had to compete with convalescent noise – creaking wicker from the Bath chairs, coughs, snuffles, phlegm hawked and everywhere varieties of physical and in one case mental discomfort, small groans, grinding teeth and sighs. The ghost turned out to be a big red-cheeked boy wearing a silver-touched sheepskin beard that made his eyes water. Gertrude and Claudius, perched on stool-thrones in front of the baroque fireplace, were a very frail old couple most of whose effort was directed at hearing what was said. Polonius had the air of a weirdly active mummy; his face was a lightly greased death-mask, his eyebrows hairless ridges, his skull as clearly marked as a stuck-together terracotta pot, a few cedarwood-coloured hairs oiled and stuck across the occiput. One eye was eclipsed by a glaucous lens and the other so bloodshot that the white had a blood-orange tinge. And yet he pottered about most spryly, never forgot a word and could only be faulted for the general relish he gave to *every* line and a liver-spotted hand motion that made him look as if he were perpetually acknowledging applause. The scene in which Hamlet talks to him of age ('these tedious old fools') was perversely impressive; two old men, one in his sixties pretending to be young (placing a hand on his hip when talking of 'weak hams') while the other, much older, those speckled hands shaking away, waited impatiently for his cue.

Not all the actors were interesting enough to excuse their perform-ances. Laertes lacked teeth and diction and Horatio spoke in the drear, unctuous tones of an archdeacon: 'gross and scope of my opinion' sounded very like 'grace and scape' and his 'And flights of Angels sing thee to thy rest' sounded incomplete for an Amen. The general favourite, however, was Ophelia, an old lady with some sparse white curls she found difficult to leave in peace. She wore a white brocade dress, the waist-tucks of which had been let out, and scuffed aquamarine watered-silk shoes still many shades stronger than the blue remaining in her eyes. She gave signs of compassionate but only sporadic involvement in the play and, rather charmingly, found her mad scenes difficult to remember.

Enter Ophelia distracted.

'They say the owl was . . . ooh [*a frown, her head turning towards the prompter*] . . . a *baker's* daughter?' At one time she tried to exit and had to be called back. At another she became concerned about Earnshaw's breathing difficulties.

After 'Good-night, mother' there was what Aubrey called a 'general *mêlée*'; instead of Hamlet leaving the stage tugging out Polonius's corpse an interval for tea was announced, whereupon Polonius sat up and asked for a chair. 'I say, this *is* a treat. Is that roe? I love roe.' We were also able to see future characters like the gravediggers, grandfather and grandson, the elder asking if there might not be a bottle of stout.

'I don't want to be mean and deny them their tea,' said Aubrey, 'but in a play in which the nature of illusion plays such a part . . . I say, is this Ophelia coming to see me?'

It was and the old lady smiled as he used his crutch to rise.

'Now I am perfectly sure, young man,' said Ophelia, 'that your love life has come on without that leg.'

I did not hear the rest of their conversation because I found Claudius and Gertrude were circling me like wizened satellites. They were, I realised, looking for signs of damage but in a don't-tell-me, don't-tell-me way. Claudius shook then cocked his head. I gave them a whistle from my lung. Then two more. They nodded and smiled. Was I enjoying the play? Yes, indeed. They were too but had found the trip tiresome. How old did I think he was? I had no idea. Born the year Queen Victoria ascended the throne. 1837? Yes. How old was I? Twenty-six. That would make him the same age as Keats, said Claudius. They had lost a son at Mons. At the same age as Byron. I said I was sorry. They smiled serenely. I mentioned this later to Aubrey, struck by the quantity of their appetites and their taste for famous dates and deaths and their easy substitutions of consumption and malaria.

'Yes, I too have some doubts as to their being quite concentrated on the play. It may have been an excuse to indulge a certain complacently ghoulish interest in us. Sanderson swears Polonius said he was finding dying harder and harder. And Ophelia actually suggested to me that girls preferred things "less crowded". I am beginning to wonder if it is a good idea to *allow* actors to perform Shakespeare. It is difficult to think that a person who considers four legs a crowd will be a sensitive conduit for dramatic poetry.' He dropped his voice. 'I did wonder if she were being *smutty*. But do you know, I don't think she was.'

Hamlet should have ended with tea. Sluggish if sometimes fitful digestion took over. Those actors who exited stage left had to go outside and round if they were to appear again stage right. Through the open windows I heard Laertes speak his clearest line: 'Lovely old house this. Wouldn't mind a spell here myself.' There were times my interest abstracted or I may have dozed and missed parts of the play. This was a *Hamlet* in which Claudius made no effort to pray. And I can remember no Osric trotting up. In general, there was such a disjunction between the lines pronounced, as if dredging memory and hesitant actions, that the play drooped, became something dutiful and fantastic, like someone trying to get back to sleep but still troubled by elements of a previous, stubborn dream. Now the usual dreamwright does not bother too much with resolution; here we had a cluster of ejaculatory, arthritic dying in front of the fireplace from the actors and vigorously relieved applause from the convalescents, closed ranks of energetic palms. I blinked and clapped. I saw Aubrey had tears in his eyes.

'I don't know that I am particularly susceptible today but I am finding it all hilarious and moving at the same time.'

I nodded, rather dully. What had belatedly struck me was how many times in the play someone says 'good-night'.

'Extraordinary,' said Aubrey afterwards when we went for a slow walk down to the pond for me to collect beech leaves and for him to stretch his leg, 'but surely an odd choice of play for anguished, ageing young men. They might have done a comedy. *A Midsummer Night's Dream*, say.'

'Do you think they considered the choice of play?'

'Quite. Still, don't you think it touching and gallant of these elderly actors to come out of retirement and cheer us up by reminding us of our greatest literary glory?'

'Ah. I'm not sure that's McKinnon's style.'

'All right. But don't imitate his voice.'

'I say, is that a *wig* Hamlet is wearing?'

'I was going to say no but . . .'

'Then how about – "No, I used the time of the play to write up my notes."'

'That's it! That's McKinnon.'

But the person to appear – on a bicycle – was the delightful Dr Burnet.

'How are you both?'

'Damn,' said Aubrey. 'I can't remember. Something about indifferent buttons.'

Burnet raised his eyebrows.

'We've been witnessing a version of *Hamlet*,' said Aubrey. 'Ghost fathers rather than Ghost pain.'

'Oh good,' said Burnet. 'So you really have been thinking about it?'

I coughed. 'Absent limb and present pain?'

'Pain that is both real and imagined,' said Aubrey.

'No,' said Burnet. 'A pain perceived when it is not physically necessary to perceive.'

'Two small thoughts only,' I said. 'First that we react to shocking things in waves, work in repetitions that we mould until we can cope with the shock – when we mourn, fear, to a degree when we dream. In other words, this mechanism in the brain takes precedence over whether or not the injured leg is still there, sporadically and literally remembers but includes a new element, a realistic stab at pain.'

'I say,' said Aubrey, 'that's rather clever.'

'Is this your own experience?'

'I have my legs.'

'But you have a patch on your chest . . .'

'About the size of a slightly nibbled postcard.'

'Which responds poorly to stimulus.'

'But which is surrounded by sensation. The second thing is that the function of the nerves in the stump remains. Originally they relayed sensation to the brain, helped transmit a stubbed toe, for example. I presume they still perform this function, can still be stimulated and still transmit. But in the case you mention the information they transmit is misread by the brain.'

'Which of these theories do you prefer?' asked Burnet.

'The second.'

Burnet nodded. 'Yes,' he said, 'thank you very much for considering it. Now Captain Gilbert, have you had any—'

'No, I have not,' said Aubrey firmly. Later, when I was breaking off a beech twig, he asked, 'Do you *admire* Burnet?'

'I suppose I do. He is single-minded, doesn't seem to care at all whether or not people find this odd and he is also most generous with his time and skills.'

'Ah,' said Aubrey, 'I suppose you're right.'

We started back towards the house in silence. The theatre omnibus was parked in front of it and was being loaded with hampers and props.

'You haven't thought of it?' said Aubrey.

'What?'

'Becoming a Hamlet.'

I laughed.

'Pretending to be crazy,' said Aubrey, 'to get out of this.'

'Aubrey, it is not a virtue but I lack the dramatic faculty.'

'I meant a gradual increase in the manic, making your *distrait* phenomenally distracted. You're a sensitive, rich young man.'

'Is Hamlet a successful example?'

'Are you equating drama with a neurotic and contemptible sense of self-importance?'

'Only off-stage, Aubrey.'

By the omnibus Hamlet's boy father, now beardless, was complaining that his face itched. Hamlet himself was wearing another wig but one which left on view a curving line of bald scalp some way below the crown.

'Ah,' said Aubrey, 'I see what you mean. A wig for real life. Damn.'

22

My father was a WS which stands for Writer to the Signet, one of a society of solicitors, a very old closed shop that has the exclusive right to handle crown writs in Scotland. In his spare time he was a thoughtful golfer – I think of him in whirling mist and rain not so much considering his next shot as chomping patiently on an extinguished pipe while waiting for a glimpse or flutter of the flag. I much preferred him in another guise, as a fisherman with a splendid wrist and tweed hat. He was, I think, keen for me to follow him in this and I cannot have been more than five when he first took me along to see him drape and curlicue a line. I watched the long length of catgut loop out over the water and through the midges. It was the action I found exhilarating and the sound, a fretful whisper, like rapid traces of a steel pen nib; it made my father look as if he were at a fluent, barely audible, barely visible version of handwriting. But it was all with the aim of dropping a fishing fly temptingly near a fish. Is Pheasant's Spur a dry fly? Dry-fly fishing was old-fashioned even then. I think he saw at once that I had no interest in catching fish; it was the effect of the twitch that intrigued me, the apparent ease with which a jerk could travel out along that line as if making a feint towards a wide, slack knot over the river and then, with a certain bite and race, unravel – to drop the fly just so.

'Do it again?'

'Oh, David, I'm not sure you've quite got the hang of this.'

He sighed, pulled in, recast. The line whispered and flourished again. I clapped my hands.

'Oh shhh,' he said. 'Fish hear, you know.'

'Do they have ears?'

'Ah. They do it, I think, mainly by tremors.'

My father's manner as a father was extraordinarily polite. He much preferred the oblique to the direct, enquiry to instruction, though he would sometimes give me a book with the air of someone handing over an important piece of a jigsaw. I remember him, after *Kidnapped* and *Treasure Island*, suggesting I leave Robert Louis Stevenson's *Weir of Hermiston* until I had read, amongst others, *Dr Jekyll and Mr Hyde*. *Jekyll and Hyde* upset me in a pre-pubertal way; I found it crude, unsatisfactory and somehow timid. Luckily, I came across James Hogg's *The Private Memoirs and Confessions of a Justified Sinner*, an earlier (1824 instead of 1886) and more satisfying book. The edition had an introduction by André Gide about which I can recall nothing except the pleasing novelty of his calling Scottish circumstances and setting 'exotic'. This was also the first time I became aware that a novel might have a structural interest (two patchily silvered mirrors not quite aligned and a short shaggy-dog story) and it had a stark sense of humour that appealed to a twelve-year-old boy. The account of digging up the Sinner's corpse cured me of thoughts of an afterlife for ever. This was possibly premature as reasoning but the decision remains. Indeed I am still half-amused when I find I have opinions and tastes resolutely, even furiously, formed in childhood. Three weeks ago at a dinner party, like a polite automaton, I turned down avocado pears. It then occurred to me to wonder why. Absurdly, at the age of thirty-seven, I had to admit that I have never tasted avocado pears, largely because my Aunt Susan claimed to have introduced them to Edinburgh. In other words my decision had been made one day out of loyalty to my mother and my dislike of Susan.

'I didn't know you didn't like them,' said Isabel, 'but if you are not going to eat yours, give it to me.'

The Sinner's body is remarkably uncorrupt but soon falls apart, when given air by prying, self-important investigators.

'Yes, I see,' said my father, unable not to look pleased, 'for you superstition and religion are merely separated by degree, not kind.' He could be a generous man, particularly in giving verbal form to my squeamish inklings. Now he gave me a rare piece of direct advice.

'Learn to distinguish, David, those who shape experience to words and those who shape experience from words.'

'Am I to prefer one?'

'What?' He looked startled. 'No, no. The knowledge can be useful, that's all.' A puzzled pause. 'How old are you?'

'Thirteen next birthday.'

'Ah,' he said, 'of course. Yes.'

A few days later, however, my father appeared suddenly in my room, cleared his throat and gave me three books: a translation of Lermontov's *A Hero of Our Time*, one of Tolstoy's *Anna Karenin* and a paperback of Henry James's *The Ambassadors*. He was a little jokey at the first, handed over the second two as if handling brittle valuables. Of *The Ambassadors* he said, embarrassing me, 'I have always had a sweet spot for Miss Gostrey. You'll find out who she is.' I think these three books made up all the sex education I received at home: a young man like Pechorin who claims to care little for himself will definitely care less what he does to women; physical passion is only half the story; Mme de Vionnet's reputation does not do her justice. An unfair summary? Of course. My father's intentions were far more anxious, subtle and restrained. But that day he was wearing his mustard-coloured work cardigan with the leather elbow patches. He sat down and crossed his legs.

'Now,' he said, 'despite what your teachers tell you, a character in a novel is not a person but a token of context. That context is the linguistic design. It is the design, the ordering and arrangement of words that matters and not some final, moral meaning. Reader or writer, moral meanings are for dictators and buffoons. Good novels, David, are adventures in perception in which text – the texture and register of the writer's brain as expressed in words – combines with the reader's brain to conjure up enthralling and exciting versions of reality.'

This struck me as quite appallingly abstract. My efforts to understand degenerated into a lurch of sentiment. And now? I should like, for example, to ask him how his design differed from skilful decoration, just to hear his reply. Ah. 'I refer to language as the receptacle of all human means' has just come from somewhere, memory, ether or the grave.

At the time I was shocked by the contempt he lent the word 'buffoons', but rather more alarmed by the formula 'token of context'. It made me feel cold and lost but for no identifiable reason other than the words. Gilmerton is a dash and two vowels away from the *Justified Sinner*'s devil, Gil-martin. Gilmerton is also an area on the outskirts of Edinburgh, a crossroads village in Fife and another one, a little west of Perth. Exactly. But in that book of doubles there is a scene in which the Sinner becomes entangled, with skeins of yarn doing the honours for a cobweb. Two nights ago I recalled a dream from about that age – or imagined I recalled it – in which I dreamt I was obliged to cast my father's fishing line but was terrified of getting tangled up in it and hooked. I contrived to cast. The line and fly floated away from me, forming translucent ox-bows in the air; and then, out of the midges – and this is why I may have imagined the recall – came a speckled brown moth which settled and stuck to the line about a yard behind the fly-guised hook. The line hit the river with the moth still firmly attached; the creature fluttered, the wings worked, but the water reduced it to a sodden little corpse. A Lobster Moth? Horatio's troublesome mental variety again? Or was that moth mostly mine? Possibly all three. I could recall with impressive clarity, however, waking from the dream with a dry tickle in my throat, swallowing some water to smooth it away, wondering if my voice was breaking. I felt splendidly and importantly confused and it was then that I understood that I should become an actor, a fine actor with a voice that would work on an audience as that original fishing line had worked on me, all hypnotic pitch and widening eyes.

The last time I took my mother out to lunch – this is the arrangement we have come to, frequently enough for her to demonstrate she has a son, infrequently enough for mutual comfort – she was unusually spry. She ate with appetite, duck on lentils, and decided to have coffee, 'proper, not decaffeinated'. I pushed a dish of chocolate mints towards her.

'Mm, your father and I were, you know, thinking of divorce.'

I nodded. I wondered whether or not she had forgotten he was dead.

'We were waiting for his retirement, you see.'

'Ah.'

'There were two reasons for waiting. The first was that you should . . . establish yourself.' She paused for a badly done moue. 'The second, of course, was that divorce, given your father's professional position and standing, was quite out of the question.'

'As a WS? Surely they are less stuffy now?'

My mother closed her eyes and sighed exasperatedly. 'As a WS who dealt in divorces!'

Dealt in, dealt with. A divorced divorce lawyer does not seem to me so outlandish.

'Dear God!' my mother exclaimed. 'If only he had had the wit and strength.'

'For what?'

'To avoid it, man! You didn't catch that creature Waddell getting stuck with divorces.' Waddell was an inoffensive, dreary partner in the firm. 'How could your father have done it? Dragged me down in that way! The food we ate was tainted with adultery!'

As an actress my mother is almost miraculously bad, especially when playing demented gentility.

'Oh, I thought the food tasted fine. Grizel was a good cook.'

My mother stared at me. 'Grizel had no responsibilities. For heaven's sake, we almost took her in. You don't seem to understand anything at all.'

'That's a possibility.'

'What do you mean?'

'It was your marriage.'

'But you had eyes, didn't you?'

'Yes, but you have to want to look.'

'Ah,' said my mother. She sniffed. She unwrapped another mint.

'Well,' I said obligingly, 'go on. What was this link between divorce and retirement?'

My mother perked up. 'But don't you see? It was the least he could do after all those years of humiliation!'

I am so used to thinking of my mother as a case that I have confined her to it. I nodded, scratched at the linen tablecloth but immediately irritated myself by remembering Gilmerton's original, oriental pillow, a wooden box with stray papers in it, a horrible version of memory. I squeezed my eyes shut and spoke. 'Oh dear,' I said, 'so it will always be a proposal.'

My mother smiled and chewed. 'You know,' she said, 'I really do think they should allow posthumous divorce. One feels cheated.' She took another mint. 'Death's nothing,' she said and popped it into her mouth. 'No,' she added, with her mouth full, 'it's the decisions that matter.'

I waited for her to swallow and wipe chocolate, mint, saliva and lipstick on to her napkin.

'Does this mean you don't want to be buried together?'

'I didn't say that! When did I say that? Oh, you're hopeless. Don't you understand anything about regret?'

'You're forgetting. I have been divorced.'

'But that wasn't a marriage! No children. You didn't stick it out.'

I nodded. Twenty years ago exchanges with my mother used to remind me of grim, old-fashioned pass-the-parcel. Now I watch her work something out, contribute a little resistance; then I nod, smile, pay and kiss her on the cheek.

'Be careful of my lipstick, dear. We don't want that wife of yours thinking you've been up to something.'

In the beginning Isabel suggested my mother was crazy with love for me but quickly changed her opinion. Isabel also suggested that my mother was jealous of me, but her behaviour was the same long before I became an actor.

'So what do you think?' Isabel said.

'That she has her own show and is in love with awful scripts.'

'Do you mean that? Who wrote *her* part?'

23

The Lobster Moth larva has, in Aubrey's term, been looking peaky. It has certainly stopped eating. I lifted it up and put it on the knuckly part of my hands for an unwitting Lobster Moth test of sensation. On the right-hand knuckles I could just make out the touch of its feet; on the left I felt nothing at all. I believe the Lobster Moth caterpillar can spit acid if disturbed but this one lacked sufficient energy. I lifted it close to my eyes and squinted. Yes. Now I have taken it off my skin and put it back on a beech twig to which it has affixed itself firmly with prolegs and claspers. It is about to moult. The skin is drying and will shrivel and split down the back and the new caterpillar will extricate itself, having got rid of the old self down to the linings of the intestines.

Most moths moult four or five times at the larval stage with more or less spectacular changes in shape but I doubt if the fully grown caterpillar to emerge from this skin will be much of a lobster. The English names I liked were those of moths that helped parody night textures like the Lunar Marbled Brown or the Pearly Underwing and the Vapourer, the Dark Tussock and the Silver Cloud, the Ingrailed Clay, the Ghost Moth, the Cinnabar and, just occasionally, the Buff Tip.

At about the age of fourteen I became fascinated by the varieties of deceit in mimicry and shortly afterwards, as it were, retreated from moths. It was an age when I was far more likely to get things wrong than right. I used to keep by my bed copies of Bates (a

harmless creature mimics a harmful one) and Muller (several dangerous species share markings and colours so that a predator that attacks
one will learn to avoid all). I'd snatch up bits of information, worry
at them exhaustively – find I could not source that information when
I went back to the books. I remember my alarm. Was I going mad?
Whole paragraphs that I could remember well had disappeared.
There were unaccountable changes in the text. It took me a little
time to understand that the vanishing trick was the result of my
anxiety to point out the flaws in their readings of mimicry. My desire
was not simply to emulate the theorists but to surpass them, a desire
not meaningless perhaps but certainly meansless. I had no equipment.
My condition was one of driven ignorance, necessarily amusing, but
at the time it shocked me very much indeed. I am by no means
sure that morality is required to be a mothist, but at that age I
realised that fraudulence and intense desire could come vaguely but
tantalisingly close to merging, perhaps melting, together. Gravely I
tried – I really can't remember such a formal other occasion in my
life – to correct myself, to steer myself away from such danger.
Possibly I was remembering my mother's distinction between gentlemen and scientists again but, at the least, it taught me never, whenever a case of falsification in biological academia comes up, to join
in any condemnation. That is hardly a virtue, simply a cautious and
self-conscious recognition that appetite can take different forms.

I have just looked in on the Lobster Moth. The new head is
becoming visible behind the old. It has occurred to me that I gave
up moths on, in no special order, my sexual maturity, our father's
death, our leaving the house near Brechin, our arrival in Midlothian.
My dislike of bright colours increased. Let me stress my sense of
glum abeyance. Because, despite my experience with vanishing acts
and my determination to be a true scientist – I remember a paroxysm
of pleasure at the word 'ontology', the science of being – I took
on the intolerant appurtenances I associate with certain religious
denominations and had the beetle-browed gall to make exclusive use
of mimicry as a standard by which to judge other people. I was
particularly irritated by those who said, 'Fascinating,' with every
sign of sincerity, because they were always the quickest to grope

for a simile when the natural one is already there and more exact. Or those who, with holistic self-regard, always asked, 'Now why should that be?' Or those uncountable buffoons who mentioned chameleons and tartan. Or all those Calvinistic ladies who could still raise a flutter and who saw moths as 'reminders of our Maker'. It was a brisk, unforgiving age. There was also something hopeless about it. For while I *said* I was intrigued, say, by certain moths performing extraordinary parodies of wasps, moving waspishly, doing waspish things, I could no longer summon up the delight I had felt before.

I found some comfort in those moths that have wings that imitate the cracks and grub holes and lichens on the bark of different trees. It is a colouring that imitates on two dimensions what is in three, and many of these moths are able, within very few generations, to adapt, say, to soot from a factory near the wood where they live. What I wanted to discover was the process by which the change in the surroundings was registered in the moth and how the change in wing shade was effected. One of the greatest frustrations for a young mothist is that so few people appreciate that individual moths vary; that is the delight, their differences. My comfort was in wondering if my examination of a relatively general change within those variations was even possible. I could describe the change, I might be able to poke quite minutely, but the substance of the change would remain indifferent or untold. Was I frightened? In a general way, yes, I think I was.

At this time I did have some plan of constructing maps of wing colours but this went one day when I got out my collection of Pebble Prominents. The Pebble Prominent has geographical variations (large in moth terms) of the Englishman, Irishman and Scotsman kind, a matter of colour, paler and greyer shades, but also of the 'pebble', in my examples at least, quite different. The so-called pebble is a mark on the forewing as if a Japanese ink-brush had been used to draw the outline of a small piece of worn mosaic, the ink, depending on the country, always starting strongly but then petering out differently, so that the English moth has a mark like a sprung safety pin, the Irish more like a child's uneven bracket and the Scots, slightly tongue out, just manages to close the mark by making it more ovoid than oblong, possibly by licking the brush.

It was then I decided to put away my moths as too vast and complicated and to move on to simpler matters – zoophytes. This was, I have the impression, both an impatient retreat and something of a rebellion, a getting rid of childhood on one hand, but a stubborn reinforcement of it on the other. I understood that it was utterly unscientific not to take cognisance of my own limitations, the derisory smallness of most of my insights (with the optimistic rider that all great ideas can be simply stated), the way my neurons worked and the nature of my desires. In other words, it was not a question of trusting or not trusting myself but of resisting simplifications and of watching with scientific rigour. Did I also have the notion that adulthood was some sort of death? It's possible.

At the age of fourteen I must have been unbearable but our mother was exceptionally patient and understanding. In fact the only time I have ever seen her in any way protest at my activities and a possible prurience in them was ten years later when I announced that I was concentrating on genetics. There was a fair pause before she said she was pleased that I had decided, as she put it, 'to tackle life-stuffs'. And why not? There was an air of correct translation about it but I liked the expression for its aplomb and irony, particularly as my small study was on the imaginal discs in the larva of *Drosophila melanogaster*, the fruit or vinegar fly. Protein is a prime but not the primal cause and all our experiments have so far been crude.

Ah. Now that Aubrey knows I walk about at night with a pen and a pillow book, he sometimes drops in.

'Ah,' he said, 'you're writing again,' and hobbled over to the Lobster Moth. 'I say, are you sure he's still alive?'

'Yes.'

'He has the most unattractive colour.'

'Patches of drab.'

'Is drab a colour? I thought it meant dull.'

'By extension. It's a dull colour. Khaki or mud.'

'Well, of course! Mind you, what we saw was usually rather

147

wetter, wasn't it? What is he supposed to be imitating now? A twig? Mm? He looks rather autumnal to me. And he is pretty obvious.'

'That's because the caterpillar is in a tobacco tin.'

Aubrey laughed. 'My regiment used to wear red jackets. Isn't that supposed to be a warning colour in insect terms?'

'Yes, but in human terms easy to see, especially if you have rifles with a range long enough not to take the warning.'

'Quite. But a lot more dashing. And surely a lot of red is much like a lot of drab if you're aiming at it. Would you notice the red going down more?' Aubrey sighed. 'Someone did tell me the red was to camouflage the blood. It doesn't show up much on trench khaki either. I suppose you can paint?'

'Not very well, Aubrey.'

'I never could. Too impatient. Used to mix my colours up. Whatever I painted it was usually a mud field.'

'What's this? The gloomy commonplaces of experience?'

'I'm having these awful dreams, Robert. I think it's Burnet's fault.'

'Ah. Have you felt pain?'

'No. I keep dreaming that in a few years' time I'll suddenly feel the leg, look down and see the thing is there. People will treat me as a fraud. I wake up feeling such a coward.'

'Aubrey.'

'What?'

'Look down. What do you see?'

'No leg,' said Aubrey, 'no leg. Of course, you're right. What are you thinking of doing tomorrow?'

'I had thought of putting the Lobster Moth larva back in the wild.'

'Oh, don't do that. I say,' said Aubrey, 'what is it you find you miss most?' It is a frequent question of his but he shows no sign of remembering he has asked it before.

'A microscope, other books, activity, variety . . .'

'Ah. I had been thinking of a taste, a perfume, soft skin . . .' Aubrey can do his common interests quite well; I laughed, enough to have my left lung wrench and whistle.

'How is your campaign for the French language going?'

Aubrey smiled, put his finger to his lips, and swung out.

I have sat down. It is a little after a quarter to three. My lung, having laughed, is twitching — not unpleasant. I am not sure why but it reminds me of Edinburgh. Yes, laughing with poor George MacFee on a very cold day with a lot of soot in the air, a similar rasp, a spasm away from a cough. George is from Ayrshire and was training to be a vet. He had had his arm broken near the shoulder by an irritable calving cow. I enjoyed myself in Edinburgh. The classes were serious and humourless but the arrangement was more coherent and amiable than at Oxford.

I am getting tired. The Lobster Moth is stock still. I have stepped outside. The air is cool and fresh. Ah, I have disturbed a small sand lizard in its flowerpot; it has slithered over the edge and along the stone into a crack in the mortar. The remains of a Grey Arches moth, *Polia nebulosa*, lie at the base of the wall. It is time to go inside and sleep.

I hope I can. I remember that at Oxford it was fashionable to pretend terror of the side of eternity before birth, particularly of the time just before it, at the photograph of a couple without children. Then there was the thrill of considering the chance combinations and trace elements that might lead to . . . the gratified expresser of the terror. Preposterous nostalgia or the water before Narcissus bent over it. I see no difference in before or after. If, as Hume says, we are a bundle of sensations, then death is an unbundling. Sleep a slackening. A nap is a mumble.

24

INT. NEAR BRECHIN — AGNES'S BEDROOM — DAY

Agnes wakes, finds one side of her face is paralysed.

INT. NEAR BRECHIN — DAY

DOCTOR ONE

We have ruled out Bell's palsy, Miss Gilmerton. We consider your condition to be of nervous origin, unpleasant perhaps but not threatening nor, usually, painful.

AGNES

It is not painful. Did you say 'nervous'?

DOCTOR TWO

To do with the nervous system, Miss Gilmerton. We refer, of course we do, to the neurological, not the common misunderstanding of the psychological or the emotional.

DOCTOR ONE

It is fashionable to say that the psychological can affect matter but I assure you that is quite secondary here.

AGNES

But you are not saying that I have some sort of infection of the nerves in my face?

DOCTOR TWO

That is a possibility we have not ruled out.

AGNES

But only one. How unlikeable. What is the treatment?

DOCTOR ONE

The best treatment is a natural treatment.

DOCTOR TWO

Patience. Time.

DOCTOR ONE

Painless but tedious.

DOCTOR TWO

It will go on its own.

AGNES

How long?

DOCTOR ONE

Now in the treatment the psychological and the emotional are of importance.

DOCTOR TWO

Be as positive as possible.

AGNES

Positive in what way?

DOCTOR ONE

Cut down on responsibilities and commitments.

AGNES

Then you mean renounce.

DOCTOR TWO

May I be perfectly frank, Miss Gilmerton? There are some, not many, whose sense of duty is so strong that it, as it were, overrules the person. I think my colleague and I agree that your nervous system has, as it were, rebelled.

AGNES

I see.

DOCTOR ONE

Accept your affliction as a warning signal, Miss Gilmerton. In many ways a most fortunate one.

DOCTOR TWO

Surely there must be some way in which you could delegate some of your responsibilities?

AGNES

Is that an order?

DOCTOR ONE

It is — if you permit it.

Agnes places one hand over the paralysed part of her face and closes her other eye.

EXT. NEAR BRECHIN — DAY

A car draws up at the portico. Gardner Price gets out and is shown in.

INT. NEAR BRECHIN — GALLERY — DAY

GARDNER PRICE

Miss Gilmerton.

AGNES
(*one side of her face draped*)

I understand you have reached terms with my lawyers for a biography of my late brother.

GARDNER PRICE

That is the case. I must say I feel most privileged to—

AGNES
(*rising, cutting him off*)

Please follow me, Mr Gardner Price.

Camera follows an anxious Gardner Price as he looks about him on their way down the length of the gallery. At the end he considers the Samurai on horse; a maid gives Agnes a lit oil-lamp.

INT. NEAR BRECHIN — EAST STAIRWELL — DAY

Agnes and Gardner Price wend their way upwards to the studded nursery door.

All films, claims Ms Nutall, are schematic and need agents to convince the audience of a sequential destiny; she will use Gardner Price, in his own way a natural. The camera will move along a row of shoes from childhood up, will close in on a moth case with a cracked glass and begin to treat the objects as a landscape, will move over Gilmerton's shaving things and will end on Gardner Price making a cymbalist's gesture and whipping off the top of a bomb-shaped serving dish to reveal a dry moth, a comb and a hairbrush. At the brush Gardner Price pauses and removes an auburn, not a black, hair, and raises an eyebrow.

The would-be biographer has touches that remind me of bedtime children's stories. The frames in which Gardner Price sits in a wing chair, adjusts a child's silk shirt as a headrest and opens Gilmerton's pillow book have the same self-centred aplomb as Mr Drake Puddle-duck in Beatrix Potter's *Tom Kitten* when he puts Tom's clothes on himself; it is a scene that gives my elder daughter obscure but repeated satisfaction.

Of course the other figure Ms Nutall has what she calls 'loaded' is McKinnon, the Lampenham doctor, though she wants him 'less a lethal buffoon than a stiff man doing what he considers his duty'.

INT. GILMERTON'S LAMPENHAM ROOM — NIGHT

Gilmerton sits reading. McKinnon knocks and enters.

MCKINNON

Ah, good. You are not asleep yet. I thought I'd have a look at that arm.

GILMERTON

Of course.

MCKINNON

I say, is that in French?

GILMERTON

It was on the shelf. *Oliver Twist*. Do you know it?

MCKINNON

The shirt as well, I think. No, I have no time for reading.

GILMERTON

Oliver Twist?

MCKINNON

No.

GILMERTON

So you do mean you have no time for reading? As I might have no time for opera. Or golf.

MCKINNON

No. I meant a physical absence of time. Please raise your arm.

GILMERTON

You do not read at all?

MCKINNON

My notes. Some papers. The *Lancet*, if I have a moment.

GILMERTON

Nothing outside your subject?

MCKINNON

Bend the elbow, please. Captain Gilmerton, mine is a vocation.

GILMERTON

Do you mean that?

MCKINNON

Why, perhaps I have a few minutes but I have many responsibilities. I take my job seriously, captain, possibly to the exclusion of many other matters.

                              GILMERTON

That's fair enough. Chekhov was a physician, I believe, but I don't know if he was a better writer than a doctor. May I put my shirt on?

                              MCKINNON

Yes. Are you stepping up the exercises?

                              GILMERTON

Yes, I am. Thank you very much, doctor.

                              MCKINNON

Good. It's important, you see, that *you* feel progress is being made, that you are getting back to what you were.

                              GILMERTON

Yes. I understand.

EXT. LAMPENHAM LAWN — DAY

                              SANDERSON

In the book trade they have 'sale or return'.

                              AUBREY

Explain that.

                              SANDERSON

The bookshop sells the book — or it returns it to the publisher. In the first case the bookshop earns money, in the second it hardly loses any, only the shelf space a faster-selling book might have occupied. I think we're sale, you're return.

                              AUBREY

Surely not. It would be the other way round. We're the returns, he's—

                              SANDERSON

Do you think he has a target to meet?

GILMERTON

Mm?

SANDERSON

A percentage of patients that return to the war.

GILMERTON

I should say something like that.

AUBREY

I say!

GILMERTON

And why not?

AUBREY

Ah.

GILMERTON

McKinnon told me he had never read *Oliver Twist*. He is a vocational reader.

AUBREY

What?

GILMERTON

Only medical books.

AUBREY

Ah. I say, do you play cards at all?

GILMERTON

No.

AUBREY

But you know the game pontoon or *vingt-et-un*. When you want another card you say 'Twist'. Does it come from that, do you think?

SANDERSON

What?

AUBREY

Oliver Twist asks for more, doesn't he? Gruel, I think.

SANDERSON

Aubrey!

AUBREY

But what have I said?

25

This part should be made up of a gamut of groans. I am so tired. What I want to do is sleep, not see out the night in the role of a man who doesn't. And who cites David Hume.

'Oh, but I like Hume,' said Ms Nutall. You know he called Shakespeare "rude"? It is the difference between the Elizabethans and the Enlightenment. Hume's version of "wild and whirling words" would be "furor of language". Delightful, isn't it?'

Perhaps it is. Right now I am only sure that a mumble is *not* a nap and that I resent the notion of Gilmerton walking slowly up and down, up and down, hand in gloved book, pen in hand, carefully writing a section for his sister to dip into and read each night before sleep while I, pursued by lax erections and the droop of fatigue, am on my back in bed, still awake after 3.00 a.m., wondering whether or not I will get *any* sleep tonight. When I breathe in, the air snags and ripples like a sigh but comes out in a flat rush. Oh, there is a groan, more breath than growl, that may attempt to imitate for the mind the clearing effect of a belch on the stomach. It doesn't work. I have the sensation of being held up. It does not feel at all like floating. It is too remorseless, there is no hint of sinking and I feel pulled up rather than buoyed up, as if my back were a rubber sheet and I were wearing a thick surgical collar.

Every so often I try to clear my mind, introduce a blackstone darkness, try to make out a chiselled SLEEP on it. But I can only do so for four or five heartbeats; first a faint network of blood filters in, then patches or bubbles of light appear, entering mostly from the left in the left eye, which then take on colour and form images. It has nothing to do with the window and the moon. I have checked. It is an apparently independent faculty, an inexhaustible but indifferent mental spawning. I have tried (I don't want to disturb Isabel) banging my head gently backwards on to the pillow, have achieved only a tiny explosion of light like a small squib – and a subsequent speeding of that spawning.

Sheets and pillow have lost all freshness and tautness, have a warm, inclusive, doughy feel that smears and blurs sensation; over most of my body, sheet and flesh feel the same except at itch points, sometimes knees, occasionally ankles, mainly my chin and cheek. I can feel sullen rings of weariness round my eye sockets and my eyelids feel as swollen as a stye looks. There is more fatigue in my throat and nose as if I were dry from speaking.

When I close my eyes there is a tingle, the visual equivalent of a huzz, under my lids. In the dark my brain appears to scurry about more, as if it had taken on the characteristics of a small animal with rapid heartbeat. I scrunch up my eyes, then relax them. I notice that my left eye is more crowded and the images smaller than in my right. In my right eye the bubble for the image is slow, large and usually single. Is this possible? The left side as quick as a riff of air bubbles rising in water, the right as slow as a blob of oil? Or is it that the brain, without sleep, begins, with an indifference near contempt, to parody its own workings?

At least when my eyes are open the spawning of images is reduced and the images less formed. The problem when my lids are up, however, is that, unlike Gilmerton, I find night does soften the edges of things. He claims to have become used to peering intently about him and of having night yield up its mothier occupants and contents. I used to treat sleep as a thick, slab-sized gap, an absence of mind very easily assumable. Awake I find, since I can see very little, even on a summer night with a moon, that it is me who takes on some of the characteristics I associate with the dark, disorientated pockets of blackish air filled with uncertainly placed objects, some hard at the edges. It is as if night thoughts were groping about *me*.

What is the matter with me? Is it only fatigue? Oh, I think fatigue is enough. But there was Gilmerton, not only strolling up and down and writing elegant prose but also scratching a great many sidelines in the margins of his pillow book. They vary. Some are simple notes of things done. As befits a reader, Gilmerton jotted down the titles of the books he read from the Lampenham library. He took them in at the rate of two or three a day and when he did not finish a volume he said why. For example, at the beginning of the larva-moulting section, he noted Renan's *Life of Christ*, *Tales of the Grotesque and Arabesque* by Edgar Allen Poe and Izaac Walton's *Compleat Angler*, the last quickly given up 'on a surfeit of milkmaids, butter and chub'. As befits someone who was preparing something to be read, he also made laconic notes, some of which surface in the body of his ten-minute sections. There are also quick sketches, Lobster Moth larva at moult, for example. And then there are others. Some look trivial. 'Genuinely good books may recommend but should not suggest others' comes from a cruel but aborted game of aphorisms, 'the very true', as he put it, apparently meant to be passed like counterfeit money. That is followed by 'A scientist without scepticism is like a priest without faith.' But the third is 'The problem with aphorisms is that they try memory – did I invent or remember that one? – and remind me I detest them.' Verbal doodles. Evidently Gilmerton had a gleeful horror of sententiousness which could rapidly become boredom. And surely, though some of his pages have fringes of notes, he flagged too. Oh. I am a stupid actor. I do not have his energy, his eye for detail, and fatigue saps my resolution. I think, too, he might have enjoyed what discomfits me.

A week or so ago I was treated to a small shock, the change of one letter in a word. Isabel brought back from the hypermarket a video of a recent film version of *Hamlet*. I became intrigued that we were getting the whole version, with all the wordy rundown of Denmark's relations with Norway, plus some quick but patronising inserts to orientate a modern, possibly school audience with texts to study, and then began waiting for Horatio to say his and my line, 'A moth it is to trouble the mind's eye.' But he did not. That Horatio, dressed in nineteenth-century tweeds and drooping moustache, played the part more like Aubrey, a bluff, loyal, occasionally agitated chap rather than as a sweet friend and witness. What he said was, 'A mote it is to trouble the mind's eye.'

Why was I so taken aback? I felt cheaply word-golfed. Less doublet, more hosed down. An actor wears his lines on breath and tongue. This Horatio wore his words as a tut-tut mutter. The film was awful, full of gasp-broken lines and others thrown away at a laddish strut; the Ghost was a gigantic Gothic stiff of bluish frost and black iron and Ophelia and Hamlet rolled naked on time-honoured, careful sheets, rendering quite a lot of Ophelia's role nonsensical. But the mote makes sense. A speck of grit in the eye, difficult to get rid of. I am reluctant to say it but it is a dull sense, an inadequate sense. The ghost of a murdered king appears and your eye waters and possibly hurts? No, I prefer that irrational, wild flutter in a mind trying to grasp what it has seen.

Am I sure that Shakespeare wrote 'moth', not 'mote'? No. He may very well have written 'mote' rather than 'moth'. The Shakespeare Moth or the Silver Sabled. I do not think I had ever considered moths as being insidious before. Exasperating, startling, but not insidious. I have just combined image and sensation: a dolmenish rock being eroded by the brushing of countless generations of moth wings. Absurd but convincingly queasy. And deposits of wing scales and grit at the base of the thing. Debris. Shakespeare's words fall off his plays. Ah. I have just seen a mouse slipping in and out of a pair of steel handcuffs. Undoubtedly an acceptable example of the reductive nature of weariness. Mm. I have just heard something, possibly from me, possibly a shrill grunt, a dip away from sleep. Slow lungs, settled tongue, drooping lids . . . and there it is again. That's not a grunt. I may just have managed lung-whistle. A fluted peep, more windpipe and nose than lung. And didn't Gilmerton say there was a moth that squeaked? I press on my eyes, massage my chin, let my lids close.

But as soon as I close my eyes, all fatigue and seep, I see something on my lids. At first it is like looking through thick aspic. Then the aspic melts. I am not used to proceeding by images, having one slip into another. Nor, along with the extraordinary flexibility, to images being quite so sharp and precise. Particularly when I am so tired. My thigh itches, I scratch and immediately let out a small, untoward belch. I wonder if those first bubble images were the visual equivalent of stifled yawns. Oh. I have just tried. I can squeeze out another small belch as if I had been drinking champagne. Damn. I have risen away from sleep but without any sign of pleasure. And I think I can just about manage lung-whistle now.

Being acceptable for a part is sometimes dispiritingly passive. The delight, the tension, is in producing, in a few seconds, sufficient energy and technique to counteract the reduction necessary to make a film. But as well as my belief there is also a matter of police basics. At present my hair is dyed black and I am becoming black haired. I have lost weight, I have my soft lenses to put in. But possibilities to escape from type are acutely limited. This is in part because an entirely passive face on film, depending on the frames around it and the soundtrack, will show joy, grief, hate or fear without moving a muscle: the viewer supplies emotion according to context and heartstrings – and type. In an action film 'the man' has the job of not looking ridiculous when running or jumping.

Let me shift and ease my back. An actor does not mimic, he represents. Two things, however, come to mind. One is the half-flattering, half-alarming prospect of Heidi Nutall considering me, hand on her chin, tapping an index finger on her cheek and asking me to say something again. I did. And a fraction before she started using her editing pencil, I understood she was bringing the film Gilmerton's intonation closer to mine. And the second is even more absurd, a desire to shake off any similarity between Gardner Price's desultory and incompetent stabs at portraying Gilmerton and mine.

At the end of his borrowed notebook Gardner Price wrote down some shortish quotes from correspondents. Some of these are by a lawyer, G. D. I. Morrison WS, sent in by his son and pertaining to 1911.

*

'Noon: Japan Bob's son. A great deal taller than his father and rather better looking. Hair as straight and black as a Japanese. Extraordinary eyes. Made me look later at the cat – not the same at all – but I cannot recall ever having met anyone before with treacle and honey irises. Is studying Science – but not the practical kind – at the University here and plans to go on to Oxford at Michaelmas.

'Quiet-spoken and acute. Disapproved – discreetly – of mother's investment policy. Quite able to read accounts. Appreciated profits lost by abandoning brewing and whisky and in losses sustained by engineering companies. Agreed investments "limited in scope and conservative in rate of return". We discussed possibilities and the moral concerns of some of his wider family.

'Amiable enough, with a dry sense of humour. But touchy I should think and probably very quick to respond. I am not sure he will be one of the future Great and Good. His father was more nervous. Cannot gauge how much real influence he has on mother et al.'

March 1st

'Morning mail: Quicker than I thought. Have today received very clear instructions from Mrs Robert Gilmerton on redistribution of investments. Have good offer for one of the engineering companies already. Robert Gilmerton *fils* will be of age in a little over one month's time. At her request will duplicate correspondence and keep him "promptly informed". Young Gilmerton lives in a bachelor's set quite close by, the soul of industrious and elegant discretion they say. Still, I wonder if what they also say is true?'

26

On my thirteenth birthday I was given a bow, a quiver of arrows with snub, brass-coloured tips and orange-dyed feathers so stiff they felt almost plastic, a leather forearm guard (bow strings can skin your inner wrist, where the palest flesh and the blue veins are) and a yellow-centred straw wheel as a target. I had made a formal decision with my first pair of long trousers a while before: I should be an actor. This gift confirmed it with the imagined sound of hitting the target. It was in no way a public decision. I did not ask for acting classes. I made no mention of it to parents or friends. Instead, I stored my archery equipment in the summer-house and retreated upstairs to my room and there, in resolute, even manic privacy, rigged up an arrangement of rickety lamps and a number of mirrors held up by stands, clamps and strings.

I have seen photographs of students in linguistics departments using mirrors to learn how the organs of speech are positioned and work. I never took up archery and my arrangement had more in common with mirrors strung up to frighten birds and a simpler voodoo altar. Anything I learnt was incidental and to do with surprise views of myself. I was easily surprised and also superstitiously frightened that if my secret were discovered before some unspecified state of readiness, then all my preparations would be for nothing.

So that when Nanny Grizel complained, 'Dear, I know your Latin is important, but would you mind not being quite so forceful after 9.00 p.m.?' I stayed as still as possible, breathing very small, for two days. What did Grizel mean by Latin? I was not even entirely convinced that one of my vocal exercises might *sound* like Latin declensions, felt embarrassed for her as I did for the fruity school singing teacher's 'Now boys, temper the ejaculatory.' In fact, I was saying the same phrase, taken from *The Justified Sinner*, beginning in a whisper, a small mirror a few inches in front of my mouth and measuring the increase in intensity and volume not so much by the sound as by the thickness of the cloud caused by my breath on the clear surface. 'It is he, it is hee, it is heee, it *is* he!', he being the devil. I once talked about this with Isabel.

'Are you really saying you were so . . . unaware?'

'Oh yes.'

There are three parts to an actor's life; the private, the actor and the actorile, this last to do with promotion and public relations, a mix of appearance and coherent character. Like most actors I have put together a few, brief replies to commonly asked questions.

'What first attracted you to acting?'

'Ah. There is an item in Elizabethan stage props – a robe for going invisible in?'

In the United States I was asked if I had written the line myself; it had culture, British self-deprecation and tickled what the chat-show person, with that sudden, somehow offhand desire to please, called 'the complicity in envy'.

Somewhere in my background lepidopteral reading I learnt that birds tend to avoid brightly coloured larvae but devour those protected by their brown or green colours or their resemblance to a twig. It seemed odd but part of the explanation given was that garish caterpillars often feed on poisonous plants and so become 'unwholesome' was the word used. I do not know if this represents some natural principle of fair warning (with a proportion of bluffs) and I take it that the twigs are eaten only when the protection fails (as it rather frequently must).

Where was I? Yes, mirrors. I began to collect them in the same way other boys collected stamps or cards of footballers or photographs of big breasts. Two years before I needed one I had a group of shaving mirrors, some on stands, some to hang – I filched the idea from a friend who had model aeroplanes suspended from his bedroom ceiling but adapted it, on the principles of a washing line that could come down and be hidden behind my curtains. I had one splendid mirror that cost me over a month's pocket money; it had an extendable arm and, with a flip, could turn in a chrome circle and give me a magnified close-up of myself.

I attended to two things: my consciousness of how I looked from every angle I could contrive, with or without mist on the mirror in front of me, twitching and angling lamps to contrive shadows and glare, then rocking or swaying my head so as to slip on and off silver-backed surfaces; and words or, rather, sounds. I formed a reacquaintance with hiccups and even had an initial spell of trying to rescue famous awful lines like 'What, in our house?' from *Macbeth*. The first actor I was ever conscious of was Marlon Brando and the second, largely by contrast, Cary Grant, the difference between a muscled magnet and a jaunty snake. Still at that 'Woe, alas!' business from *Macbeth*, still anxious not to disturb Nanny Grizel, I found I was emitting a breathy whisper, not unlike a plaintive threat.

I suppose this was all confused food for thought. I remember that age as a time of stupidity that felt almost juicy, of a sense of usually unwitting transgression. I was prone to sudden desires, remember one rubbish-collection morning when on my way to school I came across an empty birdcage on top of a dustbin, its occupant dead or escaped, which contained a small mirror bound in mint-green plastic. Edinburgh's New Town is Georgian with the result that there is a contest of curiosities; neoclassical houses are easy to look into and consequently to look out of. For a few paces I petered on. Then, in full view of row upon row of large, sashed windows, I mimed having forgotten something, turned back. The next part, by the cage-topped dustbin, was to look down and realise I needed to retie my shoelace. I squatted. I lifted my head. I was so anxious, had such a lump in my throat as I feigned an unconcerned review of the nearest windows, that it took me several fumbles for the knot to snag. I stood up and flexed my knees; as I did so I flicked open the cage door. I looked up and down the street. It was a work day, there were a number of moving shapes but I behaved as if there was no one. It was the householders who worried me. I jammed my hand inside the cage, pushed aside the perch – and a car horn hooted. I jumped, scraped my hand, but a moment later I had grabbed the little mirror and was pounding up Howe Street.

A flood of relief and delight lasted a few strides; I became aware of a tinkling accompaniment but was not entirely sure it came from me. I ducked round the corner and withdrew the mirror from my blazer pocket. There was a small, bright, acorn-shaped bell attached to it. I looked up. I was directly in front of Robert Louis Stevenson's boyhood home in Heriot Row. *Treasure Island, Kidnapped*; the least I could do was put the mirror back in my pocket and yark off the bell.

The bell I disposed of into the bushes on the other side of Queen Street Gardens railings, the budgerigar's mirror, about the size of an old half-crown, I found fit snugly into the inner palm of my hand when slightly clutched.

These things – the green of those bushes, for example – float up with a vivacity and detail I find, within the slack limits of lying in bed, mildly alarming, in part because I can't remember remembering this for a very long time. The green was privet but coated with soot. For a while I walked with the mirror held down and in front of me, self-hypnotised. I wanted, again dubiously, not so much to see how I looked to others as to see myself from the outside; I should have liked to see myself stretched out, like one of those maps of the world arranged on a flat strip. Closer to school and a greater incidence of blazers, that ended. I was about to spend a miserable day frightening myself.

I did so to avoid being discovered. The desire to hold my new mirror under the desk and consider myself was so strong that I suffered day nightmares, almost swooned at the notion of untoward heliography, ended up, quite crazily, fearing that holes were sudden and remorseless, that one would appear in my pocket, reveal a chink, flash.

I have no memory of the fear being specific; my sense of ridicule was uncertain but acute and it certainly never occurred to me that a budgerigar's mirror might be taken for a girl's make-up mirror.

I ended the day wrung out. But it was not quite over. On my way home I saw there had been some activity in Hanover Street. In red print with a small source in black that I associated with biblical declamations outside some churches, I saw a poster advertising a yoga studio. The slogan was, 'Make your body as supple as your tongue.' I got out my new mirror and looked for my reaction.

I suppose that somewhere about then I began to get a notion of the head as a volume with planes or, for the difference, a vessel with features. If I was not quite learning, I was at least becoming aware that projection had rudiments. Now I am more amused by my absolute refusal to take any cognisance of stage fright; I wanted to believe that if I controlled my appearance that would not be a problem. Tentatively, I went on exploring. A day or so after the yoga I saw on television an old film (*Indiscreet?*) in which Cary Grant parodied a good time and a sea shanty with his hands in his dinner-jacket pockets. I practised this, began to consider my body as well as my face. For fear of Nanny Grizel I did not move my feet but I tilted and swayed. I also began a series of would-be oriental movements, all in slow motion, took an interest in slow gymnastics or at least learnt to stand on my hands.

Self-conscious makes conscious. I began, outside home and school, to watch with close attention how people moved and did things, an old man sucking his dentures as he considered a price, then clamping his big-pored nose between thumb and index finger and blowing out of the side of his mouth through wavering fingers, a rough fluted sigh, then shaking his head. Or a common expression in women shoppers, a combination of grimace and pout on one side of the face while the eyebrow on the other side began to rise, the whole forming into a tuc of resignation at the decision to buy. Those stores were hot houses. I remember a woman who looked tragic with want at something her husband could not afford, a dishwasher I think, still consider her expression one of the greatest I have seen. And the make-up girls, boredom occasionally animated by trying out perfumes, touching up lipstick. And pretentious ladies, women who huddled, those who came with a friend, some who looked stunned by the heat and the smells of new goods. I fell in love with fleeting looks, people wrangling with their eyes, couples muttering.

And to be fair, my parents helped in some ways. They had an uncomfortably dressed, rather lumbering tradition of celebrating birthdays by attending some cultural event. I cannot now remember whose birthday corresponded to which function but I found I disliked mime, was not taken with the opera *The Girl of the Golden West* and am even now slightly surprised that even at that age I could instantly decide that a famous, titled actor's diction in *The Tempest* was not for me. I wanted more the apparent patina of realism that comes with film. This meant I finally separated screen and theatre and stopped the grandiose phrases I used to rehearse and began, with the aid of a tinny recorder, to pronounce phrases from films. I am struck now that, like a good Shakespearean boy, I usually imitated actresses: Glenda Jackson, Billie Whitelaw and, occasionally, Marilyn Monroe in *Some Like it Hot*. Women had for me something to do with melting, a confusion among desire, assuming and becoming. The Actor Moth would be *Ora nebulosa*?

27

On 14 June Gilmerton made a note: 'Pleasantly mounted by Messrs Wilkins & Tighe of Winchester both forms of *Stauropus fagi*. I handed them over and was surprised to see them up by supper, beside a framed piece of ancient parchment, looking well against the oak panelling in the small hall. Aubrey says they resemble small, furry scallop shells, with a silverish cowl at the head.'

I am not sure what he means by 'looking well'. But then I have seen the two forms of Lobster Moth in illustrations only and I doubt very much that seeing them dead and preserved under glass in good light, let alone against oak and still less live, would change my impression. Perhaps the verbal description of the two, 'brown-grey' here, 'deep blackish-brown' there, the vocabulary of 'subterminal', 'costal mark' and 'dentate white lines' misled my ignorance. The bite in the words promised a sharper differentiation. Stoats and ermines, peacocks and peahens are different. I blinked. To my untrained eye the moths look very much the same. Like one of those spot-the-differences puzzles for children, only a tad more difficult. I noticed a couple of very prompt reactions in me – irritation (what pedants these people are!) and discomfort (an unpleasant tug and twitch in my eyes). These softened as sighs soften. I let the illustrations sit. Dimorphism is hardly a case of *doppelgängers*. Jekyll and Hyde both look and behave differently. But on the other hand, Hogg's Justified Sinner's devil has the gift, possibly imaginary, of looking very like other people.

When I looked again, those spread wings began to yield up tiny shifts of tone and smudge; one body looked stockier and tapered more than the other (though this was not mentioned in the description and both were given the male circle-and-arrow symbol); and after a while I could see that indeed the colourings were a shade different, the stitches round the splotches differently placed.

Having closed the book, I am pretty sure that were I shown a selection of *Notodontidae*, the two-hundred-strong family of the Peleartic region to which the Lobster Moth belongs, or even the twenty-five that inhabit Britain, I would be unable to identify Gilmerton's creature(s). Study and expertise undoubtedly bolster sharp eyes in a beech wood in the dark, but I mean that for me the camouflage is doubly operative. You might say, that is surely the point. I am merely saying that study is not the same as picking out food and I suspect that the bird or whatever misses the subtlety of the camouflage because it ignores it and eats, indifferent to which form of Lobster Moth it is consuming or even – I know nothing about birds' abilities to taste – if that was an Iron Prominent it just swallowed.

An actor is neither a scientist nor an artist. For practical purposes an actor is commonly regarded as a shaped, empty box which resounds when words are put into it. Shape, usually clothes and make-up, and resonance should be enough for the willing layman to accept the deceit. The bird or whatever predator cannot or does not appreciate the enchanting delicacy of the mimicry; it merely consumes food, does not distinguish one form of Lobster Moth from the other. Let me change the position of my head on the pillow. A crick in my neck goes click. Natural mimicry, that is, is a luxury.

Can that be right? An actor is a luxury. But a moth? The young Gilmerton was attracted to the extraordinary detailing of mimicry and wished to investigate the biological means by which mimicry is effected, the impulses and responses to light, temperature and tree bark that appear in some moth wings. Ms Nutall says the fourteen-year-old cleverly noted, 'In Scotland, people paler, moths darker.'

Let us go back. A Lobster Moth is a striking example (but one of many) of the contortions a creature goes through to enable some to begin the process again. *Stauropus fagi* starts life as an hemispherical egg, pale cream deepening towards purple during the ten days in May, June or July it takes to hatch. To some observers the egg resembles a 'bird's dropping'. The first instar (an attractive word but with nothing to do with astronomy, it describes the form of an insect between moult and moult) is a larva which feeds solely on its eggshell for nine days and is described as 'ant-like'. In September it spins a 'flimsy' or 'soft' cocoon and overwinters amongst fallen leaves until May next year. Before that, however, is the stage that lends the moth its English name and the one Gilmerton kept in his scrubbed tobacco tin. The full-fed larva or caterpillar is about seventy-five millimetres long with a large head, an 'ochreous-brown' or 'chestnut-brown' body according to your source, very long thoracic legs and greatly enlarged anal segment. Kirby (1903) has the delightful sentence, 'When the larvae are reared in captivity they are liable to bite off each other's long legs if too many are kept together.' I am not sure why but I find this vision of overcrowding and leg irritation or jealousy perversely comforting – the legs have it.

Now both laymen and lepidopterists agree that it takes considerable imagination to make out any resemblance to a lobster when the creature is 'at rest' – presumably there is even less when it moves. At rest, the larva contrives to raise both head and tail. But here is the point. Gilmerton is by no means alone in considering the larva not as a far-fetched lobster but as an apparent tangle of a large ant dragging a squirming grub. I simply cannot make it out from the illustration I have but even allowing this to be so, what I find difficult to grasp is the following. Imagine (to use a Gilmerton favourite) that a bird (or whatever) sees a Lobster Moth larva in its double disguise. Why should it reject the prospect of a combined meal of ant and grub? Even if the combination is unfamiliar, an enquiring stab of the beak does for the caterpillar. Even if the imitation of the ant is of an unpleasantly bitter one, a snip still does for half the imitator.

Perhaps I am coming round to Gilmerton's point of view from

the necessary side of appetite – the richness and subtlety of the mimicry is not, in terms of survival, of that much use, constitutes a formal feint or a mannerist pose, a natural pun on gambol and gamble, or even a Lewis Carroll doublet: moth mote mole mold fold food. That is quite a nice run. But I still find it easier to understand the principle if it is one employed when, say, a bird attacks the 'eyes' on certain moths' wings and finds nothing fleshy; better punctured than dead, defence as shifting the wound.

Let me just untangle the sheet. Here is a moth as a bird's dropping (already digested), here as a miniature lobster or ant and grub (half gone, not worth the bother), here as a small cluster of beech leaves on a stem (try to find me). The apparent intelligence of all this – a cognisance of birds' digestive tracts, of the scarrying tactics of ants, of arboriculture – is contradicted as soon as the moth twitches. Movement cancels mimicry and reveals a meal. Who has not seen a moth err grievously and land on a plant of quite the wrong colour? Which is to say the moth is not aware of its ability to blend in. That the creature currently stunning itself against your bedside light is an acutely limited miracle. The ability to change wing colour in areas where barks have been darkened with pollution has not been matched by a lessening of the often fatal, age-old attraction to light, whether candle, gas or electric, suggesting a hopelessly delicate sensitivity to light.

I don't know. Is Gilmerton suggesting that mimicry is an end in itself? It seems a fatalistic, somehow aristocratic view. I am too suggestible. The two forms of the adult Lobster Moth *can't* allude to the two creatures imitated at the larval stage. I have been reading too many lepidopteral descriptions. An actor is one in clearly defined settings. It is one of the reasons I *am* an actor. The difference between transitive and intransitive. Direct object. Or object confined to the agent. Is that his old man, young man business? Ah, I have just thought: memory *is* mimicry.

No, no, no. The only sense I can get out of that would be that memory is belated mimicry; we mimic recall and adapt to circumstances. Mine are mothy and yes, I have a tendency to stick at one thing, mothing in inexpert circles. So step back. Or at least close my eyes and remember some of the crowded plates in moth books. Yes, on the whole I have found the larvae more attractive than the moths winged. Some of them are rococo; appendages, frills, outcrops, twists, spikes, horns, one that looks like the snark but the other way round, anal appendages like antennae in the form of question marks and a head like a chunky wrist-watch, hands at twenty to four, though I suppose in terms of mimicry, it resembles a freshly broken stub of a twig. My wrist-watch larva, or the twenty to four, is *Cerura vinula*, also known as the Puss moth, a Persian among adult moths.

I say my wrist-watch or twenty to four but I don't feel either Hamlet or Polonius in this game. Is the 'I see a weasel or a lobster' in a cloud radically different from working on the happenstance of a smudge on a wall or seeing formal possibilities of an ant and a grub in a caterpillar? I think not. There is also the point that Lobster Moth is only the English name and that geographical variations mean variations in concept, imagination and vocabulary as well as in the moth. For casual reasons I know that the Lobster Moth is in Spanish *El Guerrero del haya* – the beech warrior. Beech is habitat and food. But warrior? What aspect of war did the namer have in mind? Gilmerton sometimes suggests an element of heraldry in the larva's at-rest position – caterpillar rampant – or it is always possible the namer saw with Kirby that overcrowding led to aggressive leg biting. Or simply that the larvae are bad for beeches. For what it is worth, the illustration I have seen of *Stauropus fagi* reminds me of something Tenniel might have done, though I appreciate that might have more to do with the style of the illustration than the larva. In the taxonomic name, *fagi* refers to beech again (*Fagus sylvatica*) but I have not found what *Stauropus* means. And now I see from the luminous hands of the bedside clock that it really is nearly twenty to four. Absurd but dispiriting. One lunch with Heidi Nutall I made a point of ordering lobster from Loch Fyne.

'There is no resemblance, is there?'

'To what?'

'The moth larva.'

Ms Nutall is short-sighted and therefore takes off her glasses to look closely at something. She peered.

'Ah,' she said, 'I hadn't twigged that they have ten legs, if you count the pincers. A coincidental leg a minute.' She looked up. 'No, I can't see any resemblance. Should there be?'

'I don't know.'

Evidently I sounded miserable. She took hold of my wrist with plump, warm fingers.

'But what are you thinking of? It is not as if the film were about the Lobster Moth. It is merely a prop, an illustration of his interest, that re-infancy he saw in military convalescence. It is rather pathetic. A biologist pretending to be a soldier, a grown man with a caterpillar in a tin, going out to collect beech leaves for it. It's a kind of non-race between the creature munching its way towards spinning its cocoon and Gilmerton being given the all-clear. You don't have to be a lepidopterist. What you have to do is give over some sense of loss, frustration under all that fine-mannered patience. He is watching himself a lot more than he is watching the caterpillar.' Her eyebrows came up. She gave my wrist a little squeeze and let go. 'Ah,' she said, starting to look for a pen, 'I have never been happy about the effect of tobacco on the Lobster Moth. It makes you sound prissy. We could have Sanderson say, "But isn't there a caterpillar in *Alice in Wonderland* that smokes?" Then he could offer you a cigarette. What do you think?'

I nodded. I wasn't just then following her. I felt squeamish, as if ignorance were rubbery. I looked down at the eyes of the lobster on their stalks. Like black capers. Ms Nutall was writing and barely looked up when she spoke.

'Sanderson could say, "They're Turkish." Yes, what's that pipe that goes through water called?'

'Hookah.'

'Of course it is. Why was I thinking of gargoyle?'

28

On one occasion, just here in his pillow book, Gilmerton's pencil sidelines widen out into notes and instead of living in left- or right-hand margins have a page entirely to themselves. The writing is smaller in size than anything else he wrote, the pencil point repeatedly sharpened. Another curiosity is that these sidelines are written as if they were still in a margin, are in narrow blocks, but the first three are stepped across the page, each slightly lower than the preceding one and while the sequence is vertical enough for sense, the arrangement is not constant and the overall effect is of a pleasant patchwork, partly because of the silverish pencil lead that he used. I have seen Ms Nutall take a magnifying glass to one block at a time.

'Handsome as a dissertation on the curve that a dog describes running towards its master.' – A description of the Grand Duke of Virginia in Lautréamont's *Maldoror*.

I am offered this as 'an admirable line', as an example of 'indirect description which instantly brings the character to life in a way that the minute detailing of person and dress cannot'.

But does it? Perhaps I am dull today but I thought first of simple features or slight plumpness of face. Does the far-fetched lead to abstraction?

Aubrey complains that the sentence is incomplete for the breed of the dog. He suggests a pointer because, for example, a greyhound 'buckles' as it runs and does not give quite the same impression of fighting its own forward momentum as it comes round; and a spaniel, with its ears flapping off the line and its hind legs splayed and slipping would 'uncontain' the Grand Duke, introduce curl and flop. He also insists the pointer would need to be running across an open field for the curve to show up well and possibly the master would need to be a little raised to get a good view, say on the steps of his villa, looking out over his parkland, perhaps with a gun over the crook of his arm.

It is true that the solitary line we have is in translation, but still, it is clear that it is the dissertation that is handsome. If you said, 'Handsome as the curve described by a dog running towards its master,' you would miss the study of the effect.

In theory I have nothing at all against anyone writing a dissertation on such a curve; indeed, there are certain intriguing difficulties – a four-footed locus, for example and, if I have understood Aubrey right, a spine that forms not-quite-vertical waves within the line of the curve.

But in practice I loathe the description of a dissertation as handsome. Clear, certainly. Even elegant. But not handsome. Hume, in his laconic and resolute autobiography, says – I am not sure that I have the exact words – that his father 'passed for a man of fashion'.

Whether I recall well or not, it is the irony I miss. I suspect Lautréamont's handsome Grand Duke is also the master. The curve as swell. And exactly who ran? The master will unbend a little and pat his proud panting friend.

Very well. Try to praise Lautréamont's line – It is a sentence as exhilarating as the swirl of a girl's gown as she swings into her first waltz.

Unfair. Let me try at least to put us both on a footing of genuine admiration for the person observed – I once watched her working to get the precise measure of her boredom into a doodle.

Today I have a little more faith in boredom than in handsomeness. But is the measure of the doodle more immediate and revealing than a dissertation on a curve? She is certainly more active.

I imagine the Grand Duke as a man who would say, 'The stricture of a line should be a line of equal length.'

Lines always sag when singly and persistently viewed. A curve never does.

A director once approached me after a take; grimacing, his fingers clasped together, he said, 'David, I want you to be . . . porous!'
I thought of my skin, of water disappearing into dry soil, then petered out in a nod. The other actor frowned.
'Do you know what he meant?'
'No.'
'Film doesn't have pores.'
In the event I gave the director what he wanted. I imagined a loose weave as I spoke and peered at the other actor through it.
'Exactly!' said the director.
'Oh, shit,' muttered the other actor, 'are we going to have to spend all this *seeing* for the first time?'
Glamour is the glaze on the pot. Wait. Dancers and a potter's wheel, spinning and staying still. Homer. Yes, I once saw an animated short of that, with flickering pencil lines, beginning with a clay lump, spinning into an urn-like shape, going into the oven, being painted with rather Matisse-like dancers in a hand-linked chain around it, the thing (and the dancers) beginning to spin faster and faster until it settled into an image of an ecstatic static round of leaping. Film is glamour. Glamour glimmered fitfully throughout. Gleaming with finish. There used to be, maybe there still are, places called finishing schools. For young ladies to acquire a patina of restrained but obvious cost. There is also highly polished verse. And a kind of Victorian novel called Silver Fork written to encourage the fear of a social Achilles heel. Is what Gilmerton dislikes in Lautréamont's line simply that it is a fatuous flourish, false precision, careful flattery?

Oh. *Mattress Struggles*, a title for an unsprung film. In bed thought becomes effortless but very slack and I cannot help feeling that if I had managed to sleep and were now rested I should understand Gilmerton just a mite better when he talks of lines. At school the expression surely was to plot a curve. Or is he joining Yeats and Eliot; all lines, when pressed, dribble juice and drivel?

When I played Malcolm the porter told me that it is not the first and third but the second 'tomorrow' in Macbeth's famous trio that causes problems to actors endeavouring to charge monotony with ache. Even when they have no intention of doing so, they are hopelessly biased towards variety as a means of retaining interest. And in consequence will, in terms of pitch, make the line convex or concave or, if very bad, in terms of volume. 'Tomorrow and tomorrow and tomorrow.' The porter seemed to me obscurely but spitefully general and I disbelieved in him. Still, Lautréamont's curve is probably better read than said. And Gilmerton's depth of a doodle and boredom in terms of pencil lead? More modern, more private and rather better instructions for an actress. How would one act the Grand Duke? Very easy to make a fixed point look like a stiff point.

Oh, I don't know. He could smile, rather amiably. Ah, it is time to change position. I belch. Solemn owls regurgitate indigestible pellets of fur and bone. Without shaking their heads or stretching their faces. Let's see. I have pincers, Gilmerton wings. Odd. I am lying now on my front with my eyes shut and I have just had the impression that if I bent close to a cocoon, I would be able to hear the chrysalis creak. Pillow, earwax and fatigue. Yesterday morning Isabel woke frowning, told me she had had a 'silly, troublesome dream', involving an old-fashioned printing press and her inability to correct the word 'mothyfur' to 'metaphor'; every time she turned to look for the lead letters she found that the word, more mouldy than furry, had crept away into another line. I kissed her, apologised for insomnia and role and the lepidopteral books around. She shook her head. 'It was unpleasantly like drowning in slightly sexy childspeak,' she said and shook it off. Ah. Moving my neck dislodges memory. Isabel doodles. And the shapes she draws, particularly when on the phone to her own mother, tend to retorts, those glass flasks one used in chemistry class with long, thin, bent-back necks. In her case, I think, portraying containment rather than answer, marking the paper in time to her patient 'yes'es rather than her patient 'really's, an irregular pendulum-cum-yes marker. Isabel teaches at the architectural school at the university about twenty miles away, one of the reasons we live here. The base of the retort becomes thick and black, betraying how long her mother has been on the phone. Later that day she said, 'I'd never thought of caterpillars being at all sexy before. Are they?'

A yawn. I wonder if one could grade fatigue by the volume of air taken in and pressed-out jaw pressure. And some tears. The yawn as slightly noisy blotting of an excess of tiredness. Breathe in. Yes. I like to *smell* my characters. And what I am looking for is an expression of face, a pitch of voice that sets the performance when the character becomes conscious of his own smell. That impotent brushing his hair, for example, was lank Turkish delight topped by a blob of astringently scented shaving soap. That murderous family man abruptly appreciated how sweet oily grass cuttings are. Half the Minotaur still lives on the nearby farm as a (hornless) Aberdeen Angus, his horns a tied-on pair of raw spare pork ribs, too high for him to smell more than sporadically. Vanderbank was rank comfits. The smell helped me fix the point by which the rest of Vanderbank could be graded, the smile of a man offered money to marry the daughter but who sticks to the mother. Preceded by a loss of density in the muscles, the smile toothless, the lips creeping in a slow run of twitches, just saved from turning into a lopsided sneer by sinking back into small-mouthed irony, the eyes chummy, then pitying, then lost, then bored.

Do I have an expression for Gilmerton? No, with my face stuck in the pillow I have just caught myself trying to read a possible expression in wrinkled white cotton, the insomniac's life-mask. Do I even have a smell? Gardner Price surely gives off whiffs of stale old train. McKinnon is Wright's Coal Tar soap with a chill sniff of medicinal alcohol. But Gilmerton? I think there is something there of butterscotch. But I cannot see any link between that and an image of fresh-cut flowers, which is not even followed by the scent of fresh flowers but by the smell of old flower water a week in the vase. I can't explain that. It is time to turn again, carefully so as not to disturb Isabel.

29

Ghosting Gilmerton requires weight loss: 'Not kilos, David, ribs!' said Ms Nutall. 'And then it doesn't matter if you put a little on. In fact, probably better. A little plumping would suit convalescence, make him less desperate. But remember, we want you very clearly on the scarce side of robustness.'

As usual I have lost weight by eating exiguously, fruit mostly, and by wolfing vitamins and cod-liver oil capsules, drinking six litres of mineral water and by trot, trot, trotting some nine kilometres morning and evening. Eight kilometres, eight hundred and thirty-two metres my daughter says, her belief in numbers on a dial being absolute.

'Perhaps,' she suggested, 'you are not sleeping because you're hungry.'

'No. I'm not aware of missing food at all.'

In fact, whether by compensation or not, I have been enjoying cooking and often act as an abbreviated chef for Isabel and the girls.

'So *You Only Eat with Your Eyes*,' said Heidi Nutall.

'I'm sorry?'

'That was the ghastly title of the television series I started in. I think it was supposed to be scrotum prodding.'

'Ah.'

'You didn't see it?'

'Not that I recall.'

'It concerned a wonderfully ill-favoured woman in Glasgow who worked in a private detective agency. The boss was a lush – barely appeared. She carried a very discreet torch for a baby-faced lorry driver who treated her remorselessly between chum and mum.'

'Ahh,' I said. British television works on animals and detective work. It was a long time since I had heard of love and torches.

Ms Nutall smiled. 'She wore brown knee-length cardigans and moss-green ski pants, was easily thinner than you and had a lovely, shuffling walk, slightly hunchbacked, as if her shoes were too big, black Orphan Annie hair and was given a complexion, a mix of liver and livid for old acne, that should have won awards.'

'Did you write it?'

Heidi Nutall started, then laughed.

'Each episode centred on a different kind of runaway husband and ended on her ordering a double cappuccino for herself and a pie and double chips and sauce for the lorry driver. She divided her judgements into "sordid" and "not so sordid".'

'Oh, I remember that,' said Isabel. 'There was a series of books, too. The actress was called Meg Something. Meg Henry! She went off and opened a hotel in Menorca, I think. Yes, why don't we have Heidi Nutall over to lunch? You can talk and I get an excuse to eat.'

Ms Nutall accepted at once. Our children are cautious before sociable but Ms Nutall was in determinedly grandmotherly mood and having leant towards Isabel's belly – 'I'll just say hello to your sister' – she gathered them to her.

'Do you know what a pelican is?'

'It's a bird.'

'Yes. And do you know it has a crop or pouch to keep fish in? That's my crop,' she said, pointing at a stuffed, bright green plastic carrier bag she had left by the door. 'Young pelicans push into the crop.'

She turned to Isabel. 'I haven't put terribly sugary things in.' And then to me. 'I understand Lewis Carroll used to do the same, drag about books and puzzles on the assurance of meeting small girls.'

'I'm two,' said the younger child.

'Yes, darling,' said Ms Nutall, 'the wobbly otter's for you.'

'Would you like wine?' I asked her. I was about to say, 'Or . . .'

'Of course I would, David, of course.'

Heidi Nutall followed me round into the kitchen and, adding nods to her smiles, lifted lids. We had, after my lunch with her, chosen food for colour rather than anything else, halibut and poussin.

'Oh good,' she said. 'Mrs Sempill is incorrigibly milk-based. And it's you that does the cooking, David.'

I gave her a glass of wine. 'Today anyway,' I said.

'Would you like to see the house?' said Isabel.

'Of course, dear,' said Heidi Nutall.

They were away for enough time for me to make a fruit salad in which the grapes were skinned and pipped and I could mull over Gilmerton's childhood platonic fruits and the table manners he learnt.

'David!' said Heidi Nutall. 'But why didn't you tell me you slept under a painted ceiling?'

I wiped my hands. 'What have you done with your wineglass?' I asked.

'I'll get it,' said the five-year-old.

Heidi Nutall was now examining all our ceilings. 'Ah,' she said, 'would that have been the original door to the hayloft?'

'I suppose something of that sort.'

Ms Nutall turned to my glass-bearing daughter. 'It just shows you,' she said. '*Two* hundred years ago horses got rather better accommodation than people *four* hundred years ago.'

The two-year-old was nursing her wobbly otter; the five-year-old beamed in assent and thrust up the wineglass for me to pour more wine in.

The house has indeed two ages; we cook and live in a converted stable, described as a rare example of Regency building in Scotland, sleep in the thrawn, sturdy little tower house abutting.

'After lunch,' said Heidi Nutall, 'you can take me round the policies. I hope that's ginger you're adding to the halibut.'

It wasn't and I did take her round, except that she led. She peered up at the date stone over the older, dwarfish entry door.

'When you consider this is seventy years younger than Lampen-ham! It is a world of space and elegance apart.'

'Isabel found it.'

'She told me.' Ms Nutall looked around. 'You're not a gardener.'

'No. There's a man comes in to keep the grass down. He does the big house you passed as well.'

Ms Nutall was already peering through the iron gate in the wall. 'Ah,' she said, 'you have a doocot as well.'

'Empty.'

'Yes,' said Heidi Nutall, unbolting the gate. 'We could walk round the water?'

We have a loch cum pond, the reason the gate is bolted, about two shallow acres with a three-tree islet in the middle, on which a few ducks have seasonal squabbles. There are too many reeds. On the far side there is a shelter belt of rather ugly conifers put up by a previous owner against the farm on the other side which tilt permanently towards the east from the prevailing wind.

'No swans,' said Ms Nutall.

'They say there used to be a pair that nested here but they were certainly gone by the time we came. Perhaps they were put off by the people restoring the painted ceiling.'

'Shhh,' said Ms Nutall and put her arm through mine to begin our walk round.

Ms Nutall retains some of 'the bubble and pleasure' of the first film she wrote and directed, meaning, I think, some pride in getting it made on a very small budget and then seeing it enjoy some distribution. She says she particularly enjoys what she calls her children's 'translations' of the title. Her favourite is probably *Trains and Babies*, 'catching me somewhere between Charles Kingsley and Edith Nesbit'.

I have seen the film on video and like it. It plays at real time, a ninety-one-minute walk round a beautiful loch in the Trossachs. Ms Nutall has a splendid way with sunlight and water vapour. 'And no fog machines, David.' Dressed around 1860, a thirty-three-year-old daughter of a dead Romantic poet who lives with her august aunt, the poet's wife whose sister died in childbirth, and a forty-two-year-old professor of pathology with the size and look of a staid Chaplin, indulge in a mix of debate and negotiation.

The girl, Adela, is red haired with very large, almost pop eyes and despite being, in Victorian terms, shelved, argues hard with her suitor. The professor has contrived a collection of one hundred and forty-three foetuses in glass bottles in his effort 'to record the stages of development from conception to birth' but Adela wishes to know how he came by his collection. Did he buy any? Did he swap? How many were discovered during autopsies performed by himself? How many of the would-be children had had to be patched up? Their chaperone is his eight-year-old niece and their argument, carried on in urgent whispers or out of earshot of the child, centres on the inconvenience, pain and risk of having children. Given technological advances (like steam engines and railways) 'which have brought us here', she wonders whether the sexual act will be necessary for much longer, doubts that 'anything about a man can rival a sonnet' and suggests 'it is not only the sword that is less mighty than the pen'. Their argument becomes so heated that they forget the chaperone who, when they have come to 'the very beginnings of a marriage agreement', is found to have fallen into the loch. I rather liked the suitor's peeved enquiry, 'But can't you swim, dear?' before wading in to the rescue. The film did well as a festival film and Ms Nutall began to acquire her reputation as a good writer for women. Adela has some good lines and was allowed to be strikingly direct.

Two of her touches I like very much. Some frames by a small shore overhung with branches, in which reflections of the leaves play among the small pebbles in the shallows and Adela asks her professor for 'the difference between love and lust' and, since he is initially too disconcerted to answer, offers him 'a smooth lake and a choppy lake?' And a pleasant mix of the straight and the tender – 'You are not displeasing but I dislike one aspect of your face very much.' The professor has on his cheekbones 'two weak replies' to his eyebrows. Carefully he explains that the skin under his eyes and the top of his beard have, with age, 'made an unholy alliance of bristle and a stuff that parts as easily as wet blotting paper'. He has tried, his manservant has tried, even a professional barber has tried, but to no avail. Adela stops him and examines the crow's feet at his eyes and the soft skin under them closely and from several angles. Ms Nutall told me the kind of critic she doesn't like called the scene 'highly erotic'. 'I believe *I* could remove those hairs,' says Adela. 'Dear lady, I bleed with a blade.' 'What? I was thinking of plucking them, professor. With tweezers – or small forceps.'

As we pottered round my pond Ms Nutall sighed. 'I try to take a little exercise after meals because recently I have found I get depressed after *eating*. Must be age.' She looked round and up at me. 'I was talking the other day to someone who thinks actors will be replaced by computerised mammets within seven to ten years. I like that little bracket of time, don't you? The notion is a sophisticated sort of Identikit, there'll be face and head designers and market research.

After a meal I tend to grow sleepy, not get depressed. Is that what I am doing now? Ah, in bed I have too much knee. The upper one weighs me out of sleep. An unvivacious but decided jerk. Ah, I asked our daughters what they had talked about with Ms Nutall.

'Oh, you know, mostly about our dreams, Dad.'

In *The Female Fool* there is a lovely scene in which Nicolle la Folle, who measures six foot two inches and has almost albino hair, attempts to learn the walk of the camelopard or giraffe from the musicians, gradually assumes a stately, undulating gait and a look of supercilious disinterest. Belief has ragged edges. I remember once getting a lift from a lighting man and my disbelief that we should both be living in the same street, as if it were a joke when there was no need for one.

Ms Nutall stopped and sighed. We looked over the patch of water at my bipartite home.

'I like to think it was more than a calling card,' said Ms Nutall.

I had not heard her sound plaintive before and it took me a second or two to understand she had been thinking of her first film and, possibly, of its limited distribution. In the mean time she has become a lot better at titles. Her first film was called *The Wedding Train*. 'I can't believe I was so stupid,' said Ms Nutall. 'I wanted the title to fall off like a wart.'

30

For some reason Walter Scott keeps floating up tonight. I don't know why. *Ivanhoe* read at eight put me off for twenty-five years. Then I read *The Antiquary*, thought he might have possibilities, but gave up on *Heart of Midlothian*. But if I remember right, it was he who introduced the word 'glamour' into English from the Gaelic. Ms Nutall loves it. 'Ah, glamour!' she says. But it took me a little time to understand that when she talked of scenes in which Gilmerton appears as 'glamorous but off-key', she was referring to historical film techniques.

'We could use Garbo-ish lighting, make your forehead as luminous as a lightly dusted moon and your eyes huge.'

'But you are not going to?'

'Not quite. What I had thought of was shooting in black and white and then having the scenes coloured by computer.'

'You don't mean like those films on television when the Southern troops look as if they were wearing grey-milk baize uniforms?'

'Yes, David. I am particularly fond of the greens and purples. I also like that curious light blue they achieve.'

'Ah. Is the idea that this would separate out the fantasy parts of the film like . . . quotation marks?'

'More like another script for the fantasies about him.'

'A dull sort of italics?'

Ms Nutall moued doubtfully. 'The other thing is that I want a contrast with Gilmerton's night vision, that soft stained-glass look Burnet mentions.'

'So we're talking about varieties of *stained* film?'

'Pointers.'

'But you do want to separate Gilmerton from the fantasists?'

'Oh yes. And we've got to give him a level of consciousness in the fantasy.'

'Explain.'

'Gilmerton's complicity is obviously with the viewer not the fantasist. And all the fantasies are fed through Gardner Price. He doesn't always believe.' She sighed. 'I'd like the colours to give off misty tendrils as the fantasy runs into disbelief.'

Ms Nutall has an idiosyncratic use of verb tenses. If she says she had thought she means she is thinking; if she uses the conditional she is presenting a proposal that she has already rejected but is giving it a last try to see how the listener reacts. I have the impression though, that even if the reaction were enthusiastic, her rejection would persist.

'Let me get this clear,' I said. 'Gilmerton's own memories and stories . . .'

'. . . are as natural as the rest of the film.'

'I see. Could you give me an example of this colour work?'

'Of course. Sarah MacDonald?'

INT. NURSERY — DAY

Gardner Price picks up a letter from a pile and begins to read.

GARDNER PRICE
(*voice-over*)
There was a persistent rumour in Edinburgh that he employed a lady, no better than she should be, to teach him the art . . . of the kiss.

Gardner Price raises his eyebrows and continues to read in silence.

INT. MACDONALD FLAT — DAY

The flat is austere, an elegant schoolroom, bare polished floor, studio mantelpiece, chaise longue, *screen. Camera at desk height. Black and white for first frames as in a still photograph, then processed colour and movement as Sarah MacDonald comes into frame and speaks.*

SARAH MACDONALD

The kiss given to a female member of the family is an exercise in containment – between affectionate pose and labial posy.

But a kiss! A real kiss involves the organs used to eat and to speak. A real kiss involves communication and consumption.

Let us begin with the small muscles at the corner of the lips.

INT. NURSERY — DAY

Gardner Price briefly closes his eyes, puts that letter down and takes another one from the pile. (Behind him is a blackboard on an easel which shows a number of chalked lip positions headed 'Osculation'.) [The parenthesis there means this is possible but likely excessive; nor is it too likely the labial posy will survive the final cut.] *He reads.*

GARDNER PRICE
(*voice-over*)

They say that the seventeen-year-old Gilmerton brought a black woman back with him from Brazil. She was at least fifteen years older than he and claimed to be the widow of a Presbyterian missionary – hence her surname.

Gardner Price puts that letter down and picks up another.

Her name was Sarah MacDonald. Originally from Santo Domingo, she was the natural daughter of some Catholic priest.

Gardner Price goes back to letter 2.

He set her up in an establishment quite near the university.

Gardner Price goes back to letter 3.

Gave her a pleasant flat near the Botanic Gardens so as not to feel too far away from exotic plants.

Gardner Price sighs. He picks up another letter.

He was easily wealthy enough to keep a lady to instruct him in the arts of love.

And another.

He is said to have arrived at university directly from Brazil, with ferns for the Botanic Gardens, a sloth for the zoo – and a mulatta for himself.

INT. MACDONALD FLAT — DAY

On the chaise longue, *mussed hair and undone buttons, Gilmerton and Sarah MacDonald kiss. She breaks off. Processed or fantasy colour.*

> SARAH MACDONALD
>
> The tongue now, I think.

They kiss.

INT. NURSERY — NIGHT

Gardner Price opens his eyes. He is sitting in evening dress at the head of the dining table with a small stack of letters on the plates in front of him. Fantasy colour. He lifts the top letter and reads.

> GARDNER PRICE
>
> He was wearing a dressing-gown, rather Russian, made of some fabulously expensive cloth.

He shuffles letters and reads again.

> Wearing the kind of thing Regency rakes wore in their chambers, a raiment of watered silk.

He puts letter down, takes a reflective sip of port, fits a walnut into nutcrackers.

> GARDNER PRICE
> (*voice-over*)
>
> He was seen –

The sound of the nutcrackers to join sound of feet in snow in

EXT. MEADOWS — NIGHT (*Fantasy colour*)

— at four in the morning with snow on the ground dressed in the Japanese manner striding to a rendezvous with his mistress.

Gilmerton stops walking and looks with irony and patience at the camera.

INT. NURSERY — NIGHT (*Fantasy colour*)

Gardner Price in evening dress and Agnes in evening gown sit on the sofa, Gardner Price sideways.

GARDNER PRICE

Miss Gilmerton . . .

She looks round at him. He moves his head towards her — but then lifts and kisses her gloved hand.

INT. NURSERY — DAY

Close shot of Gardner Price back to normal. He nods.

INT. MACDONALD FLAT — DAY

Sarah MacDonald reclines naked on chaise longue. *The very first frames in processed colour, then in black and white.*

GARDNER PRICE
(*voice-over*)

Sarah MacDonald. Sarah MacDonald.

There is a flash as with an old-fashioned camera.

INT. NURSERY — DAY

Gardner Price examines a black-and-white photograph with a magnifying glass. Camera views through glass, closes on Sarah MacDonald's flash-opened eyes. Back to Gardner Price frowning and moving glass. He pauses and peers. Camera views through glass at lower right corner of photograph an extraneous bare black foot.

Back to Gardner Price, puzzling.

INT. NEAR BRECHIN — DAY

> GARDNER PRICE
>
> Miss Gilmerton, does the name 'Sarah MacDonald' mean anything
> to you?

> AGNES
>
> No. It's a common enough name, of course. Where was this?

> GARDNER PRICE
>
> When your brother was studying in Edinburgh.

> AGNES
>
> Mm. No, I'm afraid not. Nothing comes to mind.

> GARDNER PRICE
>
> Thank you.

INT. STAIRWELL — DAY

Gardner Price trudges upwards, muttering.

> GARDNER PRICE
>
> How much of Sarah MacDonald was just idle, envious tongues?

Something occurs to him. He hurries into

INT. NURSERY — DAY

and begins to look for something on another table.

Yes, this is it.

Shot of notebook marked 'Colours'. Gardner Price flips and reads.

Ecru — the colour of unbleached linen ... greyish yellow ...
greener and paler than chamois or old ivory.

He shakes his head, he sighs.

Ah. Her skin – the colour of Arabica coffee grains with vanilla just beginning to surface. Mm.

Her . . . like matt black raspberries.

Her . . . gleaming russet folds in chocolate.

Sarah MacDonald? Certainly degrees of blackness. But then again, he did go to Brazil.

He strokes his neck, looks down again and flips.

On the whiteness of the Ghost Moth; patchy candour, gold-rimmed wings.

He looks up.

Two things. I can't help feeling that, possibly because of his childhood interest in lepidoptera, his sense or at least his vocabulary of colour and texture is exaggerated. Dickensian in a scientific sort of way. And the second thing is that this exaggeration tends to the . . . sensual. Very well. Let us call it . . . an urgent, no, no, no, an *intense* desire for accurate description. Which may be incompatible with saving Miss Gilmerton from a certain unpleasantness. Yes. Exclude Sarah MacDonald.

Ms Nutall barely gave me time to finish reading or consider her use of processed or fantasy colour.

'Did I ever tell you that I might have seen Sarah MacDonald? I was decidedly small but I was taken with her very old-fashioned clothes. She dressed like Queen Mary, or perhaps it was Alexandra – she wore a toque and rather baggy, brown stockings and bauchled shoes. When she lifted her veil her face was as powdered as Turkish delight.'

'Sorry. Are you saying there *is* some truth in the fantasies?'

'I wouldn't know where, David. My researches only turned up that she died in 1956 aged eighty-three, that she had been born in British Guiana, daughter of Solomon and Doris, and that in 1923 she married a retired farmer from Aberdeenshire who had made his money out of horses in Gilmerton's war. Her married name was Laing.'

'So what do you think?'

'I'd guess that Gilmerton and Sarah arrived in Edinburgh about the same time in 1907. Japan Bob's son back from Brazil – by the way, he did come with animals for the zoo and plants for the Botanics – and into his elegant apartments; and an exotic woman from somewhere tropical, inexplicably well off. Enjoyable bad faith, I'd say. A mix of racism and a little spite – I imagine people found the pairing quite glamorous.'

31

It is apparently difficult to arrest the development of a larva & then preserve it so that it retains shape & colour. The simplest method given, described as not always very successful, is to kill the larva by immersion in spirits of wine. A small vertical opening is then cut at the an** with a fine, sharp-pointed pair of scissors. The larva is subsequently laid between two wads of soft blotting paper & the soft contents of the body are carefully squeezed in the direction head to tail & out through the opening made.

When the skin is completely emptied, the tube of a small blowpipe or a hollow glass stem is inserted in the opening & tightly secured to the skin with thread. The skin is then slowly inflated by blowing through the pipe till it has reassumed the shape of the larva. The instruction is given that the skin must not be inflated too rapidly or violently, lest it should become unduly distended or even burst. The caterpillar should then be dried as quickly as possible over a spirit lamp, continuing to keep it inflated by blowing through the pipe till it is dry.

The principal (!) disadvantage of this method is that the larva loses more or less of its colour during the process. To preserve the colours better, the skin may be filled with fine sand or with sawdust if previously tinted with a colouring matter which corresponds to the ground or base colour of the living larva & thoroughly dried. After the stuffed skin has been brought to the required condition, it should be attached to some suitable object, such as a leaf or a twig.

Blowing air but not life. Compare then the relatively simple but still demanding task described above with that of rendering subtle, sentient, human flesh & blood into ink on paper, of delineating the complexity of a fine mind & noble spirit in a sequence of sentences.

There are drawbacks; the comparison is shocking.

On the other hand, the idea of loss & faded colours, of opportunities scythed, of many futures obliterated . . .

I agree with Ms Nutall, Gardner Price is 'wonderfully off-key', incapable of continuity – 'He does not know what an idea is,' said Ms Nutall, 'and he is, incidentally, the only person I have ever encountered who *writes* asterisks' – but that day I was alarmed that she should think the section might do well acted out in the film. By that time I was practising cradling my left lung in my ribcage, breathing shallow, overriding snags of pain.

'I see him first in the garden looking through berry bushes.'

I said nothing, worried that she might want those statuesque gardeners in the background.

'And I'd have Agnes looking out of a window at him. He strolls in the garden, the would-be biographer musing, notebook in hand, then plucks a caterpillar and pops it into his pocket. Agnes shows no surprise.'

What makes me anxious about Ms Nutall is her inordinate liking for links, Gilmerton picking a Lobster Moth, the child Agnes eating her caterpillars.

'You're making Gardner Price something of a Malvolio?'

'What? No, no, David. Nobody sets Gardner Price up to make a fool of himself. No, he is much flabbier and more wistful. Nor is he against cakes and ale. Gardner Price is the kind of man who'd take smoked salmon and a little champagne as a social prophylactic!'

Ms Nutall was pleased by this last and I found myself smiling distractedly back at her.

'Are you all right?' she asked.

'I'm not sure. I'm feeling rather nervous. As if I had an allergy. Do you know that feeling?'

'No,' said Ms Nutall. 'Can you go on?'

'Yes, of course.'

'Some of this is too awful to miss. "Blowing air but not life"! Mm? Here he is, at the first hopeful flush of his relationship with Agnes and the poor man is, as it were, trying to try.'

'But what does he do with the caterpillar?'

'What? I think we'd have to go through the process he describes. The practicalities are grim. Dropping the creature into spirits of wine. Trying to gauge just how much blotting paper is needed. We might have to snatch-snip with a pair of scissors from Gilmerton's collection. And then there is the business of the glass tube, of blowing into a caterpillar. I don't think we want explosions but I think we do want a certain wonder on his part as to quite what sort of person would become involved in such barbarous little messes. Not that there is evidence either way that Gilmerton did. Mm? What's the matter?'

'It might be rather disgusting to see.' Was that my objection?

'Oh, I had thought we could have the caterpillar ambling about while he read about the process, went through the actions. Face-acting, David. The most we'd do is have him blow down the tube at the caterpillar and do his blowing lifeline. I'm taking it the caterpillar might curl up. What do you think?'

'I'm getting your idea. Can I let it sit?'

'Of course.'

Gardner Price's next entry – 'stiffening his jellies' in Ms Nutall's phrase – is headed EYES, his list of the colours attributed to Gilmerton's pupils. But the entry after that is simply copied from Arabella Laing's *A Lady in Japan* (London, 1888):

Today I was taken to meet Mr Robert Gilmerton who is so much admired by the Japanese. He is a Scotchman who has found his grail in marine engineering and his paradise in a Japanese shipyard. His is a most curious case. Although he affects an air of having no time for fripperies, he was a most attentive host, had had some coolies erect an awning for our party under which we were served an excellent luncheon. To a degree, he dresses for his part and proves an eminently kenspeckle figure in a Japanese shipyard. He was wearing what he described as a Perth hat, which is like a grey top hat but with a wider brim. The day we saw him he was wearing an oatmeal-coloured coat, provided with many flaps and pockets, that reached to the back of his knees, a dark blue waistcoat, and trousers of a small black-and-white check. It was unspeakably hot, being 93 degrees F and very humid. Mr Gilmerton himself however took no shelter but that afforded by his headgear and he is, in consequence, most deeply tanned. He is a lean man of about fifty, I should say, of a little above the middle height, with a thick dark moustache, a firm nose, deep lines accompanying the curve of the moustache from nostril to chin, a head of abundant, dark hair and heavy-lidded eyes one fellow visitor described as 'cheerfully sceptical' and another as 'almost challengingly indifferent'. He smokes long black cheroots or cigars which he has made for him locally. He was asked how many of them he smoked a day and replied that 'when working, at least twenty'. Did this not affect his health? 'The reverse,' he replied. In permanent attendance he has two diminutive translators, a native married couple, the male in morning dress and the female in a kimono. Though his speech is peppered with Scotticisms they show no difficulty in understanding him; while they transmit his instructions, he insists again on his main points, slowly and with great intent. He is always 'wanting a keek' (a look). The Japanese pronounce his name as Gimerutu. Gimerutu-san has his office where he is and is surrounded by an ever-changing gaggle of men and a boy who carries a drawing board.

Mr Gilmerton did not join us for luncheon but came afterwards to drink coffeee and smoke another cigar – 'The best part of a meal,' he said – and to answer our questions with good humour. His is an engineer's view of the world. He is the only white man I have encountered here who considers the Japanese 'no different from anyone else. The so-called particularities of a culture are often merely differential decoration and almost as often emotional nonsense. Like everyone else the Japanese simply required the opportunity to be involved in a manufacturing enterprise and to be treated with respect.' He thought humanity made up of a 'basic stuff' and that most of that stuff would always find 'collaboration, economy and function highly attractive'. Despite the generality of such remarks I had the decided impression that Mr Gilmerton dotes on his workmen. Another guest, however, asked if he considered that other peoples would be able to abandon a traditional mode of life and embrace a new and industrialised one with the speed and success of the Japanese. He replied, 'I did not say that government and culture were not important. It may be the impetus of the change in Japan was due to the stifling effects of the past, but that does not change my point. Of course, if you attempt to establish a great industry among people who regard machines as contrivances of the devil, you will need to explain your purposes with great care and this may take time, but if you do it well and you train your workforce well, you will have your machine.' This opinion caused some amusement but Japan Bob, as he is often called, merely smiled and apologised for having to return to work.

Our party had different opinions of Robert Gilmerton's manner but no one could question either his moral character or abilities. I will remain with an impression of an engineer 'caring only for who and what will work', an exclusive concern but one carried out with cheerful vigour and capacious intelligence.

I find it difficult to work out why Gardner Price should have bothered to copy out all this decidedly pedestrian chat into his notebook. 'Exceptional men often have exceptional parents' again? Ms Nutall says the remark on Gilmerton Senior's moral character suggests he did not have a Japanese ménage. Or was Gardner Price beginning to palpate some notion of eccentricity in his subject? Or of heredity?

The next item in the notebook – 'Absolutely to his taste,' says Ms Nutall – is as follows: 'I am reliably informed that the estate was no less than five million pounds & may have been as much as eight. Five million pounds. £5,000,000.'

At some time Gardner Price added a pencil tick above each of the six zeros. They slope slightly to the right, 'like little smoke stacks,' says Ms Nutall, 'on his own special train.' He was less inspired when he tried to tackle Gilmerton's later scientific interests.

*

When Robert Gilmerton answered his country's call to arms he had recently graduated from Oxford University with a First Class Honours degree in Zoology. His interest for the future was in the speciality of:

inheritance

genetics

what has been called the chemistry of life

those means by which characteristics are passed on from
generation to generation.

Miss Gilmerton has told me he was fascinated by 'life stuffs' & has mentioned 'marvellous proteins'. She has also said, 'Butter or fruit, usually a fly.'

The means of her brother's interest was the fruit fly or vinegar fly, an excellent vehicle for the study of chromosomal inheritance because the fly is small, cheap to keep, and produces large numbers of offspring (I am informed that a female can lay up to one hundred eggs a day), the time from egg to adult taking ten days, so that genetic changes can be quickly as well as readily seen as they effect wing morphology, for example, or body or eye colour.

And that is that. The paragraph sounds a little stunned to me, as if, when Gardner Price was listening to what he was writing down, the words had been tapping on taut eardrums. I quite understand. Neither do I have the knowledge, historical or scientific, to know what Gilmerton was doing at Oxford or whether or not he would have gone on to make a contribution to the study of multicellular organisms, chromosome evolution or morphology.

'But it doesn't matter,' said Ms Nutall. 'Think of the spectator. The fruit-fly business is background, a possible part of the *ALMOST*. What you've got to do, is not look holy when you're near a microscope.' She frowned. 'I wonder,' she said. 'Do you think that butter or fruit business, but usually a fly, is genuine? Do you think he took it as flirtation? Or perhaps it alarmed him a little. Like brother, like sister. Butter or fruit. I am going to think about that.'

*

Poor old Gardner Price went back to the nightmarish practicalities of preserving larvae:

How does one secure 'a hollow glass stem . . . to the skin with thread'? One cannot sew glass. This must refer then to raising the skin around the glass tube &, as it were, lashing the skin to the glass, something that must, in part, deform the larva. & how does one avoid cutting into the skin with the thread & yet make the arrangement secure? & that business of *both* blowing & drying over a naked flame?

A hot-faced twiddling, well this side of toast or a marshmallow? Ms Nutall sighed, shook her head and turned a sheet of paper face down.

'I'll wait about the butter,' she said. 'Drink?'

'Yes, thank you.'

'Are you feeling any better?'

'Oh yes.'

But it was not until I had left the script session and was driving home that I admitted I had spent the whole time dreading that Heidi Nutall would want to match Gilmerton's lung-whistle with a fat grass squeak from Gardner Price blowing down a thin glass tube into a caterpillar skin, a quite absurd fear and an absurd but considerable relief.

32

Is it possible to dream a novel? Everyone knows of that Person from Porlock who first interrupted and then left Coleridge with the fragment of a dream poem. I have never understood why people snort at Coleridge. Is it because they think 'Kubla Khan' a West Country opium dream that rhymes and scans? Or because they consider his famous footnote a bombastic lie? Perhaps the snort comes because Coleridge believed what he was saying; that he had dreamt the poem whole and only had time to record what we have before that Person arrived and that after he had gone Coleridge found the rest of the poem had vanished in the same way that a vivid dream can vanish with and possibly because of the arrival of wakefulness. (A sideline: If you wake in the dark are you better able to remember a dream than when you wake in daylight?) Reading someone who does not appreciate the dream terms of what he is writing makes bluff readers uncomfortable to the point of incredulity. And then there is the implication that Coleridge was polite to the Porlocker, did not send him away or keep him waiting. In short, that he sacrificed poetry for manners. A gentleman always comes out of a trance.

I find other aspects far more interesting. I suspect the footnote constitutes a brief tale that tells us stolid Persons on business from Porlock are more dangerous than Doctors Frankenstein or Jekyll since they do not require electrical storms or potions, are in no way grandiose but do appear, with some frequency, without warning, to interrupt whatever we are doing. 'The Person from Porlock' is a true, daily horror story, the most restrained and effective of Gothic tales, the poem itself an example of gorgeous and exotic imagination, the footnote as a most prosodic version of reality reaffirming the stolid primacy of the world. It is also a robbery story in which something vanishes but there is no booty. The finality of it is absolute, the consequent oblivion casual and eternally sealed with a businesslike handshake on the visitor's departure. The Porlocker trudges off, ignorant of having left 'Kubla Khan' a romantic fragment, of having pre-empted but not secured the rest, of having contrived a splendid ruin. And if he knew what he had done? I suspect Mr Black from Porlock would be offended to be measured against dreamstuffs and pleasure domes. He might even be critical of Coleridge's impersonal and alliterative sense of discretion about his name and the omission of the nature of his business. Had he called to collect a debt? Was he a druggist delivering laudanum? Whatever the case, the Person from Porlock is always an unwelcome intermitter and I suspect that Coleridge, with that distracted, more hangdog than grave air of his, understood that on occasion he too could turn out to be Mr Black to other people. Coleridge leaves me with a feeling of delightfully resigned fairness.

The Lampenham library has its sectioned walnut shelves full of books but none later than 1871, the date the last owner-reader died or lost interest in reading. Apart from a sizeable crew of Romantics, there is another flurry around Thackeray and Dickens. The collections of a father and son? There are some odd volumes. *Oliver Twist* is in French and so is *The Antiquary*. A peculiar and partial principle operates in the ordering of the books; the central cabinet on the long wall is glassed in and contains women authors only, arranged alphabetically from top left. That is, there are no men in the cabinet and no women elsewhere.

I mentioned that I found this potentially troubling to Aubrey; he suggested spreading the books around, then pairing off authors, but gave up on Austen, finding no male author suitable. I am no littér-ateur. For me 1824 is the year in which spermatozoa were demonstrated to be necessary to human fertilisation rather than the year of Byron's death. But to be surrounded by this time-stopped library and one so literary (I admit, I have ignored the legal shelves) has had its effect on me. In one volume of *Humphrey Clinker* I found a strip of paper on which the following was written: 'My Dear, you are absurd. It is not a question of billiards *or* forfeits, but of *not* using the cue as a tusk.' I am no Coleridge. When I dreamt of a book, I dreamt first of the object rather than the contents. Three matters worried me as I napped, one, as it were, overlying the other. The first was that this was somehow a book of mine I could no longer recall. The second was that I was obliged to match the contents word by word. And the third, despite my incredulity, was that I set out to do so, becoming fatuously excited at the prospect of filling in those blurred, glue-grey paragraphs. I woke stunned. I could see, not a poem, but precisely one line, a horribly poor-quality pun with something of dream doggerel about it serving as poetry – 'Cue black and pot it.' Perhaps this is one of the reasons why I am reluctant to dismiss Coleridge's explanation of his dream poem as fraudulent; though his is far finer and longer and of far higher quality, subtlety and humour than mine.

Apart from talent – is it also a matter of desire? Somewhere else Coleridge has that business of a man dreaming of paradise, of receiving a flower as proof that he had been there . . . and if he awoke with the flower in his hand, what then? Or there is the reverse principle; Coleridge was bouncing a black ball against the cushions of a billiard table, listening to poetic measures. Or again, great concentration can lead to a blank aftermath without need of drug or sleep. The critic Hazlitt describes himself as thinking himself into love and dreaming himself out of it. Coleridge might turn that around. But in either case a specious formula. And all our Porlockers continue as conclusive but indifferent third parties.

I fell in love with all her details as if, to carry on with Romantic intonations, I had found a cornucopia of them in one person. The second time I saw her I was sitting on a window-seat of her house, feigning interest in the view from the window, my mind and hearing as far as possible from the words of a tedious old don, enjoying the reflection of her in the glass. She was seated on a long, low stool, a buttoned, crimson velvet bench with dwarfish legs in front of the fireplace, slowly stirring grains of sugar in a bowl.

'I said to him,' sniffed the old bore, 'I said to him – a science laboratory is not a kitchen but a powerhouse.'

'Ah,' she sighed, 'as cooking is not an art, nor science entirely edible.' There was a pause. She looked surprised at having spoken, then by what she had said. 'No, no,' she went on, 'I mean your comparison is slack and ill-drawn. And also misogynistic.' She inserted the spoon in the sugar again and stirred a little. 'Besides, a kitchen is a powerhouse by stove and by food.'

Through convulsive, sticky blinking the don shuttled first between ignoring her and then patronising her.

'My dear, I was of course speaking of the intellect and did not, I assure you, mean to deprecate any lady nor – heaven forbid! – speak badly of cooks.'

She allowed him time for a short chortle. 'No,' she said, 'you think intelligence makes women even fishier.'

It was here I noticed that when she raised her eyebrows they showed double on the window-pane. I turned, her husband made to raise his hand but she kept speaking.

'Pots,' she said, 'you make us pots. And what have you against them? You say pots of money, pot-bellies, pot luck though I have never heard of pots of intellect. Is that it? Your complaint against women? That we are pots? But surely a pot serves as it will. And that is the case for male scientists as much as for women. Ah, I am forgetting pot roast.'

The old don was inordinately offended by this little pot speech and huffily described it later as 'ventilation improper in a lady' so that when asked for my opinion as a witness I said his original remark had been 'shamefully overbearing and vulgar'.

I enjoyed more, however, the tone of her words as she spoke of pots; it reminded me of a spinning top seen somewhere in childhood. Even when furiously pumped, the rainbow colours on it having blurred into something like pale beaten eggs, it emitted mild, almost distracted hums.

'I should have punched him,' she said to me a few days later.

'That was clear.'

She frowned at my enjoyment and told me that once as a child, much taken with the Pathfinder novels, she had attempted to cross a Sunday wood as if invisible and inaudible but had almost at once stood on a twig and spun round 'furious at the self beside myself'.

I smiled. 'He will merely be resentful. I don't think either of you need worry about him.'

'But I don't!' she considered me carefully, almost suspiciously. 'Have you never had the feeling, Mr Gilmerton, that you have been a coward? That you should have struck someone on the mouth?'

'I once did.'

'Are you humouring me?'

'Certainly not. I broke a knuckle.'

'But didn't you feel any satisfaction?'

'For a fraction, I think, as the other boy began to go down, just before I clasped my hand.'

She sighed and pointed over the terrace. 'The sneaking parapets of Oxford,' she said. She had a marvellously persistent quality of seriousness which went well with her oval face and very dark eyes. 'Can you understand, Mr Gilmerton, that I am almost pining for *not* having done something to him? Oh, not *him* with his teeth and drawl and those bristles and hairs . . .'

'I understand, I do.'

She looked surprised, even a little displeased. 'Ah. *Do* you?'

'Yes.'

I also enjoyed her husband's reaction the day after. 'There is no more bad form than a bore,' he said and then burst out, 'My word! Surely the old fool knows she is with child!'

Euphoria: a mix of hilarity and manic tenderness. I loved every pore of her, every follicle and nail, every joint and swell. I loved to watch her, the twin spots of vein blue on either side of her nose where spectacles might have but did not press, her cluster of fingertips when she held a scalpel like a pencil, twitching the handle between cuts exactly as she did when drawing, her breathing beside me while

I looked into her microscope, the day I understood she had stopped dissecting what we caught at night, that the veins on her wrists and hands were so charged they looked painful, and that holding the end of the pencil against her palm, she now, with a slightly defensive action, shaded and, apparently unconsciously, made her moths furrier and fatter. Aftermath, aftermoth and afterlife – a boy weighing seven pounds and eleven ounces. I remember a conversation about islands, swelling islands, temporal islands, nomads and nomans. My impression now is that having loved her I still do and I feel gratitude even at – perhaps because of – the natural-term nature of the thing, unforgettable pleasure and delight. Once, in the freedom of night summer air, in the small wood near her house, I caught for her a Pebble Prominent and carefully handed it over; instead of killing it, however, she held the moth in her cupped hands, allowed it to whirr and then let it go.

'That's something I have always wanted to do. Feel the wings working against my skin. You don't mind, do you?'

'Not at all. There are some berries here. Would you like some?' She nodded. She smelt her hands and breathed out. 'That moth was very slightly snuffish,' she said. She rubbed her hands, then stretched out her arms and raised her face towards the night sky.

'This is exactly how night should be,' she said. 'Are those berries juicy?'

33

Round about 1951, I think, Picasso was taken by a strip cartoon retelling of Walter Scott's *Ivanhoe* in a French newspaper and produced a series of etchings in which, rather than a knight, a vigorous rewelding of armour sits on a horse. Also in the fifties, Italo Calvino wrote a novella to do with rearrangements of chivalry, human halving and heraldic quartering. I was reminded of these when I saw a ninety-year-old illustration of the caterpillar of the Pebble Prominent, one of Gilmerton's favourite moths. The illustration shows a large head as red as a child's gum after she has waggled out a milk tooth. The head – thistle shaped and topped by a blob of milk-shake pink on one side and a small patch of battleship grey on the other – issues from what looks like a piece of bizarre armour, combining an arm piece, two royal French blue-and-gold trimmed elbows on the inner arm and then something like a Captain Nemo-like anal periscope with three coathooks. I am quite unable to think what the larva might be imitating on its aspen and have not come across any suggestions.

The scientific name attached to the illustration of this creature and indeed the one used by Gilmerton is *Notodonta ziczac*. When I looked up Pebble Prominent in a modern reference work the taxonomic name given is *Eligmodonta ziczac*. Now I think I understand how an important part of lepidoptery is taken up with classification and nomenclature, with occasional family wrangles to do with properties and priorities; in other words, names can shift as knowledge is refined. My (expensive) modern book has no illustration of the Pebble Prominent larva. It describes the head as 'large', but then briefly and flatly colours it 'green'. Green? I cross-checked with a guide for children. That suggests the caterpillar is 'odd looking' and 'pale greyish brown, but this can vary'. Vary?

Naturally it occurred to me that I was being misled by the stationary *zigzac* and that the name Pebble Prominent had shifted creatures. But when I looked at the illustrations of old and new imago, it was clear that, allowing for the vagaries of colour reproduction and age – the old illustration had tints of faded straw – the moth itself was the same. So? I am in bed. I am not going to get up to compare words and illustration again and I have no doubt my daughter's toothless gum is very red.

I am not a lepidopterist. But amongst Gilmerton's side-notes is a list of surnames that 'ill serve the theory'. He calls them sound clouds. Thus Darwin is too easily he who dares wins. And Dalton reduces to dull tones. Gilmerton suggests this is why the English call colour-blindness what Europeans describe as Daltonism. I certainly remember a test about the age of fifteen with green and orange dots, a green three and an orange eight. I can't really accept that the shift from *Noto-* to *Eligmo-* has meant such a toning down. Still, I suppose that a colour-blind illustrator, when concentrating with enthusiasm, might translate shades of grey into spectacularly bright fancies and that what I have come across is merely an example of poor proofreading a long time ago or a checker of illustrations who had not seen that caterpillar but who was quite prepared to admit that some are fantastic. The illustration as singular anecdote, a sport or aberration amongst illustrations, rather than any mutation in the larva itself.

Of course there are many other Prominents. Pale, White and Plumed. Iron, Coxcomb and Swallow. Scarce, Maple and the Three-humped Prominent. I have no idea what the three humps refer to. In my modern book the Pebble larva is described as having pyramidal 'humps' but I do not know if these correspond to my armour elbows and in any case they are numbered as three, not two as shown in the old illustration. By the way, the Iron Prominent is *Notodonta dromedarius* which is odd, since I think a dromedary has one hump and its larva is described as having two. Or sometimes four. And the Three-humped or *Tritophia tritophus*, it is only fair to say, is a 'rare immigrant', only four being reported (this too is from the modern account) between 1842 and 1907, in Essex, Suffolk, Paisley and Bedford respectively. I'd check that Paisley, several hundred miles farther north than the others. The *zic̣zac* (Latinised zigzag) is widespread and I still have not found any other Prominent larva described as having a red head.

At the beginning of *The Ambassadors*, the hero (Strether) cheerfully describes himself as suffering 'prostration', meaning fatigue or nervous exhaustion or dog-tiredness, and there is some disagreement (with his friend Waymarsh) as to whether prostration encourages or discourages sleep. My mother has always had problems separating the words 'prostate' and 'prostrate' and is supposed to have said, of her father, that he was prone to the prostrate. Prone as flat and susceptible. I have been Pebbled to prostration – or at least that is the way it feels when you are awake in bed. I once heard two men on a train sing the praises of pebble-dash – I have a good imitation of the stuff on my inner lids now.

The ceiling above my head is painted. Or perhaps decorated with pigment would be a more accurate description. It is not a delicate scene of nymphs and goddesses and pink, puff-cheeked cherubs blowing into clouds and blue skies from the corners of a stateroom. This ceiling is low (eight feet), made of wood beams crossed with planks, and it provides the floor to the attic rooms above. The beams are decked out in a redcurrant-and-white pattern, reminiscent of the anthemion or Ancient Greek honeysuckle device, but less than honeysuckle, the painting on each beam suggests the underside of some fossilised centipede with tucked-in apostrophes for feet. Even so, I find the design attractive. The red is now a thin, rust-coloured clay red and the white is grubby, like thin plaster of Paris, both colours having drained into the wood, but the brush marks are pleasantly visible and pick up something of the swoop and twist missing from the device itself.

The cross planks are more colourfully rendered and roughly

heraldic. At least I think that is what the various animals, shields and implements are, though there is a leavening of inept figures, classical, biblical or heroic. Maccabeus, for example, about whom nothing at all comes to mind. And that is, we are assured, above the garderobe door, Santiago, peering out of a grey tower with a stylised heart in the middle, breathing fire on a Saracen who, in comic-book style, is made up of little more than a bristling black beard, turban and scimitar. There are several Virtues, identified by the instruments they carry, spade-faced ladies, with ruffs at their necks, floor-length gowns, but very decidedly shod and with bare forearms as subtle as white sausages. Gaps have been filled with prying faces which at least have the energy of freer lines. But the most striking thing is the use of colour, in which the order and spacing of the pigments is of more importance than any sort of verisimilitude. Thus there is a red lion and a pair of yellow elephants with the look of soft-eared dogs and battered brass trumpets for trunks and there are three blue, smiling fish. Our five-year-old daughter was the first person I ever saw smile back at them – though it is quite common to see visitors, heads right back, return the smile before they know what they have done.

I am on the side nearer the window, open tonight, which over-looks first the doocot (empty, tilting like a miniature, random rubble Pisa) and then the pond cum loch. Tonight there is a moon (not generally good for mothing) and bit by bit, the moon and water have combined to illuminate a three-headed dog. Its muzzles resemble bauchles or old, soft bedroom slippers, once gold, now beige with luminous specks and black cracks, and large, plump, grape-like eyes just beginning to turn into raisins. Each mouth grasps a quoit.

Ah. There is, when you are flat on your back in the dark, looking up at a ceiling daubed and dated 1617, a proneness, a susceptibility – to ridiculous heraldry and pregnant women – and to swimming turns of the mind that have no existence outside summer-night insomnia. I have just seen from the window, in the little loch outside, in the reflection of the moon, quite near the islet, a fish rise. Almost at once a large Swallowtail came down and, for a few moments, settled on the fish's head, before the butterfly vanished into the shadow of the trees on the islet.

A summer hallucination? Let us replay it in slow motion. The fish rose in a moist disc of moon, its head just breaking the surface film of water. The butterfly ducked down out of the darkness and with a movement like a bird of prey braking its flight, rested its feet on the sliding, gleaming head. How can I know that? I am some sixty to sixty-five feet away and while my eyesight is good the close-up zoom quality is quite fantastic, the vision of the butterfly's feet touching the head and rising with a globular pulling at their extremities of sticky slime, impossible. And all this on my back and looking not even towards the window but up at the ceiling.

I can smell beeswax. The soles of my feet itch. The moon has moved; one of the quoits is in shadow. It is an illusion, I think, that I can see the rings round my irises when I blink. The rings in the water caused by the rising fish ebb away. And then, of course, that was a butterfly. There is a Swallowtail Moth (*Ourapteryx sambucaria*) which has attractive Mediterranean colours, pale lemon yellow with thin olive-brown transverse lines that waver as if in heat. And yes, if I remember correctly, it feeds on honeysuckle.

But what I saw was definitely the Common Swallowtail butterfly (*Papilio machaon*) with the scallop decoration on the hindwings and long black points as fragile looking as the smooth, carved tips of carbonised twigs. And it likes carrot, vitamin A – to help it see at night. To trace one's thought processes on a pillow is as much tangle as tingle.

Preparing a role is trawling, letting the character reveal his possibilities till a convincing impression of roundness or completeness is arrived at. I have just thought of a fish's mouth there, working away. Gills and ripples. I once heard my father say, 'No, no, no. *All* evidence is circumstantial unless judge and jury were there at the scene.' Would Gilmerton have smiled at that? Or looked bored? In a letter to his mother written in September 1913 to explain why he was going to concentrate on genetics, he says, 'I am not an intelligent but a notetaker. I try to be as observant as I can, which means, in part, that I stretch patience to unconscionable degrees. I consider an open mind, possibly wrongly, to be a rather vigorous position . . . I have never understood those who consider imagination and the associative facultics as having borders. Surely the limitations of imagination are more notorious than commonsensical; they often appear to be based on fear, stolidity and beetle-browed faith.'

Sometimes he seems to me prim and stiff. Isabel tells me I now speak in more than proper sentences. That I am far too deliberate. That I now consume a cup of coffee rather than drink it. That I never look even remotely surprised. That I handle knife and fork more like a puppet master making his puppets bow and dance than either a scientist at dissection or someone eating. I am not sure she is entirely right. I eat an orange with a knife and fork because Gilmerton would have done so – and also to make more of a meal of it. The first photograph I ever took repeated the sun several times across the print. My subject was Grizel and she was transversed by miniature suns. My Aunt Susan said, 'Oh, what a clever effect, dear. Perhaps you've something artistic in you.' It was the first time it had occurred to me that art could be a fraud.

34

Today it is hot, and the sun, while it may make my plumage gleam, comes through to my skull as hot as an ethereal graze. I am more comfortable directly over the river.

From her view the scene is a pretty one. In the haze over the water there is a busy sediment of insects above the dappled gleam and sugar scum of a wide, slow river. On the steep opposite bank old beech green fades upwards towards grey but at the towering clumpwork canopy breaks into bright sun patches and waxy shadows. A long stone on the river bed shows itself by its effect on the current at the surface; in another patch by a fallen branch, insect wings and twigs clog the water. The air is close and warm. The naked girl steps into the river pool; man-made, it is little more than a scraping of the river bed and a few bordering stones arranged in a curve. She uses her hands as a loose-fingered ladle, scooping up refreshing trickles of water, body crouched, face lifted, gusting the stuff towards her head and shoulders. She has goose-flesh on the upper parts of her ripe, undulating form and on her thighs (the water comes no higher than her knees). In the warm girdle about her belly nestles a pair of recently conceived twins.

We enter from her left. The swan flies some seven feet above the water, neck at full extent, wings thumping; swans are perhaps more graceful, certainly more stately, when swimming. In the air something of their considerable power comes over. But that is a personal appreciation. In this case, I, as an eagle, plane in and attack.

I tuck in my wings, tilt and drop. As we pass her I am six feet above and behind the swan and in the act of pulling back my wings and stretching out my talons. Instead of striking I merely touch the swan and for a moment there, as my claws caress that long, out-stretched neck, I have a delicious sense of power; the swan gives a warning twitch. And to be fair, he plays his part well, crashes spectacularly into the water. I rise, flap wings, turn again for another pass.

Since the show is for her we tailor our activities to her field of vision. It did occur to me, when we were out of sight, that I could not recall ever having seen an eagle attack a full-grown swan before. Swans are larger and considerably heavier than eagles and have wings powerful enough to use as weapons. Anyone who has seen a swan in a rage will know they are more intimidating and dangerous than the most vicious of geese and anyone who has seen an eagle pounce on a hare or a grouse knows what care the eagle takes to avoid injury. If an eagle killed a swan on a river it would need help from the current to bring its meal ashore. Divinity always implies an imposing degree of indifference. Though I notice, even in his guise as a swan, that he still has a cold in his right eye.

Against a screen of thick, summer leafery, we fly back and forward over the river. And of course he is right. She sees nothing incredible, nothing ominous in our performance. Instead, she sees a desperate affair between a pitiless bird of prey and a once graceful white bird striving to save its life. A round pebble whizzes startlingly close to me. Leda rebels against natural cruelty and is already scanning the border of her river pool for another stone.

It may be, of course, because I am in the know that his perform-ance strikes me as crude and overblown. At one time he spews white feathers on to the water. At another he throws back his wings in some frantic sort of backstroke. And then – one of the more sus-penseful moments – his wings beat the river like a pair of rhythmic oar strokes as he feigns fatigued, silent struggle. Will he rise? Will he take to the air? Those wing-tips dip ten times leaving diminishing circles behind him as he beats downriver; when almost clear, his feet just trailing, the eagle swoops down once more and he tackles the river bend at a prowish rush and thrash. It is time. His next rush is directly towards her, he mostly in the water, eagle behind and closing. Another pebble whizzes by and I take it as an excuse to rise in the air, turn back and prepare for another sweep.

He is shameless. He barely but most determinedly reaches her river pool and collapses on to the border of stones, still half in the water. She is brave. Rather than hold up her hand to ward me off as I come in, she strikes at me. I like to acknowledge such things and have my wing-tip feathers touch her hair. She gasps. And that is my part over. I turn up and away to settle on a treetop and look down. His neck droops, a webbed foot beats weakly but she is not quite prepared for the hefty turkey weight of the swan; still, she drags him through the shallow water to the bank and there embraces and holds up that flopping neck.

Doubtless he is enjoying himself very much, enjoying her unconscious nakedness as she tends to him, enjoying the warmth of the sun on her flesh. I watch him as he sidles his head between her breasts. Sorely tempted to nibble, that bill works, clacks briefly like wooden calipers, then stretches up to her neck as if about to nuzzle. The poor girl smiles and moves her head as at some affectionate pet.

And then it occurs to me on my treetop perch that Zeus has been so obfuscated by lust that he has forgotten how his objective might be achieved. For though a whole swan may have a grossly suggestive shape with the improvement of a most flexible neck he has forgotten particularities and practicalities, that male swans are, in terms of humanly sized genitalia, more Sapphic than Priapic, and he has also forgotten how swans mate – a treading arrangement, unsuitable here.

I cannot pretend. I shift my claws in pleasure. I love to see him stymied. But that is my part and merely discomfort at having acted the eagle and the bawd. Divine rape and mortal confusion. What is here constituted? Zoomorphic anthropophilia might be the term.

Zeus stirs. His feathers rattle down to the quills. I should like to say that Leda appreciates that she has, cradled in her arms, a creature of great strength of whom it would be unreasonable to expect human gratitude or reactions but I doubt very much that she has any inkling of what is going to happen.

My view, though a little foreshortened, is unobstructed and excellent. On his resettling a wing, two stiff feathers brush against one of her upper shins. She has beautiful pregnant skin, plump and smooth with, particularly at the shoulders and the upper slopes of her breasts, a slight sheen of sweat from the effort of lugging him in this heat.

I may be wrong; I suspect him, however, of the rapist's desire for a measure of connivance in his victim (to justify his subsequent rage) when the only complicity offered is sentimental, relief that a slaughter was avoided. She sits, legs to one side, feet still in water, with the swan half-draped across her lap. His neck no longer feigns limpness. She smiles and pats, amiable and encouraging. I think she is about to ease him into the water again and stand and watch him go but he gives her no chance. Those huge wings, creaking like masts, thrashing and tugging like sails in a white squall, burst outwards and beat. The girl sways backwards, at first startled and frightened, then as if *she* felt responsible for some unknown but untoward gesture towards a dumb creature. That is brief. The girl scrabbles backwards in an effort to get away from those flailing wings and lunging beak. The swan surges after her, making frantic use of his webbed feet, paddling on her thighs in his efforts to loosen them. That bill now pecks hard at her head and the nape of her neck; I hear the sound of bone when she holds up her forearm to ward it off. She tries to get up and for a few moments the wings slow, enough to allow her to rise. As soon as she has, the rapist rushes at her again, feet still paddling because the only way he can copulate, although swans can hardly hover, is in the air. The poor girl is driven to adopt a straddling stance; the tail ducks and wags between her legs – briefly, in the time it takes for a single spurt or an eagle to blink. He just saves himself from crashing backwards and lands heavily on one side. Then Zeus rights himself, settles his wings and waddles into the river pool. He swims across, tackles the border of stone and afterwards proceeds downriver in the stately manner of swans.

Leda is dazed. The wing buffeting has affected her hearing and balance. She puts a hand to one ear but staggers. Her thighs are spectacularly scored and scratched; his webbed feet have cut thin strips of skin from her and caused blood blisters. She stares down at her legs. It is rare but conceivable to be attacked by a swan, but I do not think she knows she has been raped. Incredulous, she looks again at the swan swimming away, just before it disappears round the bend in the river. She shakes her head. She looks about her body, is surprised by the blood and bruises, winces, examines her arms. Buffeted, battered with nips at her neck and shoulders that are already turning madder and black. She closes her eyes and uses her fingers to feel out the nape of her neck. Tears appear on her face but they are tears of pain and there is no movement of her chest and no sound beyond sharp intakes of breath.

It is a condition of divinity, however it is disguised, to engender with each and every sexual act – here, Zeus not only adgenders but also encloses both his children and Tyndareos's (Leda's husband) offspring in two eggs as two sets of twins. From which egg are you? Castor and Pollux, Clytemnestra and Helen. At the beginning the confusion as to who is divine and who not, will favour one male and one female. Then the males will be divine, the females go on as mortals, Clytemnestra to marry and murder Agamemnon, Helen to abandon Menelaus for Paris and the Trojan War. All this from a divine swan. What was to stop Zeus impersonating Tyndareos in a matrimonial tumble? Why was this avian rape necessary?

And what of Leda herself? Honest, faithful – but I cannot remember what will happen to her. Clytemnestra will be killed by her own son, Orestes. Helen I will help and she will finally join her womb brothers, the Gemini, helping sailors at sea, a reformed sort of job. But Leda. Leda gives birth to two eggs, presumably as soft as a reptile's, to allow the children to claw their way out and breathe. And then she vanishes.

Still, she surprised me. Instead of breaking down, instead of running away, she stepped into the water, walked slowly across the pool to the bordering stones, stood on them and then stepped into the river itself to wash. I should have left it at that but I noticed that downstream swam a small snake, small but bright and poisonous, one of those that swims not sideways but undulating downwards in the water. I considered it the least I could do. I flew down, caught the creature just behind the head, plucked it from the water and, with the thing writhing in my claws, flew to where Zeus lay in his post-coital nap and dropped it beside him. He opened one eye on me.

'What's this?' he said and grunted. He tossed it into the bushes. 'My dear,' he said, 'that is absurd. That was a snake. I was a swan.'

And so he slept. Ripe with divinity, devoid as a debtor of common sense.

35

'I think for privately printed reasons, David', Gardner Price did not research Gilmerton's Oxford years either with much enthusiasm or 'push'; he preferred a squeamish, skirting approach to them or, as Ms Nutall puts it, 'the discretion of exaggerated fear'. But then Gilmerton himself hardly showed more enthusiasm for his time there. Gardner Price finally plumped on the formula 'aloof but amiable' for Gilmerton at Brasenose. I am not sure what he means; not sociable but amiable when approached? Evidently he was not much approached. He had no close friends, or at least none he considered worth mentioning as such, and took little part in what Gardner Price calls 'varsity life'. Interestingly (for Ms Nutall) the biographer wrote the words 'monastic dedication' and then scored out the first, 'leaving the dedication rather bereft'. We know from a Gilmerton letter that he spent many hours 'in the Radcliffe Science library' and that, in his words, he was 'probably too serious in my studies. It is one thing to be applied, another to be such a diligent owl.'

Despite this unpromising stuff, Gardner Price received one or two anecdotes from self-described friends – so close, they thought Gilmerton had recently arrived in England from Japan and that his mother was Japanese. One of these describes Gilmerton 'most reluctantly' performing the Japanese party trick of throwing a 'white silk scarf into the air' and converting it to a 'flutter of petal-sized pieces' in a trice with a long sword 'with a slightly curved blade'. Ms Nutall likes that 'slightly curved' but otherwise calls this the 'stand-well-back letter'. And there is another anecdote, just as unlikely, possibly my favourite, that describes Gilmerton being 'inveigled into playing the game of lacrosse, quickly understanding the violence of the sport but rather misunderstanding the spirit, holding the stick as a sword, using one end as a cudgel, the other to send the ball at terrific speed to his team-mates. He looked lost but dangerous.' The same correspondent suggests Gilmerton was distressed by British standards of hygiene, could not understand 'body and suds in the same bath'. Another informant claimed Gilmerton had been a skilful tower climber and 'excelled at playing the bagpipes'. Even Gardner Price put two question marks against this.

There are two other notes that Gardner Price troubled to write down for his Oxford section. One was, 'Gilmerton treated himself as both scientist and laboratory animal, experimented on himself with a resolution that took the breath away.' And the other was the fatuous, 'He was unshockably curious.' However, Gardner Price did not think to take down any more to demonstrate either claim, though as Ms Nutall says, at this time he may have been more interested in finding items for his almost heroic protection of Agnes, preferring to save her from anything he considered might prove distressing, rather than finding out what, if anything, such phrases meant.

A couple of things. For three academic years between 1911 and 1914 it struck me as a meagre collection of stories. Of course a number of his teachers – we know Gilmerton particularly admired two, J. W. Jenkinson who taught Experimental Embryology and Geoffrey Smith who taught Zoology – as well as a number of his companions, were also killed in the war. 'Yes,' said Ms Nutall, 'but he does mention some names. For example, there is a grateful reference to Julian Huxley in a letter of 1912 for putting him in touch with Muller when T. H. Morgan's team at Columbia produced the first genetic map of the fruit fly. Muller's subject was the effect of radiation on genetic development.'

'Are you talking about that business at Darwin's anniversary celebration at Cambridge?'

'That must have been Julian who imitated the dray-horse.'

'But not Muller who talked of noodles?'

'Yes,' said Ms Nutall, looking pleased with me.

The other thing that intrigued me was that the few Oxford correspondents thought their anecdotes worth sending in at all.

'Oh, I don't know,' said Ms Nutall. 'You are forgetting how bored people get and how wistful they become when asked to contribute a memory. Besides, almost the whole of Oxford comes to us funnelled through someone who went there, printed his poems and fled.'

After the Person from Porlock part of Gilmerton's pillow book, a number of pages have been cut out. Ms Nutall has carefully counted the stubs and has found they make up precisely enough pages for two spells of ten minutes each. There are other cuts, usually at the end of a section but sometimes within, though not affecting the body of a ten minutes. It is true that no other cuts are as large or as consecutive but I see nothing special in that.

Ms Nutall, on the other hand, believes the pillow book to have been censored. We can agree that Agnes was not responsible. Indeed, both of us are sure that Agnes could not even bear to open the damson leather-covered book she had given him on his last birthday, let alone read anything he had written in it. Ms Nutall believes, and insists in her belief, that H. Gardner Price was responsible for the cuts. 'I can imagine him getting some satisfaction out of using a razor-blade and slicing the pages. He'd like the feel and the sound.' She thinks Gardner Price mistook the term 'pillow book' as 'something inguinal', had heard something of its later guise as the book of sexual postures, ostensibly provided to help innocent Japanese brides on their wedding night.

'I think Gardner Price was one of those people who go deaf by association.'

'How do you mean?'

'The words "pillow book" made him shut his ears. I saw the same effect once when Nabokov's *Lolita* came up in a conversation. The other person went pink and said, "You can't seriously be suggesting that pornography can be saved by style?" It turned out she knew only the title and the sleazy kerfuffle. Nabokov produced a marvellous book that made most of its money out of prurient people. It is a rare example of the revenge of the littérateur and the cash possibilities in irony. I pointed out to her that she feared what many of those buyers had hoped for.'

'But in neither case did they read the book.'

'Ah, but in one they scurried about the pages looking for juicy titbits. And in some cases leafed at dictionaries in case unknown vocabulary contained a stimulus or something delightfully disgusting. David, Gardner Price cut what he *thought* might be offensive or might harm Agnes. That's all. Precisely two spells of ten minutes. You don't think it is odd? And out of balance that Gilmerton should write so little about his Oxford affair?'

'Given Gilmerton's non-consecutive way of presenting his pillow book, we are talking, at most, of one of those ten-minute spells.'

Heidi Nutall beamed. 'But David, don't you see? It explains things. Gilmerton preferred women to friends.'

Ah, I am a wretched arguer and Ms Nutall is particularly good at rounding out her arguments for Gilmerton's character by appealing to mine. But we have little evidence that Gardner Price was a great deal more curious than Agnes or that he did much more than pick about all the stuff stored in the nursery. At no time does he mention the pillow book in his notes. ('Well, of course not,' said Ms Nutall.) Second, the cuts are done with a sharp-edged precision I associate with Gilmerton, not with his lax biographer. (Ms Nutall shrugged.) It seems to me far more likely that Gilmerton cut out his own notes and drafts. In other words, all he did was edit himself.

Ms Nutall considered this but shook her head and came down against 'self-censorship'.

'But I am not talking about censorship at all! He may simply have jotted things down that belonged elsewhere. The pages may have held notes and he cut them out. The cuts are in the centre of the book, bracket the threads there.'

Ah, I have a tendency to booby-trap myself when arguing, remember things that feel as if they are weakening my stance but are not obviously to the point; in this case I recalled a scene in a film by

Eric Rohmer in which a man picks up a book the woman he desires has been reading and inhales, buries his nose in the centre of the book as if it were the seam in her heavenly underwear. I closed my eyes and grunted.

'But you are not,' I said, 'suggesting that Gilmerton wrote his ten-minute sections straight off, directly? Surely he'd have fiddled, tried phrases out, ordered what he had written?'

Ms Nutall looked interested but said nothing.

'And what about the other pages that have been cut out? Some are in the middle of a ten-minute section but there is no break in that section.'

This seemed clear enough to me but Heidi Nutall shook her head again, this time pushing out her lower lip.

'No,' she said, 'I've not said there might not be a *coincidence* of cutters. In fact, I can imagine Gardner Price rather enjoying snuggling up to Gilmerton's book with a razor-blade and imitating the subject of his biography – for the subject's own good, of course. Besides, perhaps Gilmerton drew or made illustrations in his pillow book. He does have sketches in the margins.'

'Yes. But always of moths and caterpillars.'

'Mm,' said Ms Nutall.

'But does this matter?' said Isabel.

'I hope Ms Nutall doesn't want to show Gardner Price censoring away.'

'Meaning?'

'Oh, lovers' scenes coming unhinged from the frame as Gardner Price cuts them out of the pillow book, crumples them, sets fire to them, sweeps up the ashes.'

Isabel laughed. 'But what's the problem?'

'I don't understand why she insists there is evidence for an affair because there's a gap. If Gardner Price acted as a censor, why should he leave the pot part? Or for that matter, that line in the old man/ young man section, about exploring other parts of women's bodies? Ah, Gilmerton doesn't go on to explore, does he.'

'Don't you believe there was an affair?'

'I don't know. There's a possibility it was rather one-sided.'

'The broody young man?'

'It's possible.'

'Chosen *because* she was pregnant? Are you suggesting a very safe kind of worship?'

'I don't know. I once heard a misogynistic old don who graced his dislike of the smell of women with Latin. He said Edwardian young men of his background received an admirable academic education but were kept in an emotional kindergarten. Gilmerton? He doesn't give me the impression of fearing or hating women.'

Isabel nodded. 'Then an affair would be rather intriguing, surely? I can't recall ever having heard of anything similar. Mm? Ideally prophylactic. With an advantage of a set term to the affair's duration. Extraordinary. And they'd have had at least an element of social camouflage. Who could object to a young man attending his professor's pregnant young wife in a shared interest in mothing? Very good of him to attend her. There might have been the odd sadsack to accuse him of sucking up. At least professionally. On the whole, though, I'd have thought they would have been considered at most eccentric. Going mothing again? Unwise in her condition perhaps, bizarre, boring but not censurable. He could also have hidden behind a measure of broodiness. Isn't she supposed to say something about the sneaking towers of Oxford? Sounds like complicity.'

'Then what would persuade her to start an affair?'

'Oh, I'm not sure I'm the right person to ask. But let's see. She may have woken up to their being much closer in age than with her husband. Gilmerton was a very presentable young man. A gentleman. Discreet. And there may have been other matters. She may have had considerable sexual urges which she felt might not have pleased an affectionate but elderly husband. She may have felt heavy and unattractive and in need of reassurance.'

'Gilmerton as a lusty detour?'

'Oh, surely it would be more than that. They had an opportunity, within very clearly marked time limits, and they made the most of it. A private experiment, a sensual sort of science. And if I have understood right, that's what Heidi wants to bring out. A sensual bump and island, a wood at night, summer, some berries, a moth. It's the Pebble Prominent she's doing, isn't it?'

I groaned. 'I think so. My problem is that if she is suspicious of the

36

brevity of Gilmerton's treatment of his Oxford affair, I think it fits his sense of proportion.'

'But that's a sensual sense of proportion.'

'Precisely. But don't you think part of the sensuality comes from the care and discretion he takes? All he is saying is, "I fell in love, I enjoyed myself very much, here are some carefully arranged details."'

Isabel smiled and put her hand on my cheek. I kissed her inner wrist.

A while later, when I was staring at the two forms of Lobster Moth in an illustration, it occurred to me that Gilmerton had not cut the page of pencil notes on *Maldoror* and that line about a doggy curve. I sighed. Almost at once, Isabel leant over my shoulder, pushing a plump, weighty seven months against my back.

'Mm,' she said, glancing at the illustration. 'Attractive creatures.'

It did not come to me immediately – her shoes on the flagstones had already gone – but it came to me suddenly, as a flash of understanding. I raised my palm to my forehead – of course! Gilmerton's curve is not described by some dog but by a swollen belly. His curve increases. The taut skin grows tighter. Of course! The navel prominent.

I liked it. I felt as if I had solved a puzzle. I thought I appreciated it. But, for some reason, this little effort made my mind go blank. What did I have for the film?

I have nothing at all against love stories when one person is pregnant and nothing against film love. Wait a moment. The Lautréamont business will not be in the film but when we were talking about it and film aristocrats, Heidi Nutall said, 'One of the differences between novel and film is that one suggests, uses innuendo and nuance and the other gives a demonstration. In the novel *The Leopard*, the onlookers do not dare clap when the Prince dances; in Visconti's film they go at it like an opera claque.' She shrugged. 'The book is wistful enough. Burt Lancaster turns out to have been a shy, pudding-faced fellow.' Give me a part and I will act it. So why should she attempt to persuade me that her love story for Gilmerton has historical evidence, deducible from his pillow book and a gap in it?

'One of the things I am most anxious you take on in the right measure,' said Ms Nutall, 'is Gilmerton's cherishing a sense of his own ridiculousness. After all, the pillow book is proof of it. And we want to bring that out.'

'Do I understand that?'

'Of course! The idea of a ten-minute book in itself is intrinsically silly. But that was his challenge. To make it something else.'

'You mean it *is* his version of a pillow puzzle?'

'Oh, not quite. But there's something of that there. And something of a frightened bet with himself. An account of what might turn out to be the last few weeks of his life. He doesn't know the end of it,' said Ms Nutall. 'It's rather charming and very brave. He wants to leave something suitable – and faint. Now. What activity would be mean if limited to ten minutes?'

'I'm sorry.'

'Sex, David. That would be worth a minimum of twenty, surely?'

'Ah, this is your gap in the pillow book. Two sections together.'

'Summer-night air. Stimulating and insinuating.'

'Ah.' Vanished pages fluttering off to mate.

Ms Nutall picked up the pillow book as I might a dictionary. At the very end of the Porlock-and-pot section Gilmerton made a marginal note. It is 'aspergillum'. Or rather, 'Asper-Gillum'. An aspergillum is a religious artefact, used by a priest to scatter holy water at, for example, a christening. In due and natural course in 1913 the professor's wife had her child – and Gilmerton was one of the godfathers. Yes? Ms Nutall made rippling movements with the stubby fingers of one hand.

'It may be a little tasteless, of course, at least to outsiders, but then that is always the risk in private languages.'

What did old novels used to say? 'It was suddenly borne in upon me?' Yes, I *think* Ms Nutall was suggesting a private language for privates; Asper and Gillum.

I nodded. I have always been rotten at working out who is having an affair with who. 'Which is which?' I asked.

Ms Nutall laughed, complacently enough to omit a reply. Did she think I understood? By this stage I was beginning to feel, in a light-headed way, through insomnia and Ms Nutall, out of time and tune.

'Just hang on,' I said. 'Imagine that Gilmerton cut those sections himself. He rejected them, didn't want them to represent him.'

Heidi Nutall laughed out loud, as if delighted by a strain of waggishness in me. For some time afterwards she made pleased little noises. Then she paused and frowned.

'Have you ever seen moths mate?' she said. She smiled that fond smile of hers. 'It's a sticky whirr, a sporadic flutter and tug.' She smiled again and returned to the script.

There is a certain ruthlessness in directed love, particularly when someone wishes to change career. Shortly after this, Heidi Nutall arranged a meeting with the other ex-model she is using, this one to play the professor's wife. The new actress came with her husband/ manager, a tall Argentinian in a chalk-striped suit and with slicked-back hair, a complexion with the texture of pumice that may have been powdered and proud, languid hands; the ex-model was just pregnant enough to have put on maternity clothes.

'And why not?' said Isabel. 'It makes nude scenes much less hassle. No false bumps. No stand-ins.'

It seemed to me a different matter from black hair dye and saffron and mint lenses for my eyes.

'Is this what you call throwing yourself into a part or doing anything to get it? These people have planned a baby to a film schedule?'

Isabel laughed. 'Don't be so po-faced. You're not going to say you can think of better reasons for having a child? If they're living off her looks and they wanted a family, they must be delighted. It all fits. Oh God, you're not going to be one of those terrible fathers who don't allow their daughters a sex life?'

'What? No! Certainly not.'

Dasychira pudibunda is the Pale Tussock. Locally known (though I cannot recall any locality being given) as the 'hop-dog' in the larval stage. In recent years there has been an increase of melanism in the male. The Dark Tussock is *Dasychira fascelina* and in both Tussocks the female is almost twice the size of the male. The Dark Tussock does not overwinter in the cocoon but, still as a caterpillar with its four black-tipped white-haired tussocks, hibernates and resumes eating the next year on heather, hawthorn, sallow or broom. Mewlmoth the Wonderer. I am dog-tired.

'It's a boy,' said the professor's wife, 'and we're going to give him the same name.'

'Oh, that's delightful,' said Ms Nutall.

Her insincerity seemed to me breathtakingly obvious. It sparked off two things in my mind, fear and suspicion, one immediate, the other more general. The first was that this languid couple, all droop and drape, would turn, expecting an offer from me of godfatherhood. The second was slower, I provided more resistance; that, like the couple with us, Ms Nutall had all along been treating me as a character, providing me with bits of self-knowledge that I might like to consider, that she had brought aspects of fiction to the director's skill of actor management.

For reasons to do with gestation, the love scenes are the first that will be shot in *Almost a Hero*. I have taken off my clothes twice before in a film, once in the US and once in Europe. For reasons never made entirely clear to me, it is the practice in several European countries to do sex scenes first. I assume the reasons are economic (few actors, skeleton staff) because it does not make it particularly easy for actors to begin this way. Bed scenes are more or less humorous anglements of limbs and camera, sometimes with contractual bits and pieces, summed up by satin sheets that never slip off breasts or that elasticated funeral sock worn over the privates by more than one actor; if the sock shows the scene is ruined, even for the most unscrupulous of directors. In one film I refused to do some frames of doggy thrusting with my face in close-up but in general, it is simply easier not to begin by simulating sexual activity, wearing body make-up and negotiating a passion millimetrically designed around a rating principle Heidi Nutall calls 'dynamic discretion' and combine it with the type of sexual relations required, whether initiatory, hasty, elegant or a-tremble – all with a more or less self-conscious person, sometimes very nervous indeed, who you may have just met.

Doubtless Ms Nutall would disagree. She thinks it helpful 'for everybody' to establish 'an emotional gauge' directly, first thing. In this she is like Gilmerton's Mr Cameron and his clanking, orchestral watercolours for surely it is the same idea of scales; fix one element and you have a yardstick for all the others. She is extraordinarily persistent.

'Of course, what I really want from you, David, is all the ache and delight you can manage.'

I nodded. The problem of caution is that it is not an energetic state and tires relatively quickly.

Ms Nutall has told me she went to art school, in her case Gray's in Aberdeen. 'Lovely name,' as she says. And one of the reasons she has so many work tables in her studio on the Fife coast is that her first references for a film are 'pictorial', that is, she makes some fuzzy coloured sketches. 'Visual notes' she calls them. She then listens for 'an echo', jots down possible dialogue and from there works towards a script and a storyboard. In other words, those first note-drawings never appear in the film, in part because they lack focus. She has shown me how she works just once, first showing me a drawing that was mostly misty patches of colour with a pale inset; she then used a pencil to turn the inset into almost featureless actors, stand-ins for Gilmerton and the professor's wife, both naked in a shrouded sort of way, she standing, he kneeling and clasping her around that swollen midriff unmarked by any prominent navel. I have to admit, the arrangement seemed to me rather prissy and impractical, without regard for joints and bones and creaks. But Heidi Nutall immediately set to with black ink and in a few twitches and crinkles, produced recognisable representations of us both that made the pose startlingly, slightly painfully, realistic. Ms Nutall draws naked naked.

She put down her pen and pushed my chin up until the back of my head was squeezing on my top vertebra, the protruding navel just above my chin, the swollen breasts above the belly. It was only then I realized that, for all her ache and delight, she wanted a Gilmerton who saw first, touched later, the touch referring back to the sight, possibly with his eyes closed or half-closing, a constant, tight cross-reference. To a degree I was right. I never saw that drawing again and no such scene is planned for the film. And I even felt touched that she should take such trouble to convince me just how Gilmerton set up a network of sensual references and how his manners and restraint played their part. I remember thinking – the most barely of quivers.

Isabel says one of my two film sex scenes is 'as ridiculous as usual'. But she likes the other one. 'You get it just right. There's a moment when your face takes on that look of amazement and incredulity when you realise the time-scale is all wrong. You even appear to be calculating, in a depressed, surly sort of way, the exact time between your ejaculation and her orgasm.'

Gilmerton has a positive dribble of moth names in his margins. I always liked his Moister Moth. And at one time I suspected, from the Moiety Moth and the Double-goer Moth, which is not dimorphic, that he might have had some game in mind or been toying with names for his pillow sections. There is the Scintillant Moth. The Tint and Taint, difficult to find, the Swollen Conical. The Spring Moth which has nothing to do with the season but to a resort when under threat. The Plush Moth. All (I think) imaginary creatures, some with small sketches of the adults and others, my favourites, of extraordinary caterpillars, the Stir and Star, for example, which, ignoring the fourteen legs and the twig supplied, has something of the sea horse in it; or the Water Rug, which appears to be moss in a ragged crack.

37

In bed or at script table I am plagued by parodies of rules of three. There is no apparent stimulus. The things float up, ready-made, rather heavy. An example? Lobster is to ten as Shakespeare is to the iambic pentameter. I find them exasperating. But my mind simply furnishes another one. The next linked the number of lines in a Shakespearean sonnet and the number of legs on a caterpillar – both fourteen. So what? It was just coincidence then that Ms Nutall told me she thought Sanderson 'something of a Shakespearean touch'.

My bags were in the car. I had an evening flight to the US. I squinted at her.

'But how?'

'Oh. Appearing, then disappearing. Like the fool in *Timon of Athens*.'

'Or the one in *Lear*.'

'Yes. Sanderson just drops out of the pillow book. Or is dropped.'

'Is that significant? You're going to handle that?'

'Mm. I think so, David. We can see him doing his best to write his five-year-old's scrawl to Gwendolyn. Later, Gilmerton can ask Aubrey what's wrong. Has Gwen turned Sanderson down, broken off the engagement? No, says Aubrey, it's the reverse. Her reply was appallingly bright, nothing-has-happened stuff.'

I nodded. 'How do you see Sanderson?'

'Quite slight. Blond. More crushed hope than presence. There is not much Gilmerton can actually do. But it might encourage him to remember the professor's wife. And at Lampenham, Earnshaw can take over from there.'

I was not at all sure what she was talking about. But Ms Nutall smiled and nodded. I have sometimes suspected that she explores in order to explore and that her explorations take on violently lush forms before they settle, fairly well restrained, usually somewhere else in the script. There is also her related habit of looping on something unrelated to the matter in hand in one of her almost entirely one-sided chats. Here, I admit, I was still mulling over the number of actors in an Elizabethan company when I understood she had moved on to talk about the word 'sting' when applied to a woman's breast.

'I think it is there because "nipple" is not a moving word. "Nib"? "Nub"? There may be something of "dimpling" but it is too near "nibble" and too far away from "suckle". The word "sting" is surely a word for arousal, not for food. And I think it has heat in it, doesn't it? A bee sting does not chill. It may be the effect, of course. A breast pricking, even from cold, stings the sight. What do you think?'

'You want a discourse on the nipple?'

'Some help only. From an adult male point of view.'

'Ah. In a warm room an erect nipple encourages, sometimes flatters. It may not be as warm as you think.'

Ms Nutall laughed out loud. Our relationship has come on, but rather more generously on her side. 'Double vision,' says Isabel, 'with some gelatine'; she says she has seen Ms Nutall complacently watch an image of me walk away from where I am and claims that when she picked up the telephone a few days ago, a very quiet voice asked if Robert were there. No, replied Isabel, but David was. There was a pause. 'Then I think I'll wait for Robert,' said Ms Nutall. I know what Isabel means. My director has recently begun to touch me, usually with the tips of her fingers, not a tap exactly, but a press followed by a small pull towards her, a flattish tugging, usually on my arms or the backs of my hands where there is skin to move. She does not kiss but she bumps cheeks. Here she pressed soft-water skin against mine, rocked back in her chair and, in a moment, had looped back to Shakespearean rules of three.

'Don't you feel there is a wry element in the pillow book, very British and self-conscious, that Gilmerton is to caterpillar as Shakespeare is to the imago?'

I was too tired and nervous to be whimsical. Was what she had said much different from saying Lewis Carroll's doublet rhymed with couplet? And I don't care about Sanderson.

It's Gilmerton I fear losing, of having him disappear into belated motives and dried-out appetites; there is a muesli that my elder daughter likes which has slices of desiccated banana amongst nuts and raisins and oatmeal. I have tried this stuff; with milk the bits of banana become slimy and horribly sweet.

'Did Shakespeare write anything on Leda and the swan?'

'What?'

'That's the weakest ten minutes in the pillow book, surely? I know I haven't met Aphrodite as the narrator before but the novelty of that doesn't save it. It doesn't work. It's somehow arch and truistic at the same time. A degree of realism in a mythical rape proves what exactly?'

Ms Nutall cocked her head at me. 'Go on, David.'

'Uhm . . . it's the nearest Gilmerton comes to leaking. It makes me think pessimism might be all of self-pity. And, however ruefully he has done it, why has he introduced a chunk of adapted myth when he has already made his point with more irony and grace elsewhere? It's just not sly enough.'

Heidi Nutall raised her eyebrows and nodded. She sighed.

'People vary, of course,' she said absently.

I winced. Does an actor's desire to believe involve as much self-preservation as a desire to do justice? The Leda story may be a mistake but had I been unjust? Oh, had I attacked the character I was to play because I was miserable with anxiety? I was tired, too tired to think clearly.

I am not at all sure about levels of the conscious and subconscious and I can't say why, but when I let myself droop, a misty image from the Leda story, head and neck, turned itself into that old French gesture, fingers to plosive lips, a juicy kiss of anticipation to sell any dish from an omelette on – but here sardonically done. But from there I was reminded of an egg given to me by Nanny Grizel, hard boiled though I carried it as if it were raw and was most reluctant to throw it high into the air like my school companions with theirs.

'Why?'

'Didn't you have a teacher who threw eggs up in the air to demonstrate something on types of strength and who'd say, "Ooh. I think that one must have had a weak part," when the yolk dribbled out on to the grass?'

'Oh yes. A Miss Carmichael. I think there was a moral point to go with the natural science one. Whatever it was I missed it. And there was something about a shelly sort of osteoporosis to go with the form of an egg and Galileo and Newton. Miss Carmichael was a believer in the wholesomeness of the eggs of her youth. And for a time I had the notion that eggshells were an unreliable kind of weave, like kapok and plaster. There was a girl who asked why birds bothered with nests.'

'Yes, we had a boy like that too. Though I think most of them were more bomb orientated. Hard-boiled eggs were flying up everywhere against a patchy blue sky. I clung on to mine. It wasn't that I liked hard-boiled eggs. I found them palate clogging and I could never quite manage to get all the shell off. I hated the sound and feel when my teeth crunched on a bit of shell. It was worse than chalk squeaking or a knife on a plate. Instead of a coming sneeze there was a coming shudder. So that day I didn't break the egg. It had a nice pale, oaty colour but it was the feel of the eggshell, the smooth texture warming in my fingers, that made me want to bring it to my lips. I didn't dare do it, though. I was conscious, despite the egg having passed through boiling water, that I should "think where it has been".'

'Oh, David,' said Ms Nutall, 'that's lovely.' She gave me an ample smile, took hold of my left wrist and squeezed. It was not just a squeeze of companionship; there was, though I had stopped, an instruction to pause there as well.

Actors are accustomed to being examined, to having their features quizzed, but I still find it uncomfortable when someone, holding down your wrist, tilts her head and concentrates on your eyes. It made me remember a reply I once gave in the US which I regretted almost instantly. Isabel does not see why, Grizel found it funny. But it has stayed with me as a regret.

'I had a very correct Presbyterian nanny. I think I got from her that if I was going to lie I should dress up and be paid for it.'

I do not know how many people regard themselves as trustworthy. I don't, certainly not when trying to please in a profession that tries so hard to do so. What does the expression 'egged on' come from? Probably from edge. Edging myself into a version of Gilmerton. Grizel and Heidi Nutall share a gesture when considering someone: a slow, distracted, pinching movement of the skin at the base of the throat between thumb and index finger. Grizel was more self-conscious; when she realised what she was doing, she would turn it into plucking fluff from whatever woolly thing she was wearing.

When I arrived at my hotel in New York I was given a security bag marked 'Extremely urgent'. It contained a fax from Heidi Nutall and a 'How about this?'

INT. LAMPENHAM — GILMERTON'S ROOM — DAY

AUBREY

How much have you explored?

GILMERTON

Just the bookshelves.

AUBREY

Nothing else?

He begins opening cabinet doors and drawers.

I say!

GILMERTON

What?

Aubrey shows Gilmerton a drawer of marble eggs, takes one out, then another. Gilmerton sees something, removes a peeling blue darning egg.

> AUBREY

Architecture and darning. Perhaps you should hand it in to the seamstress/ the sock corner/ for the war effort.

Gilmerton smiles and shakes his head. He puts the blue darning egg in his side pocket. He puts the marble eggs back and closes the drawer.

Are you saying that is the exploration over for now? We'll ration surprise?

> GILMERTON

Mm.

INT. LAMPENHAM — GILMERTON'S ROOM — NIGHT

Gilmerton sits by the window, the blue darning egg on the palm of his left hand. He closes his fingers round it, shuts his eyes, raises his face.

EXT. RIVER — DAY

Professor's Wife bathes naked. Camera pans to swan on river.

INT. LAMPENHAM — GILMERTON'S ROOM — NIGHT

Gilmerton lifts fist and darning egg and presses them to his lips. He opens his eyes and his palm, looks at the darning egg, closes his fingers and eyes again.

I spent a restless American night, feeling jet lagged and guilty, as if I had shamefully let Gilmerton down and misled Ms Nutall. Shame seeped into my dozing. A swan landed on Lampenham lawn and crutches and khaki legs hastened away. A woman's breast leaked not milk but yellow yolk. I also heard the name Thinka, Thinka and it took me an hour to trace it to Eric Rohmer's scrupulous and beautiful version of von Kleist's *Die Marquise von O . . .* Thinka is the name of a swan Bruno Ganz's character remembers from childhood and Thinka becomes confused in his delirium – he is another wounded soldier – with the Marquise. My teeth began to ache and at about 5.30 I got up and drafted a fax reply: 'Don't you think it would be better for the professor's wife to be washing inside at a washstand? A movement of a swan on the river outside catches her eye. Is this your sting? I think she'd probably cup her breasts almost before she knows it is a swan. If Gilmerton then pressed fingers and darning egg to his lips, that would be enough, surely? We don't need a view of her window from the swan's position. She'd look at the swan, go back to washing. As to the three possibilities for Aubrey I'd take sock corner – but would prefer a fourth.'

I regretted that fax almost as soon as it went off. I think it may be the only suggestion I have written down for Ms Nutall. That evening an ample, exclamatory OK! was waiting for me. I am an actor. I can produce goose-pimples on my face, in the hollow of my cheeks.

38

'A man falls asleep in church. He dreams that he is an aristocrat during the French Revolution – and that he is about to be guillotined. The crowd bays as he is pushed up the steps. He is manhandled on to the machine, his legs are strapped, the wooden yoke is fixed around his neck. The crowd falls silent as a drum rolls – and stops. The man hears the metal blade begin its downward run with the sound of a sledge on snow. A frightened snore escapes him. In church, his embarrassed wife, smiling about her apologetically, taps the back of his neck at the moment the guillotine would have sliced into it. Instantly the man's heart stops. He slumps from the pew quite dead – an expression of unspeakable terror on his face.

'Now, gentlemen – what is wrong with that story? Yes. You, Weir.'

'I should like to know if there was any blood sir, because—'

'Don't be silly, boy. Well? Anybody? What, do none of you know? Ah, how remarkable! Privy to other people's dreams. You must all try to make use of this marvellous ability more often. You know what someone else is dreaming.'

Did I look asleep during the sermon? I wasn't snoring. Was someone else? Or was this an obscure prelude to something? Or a warning? It is better to kick a church snorer than to touch his neck. Might any jolt be fatal? Or was this something to do with respect for the dreams of others? Or a dramatisation of the subconscious dangers of aristocratic pretensions and time travel? Worse, how can anyone avoid nightmares and the consequent risk of dying by whatever form of execution? Or was this some twist on the mote and the beam, of God not minding a snorer because it was dangerous to wake him? Unlikely. More probable would be looking exclusively after one's own talents and minding one's faith as the height of responsibility. It did not matter. The teacher was content to look replete and shake his head at our stupidity.

That is not my memory but for the life of me I cannot remember whose it is. I can see the schoolmaster, a man of fifty with a high-bridged nose and sparse but rather long hair carefully arranged over his scalp; with a neck more intriguing than the face, a mix of wrinkles, wattles and engrained geometry. I can even make out a most intriguing couple of small patches in the skin, areas left over from the muscles underneath, one low on the right side of his neck, the other higher on the left, that resemble tiny collapsed soufflés. He was never a teacher of mine. Mathematics, certainly. But I can recall no film or book either. One of memory's actors, perhaps. But why do I feel some correspondence between that school guillotine and Gilmerton's dislike of the line in *Maldoror*? Strictures on fatuity and complacence? I am beginning to feel some alarm at the quality of my thought. Rather than getting into his head I appear to be caught in mine.

One of my earliest film parts was in a clotted thriller (hand-held camera, stumbling focus, the protagonist's fears swimming into frame). I played a once-famous child actor grown into a vengeful drama teacher, so inverted he could, without knowing or caring, break down an insecure personality. 'Be elongated,' said the playwright-director, 'and imagine you are going to batter him with balloons until he is deaf.'

'Now what does an actor believe in?' was my first line. 'Mm? Being other characters? I think we can take out character. Being other will do for just now. So let us first learn to do justice to things. You be a pen with too much ink. The pathetic person handling you wishes to be taken for an intellectual. But remember, you are not that person. You are the pen, neither pleased nor displeased to leak ink on those manicured hands.'

'I don't understand,' says the victim, 'I'm sorry.'

'Pens can be sorry objects, dear, but do not apologise.'

'What?'

'There are three rules for an actor. Be ridiculous, be precise, be free.' (Laughter and sycophantic applause.) 'Now let's all have our senses tingling, shall we? Uhm, try being a chair, dear. A comfortable one if not elegant.'

There was a fair bit of camp balloon-work but the drama teacher ended by draping an arm round the protagonist's shrinking shoulder.

'Come, Sidney! You are a condemned man mounting the steps of the scaffold. You look around you. Is the scaffold made up of your correlatives to the situation you are in? Will they hold the structure up? My dear boy, they do not matter. Why? Because you have never been condemned to death before. The real question is – *how* will you die? "Oh look, there is a crowd." Then it is a double performance. Last words, last words – that's all you have left. Your legs tremble. But now, *what* do you say? "Well, thank you for this quick death. I'm not sure I quite deserve it"? "I'll meet the faithful later"? Mm? "I don't *understand*"? In a minute you'll be dead, man. Now. Give me that moment, just before you speak, just before the words – that the author has already written – come back to you! *Feel* the fear! Enclose it, do *not* let it escape!'

There is a touch of accuracy in that fruity madman and his balloons. Actors are, however restrained, dealers in emotion. I think Ms Nutall might say I fail to distinguish between sentiment and emotion. I am not sure I can. In a film, it is not even entirely up to me. Take music. In film terms, music and emotion are close to being synonymous. The perception of emotion in a film face is more than channelled by music – it is supplied by music. A face without a chord is, in effect, blank. I have seen an actor criticised for over-acting when it was the music that was clumsy and overblown. For *Almost a Hero* I have heard early tinklings and inklings by James Soutar, a thirty-year-old with an enormous, pale bald head and a fringe of very long, fine, Flemish red hair laid over his shoulders; when we went to visit him at his home near Aberdeen, some archaeology students were picking up a dead deer. Apparently they bury dead animals to learn about 'decomposition in different soils'. James Soutar said his wife was distraught – the deer had been visiting them for a couple of years to lick salt. He had got out Marvell's poem on a fawn and would think about it. Otherwise he was enjoying his commission to do an opera on Thomas Reid, founder of the 'common sense' school of Scottish philosophy. For us he was working on four notes, 'close to rhythm and pulse' in Heidi Nutall's phrase – I thought of an athlete's pulse in repose, and it sounded tun, tun, tatun to me – and a number of what they both called 'voices'; Agnes reminded me of an oboe, Gardner Price tilted more to a bassoon. 'And this is yours,' said James Soutar, mousing away. Gilmerton is a flexible, hoarse, flautish hush.

It was an intriguing, slightly goose-pimpled visit. Actors do not usually get to hear beforehand the music that will be put to them. Nor to hear their director talk to the composer.

'Mm,' said Ms Nutall. 'I'm not sure you're quite there, James. Very nearly. But I am missing something. You see, he was schooled not to be possessive. There is the obvious point that he is a rich young man and that therefore to show attachment to possessions would be ignoble. I suppose possibly even insulting to the poor. But it goes much further than that. Gilmerton would have considered it frightfully bad form to allow his emotions to affect his treatment of other people and he would never, ever, have made an emotional claim on someone.'

James Soutar sucked on his teeth. 'You want another pluck on emotion?'

'A little more uncertainty or tension,' said Ms Nutall.

'Are you sure?' I said. 'Surely his possessiveness went into his studies. And aren't you turning any emotional claim into a splendid memory of emotional and sexual service?'

'I couldn't have put it better myself,' said Heidi Nutall.

I winced. Their problem was solved to their satisfaction by the introduction of something not half a hiccup long. Mine is a dislike of too much description. Any actor works on a different type of replacement, not description, however acute, but on what comes down to a mix of ripple and twitch in voice and face. Film rush; brief brain belief flooding through tone and expression. Urgent effect. Too much description makes me choke. Nobody employs an actor to describe. Ah, I am sweating a little. A slight panic attack. Breathe in. What is it she says? How do I play a rich young man, hanging about in a convalescent home waiting to get better enough to go off and be killed, who keeps a Lobster Moth caterpillar in a (scrubbed) tobacco tin, who has eyes based on yellow, who sleeps little and who has exceptionally practised night vision? In the car, driving back, Ms Nutall smiled most amiably.

'The point I want to consult you about is this. Here was Gilmerton affable to almost everyone but, shall we say – rather prickly to those of his own circle? Men only, of course. I suppose you know that before the First War, the Germans revived duelling in universities and a duelling scar was thought of as an attractive badge or status symbol. The British went in for the heavy put-down. There was a man called F. E. Smith who was much admired for his ability in this way. His talent has dated very badly. Read what Smith said to a slow judge at the *Lusitania* inquiry and he sounds overbearing, as nasty as a drunk. He was also lying. Of course, Gilmerton was not like that, but some of his comments and replies have a certain snap to them. I mean, to describe Oxford University as "ridiculous and lazy" shows a certain confidence – even if the remark was justified. The point is that a number of correspondents sent anecdotes to Gardner Price on the lines of how verbally clever and quick Gilmerton was. And I want to know how you would feel about them, whether or not it would be a good idea to include one or two and also whether or not you think the language is even possible now.'

It was drizzling and I was keeping my eyes on the road. 'Give me an example.'

'All right. Classics don on hearing of Gilmerton's field of study: "I fail to see how anyone could be fascinated by infinitesimal variations in small flies." Gilmerton: "That merely shows your perceptions to be stunted and your arrangement of them infinitely complacent."'

I think this is the nearest I have come to disliking Ms Nutall. I once saw, almost certainly in a documentary, a basic operation in which a whitish maggot was extracted from the sole of a foot using a pin or needle; the maggot was in a sac and twisted and writhed as the pin poked and pricked and teased.

Ms Nutall cocked her head at me. 'I suppose it is a kind of verbal glove smacking, "words at two paces".'

Or a camera even closer. Camera, chimera and the final cut. A character is look, manner, walk. Gilmerton is a head-down person who raises his eyes to answer or look. Public aplomb, private pleasure. Publicly private, privately supple. Would that make sleep too pleasurable to indulge in more than briefly? Perhaps not. He seems to me more restrained than puritanical. And his walk? An athletic stride would be quite wrong. But he is not flat-footed. When writing in his pillow book I could add a little of a smooth, slow march. Unhurried movements, perhaps even a little dreamy self-observation. He'd behave very much in the same way when thinking. Sensual, a touch pernickety, he'll blow away specks, brush the paper of his book with his penultimate finger, before beginning to write.

39

Earnshaw is a most embarrassing convalescent. It was our side mowed him down. They did it thoroughly. And he should not be here, should never have been classified as a convalescent. His scars are as spectacular and as intricate as an overworked tattoo. Aubrey, who takes enormous interest in such things, says he has never seen such a variety of bullet marks on someone's skin. Earnshaw has, for example, a groove across his chest, at no point more than half a bullet deep, which demonstrates quite conclusively the calibre of ammunition used on him; it shoots from left to right, diminishing as it goes, so that by the time it reaches a little above the right nipple it is barely more than a slightly indented burn mark. Aubrey reckons you could run a small marble along the track with little risk of it falling out. Earnshaw's legs are entirely spotted, an effect increased by the quantities of hair he has on him.

In his Bath chair, those legs covered by a pale blue blanket, with his thinning, dry, wiry hair, his thick-lensed spectacles, his greyish skin and blue-black chin – shaved inexpertly by a nurse every morning, so that his face is often mottled with sticking plaster – he has the tilt of a moribund heart patient. He finds it difficult to sit up because, Aubrey says, his midriff looks as if it had been stitched together by Dr Frankenstein. Earnshaw, however, is twenty-two, something much clearer in his tone of voice. Aubrey says he sounds like a plaintive crowlet or whatever an infant crow is called but there is nothing complaining or raucous in his words. The effect

Aubrey has noticed is due to Earnshaw's pressing or pursing so hard on his lips that they whiten; when he makes ready to speak, blood comes into his lips and he makes a sticky, clocking noise as he sucks air into a dry throat, then exhales words that are as much breath as an expelled drone.

Those able take turns sitting with him. The turns have become very brief. If he gives his attention, tries to join in a conversation, his breathing becomes alarmingly sought for, as if his windpipe were disconnected.

'That is odd, surely,' said Aubrey. 'It's as if you had to ration your blood supply.'

Earnshaw tapped his forehead. 'Blood where needed.'

'What do you mean?'

We looked at Aubrey and he flushed.

'Oh right,' he said. 'Yes, of course you're right. What am I thinking of? Of course, blood . . . varies. Yes, it's a question of circulation and oxygen, isn't it? This is a silly question I'm going to ask, personal, too. Now that I am one leg short, do I have the same quantity of blood as before? Do you see what I am driving at? Do I have a pint less? Or . . .'

'Asthma young,' said Earnshaw.

'Has asthma got something to do with blood supply?' said Aubrey.

'Doctor . . . asthma . . . injuries.'

'Yes? What do you think?'

'Doesn't feel same.' To show he has not finished speaking, Earnshaw has taken to holding up a finger like an English cricket umpire when declaring someone out. 'Feels . . . pump . . . uproot . . . heart . . . faint.'

Earnshaw arrived a few days after me at Lampenham and in the bare fortnight he was there, it was clear, even to unmedical eyes and ears, that far from convalescing he was deteriorating. His skin took on a white-ash dullness and his breathing the tones of someone suffering a nightmare. It was necessary to learn his extreme telegraphic form of conversation.

'Your room – library?'

'Yes.'

He pointed at himself. 'Billiards.'

'Yes.'

He waggled his head. 'Table,' he sighed. 'Books?'

'Oh yes. It's not a wonderful selection but I can look for you. Have you anything particular in mind?'

Earnshaw nodded and got his breath. 'Classics?'

'There might be a translation or two.'

'Would you?'

All I could find was Pope's translation of *The Iliad* in three volumes.

'Splendid,' said Earnshaw.

'Do you know this version?'

Earnshaw's nods and shakes are minimal. 'Only Greek.'

'I think I read this as a boy.'

He tapped air as if it were my forearm. 'Would you?'

'Of course. Have you a favourite passage?'

'*Odyssey*,' said Earnshaw. 'Not grand. Not tragic. But . . .'

'You prefer it.'

'Just begin. But . . .'

'What?'

'Slowly.'

I nodded and began reading a brisk, elegant eighteenth-century version of the quarrel that caused the Trojan War. I was pleasantly surprised; the verse had far more vigour and bite than I remembered. I looked up. Earnshaw was mouthing the ancient Greek. He was near tears. I stopped. He raised his face. On the right of his slightly lanterned jaw the beard was broken by an almond-sized area of white skin. I was aware suddenly of his thumb feeling about his chin to cover it. He looked down his cheek at me.

'Fell . . . tree . . . York . . . seven . . . eight.'

'I have one on my knee. A small circle.'

Earnshaw nodded. 'Yes.' And essayed a smile. He started to stroke the hairs on the backs of his hands. I put two of the volumes on the side table, gave him the first volume and he patted that.

*

Aubrey was waiting for me. 'How's Earnshaw?' he said.

'Poorly.'

'Yes. I say. Do you think people know when they are going to die?'

'Some. Obviously.'

'Ah. You see, I am not sure it is so obvious.'

'Aubrey.'

'What I am driving at is this. I have had the distinct impression this last day or so that Earnshaw is almost in mourning for himself. At least, one part of him is. The other part plods on dutifully.'

'He should be in hospital.'

'Well, that's the other thing. You don't think it's deliberate, do you?'

'What?'

'Putting him here.'

'I don't follow you.'

'Haven't you seen McKinnon? He looks grim with satisfaction. I say.'

'What?'

'You don't think Earnshaw's here to rid convalescence of complacency, do you? Stir us up a bit?'

'No. I doubt if that's the policy, Aubrey.'

'But why don't they do something?'

'Mm.'

Aubrey leant a little closer. 'Yesterday Cummin's father came to see him. I almost hit him with my crutch.'

'Why did you want to do that?'

'I think for being plump and middle-aged. And for shooing us on.'

'Yes.'

'I don't mind things being intriguing or lively but this ghastly Earnshaw business is upsetting.'

'Why don't you give me a game of badminton? I have been neglecting that bit of my exercise schedule.'

'Oh. All right, I suppose. What's Earnshaw reading?'

'Pope's translation of *The Iliad*.'

'Ah. They say he won a prize for translating some of Sappho's poems.'

'Really?'

'Oh yes, apparently he is something of a brainbox.'

Earnshaw died at about 1.20 this afternoon in the dining-room. McKinnon insists on calling the place 'mess'. It is, allowing for adaptations in the seating arrangements for those convalescents in wheelchairs or those unable to sit on a bench, like eating in college. McKinnon always pays us a visit, makes a tour of the long table, consulting various pieces of paper to make sure that his dietary instructions have been carried out. He does this with the head nurse and the cook, an irritable and irritating display, though it is not always the staff who are blamed. Today, what McKinnon described as 'broth' but what looked to me like beef tea, was on Earnshaw's prescribed menu. He had waved it away. He was sitting on the other side of the table in his wheelchair, four places to my right, with his eyes shut.

'No broth?' said McKinnon.

'No,' said Earnshaw. He did not open his eyes and McKinnon began blinking.

'I cannot be responsible for your well-being, lieutenant, if you refuse the nutrition stipulated!'

A maid was summoned and beef tea ladled out on to Earnshaw's plate. Earnshaw opened his eyes a little or, rather, rolled them and let the lids droop again.

'Well, lieutenant?' said McKinnon.

Earnshaw sounded almost judicious. 'Cannot . . . breathe,' he said.

There was a pause in voices and spoons.

'How wretchedly pompous,' said Aubrey.

McKinnon turned his head sharply. I think Earnshaw tried to make a calm-down gesture but then his eyes started open. In an effort to clap his hand over his mouth he pulled one side of his spectacles away from his face. Blood began to come up through his nose and mouth. He lurched forward and sideways and the hand he had brought up ploughed through his table setting. The noise, the clatter of crockery and glass and his liquid-filled death rattle, a mix of cough and vomit, was stunning; I had the impression those sounds crept, as if hiding, under the skin of my hands.

McKinnon pulled Earnshaw's head back, the senior nurse ran, orderlies hurried him out of the dining-room. I heard some time later that they tried a tracheotomy even though he was clearly already endlessly dead at the table. I saw a maid shrinking when she was told to clear up. Earnshaw had spilt his beef tea and it was mingled with a whitish bile and strikingly different-looking blood, in parts a vivid red that looked honeycombed with gelatinous bubbles, and some much darker stuff, crimson and black, barely liquid. Someone dropped a napkin over the worst of the mess and those nearest began collecting pieces of glass and china. Then the girl, with a bob of gratitude and a grimace, stepped forward, crunched china underfoot; she began instantly on tears. She made no sound but the tears jumped from her eyes on to her plump slightly downy cheeks. Abruptly, she was given a ringing slap by much older womanly valour.

I don't know. The wildest creature I ever heard was a diminutive stoat; it emitted an appalling concentrate of sound, a shrick cut by a snarl. 'Stop that!' rang through the dining-room and a moment after-wards I saw Aubrey giving me an approving wink. How sickening.

The early afternoon hush has been thicker than normal. I usually nap, of course, but today I was sent riding. Whether I like it or not – I do not – I had been put in the role of Don Quixote on Sancho Panza's mount. I am a reluctant rider but at least, while the animal had no intention whatsoever of taking instructions from me, it never went faster than a precipitate amble and I was able to use my feet on the ground to counteract the roll. Luckily the creature stopped at the copse and allowed me to dismount there. I sat while the diminutive stallion grazed amongst the buttercups by the pond. And I found myself remembering, of all things, ears, remembered during a Zoology exam in Edinburgh when I finished a little ahead of schedule and looked up to see in front of me a collection of ringing red ears in the hall, with considerable variations, from a glaucous, congested violet to a pale, downy pink and one ear in particular, the upper part a pinched white, then a number of purple-crimson capillaries and an ear lobe like a blood-filled sac, fat as a gorged leech. I could not think what this memory had to do with Earnshaw – unless I was half-remembering the faces in the dining-room, one or two flushed but most pale with patches – and Aubrey, of course, patchless with rage.

40

Ms Nutall has made so many changes, treated the script as if she were rerouting liquid, that she has left me with script hangover. I have the dregs of countless lines, variations and quick differences, a sticky tongue and a head that feels shrunken and dry. I have imagined liver salts, the fizz bubbling up in a tumbler of water. Yes. One of my problems has been Sanderson, or rather the startling ease with which Ms Nutall has changed him. Having commented that in the pillow book he is given an unattributed Shakespearian drop, she looked up and suggested suicide might be better. She flicked at the pillow book. Sanderson is mentioned for the last time when the makeshift players come to Lampenham. What did I think of an image of Sanderson hanged from a tree in the grounds? Some morning mist, she suggested, Gilmerton peering out at the day.

My references are filmic. 'Not bad for a man with only one arm.'

Heidi Nutall laughed but said it was quite possible and added some one-handed tie-tying gestures.

'But wouldn't he need a chair?' I said.

Ms Nutall sighed. She dislikes clutter. A week later, however, she had decided he should, like Ophelia, fail to swim and suggested an image of Sanderson drowned in Gilmerton's pond – 'just the puttees unwinding in the reeds'.

Now it is true that films, like heroes, have characters who do too much rather than many characters each contributing a little something. But I could not understand how Sanderson's suicide would help the film. Ms Nutall said it would make a good scene – and lead to another, when the other convalescents as one entirely ceased to mention him. I still did not understand, began to wonder if Ms Nutall were trading off, getting me to baulk at Sanderson and accept the love interest. But, to be honest, I also began to find it peculiar that Gilmerton should drop him and do it so thoroughly. Bored with him? A falling out? Or had he left, been declared fit and gone back to Gwen?

'No,' said Heidi Nutall, 'Gwen's letter did for him. Depressed by the upbeat. Killed by callow cheerfulness.'

'He can't just tag along till the end?'

'Mm,' said Ms Nutall. She began to lay unsharpened hexagonal pencils on her table in the shape of a sparse eyebrow. 'You think it's too much?'

I shrugged. Then, to my surprise, she got out and spun a coin. It came down tails.

'Perhaps,' said Ms Nutall.

I have sometimes had the impression that Heidi Nutall is pushing my faith in her to the limit, that she enjoys prodding at my capacity to believe, in her, her arrangements, the film.

'David,' she said, 'I am really most anxious not to kill the already dead. Does that make sense to you?'

Good faith. And I think it probably does. I have difficulty, for example, in retaining my father. He has been doubly buried, the second time by other versions of him, a collection of fathers, most of them clumsy, pious and, worse than inaccurate, unbelievable. The discomfort caused by death becomes someone else's self-affirmation, part of their often dreary fantasies and fears. My Aunt Susan, for example, behaved as if she had been involved in a version of *The Master of Ballantrae*, Robert Louis Stevenson's rather tedious story of two brothers and one woman. The woman in question is frequently and accurately given as an example of how, at that stage, Stevenson had not yet learnt to portray a convincing woman character. That kind of thing never stops a Susan. It may even encourage her, give her material to think about and work on.

Some families appear made in moulds. My father and his younger

brother Archie were physically extraordinarily alike – and Archie
too is a WS, though with a taste for chalk-stripe suits. There were
only the two of them but only eleven months between them. Archie
married a now champagne-blonde lady, my Aunt Susan, and had
two daughters, respectively five and three years older than me, one
plump, Marion, and one slim, Linnet. In shape Susan has moved
from Linnet to Marion. Marion is a nurse in Fiji, Linnet had blighted
hopes as a singer and now has a franchised perfume shop. Marion
has never married, Linnet has a stable relationship with an actuary
called Eric Keir and two small boys, Hugh and Hamish. At Christmas
they send 'to all our friends' a printout as narrow as a supermarket
checklist of 'this year's doings'. Hugh is 'into Judo' and Hamish is
'the sensitive one', at present caught between pursuing 'his music
or his undoubted talent for colour'. Susan describes Marion as a
'genuine carer' while Linnet 'enhances the quality of other women's
lives'. She has a tremendously sweet tooth, is the only person I have
met who adds sugar to bought shortbread, though not, I think, as
my mother claims, in a crude attempt at pretending she was responsible for baking the stuff. Susan used to give many dinner parties.
I remember, a long time ago, being used as a guinea pig for some
of her sauces; one was made of leeks, pistachio and cream, with
curls of raspberry. Now she discovers restaurants for her opera
parties and will wear what Isabel calls 'aggressive' tartan evening
dresses. After my father's death she insisted we meet so that she
could explain some things, but first she had Archie talk to me of
childhood brotherly memories – after the legal bits and pieces.

There is a certain insidious reassurance when family memories
come up. I have heard so many versions of a fight between two
brothers aged ten and ten, that some years and versions ago I asked
myself why I should be expected to care. Now I tend to think that
this is some perversion of passing matters on, a sentimental bob at
the past and lives running out. The story is about a Stone Age axe
applied by the younger brother to the elder brother's head. Any
biblical tones are quite incidental and there is nothing grand or
mythical about the story. It took place in a byre or barn with the
summer hay just in and it is that detail, possibly the only constant

257

amongst bits of basic physics, the jump of the ambusher, the swinging arm, a more-or-less glancing blow, that has stayed. And for some reason I see the weapon as a perfectly smooth lump of stone. There was an element of apology in the story that was dificult to identify. That a father and uncle should ever have behaved like that. Or that they had not always been so civilised. Or were they telling me they appreciated the wildness in childhood? Or warning me of the inherent thinness of civilisation? Probably all of these and possibly, not as an excuse or a cause, but as a contrast to their polite indifference to each other; 'I have never seen,' my mother once said in one of her grander moods, 'an indifference so utter.'

Susan, on the other hand, found something titillating in my father's death, a sharpening of sexual memory, almost a detour round tears; though what might have been, however fantastic and private her notion of herself as a girl fought over by two brothers, finally broke down into a snuffle. 'I'm just a silly old woman. My hair is like candyfloss. My eye make-up has run.' Under the circumstances three fine lines. Even the second. Her hair has thinned with all that ammonia and champagne dye so she employs furious backcombing and fluffing out, followed by immense quantities of lacquer. In certain lights, her hair looks covered with drops of gossamer, except that the dew has an oily spectrum. I embraced her, patted her plump back. 'It's all rubbish,' said my mother. 'The weddings were years apart. Susan was pregnant with her second child before I even met her. In any case, I *know* your father never even looked at another woman in all our married life.'

Whether due to age or to carrying small children, I notice that I have an increasing tendency, whenever someone is distressed, to cup my hand. With a baby, my left hand holds the head to my chest, the right cups the cranium. With Susan, of course, my right hand stopped as soon as it felt the rasp of dried lacquer. Heartbeat and cradle cap. Susan had applied a lot of perfume or cologne. 'Paloma Picasso,' she said, 'perhaps a little young for me.' I nodded and patted silk and soft flesh.

For my last birthday my elder but still five-year-old daughter gave me a large tube, a very heavy version of a cylinder I associate with oatcakes. It contained reddish clay. 'I thought you needed something to do with your hands,' she said. I was a little taken aback because Isabel must have connived or at least approved the purchase in Perth. Children leak and impose. I have never wanted to be a sculptor and I dislike the word 'modelling', too much fiddle, mould and therapy. But dutifully I retired and twisted and shaped clay. I liked the colour of the stuff and liked it better when dry and smooth. I made nothing bigger than would fit into my hand and produced a short run of smooth, stubby, shrunken heads. I like the feel and the weight of them. I suppose I can imagine that someone might use clay to help with a character, not producing the right face, but shaping clay worry beads till the heaviness and form felt right, a blind exercise while mulling, using the ball of the thumb to squirm nearer the part. In my case, letting my hands run over the smooth dry surface of a head might do just as well.

But the next time I went to see Ms Nutall I took a letter my five-year-old had written. 'Dear Dad, have a nice film.' Each letter was in a different colour, printed separately from the rest. Ms Nutall was delighted.

'Yes, of course! It's essential we show Sanderson writing to Gwen. Now how does a one-armed person secure the sheet of paper? Mm? Slipping it under the leather edge of a blotter, perhaps. Then there is the problem that we use one arm as a strut and rough guide, the other to wield the pen. Let's see.' She took up a pencil and wrote 'Dear' – rather like my daughter. 'Oh, that's wonderful,' she said. 'We really must use that.' She added a clumsy 'Gwen' and held up the paper. 'Yes, that's it exactly.' She looked round at me and cocked her head. 'How do *you* see him?' she asked, 'how does Sanderson look to you?'

'I think you said he was blond,' I said. 'I don't see that. Mousey. Frank faced rather than handsome, younger looking than either Gilmerton or Aubrey. He *was* cheerful and rather eager to please, would still like to please but is finding his new circumstances do not sit well with the boy who has all the supplies.'

'You're saying you don't think he was very tough?'

'No, I don't have the impression he was tough.'

'Yes, I think I agree. A good candidate for suicide. It really does explain why Gilmerton shifts his attention from Sanderson to Earnshaw. Sanderson does something unforgivable. How many have they seen die in the war? He kills himself because he has survived incomplete. Earnshaw is far worse off. Sanderson kills himself because he feels humiliated. It is not a good enough reason for Gilmerton – but he won't criticise him.'

'Wait,' I said. 'You did say this was a comedy.'

Ms Nutall raised her eyebrows. But then something else occurred to me.

'As a matter of fact, *do* you know what happened to Sanderson?'

'No, I'm afraid I don't,' she replied. 'I thought I had a reference for him much later when I read of a one-armed director of the family tobacco company. The problem is that Gilmerton does not give us his first name. The one I found was called William, was in the First War but lost his arm in a biplane accident. Of course, there hasn't been a family firm for years but there was a book published about it and that gives the name of three Sandersons who died in the First War, two brothers and their cousin. One brother was killed in 1915 at Loos, the other brother and the cousin died in 1917, Arthur at the Somme, Jeremy "of wounds". Given our schedules I have left it. After all, this is not Sanderson's pillow book, is it? I don't even know if these are the right Sandersons. The name is not uncommon.'

I blinked. Uncle me no uncles, cozen me no cousins. Ms Nutall is an excellent cozener. She brought out her pencils again. Narrative markers. If we have Sanderson dying in the background (one pencil), everyone resolutely ignoring the business (another pencil), perhaps a suggestion of a whitewash (no pencil), while we move towards Earnshaw (third pencil), we strengthen Gilmerton's decision to get out of the place (pencil placed like a dash). There was no curve this time, the pencils were neatly lined up and straight.

41

Heidi Nutall loves the word 'mingle'; I have heard her use the adverb 'minglingly' and on one occasion, accompanied by a slow-waving hand, the noun 'a minglement'. I am not at all confident I know what she means and have often felt 'whirr' might be more apt when she uses it. Take that section Gilmerton wrote with an older self answering a younger one. Mingle the elements. Gilmerton removing an old man's wig, Gilmerton as an old man watching a female child with distaste while she casts shadows on a wall, Gilmerton young and dancing with an eighteen-year-old girl, then old, minging at rather than mingling with, the young version who breaks off the waltz appalled at the bruise on the girl's arm.

'That wasn't me, was it? I'm—'

'No, silly. I bruise like a peach. [*Cocking her head, offering the inside of her arm.*] Do you want to try?'

'What's that?' [*Nervously referring to the other arm.*]

'Mm? Oh, that's just a little birthmark. [*Offering her bruised arm again.*] A little pinch will do.'

Gilmerton takes her gloved hand. A close shot of the powdered upper arm and bruise, so close the talc on the hairs shows. I make to move up and kiss it.

'Oh, not so high please.'

And then a cut to the old Gilmerton wincing. As he speaks he brings thumb and index finger briefly together.

'Young women require the most *delicate* of pincers.'

*

I can see how the old man and his wig might fit in or mingle with Hamlet, am less happy with Alice and predatory pincers and teasing girls and shadows. But Ms Nutall's objections to the scene were surprising.

'It's the powder, you know. The whole powder business is meaningless now. No nicely brought-up girl would have used powder then.'

By which she meant the whole of that section of the pillow book was dropped from the film. No talcum powder when you have fantasy colouring. And yet after all, it is Gilmerton who mentions it in 1916, not a living expert on mores then. The boyish pebble at the beginning of the pillow book; Ms Nutall speaks when the stone (I'm forgetting, it's a large stone) hits water. I am not getting the bits in the middle. In fact, I suspect she does not mean mingle but a texture to compensate the whittling down necessary for film. She turned and took my hands again, something she does when emphasising something to herself.

'This is a love story,' said Ms Nutall.

INT. STUDY — EVENING

A woman of thirty, the Professor's Wife, is dissecting a grasshopper. The scalpel slices. She has around her solutions and boxes and, on a sheet of ground glass, various dead insects.

Enter her mature Professor and Gilmerton at his most varnished, that is 'make-up like the glaze on some fresh bread, hair as slick as a stag beetle's back'. Smiling, she rises to greet them. The camera establishes that she is pregnant.

'Is that acceptable?'
    'I think so.'
    'Then I want to do pots, almost directly. You looking at her reflection in the window, the old don mincing and being minced, her husband's reaction, the self-beside-myself business and then a repetition of the very first scene but lengthened out into juicy berries. Is that all right?'

'Yes, I think so.'
'Then this.'

INT. BEDROOM – DAY

A naked Gilmerton considers the Professor's Wife's naked belly. He kisses the swollen navel. His finger runs.

> GILMERTON

Ah, this is beautiful. This stretch mark has the look of silver and—

> PROFESSOR'S WIFE

Robert.

> GILMERTON

Yes?

> PROFESSOR'S WIFE

A little brisker in the poetry?

Gilmerton smiles.

INT. LAMPENHAM – GILMERTON'S ROOM – DAY

Gilmerton turns from the window. He opens and slowly closes his left hand. It is a little painful and when he has done it, he blows as you might blow out a candle and smiles.

'Uhm, how much of this—'
'Shhh,' said Ms Nutall.

INT. GALLERY – DAY

> GARDNER PRICE

Miss Gilmerton, have you ever heard, did your brother ever mention a . . .

> AGNES

What?

GARDNER PRICE

Lady Glanville.

AGNES

No. Not that I recall.

GARDNER PRICE

This would have been at Oxford.

AGNES

I am not sure. My brother often had private names for people he valued. Are there variations?

GARDNER PRICE

Indeed. 'Lady G' is one.

AGNES

Quite. But are there no others?

GARDNER PRICE

Ah. Yes. There are some, yes.

AGNES

Well?

GARDNER PRICE

Uhm. 'Lady Glanswill'. 'Lady Gruntuntil'.

AGNES

Exactly! My brother was very fond of women.

Gardner Price stares.

He knew how to talk to them.

Gardner Price shifts.

He had none of that absurd masculine superiority rife in places like Oxford.

GARDNER PRICE

I was at Oxford, Miss Gilmerton.

Then you will know what he meant.

She leaves.

GARDNER PRICE
(*voice-over*)

How awkward. I will have to suppress it. Out of decency. What I cannot understand is that he should give such unforgivably clear identification of a lady. Out of the question then to mention the matter. But I am wretchedly with the evidence of . . . adultery, after all. With a woman . . . *enceinte*. With child by another man. Will I burn the letters? I think I must.

Enter Agnes.

AGNES

Mr Gardner Price.

GARDNER PRICE

Miss Gilmerton!

AGNES

You asked me if I remembered the name 'Glanville'?

GARDNER PRICE

Yes, indeed.

AGNES

I think your name is a butterfly joke.

GARDNER PRICE

I beg your pardon?

AGNES

A Lady Glanville lived in the seventeenth century. When she died her will was contested on the grounds of her insanity. The single proof offered was her inordinate liking for butterflies. The Glanville Fritillary is named after her. (*Pause.*) Fritillaries are . . . a rather common sort.

Ah. I see. Yes. That might explain the rather . . . Restoration nature of the other names he gave her.

AGNES

No, Mr Gardner Price, they are pet names. Code-names. I think the person you are after is a Mrs Ovington. Though I am not at all sure her husband did not die and that she has since remarried. Another professor, I think. Well — Professor and Mrs Ovington asked Robert to be godfather to their little boy. My brother accepted and left him five thousand pounds in his will. You might like to put that in. The boy's name is Gerald, I believe. My brother gave him the usual silver quaich at the christening.

GARDNER PRICE

Ah. Yes. Thank you very much indeed. I'll make a note of that.

Agnes nods and leaves.

GARDNER PRICE
(*voice-over*)

But this is even worse! I now know the real name. Oh, and for Miss Gilmerton's brother to be godfather! And five thousand pounds!

He pulls up. He has thought of something else. He scrabbles about his papers.

The child was born on 5 September. He met her . . . in April. Thank God. Oh, but in any case the affair is . . . disgustingly delicate.

He picks up a heavy book under which he has secreted a piece of notepaper.

PROFESSOR'S WIFE
(*voice-over*)

My dear Insanity —

INT. STUDY — DAY

The Professor's Wife at her work table writing.

My dear *temporary* Insanity, a note only. But I so wanted to have my fingers and hand work nib and ink on paper to write down how happy you have made me, of how much I have *enjoyed* our exciting, strange few months. *Our* island has been lovely.

INT. GALLERY — DAY

GARDNER PRICE
(*voice-over*)

Island?

EXT. OXFORD — GARDEN — DUSK

Gilmerton pauses to take in the Professor and his Wife sitting over tea on the lawn. Gilmerton has a net and a canvas bag.

PROFESSOR
Ah, Gilmerton. Splendid. Now my dear, you will take care.

PROFESSOR'S WIFE
Of course I will. But a little exercise will help. I am becoming ponderous.

EXT. COPSE — NIGHT

PROFESSOR'S WIFE
I can't kill them any more.

GILMERTON
Then we won't. We'll watch them.

PROFESSOR'S WIFE
That's unfair. You can see better than I can.

GILMERTON
There is a moon. And it is a private wood.

PROFESSOR'S WIFE

You'll look after me?

GILMERTON

Like the self beside your self.

PROFESSOR'S WIFE

Or a wraith with nerve ends. In my bath my belly looks like an island.

GILMERTON

A prospering island.

They kiss.

PROFESSOR'S WIFE

Does saliva retain words?

GILMERTON

Very, very faintly. Moonlight may help. Gleam, traces, your lips.

They kiss. Fade.

42

Undoubtedly it would be delightful to say I had managed, mostly on my back in bed at night, to assume and assimilate an intelligent role, enough to project a believable image of him on to film. My face is itching. Is that a stab at Gilmerton and his clogged patchwork of pores getting ready for his pillow book? The bookish pillow. He invoked a storm and the consequent aftermath of moths and words. What have I got? Something compensatory, I think. I always try to keep a quality of self-surprise in my performances, remember people can surprise themselves, become aware they have leaked or issued outside the confines of their own self-image. This is ridiculous; I can hardly feel more insecure than Gilmerton did.

Let me grunt and wassle. Isabel is flat out, breathing deeply. And an actor is as much as a glamorous plumber, uses a collection of pipes, joints, washers, rubbery membranes and silicone chargers. Not more. I find it comforting to think like this, before I am made up, have my black-dyed hair combed, put in his saffron-and-mint eyes as thin as onion skins and rise from the chair to behave as a version of Gilmerton, as if I were living in 1916 and my left lung hurt. A question of informed belief – and energy. A question of casting my voice on the right pitch, in exactly the right range, with no insomniac suet in the brain. The opposite of energy? Insomnia. My bones feel like old celery, my flesh feels ready for seasoning and the oven.

How is it I try to get the voice right? I imagine how the other actors will speak – which is where the secondary surprise comes in, when private rehearsal meets how the actors actually say their words. I rehearse first with the characters. With Aubrey. McKinnon. And naturally I have run through lines with tweeded, bearded Burnet; he has an attractive, barely audible snort cum whinny when he has said something that pleases him, just before he closes his lips and his teeth, snuffles and strokes his moustache down into his beard. And of course I have referred back to the pillow book and what Gilmerton wrote. I have mentioned Gilmerton's liking for sidelines. Some of these are decidedly obscure, some not even sentences; I took them as verbal doodles. In the margin by Burnet's first appearance comes the following: 'cyanide, see and hide, eye and hide, ironside'. Of these, I have to admit it was ironside that stuck. Iron lungs? Well.

Now it is true that several times, while reading over Gilmerton's ten-minute entries, I have had the impression that, even in the diaritic parts, he was flirting with fiction or, egged on by that small library around him, with literariness, an often amiable, but very sceptical, biologist playing with words, sometimes ruefully self-conscious, on occasion disconcertingly dry eyed, treating himself with some indulgence, as faintly derisory. But, as he says of that summer storm he stages at the beginning, I had 'not yet formulated' these impressions. This was in part because Aubrey and McKinnon and Burnet seemed almost immediately familiar; I rather liked Burnet. It was not until the script was in its umpteenth version and some time after our conversations on Sanderson's disappearance and Heidi Nutall plumping on suicide by drowning, that I abruptly realised Burnet disappears too. He had had more staying power, somehow. But I consulted the pillow book. Sanderson very briefly and in reported form (Polonius finding it hard to die), and Burnet talking over ghost pain with Rosencrantz and Guildenstern, both bow out with Mr Marshall's makeshift Hamlet.

I don't know. It may be that my impressions have a tendency to shade into suspicion but I was particularly struck that Ms Nutall had not mentioned Burnet's disappearance when mulling over Sanderson's method of suicide. She raised an eyebrow at me. 'Oh yes,' she said unhelpfully, 'Burnet disappears down the rabbit hole. Hadn't you fixed on that?'

'No.'

A while later, having practised conversations with Aubrey and Sanderson, McKinnon and easy-go Burnet, I picked up some of the books I had got in for background reading. Under Buchan's *Greenmantle* and on top of a history of the First World War and a *Dictionary of Fashion*, I came across a book I did not remember choosing and could not think why I had chosen it, the late Gerald Durrell's *The Amateur Naturalist*. Perhaps it was the word 'amateur' that had prompted or encouraged me. I opened it and turned pages. Near the beginning there was a very pleasant photograph of Le Fabre's study. It set me thinking on sunlight and a memory of the Loire Valley and a painting I had seen on glass that I had found repulsive, not for the subject but because of the light behind the paint. When I turned and looked towards a window in the château the light looked golden and when I returned attention to the book I found I had replaced the great naturalist's study with a plate of butterflies and moths. The most eye-catching of these creatures, with wings of silver and dusted black on which someone looked to have placed crimson crayon dots, was spectacularly unfamiliar. I followed the clockwork indications – it was identified as the day-flying Six-spot Burnet Moth.

Intrigued, I consulted the index. And on page forty-two I learnt that, for some as yet unexplained reason, the Burnet Moth is immune to cyanide. I am a stupid actor. I went immediately back to the pillow book and found 'see and hide'. Why was I so agitated? In anticipation of another misunderstanding? I had somehow got the notion that lepidoptera are often named after people. Glanville, for example. I had taken Burnet as the same. It is not an uncommon surname. Neither is Campion and there is a Campion Moth. But I should have been a gardener. Bladder Campion is the plant that the creature feeds on. And Burnet, burnet? Burnet is a plant of the rose family and Burnet is for the moth that eats it, the word, according to the dictionary I looked up, obsolete not for red-gold but dark brown. In one of my reference books I found thirteen different

Burnets illustrated. I preferred to fax Heidi Nutall rather than call. My very short note went through a number of versions and I took some three hours to complete it. 'Dear Heidi Hyde – I had not before appreciated that there is a Burnet Moth and that at least one of the tribe has the peculiarity of being immune to cyanide – Yours D.'

The machine bipped and ran in reply about a quarter of an hour later. 'Dear D – Whether Burnet was a coincidence (it is not that uncommon a name) or the name Gilmerton hid someone behind or a complete invention does not matter. If one of the first two cases, good. If the third, I don't see why Gilmerton should not be allowed his summer ghost or moth when just about everyone else in the film has theirs. Are you suggesting the script needs the information? I am inclined to think not. It is a small thing and would slow things down – love Gertrude Jekyll.' It was Isabel who told me that Gertrude Jekyll was a famous garden designer around Gilmerton's time. What was it Gilmerton said about names?

Oh, insomnia makes for instant dreams, dreams enclosed in no clock time. They remind me of those Holy Infants in paintings in which there is no newborn child but a little man or ventrilo-quist's dummy raising a hand to welcome the Magi. They match that shift of sounds, the jumble of syllables and, I am not sure it is not my training, iambic pentameters that take form but little sense. Or the sense of nursery rhyme. Or the sense of fatigue. The fatuous eloquence in almost forgotten things, the blink in simple ones.

But wait. McKinnon and Aubrey existed. Ms Nutall has, at least, dug about for Sanderson. Surely then, she could trace Burnet. And surely it matters. Even from her point of view. If Sanderson did commit suicide, might that not explain Burnet's vanishing as well? Gilmerton lacked the stomach to carry the invention on.

Then again, Burnet has a relatively large part, is more carefully rendered than Sanderson. Sanderson is a bit part, a dispensary, has to write to Gwen. That is to say that a fictional character is more important than a real one. And also influences the content and manner of how real people speak. I am acting Gilmerton, Burnet was Gilmerton's device and we are about to make a film in which Burnet will appear without fantasy lighting. In film terms he will be portrayed as real.

Very well. But it took me a little time to rearrange this in my mind. The notion that Burnet was an invention depressed me. How dull Lampenham and convalescence must have been! Absurd. You cannot pity the character you play. And unfair. I am an actor, I act. Gilmerton was a biologist, schooled in lepidoptera, once wrote a pillow book. A self-described observant, he could write clearly and elegantly, denies being a littérateur, but invents. And why not? It reflects back on him. And perhaps that notion began to explain my worry. No mention is made in the film of what finally killed Gilmerton. 'Absolutely not,' said Ms Nutall firmly. My scruples were doubtless inartistic and unreasonable and, if Gilmerton were entirely fiction, the lack probably would not have mattered. And the fact is very likely more important than the cause; Gilmerton knew, as Ms Nutall puts it, 'that his health was delicate and that the conditions of war were not'. That is the background and the stimulus to the pillow book. But it was not Ms Nutall who found that one of the reasons she could not sleep was a fear of being gassed.

'Oh, I am so sorry!' she said. 'For God's sake. My dear David, he went back to the trenches all right but he died of pneumonia. He was declared sick on 14 October and died on the 19th.'

'Ah. I suppose I'm glad he was not shot either.'

Ms Nutall raised an eyebrow at me.

'You think that's sentimental?' I asked.

'My dear David, films, this one included, are absolute *processions* of sentiment. Mm. I'm thrilled you are getting into the part.'

I nodded. Ms Nutall helps maintain the tension between actor and part. She is decidedly brisk though, at dividing fantasies into categories of quality. Rather charmingly, I think, she considers herself a professional fantasist, someone who plots out fantasies with rigour and balance as against the usual amorphous and wistful nonsenses. Within that, her cultural references are always the best. It can give her a certain, almost embarrassing innocence. She asked me once how I had got on with a famous, now elderly American actress. The old lady had just divorced again, for the seventh or eighth time, from a young bricklayer.

'On my back,' she said, 'I began to feel as tacky as a turtle. I just had to get up.'

Ms Nutall nodded and smiled. She wondered how much the feeling of being too long in bed and the fear of age had been behind Gregor Samsa in Kafka's dung-beetle story and Irving's 'Rip Van Winkle'. 'I hadn't linked them before. She laughed and leafed at the pillow book. 'Ah yes,' she said, 'Gilmerton's sidelines are wonderfully *chartable*.' I was not at all sure what she meant. Mappable? Or was that nautical, tacking between the plotted points of a voyage? She pushed the book over. 'Look at that.'

'Epiphanies are piffle, *Twelfth Night* is a play,' is a sideline to the Leda section.

'It's a young man's remark, of course, but delightfully sharp and full of energy.'

I was watching her more than listening to what she was saying. Ms Nutall is a bluestocking? I am not sure I know what that means. A person for whom ideas are more important than experience? Then that is probably not true. Ms Nutall's readiness is to consider anything from another point of view. And I see that I got into the habit of having day nightmares, fearing, for example, that she'd make Earnshaw's mother in widow's weeds every mother, Gilmerton's included, not so much for protection; they were akin to taking a breather. Ms Nutall has been most resolute in keeping elements of the project free to circulate about the film. She also keeps jumping. Just after that piffling-epiphanies remark, she looped back to Sanderson and, I think, Gilmerton's very first section. She suggested a scene in which Sanderson tries to skip a stone on the trawler-shaped pond.

'He fails, of course. And then perhaps he might scatter grit on the surface of the pond, like an incompetent circular net. You'd get a variety of rattling sounds, on water, on fleshy leaves . . .' She raised her eyebrows. 'And *then*, he turning to look, Burnet quite unaware he is being observed, Burnet riding along and past him on his bicycle.'

Watching her, I nodded. She has extraordinarily soft skin; it gives a faint impression of depth rather than defined surfaces.

'Oh, David,' she said, with a small intake of breath, 'of course!' She held up a plump finger. 'Burnet's bicycle,' she said, 'always squeaks!' She turned her finger in a circle, stopping at the lowest point, turning again. For some reason it made me wonder how many spots Burnet appears in. Five spot, six spot?

'Oh yes,' she said, 'the squeak is exactly right. I must tell James Soutar.'

43

According to Ms Nutall, the person I have got used to thinking of as one-legged Aubrey found the rest of his life a chore. He never married. He had money 'enough to get cantankerous and mope around his London club and get very fat and die at the age of fifty-one in 1938 from a heart attack. Apparently he adored oysters.' When approached first, in 1922, he was briefly and bluffly in favour of making Gilmerton a hero but did nothing about it. His memory did not improve until ten years later when H. Gardner Price contacted him; then he wrote a maudlin letter suggesting he visit 'my old chum's little sister in her moraine'. *Sic* as Ms Nutall sometimes says. Agnes in Angus politely but firmly declined any meeting anywhere.

Aubrey, however, had decided to collaborate. A few days later he sent Gardner Price what he called a 'lepidopteral anecdote' on club notepaper. Out for a walk in the sun, Aubrey asked Agnes's brother to identify the creature that had flown over the kitchen-garden wall.

'Two things,' said Gilmerton. 'I am not a performing dog or a horse that counts. Second. Aubrey! That is a Cabbage White!' And then a few paces later, 'I am always amazed that people behave as if butterflies and moths do not exist. They do not see them. I put it down to dull self-concern in most cases, in the others, to a habit of mind in which any possible flutter or figment has been resolutely excluded.'

276

'Isn't that just awful?' said Heidi Nutall in that tone that manages some shock, some tenderness but mostly glee.

Aubrey, however, had merely been performing the anecdotal equivalent of clearing his throat. A few days later, when he 'had had time to think', Aubrey sent in something 'rather more substantial' in his own words and 'worked out'.

'In the spirit of the war effort' a neighbouring landowner offered to the convalescents at Lampenham an elderly pony which one of his now-married daughters had ridden as a child. The pony was called Hannibal and, as part of his course of exercise, Gilmerton was sent out to ride him 'by the doctor in charge of us, a certain Charles McKinnon, a person, I believe, now great guns in the Medical Corps'.

'A quite extraordinary small amount of observation' in Aubrey's words would have seen that the instruction was absurd. Hannibal was a pony and an elderly Shetland, Shetlands being 'a small breed in a small race' and Gilmerton was tall. An 'amusing incidental', presumably unknown to McKinnon, was that Gilmerton loathed 'anything equine'. He loathed horses and ponies for their eyes (hypertense bulges), their hoofs and shoes (slack but hard rimmed), their hindquarters (powerfully skittish), their smell (thick and cloying) and particularly for their (large-toothed) desire to nibble imaginary parasites off their handlers.

I do not know how much of this, despite the facetious enumeration, was a token dislike. I am not suggesting Gilmerton's loathing was not genuine but he may have taken advantage of it, used it to hold off those who think biologists necessarily like all animals and to protest mildly against those who imbue horses with qualities like nobility. That is Ms Nutall using me as a medium. The dislike, however, is one of the few characteristics actor and acted share from the start. The hoof of a horse is attached by an alarmingly thin piece of something to the leg and they wear their nerves in their twitching skin. I try to avoid them.

Aubrey describes Gilmerton's height as 'pretty to intimidatingly tall'. The result was that when he managed to get into the saddle, his feet rested on the ground, 'even when he bent his knees'. The sheltie we have for the film is called Kris, the wrangler insisted on the spelling. Ms Nutall took it down for the credits. 'That's like the Malay dagger?' she said. The wrangler showed he was not amused. 'But what have I said?' asked the director. The pony was named after a person, a famous country singer and actor, and Aubrey and Gilmerton were quite right; it is absurdly uncomfortable to sit astride the pony, the girth of the belly contriving an extraordinary pressure and creak on either side of the groin, then the thighs, then the knees.

According to Aubrey, all of this might have been 'pleasantly and briefly ridiculous', a matter of McKinnon not looking up from his desk, a sly old landowner getting an old pony fed for nothing and Gilmerton's 'amiable protests'. After his first ride he told McKinnon that if he sat up he had to treat the pony's belly like 'a greased pole in a pillow fight' or adopt the position of 'an incompetent jockey which is agreeable neither to me nor, I suspect, to Hannibal'.

McKinnon irritably pooh-poohed the objection, mentioned the war 'once more' and also the 'condescending gesture' (meaning gracious kindness) of the landowner in lending Hannibal to Lampenham for the benefit of the convalescents.

The next day, 'an unfortunate young man called Earnshaw died at luncheon'; routine continued, however, and Gilmerton was sent out on Hannibal again that afternoon. He rode as he could until they reached the copse, a distance of about two hundred yards covered in 'not less than a quarter of an hour', Hannibal being of an 'ambling and meandering disposition', but once in the cover of beech and lime, he dismounted, led Hannibal on to the pool and let the pony mumble about the flowers and grasses while he sat with his small notebook and observed other forms of life and napped. He then led Hannibal on to the main entrance to the park, a distance of about four hundred yards, turned back, let the pony drink at the pool and at the copse remounted and returned towards the house.

From behind clipped yew, from behind leaded lights, from under the brims of khaki hats, Gilmerton's erratic progress was observed with indignant and vindictive pleasure. This time McKinnon looked up – and promptly considered that Gilmerton was ridiculing his instructions and in consequence him. Evidently so did the other convalescents. Someone ran for a camera and Aubrey, though he gave no description of what Gilmerton was doing, enclosed a snap taken from the parapet at Lampenham of Gilmerton writing something down in his nature notebook. He is standing awkwardly over rather than astride Hannibal, carefully writing while the pony has turned his head to view something off right. This is scheduled to be in the film, with the shadow of the house (and that might just be the photographer) almost reaching pony and rider.

Two days later, on 19 June, Gilmerton on Hannibal coincided with a motor car at the gate to the house. 'Both stopped where they were.' And Gilmerton learnt something new. When faced with a motor car, Hannibal turned sideways across the drive. 'Naturally', Gilmerton dismounted and walked the passenger, 'a lady in a mourning veil', to the front entrance, leading Hannibal behind who chose that moment for 'a dubitative but undoubtedly remarkable virile reaction'. McKinnon, 'at the front door and already in something of a state', was 'sufficiently embarrassed' and annoyed to brush aside Gilmerton's introduction.

'Captain Gilmerton, that is a pony, not a dog. It is not to be led. It is to be ridden. And when it is ridden, it is not to be ridden as some Regency rake might have ridden a bicycle without pedals.'

Gilmerton turned to the lady. 'I am very sorry,' he said. 'Will you forgive me for a moment? Dr McKinnon, I hardly felt justified in remaining seated on a recalcitrant pony when addressed by the late Lieutenant Earnshaw's mother.'

As even Aubrey himself says, it is very probable that McKinnon had already understood that he had 'mis-spoken'. Ineptly and hastily, he endeavoured to correct himself.

'Very well, captain, I take your point. That will be all.'

'No, it will not,' said Gilmerton. 'I take exception to your calling me a rake. The word you wish is "beau" perhaps, but in either case, the term is inaccurate.'

'Captain Gilmerton, there is a lady waiting!'

'That was my point entirely. Madam. I am very sorry. I knew your son a little and I always found him a brave, congenial and interesting companion.'

Aubrey does not say what the lady's reaction was. In the film she will also be a veiled, silent part. Ms Nutall 'loves' Gilmerton's last sentence; in other words she will not use it.

'Aubrey's pretty worked up, isn't he?' said Ms Nutall. 'I wonder if he carried the grudge all that time or if it just welled up as he wrote. I hadn't thought of him as being passionate before.'

The exchange, gentlemanly and gangsterile, reminds me of a ghastly school tussle.

It is practically impossible to say from Aubrey's account just how much Gilmerton was now acting for himself or for the common revenge of the other convalescents. If either. But what does seem clear is that from then on, he no longer felt obliged to mount Hannibal. Instead he trotted, pulling the portly old pony behind him, usually with his left arm. On hearing of this – 'McKinnon being the sort of person who preferred to hear of rather than to see for himself', as Aubrey sniffily puts it – the doctor called Gilmerton in, to ask him if it were true. Gilmerton replied that it was, that he was endeavouring to strengthen his left side and also to gauge how much he was using his left lung. He had, accordingly, made a design for a simple apparatus, a rudimentary spirograph, which might give some notion of it, to wit a mouthpiece of rubber, two conical metal tubes soldered at the narrow end . . . McKinnon removed the pony.

Gilmerton himself said and did nothing; he had, after all, never wanted to ride the pony in the first place. He 'merely resumed his life'. Aubrey, however, thought it 'interesting and in character' that McKinnon should hold Gilmerton personally responsible for the 'brouhaha' and give up any idea of having someone else ride Hannibal. Instead he gave instructions that the pony be put to providing power to a lawnmower. There was an immediate mutter of protest (not by Gilmerton) and a subsequent letter from 'an anonymous horselover' to the landowner who then removed Hannibal from Lampenham in 'very huffy terms' – Hannibal had never worked in his life.

The film omits the landowner's reaction and, indeed, Kris is a gelding. Instead, it cuts from McKinnon removing the pony from Gilmerton to Hannibal pulling a lawnmower with a white-whiskered old man behind and then follows Gilmerton in Japanese dress on his way to the orangery.

I agree with Ms Nutall. The fantasy image is delightful. Gilmerton amongst boxed orange trees practising Japanese sword exercises to strengthen his left side. For McKinnon (to be seen staring in at one end of the orangery) it was everything he loathed about Gilmerton – the exotic movements and control, the outlandish clothes and impassivity, his individualism and his indifference to what others might think.

Gilmerton despised what he called 'Japanese dreamerie' and laughed at the dream of 'women who are delicate but compliant and, in private, invigoratingly untroubled by decorum.' But evidently this was not widely known. Even Aubrey ended his effort with a little eulogy.

'I never saw him complain or act grossly. He always bore up cheerfully and with dignity. The most I could say was that when in pain he assumed an extraordinary passivity, but I think – you can correct me – that is the Japanese way.'

44

I woke up this afternoon to find I had been dreaming of lobsters – the crustacean, that is. I was unable to break open the claws. I woke with a start and saw that my thumb and index finger were arranged as pincers; I was chasing a feel, already almost gone, that my hands had been cut and bruised. There was no mark on them. I had not, in the fuddle of dream, been pinching myself. Blood crimp as quick as a cloud's shadow. And I suddenly realised that what I had said to Burnet was untrue – or only in part true. That I could not quite remember pain was accurate. But I cannot remember many other matters to do with the senses either. I could recall something of the feel of my teeth biting into the flesh of lobster but the taste was reduced to a marine quinine, more medicinal after-taste than flavour. I grunted. Notionally awake, my mind then presented me with a plate on which there was a crustacean lobster, a locust and an adult moth, all in scale. A dab of something – the way some dab mustard – turned out to be thick, whitish honey. My mind's palate then combined them, a dizzying, white-backed spin of dusty wings, crunching segments and warm, grit-charged sea. I shuddered.

'What? An afternoon mare?' said Aubrey.

I nodded and let my eyes clear. It was hot on the lawn.

'Are you all right?' said Aubrey.

'Yes.' The pores on his nose glistened with small specks of sweat. I rubbed my face and sat up. The chair creaked. 'I'm parched,' I said and hefted myself up. I threaded my way through khaki convalescents dotted about the lawn to the refreshment table and washed sleep and various lobsters out of my mouth; the water was just cool enough to feel running down my gullet to the mouth of my stomach. I closed my eyes, opened my eyes. My head ached. But I also had the certainty that I had had quite enough of Lampenham. It was one of those dull, unexceptional certainties, in one way depressed and gloomy, in another, rather cheerful. Hm. I drank some more, swallowed and waited a moment as if I wanted to plump out like a charged sponge. Memories are by no means always welcome and rarely apt. I recalled an episode, however, long ago, a memory of striving to imagine the world through the eyes and organs of a moth.

I suppose the first point is that the eye of a moth is compound; it is made up of a number of small eyes. Of course, all I was doing was beginning to tackle the realisation that the world is made up of millions of perceptions amongst species, each radically different from those of human beings, but each equally striking. Each species receives different stimuli in different ways and each species perceives a different image in a different space. Each species, that is, perceives a different world, whole and unique.

I did not think only of moths. The shrew's world is not a spider's world. Nor an eagle's. But it was a moth I concentrated on. I imagined one of the Noctuid or owlet family and asked my brain how the imago would register the approach of a bat. Would it see a series of bats? The more bats, the closer the danger? Or did the moth register a warning riot made up of parts of bat's wings, a sudden surfeit of hooked elbows and leathery skin? Or is the owlet tribe's fame at escaping bats little or nothing to do with eyesight? If a moth can perceive the scent of an approaching storm, could it not register the shrill attack of a bat, the squeak and rush of agitated air by other senses? I felt I could imagine that. I have heard people say owlets have exceptional hearing — but that is another question. It is not possible to talk of an owlet moth's ears so much as tympanal organs situated laterally on the posterior part of the metathorax.

I was so anxious for information at that age. I turned to and explored my books. But here I was, for the first time, struck by the vocabulary often used; though notionally scientific, it was commonplace to imbue lepidoptera (bright butterflies in particular) with appreciative sensations – delight as the larva munched, a thrill at the growth of the wings in the cocoon, in short, the abundant energy and eye-catching colours of moth and butterfly growth were translated into a joy at being. The language seemed to me conspiratorial. I remember the phrase 'a maze of ecstasy'. Ah, and I have just remembered poor Earnshaw and his antish Ariadne.

Almost before I knew what I was doing, I began putting aside the books that showed what I thought of as a craven eagerness to believe. I could see something of the energy, follow the sequence, from egg to imago, could delight in the gamut and designs on the wings – but I could see no labyrinth I recognised. A caterpillar might squirm in an invisible maze?

I was puzzled and glum and you cannot know how irritated I was when you looked up around this time and said, 'Ah, he's mazing again.'

'Musing,' corrected Uncle Andrew. 'What are you thinking about, Robert?'

'I was thinking as to whether or not moths feel pleasure. And the degree of energy, if any, required for them to do so.'

'My dear boy! Some questions you *cannot* ask,' he said and taking you firmly by the hand, led you away.

Since he did not appear to be joking, I wondered briefly whether he meant I must not ask or whether he meant I lacked the ability to do so. A mix of rebellion and contempt made me a little deafer still and rather miserable. But, in my prim-sprung way, I stuck at it. At Oxford, I heard someone say that it is not really that the young have good perceptions but that they can have radical conceptions, particularly when freshness and ignorance combine, and that these can develop. Usually not. 'But when they do!' said the old fraud.

I got out a good pile of paper and began to sketch. I tried to do this from two sides; what the moth saw and how the moth's world would look if seen from the outside. I am amused that my recall of these sketches is much less crude and stubby than they undoubtedly were. An early view of what the Ingrailed Clay, *Diarsia mendica*, might see, produced something rather like a carnival mask, a pair of concave blinkers and a starry night sky.

It took me time – and you'd do well to think of me snatching at occurrences and paper – to appreciate even something of what I was attempting to do. I am not sure 'appreciate' didn't quickly become too timorous a word. I became drunk on a notion of the world as a geometrical riot, with cross-references of smell, temperature and air sharpening into interstices, a kind of gorgeous map of undulating senses, with contour lines, strata and cross-sections where prey and preyed coincided. And the main characteristic of this world was movement and energy, an intermingling of extraordinary numbers of perceptions. I am no artist but later, when I had seen paintings first by Seurat and then by Cézanne, I was reminded of that adolescent tingle. The first resembled a fabric of coloured drops, the second was made up of coloured planes formed and deformed into other perspectives. Imagine these two elements spiralled together, here thickened, here stubbed, delightfully weird fabrics, touching, billowing, ballooning, apparently on the edge of coming apart, now on the verge of imploding.

All of this was rather a shock to me. Was I going mad? I did not find that a thrilling question. How did other people see the world? And was I as self-concerned as them? It is no coincidence that I went on to study the simplest creatures available, untroubled by *their* view of the world. And yet I think what most shocked me was something akin to sudden nausea caused by my previous desire to collect, the absurd arrogance of possessing dead creatures. It occurred to me that there was something funereal about my collection, a ghastly fixing. I no longer felt pride at all my pinned and labelled creatures; rather they were revealed to me as being in a process of delayed decay and that my part in that was, apart from shabby and cruel, intrinsically stupid.

By the refreshment table on the lawn, still with a glass of water, I smiled. What was I thinking of? I looked around me; languid or lackadaisical or bandage-broken khaki. My mood had gone but my decision remained. Could I justify it? Probably not. I saw Aubrey quizzing me with his face – Are you all right there? – and nodded back at him. I drank the remaining water, put down the empty glass on the tablecloth, and strolled across the lawn towards the house.

Outside McKinnon's office I told the nurse I wanted to see the doctor the next day. He heard me and came out.

'What is the matter, captain?'

'Nothing at all. I have a request.'

McKinnon frowned and asked me to come in. He closed the door. 'Well?'

'I don't think there is a need for me to stay here any longer.'

'What are you saying?'

'I consider myself to be better.'

'Are you asking me to declare you fit?'

'Precisely.'

He sat down and considered me. Evidently he required more. I endeavoured to click the fingers of my left hand, finally and unembarrassedly, did it. Click.

'Ah,' said McKinnon.

'Obviously I am not quite what I was but I think I am fit enough.'

'To return to your regiment?'

'Yes, of course.'

McKinnon nodded, rubbed his chin. 'Of course. Yes. And you are due for some leave, aren't you?'

'Yes.'

There was a pause. 'Well?' I said.

McKinnon rocked his head a little.

'Have you any objections?' I asked.

McKinnon looked up at me. 'No,' he said, 'none.'

'Good.' I smiled and offered him my hand. 'Thank you, doctor. And thank you for all the—'

'No, no,' said McKinnon, 'there is no need for thanks.' He gave my hand a tug. 'Only doing our job. I'll see to the paperwork, captain.'

'Thank you. You are most kind.'

Outside I felt more than relieved, I felt free. Aubrey was hobbling towards me.

'I say,' he said, 'have you been *doing* something?'

I laughed. 'Well actually, Aubrey, yes, I have.'

45

Maybole

Dear Mr Gardner Price,

I have received your letter anent the late R. L. Gilmerton. Indeed I knew him and knew him well. We were first introduced in the spring of 1909 when both of us were undergraduates in the University at Edinburgh, he studying Science and I Veterinary Medicine. It was the fashion then for us 'vets' to be given a small piece of research to do, in my case on tick fever in cows; Robert Gilmerton proved most helpful on some quite basic matters of scientific procedure to do with slides and microscopes of which I was ignorant and which enabled me to trace the structure of the tick. Our relationship continued outside our respective subjects, whether in person or by letter, until his death in 1916.

I see from my diary that in February 1910 he invited me to a dinner at which I met his sister, at that time a charming, rather quiet young lady of perhaps thirteen or fourteen years of age. From your letter I understand that Miss Gilmerton is now your employer in the venture you mention.

I wish I could say that I understood the urge to produce a biography of Miss Gilmerton's brother but I cannot. Robert Gilmerton was, despite his fortune and background, one of the most modest men I have ever met. This characteristic was, I am sure you will understand, easily misunderstood. Indeed, I once heard him described as 'quite the gentleman scholar'. I suppose there may be an element of truth in this, but the other characteristic I associate with him is a disarming and unassuming irreverence; it was part of his curiosity to take little on say-so and he was inquisitive as to a great many things. Without reference to any diary I can remember conversations on the biological roots of language, of how sounds could be considered to have meaning, from matters as arcane as the self-protective habits of dung-beetles to matters as popular as the public taste for a good murder. He had a capacious, precise memory and a sometimes startling nimbleness of mind. This could shock. I remember him squinting at an oil painting in a visiting exhibition; the subject was 1848 in France and the painter may have been Delacroix. It showed a half-naked young woman wearing a revolutionary hat and leading the way forward with a flag. He suggested her breasts were 'striving to be wings. Better than the milk of human kindness at least.' Neither did he show much reverence towards monuments. He much enjoyed David Hume's grave, a neo-classical turret with a pious message for an unrepentant sceptic erected by anonymous 'friends'. I also saw him laugh on one of those Edinburgh days of stone and snow in which people are reduced to shapes not unlike moving hay stooks as we walked about the monument to Sir Walter Scott and he looked in on the statue of the author and of Sir Walter's small, stone dog.

You might, I suppose, argue that, had he lived, he should have outgrown his sharpness about such matters. I like to doubt it. Indeed, Robert Gilmerton's sense of himself as part of a natural process, his deep-rooted sense of his own insignificance, was a large measure of his strength of mind and a seductive combination of robustness and delicacy. He would never have complained at his fate since he asked why not quite as often as why. Does it not strike you then that a biography can hardly avoid combining monument and complaint, something he would have loathed with all his soul?

I saw him last on 21 March 1914 in London. He was, as always, good-humoured and considerate. If I remember correctly, he was at that time considering an offer from the United States or returning to Edinburgh. I fancy he was attracted by the first but had other responsibilities – on reflection, I see that is my reading of the situation and I cannot recall that *he* said anything of the sort. Instead he talked of his desire to study, as it were, the chemistry in biology, something for which, he was quite aware – in fact, it was a large part of the attraction – we still lack the technology required to enable knowledge. 'Marvellously ignorant' was his phrase for himself.

Now I do not know what he would have done had he lived. I doubt that he was to Science as Keats is to Romantic Poetry. He may well have been too much of a generalist to have been really useful in research. I was going to say that he might have been too generous as well – but that is to stray from my point.

It may be that you think I am guilty of a certain possessiveness, of having allowed an acute nostalgia for a friend to influence my advice; I cannot help but think, however, that the dead are important, enough to take them into account, and that it is time they had more rights than those who grieve. Why do you not let him remain with all those natural secrets he so admired?

I enclose a copy of the last letter he wrote to me, when I was in hospital having suffered a kicking from a horse on board a troop-ship, which shows him at his most tried; even so, his sly, ironic sense of humour and his efforts to amuse the recipient, shine through.

Yours faithfully,

George S. MacFee, BVM&S

This letter is, of course, the one describing the night of 5 June 1916, when McKinnon offered Gilmerton a pillow puzzle to combat 'the kind of despair we all feel sometimes'.

'I like MacFee,' said Ms Nutall. 'The poetry of the vet in those Edinburgh days of stone and snow.'

'Yes.'

'Of course, he makes Gilmerton a slightly different kind of hero.'

'Slightly.'

'You don't agree?'

'Yes, I think your Gilmerton comes through the letter. Yes. What did Gardner Price think?'

'I think he did agree, David, that the biography shouldn't be written. Mind you, he would have done. And once he had got over his fantasies about marrying Agnes and being Laird of the Manor, there was nothing much left for him to do but wait for the lease of his little fortified house to run out and he with it.'

'Seven years and no biography? You don't think Agnes knew?'

'I don't know. It may have been convenient for her to connive.'

In life, Agnes contacted her lawyers who, after due enquiry, informed her that Gardner Price had first fled to a sanitorium near Peebles but had then left no forwarding address. There is not much else. Agnes later commissioned an architect to plan a large memorial hall in Edinburgh but there were site problems and then the Second World War. No biography, no chair, no building. Agnes had spent, in a manner of speaking, almost all the interwar years trying to do something for her dead brother. After that she ceased trying. She died in 1981, leaving the house in poor condition (someone tried to start a school there) and a relatively exiguous £500,000, proof, Ms Nutall says, 'of the squaline nature of so many notaries and financial advisers'.

For film life, however, Ms Nutall has dealt with Gardner Price rather differently.

Reverend Ramsay looks at the little fortified house. Everything is shut. He squints in at the kitchen window. A scrubbed table, a milk bottle, a wire clothes brush.

INT. NEAR BRECHIN — DAY

REVEREND RAMSAY

It would appear that Mr Gardner Price has left the area. Entirely.

AGNES

But he cannot have vanished.

REVEREND RAMSAY

I understand his lease had run out.

Could he not renew it? Minister, would you mind fetching the telephone?

Agnes's hunt for Gardner Price is carried out by chauffeur-driven Rolls, a 1926 Silver Ghost with white-walled tyres, through some very beautiful highland country: hills, winding roads and deep glens. The car draws up at a whitewashed cottage. The landlady tells her that Mr Gardner Price is out walking. The car moves slowly on, Agnes keeps her eyes open – we are not sure here whether she should use binoculars or at least have binoculars in her hands or neither – and tells the driver to stop. Agnes gets out with her shooting-stick and clambers over a dry-stone wall. In the distance Gardner Price freezes, looks behind him up the hill but stays where he is as Agnes strides towards him. A few yards short, she stops, unfolds her shooting-stick and sits on it. Gardner Price doffs his hat.

AGNES

Mr Gardner Price.

GARDNER PRICE

Miss Gilmerton . . . my apologies . . . my psyche . . .

AGNES

My brother died so that you could run away with your psyche?

GARDNER PRICE

Not your brother, Miss Gilmerton. My nerves.

AGNES

I wish your guarantee, Mr Gardner Price, your word of honour.

GARDNER PRICE

Miss Gilmerton?

AGNES

For as long as you live you will make no mention of me, my family, my circumstances, the contract between us, nor anything to do with my brother.

GARDNER PRICE
(*blinking, finally grasping that he has been let off*)
Oh. No, no. I will not.

AGNES
Then that is an end to it.

She turns, lifts her stick and starts walking back to the Rolls.

GARDNER PRICE
Yes. Quite. No more.

Agnes reaches the dry-stone wall and waits for the chauffeur's help.

CUT TO:

EXT. THE ROBERT GILMERTON VILLAGE MEMORIAL HALL — DAY

REVEREND RAMSAY
Miss Gilmerton, your brother was indeed a hero.

AGNES
I do not know what good being a hero does.

REVEREND RAMSAY
Oh, I beg your pardon, Miss Gilmerton. His service to his country, this service to the community. These are not small things.

AGNES
I treated my brother as a hero too long. It is to treat someone as a doll. It is a grievous forgetfulness of someone's particularities and it betrays both our memories.

REVEREND RAMSAY
Ah. You are perhaps remembering childhood games with him? Dressing up?

AGNES
You think?

Pause. She looks at the hall.

Yes. I like the colour of the stone. I think Robert might have liked it too.

REVEREND RAMSAY
Miss Gilmerton, I have the scissors here.

Agnes snips the ribbon and then we go back to Lampenham. The run of farewells will be settled in the cutting room but will end on Aubrey's last photograph of me as Gilmerton. Ms Nutall considered at one time replacing me at the end with the photograph of the real Gilmerton but as far as I am aware she has dropped that. The camera will close in on my face and will freeze into a still when the camera shutter clicks, then lose colour and the shot become granulated to end on:

Robert Gilmerton 3 April 1890–19 October 1916

One of Ms Nutall's sketches for the storyboards she describes as a doodle merely and nothing like it will appear on film. I asked if I could have it but she has proved reluctant to hand it over. She claimed it was 'just a pretty note' but immediately took it away and secreted it in her files. It sounds like a poster but it is not; the faintest indication of a skull with a Lobster Moth imago and its wings spread over the eye sockets.

46

I don't think I could say that my eyes have sprung open; my lids
are simply wide apart. I narrow them, in part because of the so-called
dawn chorus, a ragged avian twitter; something is chirping inces-
santly in the eaves, there is a demanding, monotonous peep from
somewhere a little beyond and there are shrill, erratic pipings that
sound airborne. It is time. I roll, squint at the clock and jab my
thumb on the button before the alarm starts ringing. Above I hear
the scud of quick feet; that's the smaller daughter running to the
larger one's bed. A giggle, a complaint, silence.

Stiffly, I slide out of bed feet first and stand up. I ease my
shoulders while hankering after sleep, less as flutter than as flow,
bone-deep, flesh-slackening sleep. A groan-touched sigh. Ah, I rub
my eyelashes, flex my fingers, feel slightly unsteady on my feet.
Yes. Actors are actors, not artists. I dislike the word 'player'; it has
become weighed down by bum-numbing dissertations about the
ludic. There are times I have thought that the absence of a good or
apt synonym for 'actor' demonstrated that it is better to act than
describe, that the absence meant a healthy urgency and value. Ah,
pompous thoughts from an increasingly agitated zombie. The carpet
under my feet feels as if I am wearing the stuff as I totter round
the bed and make sure Isabel is covered and tucked up. She gives me
a polite, demure grunt as acknowledgement. I nod. I am beginning to
feel wretchedly hungover from my sleepless summer night.

I turn, remember to lift my feet on the way to our bathroom and negotiate the three worn, sandstone steps. I just cannot say how much I prefer to do my shaking in private. I shut the door and instantly have my apple turn pear. Where did I read that? It is an excellent description for a nervous lump in the throat, the pear badly peeled, slippery with juice in some parts, still with abrasively dry patches of skin on others. Am I going to gag? Let me think. No. This is set fright in the bathroom. A cloud passes over and I lock the door but resist burying my face in the soft towelling robe behind the door that belongs to Isabel.

Absurdly, I have found I need all this performance, even the grogginess; when I do not tremble and gibber beforehand, my acting feels dull. An illusion? Very likely. Self-drama? I am quite positive. I may even be trying to get rid of all my bad acting before I begin, which may be one of the reasons I do it alone. I let the bath mat flop to the floor. And I know I am properly nervous when turning on hot and cold for a bath hurts my fingers. The water gushes. My throat is parched. My heartbeat is more a ripple than a pulse.

While the water rushes and runs I think, blearily, of shaving, but I can see myself scraping off foam and bristle with a latitude in my hand that would easily manage a spoon tapping on top of a soft-boiled egg. The elder daughter prefers that and does it herself. The younger likes me to behead her egg tops with as clean a blow as possible, takes up an encouraging karate stance while the other sets to picking off bits of shell with the air of someone pulling petals off a membranous forget-me-not. Ms Nutall gave them their own horn spoons 'to save your silver'. Enough.

I close those pipes, breathe in. I am not about to vomit but a belch would help. My forehead aches as if clamped on either side. My neck feels stiff, brittle and fragile. At this stage, I have a small test. I have my brain instruct my heart to slow down. Ah, there – small, rumpled air, a helpful rift comes up my throat. Good. The test usually works, though I dread the next sensation, possibly imagined, that my heart has slowed but that small fits of twitches are radiating out in my chest.

I shrug off my pyjamas and step into the bathwater. My joints are stiff and I ease myself down. Then, sitting marooned in a hot clear puddle in an enamelled, cast-iron bath, the water somehow feels unconvincing, disappointingly thin. I have never suffered from butterflies in the stomach. I take a tablet of cream soap and begin rubbing. We have what my daughters call a telephone shower that produces weak, watery needles; I bend them around me. I unplug the bath, stand up and finish rinsing. I turn off the water, replace the shower attachment. I am, without a doubt, thin enough for the part. I can see that my rib bones are properly flat. But then again, at least for now, I am not particularly worried at having to impersonate a man ten years or more younger than I am. I unfold a towel, begin drying myself, step out.

There is something inherently melodramatic about Scottish bathrooms early in the morning in a fitful sun. A cloud passes, the mirrors turn greyish green and I catch myself looking wild, haggard and stunned – like Jekyll when he has swallowed his potion and is waiting for the effects to seize him. I am professionally vain. I tuck the towel round my waist, work my jaw, slap-pat my face and at least stand up straighter. Time? Yes, I must shave.

But this is ridiculous. Gilmerton used brush, soap in a silver bowl and a cutthroat razor stropped to bring up a lethal edge on the blade; I have a gel for sensitive skins and a plastic thing with a slightly sprung head that wobbles its pair of small blades over my face. I think I have nicked myself two or three times in as many years, usually just under the right jawbone. In a film you are shaved already; foamed and the cutthroat does not cut, you use it as a modified, gleaming steel wiper. Listen for the bristle sounds. Still, this will do; my first contact with him today. We shave together, he one way, me another; that is, I shave, interrupting my actions to feint at what he might have done. Doing my upper lip, I wonder just how much he valued his face, of how I would calculate the pressure needed on a tongue-padded or stretched upper lip to remove the hair without opening the skin.

I pat my face dry. I try out his lung. I have always taken the mystery or oblique line when asked for my acting technique. Research, rehearse – then let the subconscious work. Two matters. With insomnia, how? I lift my head and feel my neck. Still two or three patches that rasp. I dab gel and scrape. And I have never liked being questioned about it. 'Oh, I bumble about in character, waiting for insights' is both suitably modest and true enough. Occasionally I am pursued, in which case I half-do by imitating one or two well-known actors. But, to put this in morning perspective, it took me several years and at least seven viewings to understand that in *Some Like It Hot*, Tony Curtis's imitation of a millionaire is done in Cary Grant's voice. But I have also encountered perseverance in public, once landed up on the stage of a university theatre in the US. 'Are you seriously claiming you intuit everything?' said the student interviewing me for an audience. 'No,' I said, 'panic causes *some* thought.' Ah, this is revenge on the ingratiator. I have never been an insomniac and had to play a markedly intelligent role at the same time.

I put toothpaste on the brush. This is the awful stage. What if my tries at assuming Gilmerton are quite mistaken? There is a particular image in the pillow book that sticks with me, in the nursery when a burnt moth imitates a missing piece of a jigsaw fish. It nags, flutters at the base of my brain. I have even thought there may be a missing section to his pillow book that I should be able to provide if I had understood it as meant. And I am miserably suspicious that, with all his references to ghosts and moths, Gilmerton has not developed the Ghost Moth, *Hepialus humuli*, the male of which is silvery white and dances near to the ground at dusk, being one of the few moths that does not use scent but visual display to attract a mate. Have I entirely missed a sense?

I spit out. I am getting lost between some notion of comparison and a lack of accurate simile. Is that his Lobster bite? A slight after-taste. Words as mouthwash. And that extraordinary, apparently hierarchical arrangement of skin and jelly posing amongst leaves is a caterpillar. What is it that Stevenson said about thoughts not clearly expressed nor clearly apprehended? The half-formed or larval sentence.

I breathe out. Use deodorant. I glance at my watch. I am grateful for time. I need to hurry. When I am shooting I wear casual clothes, a collarless shirt so that my neck doesn't chafe on the way to the studio, chinos, thick cotton socks and loafers.

Isabel has woken and is watching me. 'You seem to be doing fine today. Good. Have the girls gone down?'

'Probably. I'll do them.'

I go downstairs. Both are sitting at the table with their bowls in front of them and their spoons raised.

'Oh no,' says the smaller one, 'not *another* film.'

This is evidently their joke. They laugh.

'My dear, I was shaking like a leaf,' says the elder.

'Do you want orange juice?'

'No, just muesli, please.'

'I'm not sure I could eat anything at all in my state.'

'Muesli then.'

'Actually,' says Isabel, coming in, 'they're quite proud of you for not doing the heroic-Daddy-going-out-to-earn-more-pennies routine.'

'Yes?'

'Some children get both parents doing it now.'

'Ah.' I put my hand over the third child. 'And this one?'

'Exercising.'

I pour muesli and milk. The girls clank and munch. I am suddenly taken by a shiver. The elder looks up and gives me an inexpert wink. I close both eyes in a squeeze, drink some bottled water.

When I film I don't drive. A car picks me up. It is always the same driver, the car is usually dark green but the make changes frequently though the car is always large and sleek, the seats leather and the tyres have a heavy but somehow delicate tread on the grit. I know the car is coming when the girls quieten just so; evidently they find the sound exhilarating and soothing at the same time. They run to the window, watch the driver easing the car up to the door and wave.

I kiss my nightied wife and daughters. Small, chubby female flesh stands on a chair, opens her arms and says, 'Darling.' Her elder sister says, 'It's Japanese, Dad,' meaning the car. Though I am not superstitious I have nothing against even slightly good omens. I go directly outside, get into the car and buckle up.

'Take you away now, David?'

'Please, Graham.'

I have the script on my knee. I'll look at that later. Just at the entrance to our drive, some trees have made a short, wild, leafy tunnel. It depends on the day and the sun but under them the light effects are strikingly beautiful, shadow and plump chlorophyll, with a lush gamut of greens, touches of pale gold, silk-shot lime and mint; under it there is an almost subaqueous feel of tints and glow and deep quiet. The car has to slow and pause for the corner. I close my eyes briefly, then open them, lift my face and make a fish's mouth and a small popping noise. Graham turns his head.

'It's my part, Graham.'

He nods and accelerates.

47

Last night I slept. In a chair. From half past one to four. Nearly two and a half hours in a moment; I woke abruptly, with no memory of any dreams but a slight stiffness to back up a clock version of time. When I had stood up, however, and brushed my hair, teeth and fingernails, I began to feel decidedly refreshed and by the time I had shaved (cold water) I felt, in a rawish way, wide awake. I changed my clothes and finished packing – except for a couple of last-minute items, including this notebook. Then I went outside into the dawn mist, the windowed door giving a last, soft, wet-wood moan. I breathed in; there was enough chill in the mist to make my left lung ache. Rather pleasant. Off the wet flagstones, the dew on the grit lent a most sonorous crunch to my feet so while I was still near the house I crept, raising my knees, ah, rather like that pawn-broker in the amusing German horror film, and proceeding on slow tiptoe. A sleepy-eyed maid carrying empty milk cans came round the corner and started, enough to set off a clatter. Since I was carrying a beech twig and a fat caterpillar I understood perfectly, winced, smiled, mouthed 'Good morning' at her and the startled girl included a hasty bobbing movement in her short-stepped scurry to get away.

Once on the drive away from the house, I was able to relax, stroll and enjoy the sounds. Grain and grit, a sodden variety of grinding under the pressure of my shoes. A pair of hunting swallows dipped down, one of them coming close enough for me to hear the creak of a wing. One of the sheep in the field to my left coughed, the sound entering but not issuing from the mist. Nearby, a blackbird pecked speculatively at the ground and looked up at me, weirdly as if seeking approval rather than a meal. Of course, the Lobster Moth larva! I checked on it; the bizarre little creature was still there but the twig seemed to be trembling far too much. So I tried walking as if the entire point of an egg-and-spoon race was that the egg should not jiggle; then I attempted a waiter's glide, to find I could only manage a swoop of the arm and a bent-kneed little rush. I stopped. The caterpillar remained splendidly indifferent. Just before the copse and the trawler-shaped pond, the huge lime was dripping as if it had been raining. I skirted it and walked on to the grass; I have always enjoyed drops of water on waxed and polished leather.

So with no ceremony at all but with some care I put the Lobster Moth larva back on the young tree I had found it on. At first, it paused and shrivelled, then slowly relaxed. I have forgotten bits of my moth lore but it should soon be ready to spin its cocoon and drop and wait for 1917. I think the cocoon is described as 'flimsy' and makes use of two beech leaves. The water of the pool looked topped by glaucous gossamer, except at the entry point where the water darkened and the green slime gleamed. Behind me a fish swirled – surely a definition of the sound of liquid – and left dark tracers in the scummy silver. And shortly afterwards the caterpillar resumed eating, began working its way up a fresh leaf.

Well, goodbye old friend, farewell. I was delighted. And relieved. Lobster Moth and Lampenham. One handed back. The other about to be. I walked out of the trees and looked back towards the convalescent home – a mellow enough place anyway, particularly attractive in the mist, but I preferred the house near Brechin at the same time of day, with the air a little sharper and with more sting in the grass and dew and those absurd turrets and towers gleaming patchily in the sun a few minutes before the tops of the cupolas on the central section threw off dull, sometimes green-tinged sparks. Aubrey came out and waved his crutch at me. Time for handshaking and thanks, time for breakfast. And now a wait for transport.

I have looked over the small pillow book to see what has turned out. And I really should make acknowledgements. Dr McKinnon was partly responsible for the idea of writing in ten-minute sections; he said he had no time for reading and made it clear he meant a lack of time, 'except for a few minutes perhaps, at the end of the day'. Not, I admit, that I wrote with him in mind. I also took into account the length of a reel of cinema film, the so-called short. And Burnet also told me that 'human beings can concentrate for ten minutes, twelve at most'. Of course, it depends on the stuff you are reading whether you have to concentrate or not. And of course, the pillow book is for you. Though not yet, I hope. In any case, to grow old with a permanently young brother would be a mistake. No, when I had recovered enough to come to Lampenham I thought that if I did not say some things to you, then when would I? I wanted to be amenable and never long; wanted, that is, as much as a non-littérateur can, to provide a bedside book you could dip into. To fit in with my memory of other people I have tried to impersonate a reduced, pale-coloured ghost. This is how I see you – turning your head, lifting your eyebrows in mock surprise, quietly checking your fingernails when someone tedious is speaking; in other words the quiet observation of small, night-dressed things, a little night reading, thinking more of the form and sound and rhythm of your soft laugh than of what you were laughing at.

Enough of that. Let me tell you what really started me writing this for you. A little after McKinnon had gone after his no-time-for-reading remark, I very nearly passed out. The sensation was of swoop and swoon. Now when I was first shipped back from France, the salt and the cold in the air made for a heady misery; it felt uncomfortably close to experiencing what the process of rusting must be like, a corrosive nausea amongst all those grey-painted rivets and oily reverberations. At the railway station logistics had failed. We were parked at the platform entrance, in my case near the buffers. After a time a handkerchief was placed over my mouth, there to acquire a speckling of soot, shaped like the shadow of some basic wing, a good illustration that though we have one mouth, we have two lungs. In the smell and stately chuff of steam engines I watched pigeons on a grimy ledge; they resembled stumpy misplaced finials. I would close my eyes for a spell and then open them to see how the pigeons had jostled themselves into another arrangement.

After a while, the medical orderlies began to become nervous and to nag at us. I gave up the pigeons and closed my eyes. I remembered a Presbyterian minister in Brazil called Gillespie who had, in the absence of converts, plenty of time to study group animals, chiefly ants. He showed me a tribe of his favourite creatures who, instead of employing other materials, use themselves to construct their nests, hanging together from a branch of a tree in a living chainwork several thousand strong while the other ants colonise the space they enclose in the usual way of queen, nursery, dispensary and so on. The overall shape of the nest was a slightly elongated oval and he pointed out, if I remember, that the building system was duodecimal, meaning that twelve ants formed each unit of construction, 'between molecular model and black crystal', living clamps and struts – and he was pleased the nest was as long as his forearm, a cubit he called it. I opened my eyes. A woman walked by us, head in the air, wearing a coat with a fur-rimmed neck which emphasised the waddle of her hips. Beyond the gates I watched a couple embrace and kiss with a most ignorant delicacy, he very red cheeked, she with a brave pout. A number of women auxiliaries began threading through us with smiles and offers. A pleasant, plump-faced girl leant over me.

'Are you sure you're quite comfortable there?'

The question struck me as quite unanswerable. She smiled and began pulling me up. I felt, even with my eyes open, that consciousness was being stripped off me like a too-tight garment. I wondered if having my eyes open rather than closed would make my blacking out different in any way. It did not but I can recall vague voices and someone working my arms like old-fashioned water pumps.

I have tried not to make the subject of my pillow book convalescence but understand that it was not until McKinnon left me in my room at Lampenham that I even recalled that railway station and the Presbyterian ants and the stumpy pigeons and the soot. It is clear to me that I did so because I had moved again and was in some way marking the stages of my movements from one place to another, that this was another step in my getting better, that I was now out of France. What I had not expected was to swoon again. I was getting better. I was alarmed but as I puzzled over what I had just seen, I understood that I had gone much further back. I have never had much time for Japan. More resistance than resentment, I think. It was where our father disappeared. I found it distantly but decidedly boring. The house near Brechin was stuffed with pieces I found neither interesting nor particularly beautiful. And when those Japanese fashions came into vogue a few years ago I found nothing to change my mind. I never found Japanese art attractive, find almost all of it flat and fey. The connection with Japan which I valued was personal and temporary – my adored Tsuru.

Yet clutching the library table, in front of me I see a cluster of Japanese calligraphy in the air; the characters appear to reduce, become more compact, take on the form of a ghostly moth – the residual ink, as it were, clotting at the edge of the forewings. There is a lovely Scots word, 'fleg' or fright; doubtless in an entirely personal sense, I have always taken fleg as the kind of fright that you do not immediately recognise. Instead, a second or two later, the fear expands, blood rushes to the skin. I had a fleg and amongst all that blood running about my scalp, saw an old oriental poem and its reading become a moth and take to the wing as if freed.

But what was this? An impression in space fed by allusion and a stab at sense? A tendency for the eye, no matter what the circumstances, to search out form?

Neither of these, I think. My explanation is based on that sensation of fainting, witless fear and the fraction of time in which impression becomes interpretation. As in, I can't help feeling that it is that often most diverting, undeliberate interpretation of impression that makes us what we are. It is hardly a grand point. But I can think of other similar if unrelated gaps. When wakefulness turns into sleep. Or, I suppose, in the gap between relation and coincidence. They are not the same. As fainting is not sleep. Nor sleep death. Do not despise the psyche. The dead do not have her.

May I suggest, then, for the time being at any rate, that the term 'phor' from the Greek 'to carry' be included in the name of the moment I describe. Phosphorus is light carrying. Flegphorcrumbs,

Flegphorworms. My phor would include the turning of some black specks into Japanese writing and from there, with a certain haste – I did not want to faint, consciousness always gropes vigorously for a context – my mind informed first a receding, then a returning consciousness by turning oriental calligraphy seen in the past into a sensation of a moth and a wild, delightfully amusing notion that its wings could be read.

No, I am not forgetting all those moths whose wing markings have passed through a runic filter to become Gothic, *Naenia typica*, Hebrew Character, confusingly *Orthosia gothica*, or even the Silver Y, *Autographa gamma*. I think one of the caterpillars you used to eat was Kentish Glory, *Endromis versicolora*, again confusingly, in these isles only found in Scotland. And I can see how blood, light and brain lobes can easily portray themselves as forewings with script impressed on them.

I drank some water. I checked, cautiously, that my left lung could still be made to whistle. But then I was most timorously confirming that I was conscious. Hardly the point of a bedside book. My dear girl, let black-and-white ink and flegs recede. Think of pillows and rest. Think of strange and friendly books, of ebb and flow and the whorls of your fingertips. And think too of touch, much lighter than down, as light as featherish antennae on your forehead.

You will, I hope, let me finish as I ended the first ten minutes on the pillow, where waft and weft and linen and skin begin.